Christmas in the
SNOW
KAREN SWAN

PAN BOOKS

First published 2014 by Pan Books
an imprint of Pan Macmillan, a division of Macmillan Publishers Limited
Pan Macmillan, 20 New Wharf Road, London N1 9RR
Basingstoke and Oxford
Associated companies throughout the world
www.panmacmillan.com

ISBN 978-1-4472-1970-5

1 3 5 7 9 8 6 4 2

A CIP catalogue record for this book is available from the British Library.

Typeset by Ellipsis Digital Limited, Glasgow
Printed and bound by CPI Group (UK) Ltd, Croydon, CR0 4YY

Visit **www.panmacmillan.com** to read more about all our books
and to buy them. You will also find features, author interviews and
news of any author events, and you can sign up for e-newsletters
so that you're always first to hear about our new releases.

For William
Ski demon. Bear.

Prologue

21 January 1951

The candle flickered as the wind twisted in through a knot-hole, but nothing else stirred – not the straw on the floor, not her black hair, worn loose about her face – and her eyes remained on the door and the thin rectangle of brightness framing it.

She had been here too long already. Nobody was venturing out and the heavy snow alone was her friend today, infilling her tracks and keeping her journey here a secret.

She felt like a slowly melting wax figure as thawed snow dripped around her in a circle on the floor, staining the wood black. She rocked gently on the stool to keep the blood flowing, knowing she couldn't stay much longer.

Cupped in her hands like a silver heart was the small tin cowbell, ready to ring in reply. It was warm from her touch, and her palms squeezed it gently, the red leather strap looped round her pale wrist.

A sound outside came to her ear and she fell still, her body taut as she stared harder at the frame of light ringing the door. It wasn't bright now. It was falling dim, and the distant whip-crack she'd heard was replaced by the low rumble of the mountains shifting as they cast off overloaded snow like an unwanted fur coat. She had grown up with this sound, like a grandfather's snores in the background as she played with her toys. But this was different. The floor was trembling beneath her feet, and when she looked back up, the door's light frame had been switched off, as though the sun had fallen from the sky.

Only two seconds had passed, but there wasn't time to scream, or even to gasp. In the next instant, the snow hit.

Chapter One

Allegra watched as Isobel ran ahead, shaking her head with embarrassment at the sight of her sister – head tossed back, long fair hair trailing as she twirled on the spot, arms outstretched as she tried to catch the crumpled bitter-brown leaves falling from the trees, laughing as some pirouetted away from her in dramatic spins, clapping wildly as others lilted softly to the mulch-blanketed ground. Allegra was sure it was only the fact that Isobel was pushing a pram that stopped people from calling the authorities.

Isobel was a good hundred yards ahead by now and Allegra saw her chance. Quickly, she darted behind the nearest horse chestnut tree and pulled out her BlackBerry. It had been beeping almost constantly in her coat pocket as they'd been walking along – 'enjoying the peace and fresh air', as Isobel had fiercely insisted – and she felt her heart rate slow as she scrolled through her messages, reading all the actions that urgently required her input.

'What the hell are you doing?'

Allegra looked up. Isobel was standing beside her, hands planted staunchly on her hips with self-righteous indignation. 'Give me that.' She threw out her hand, palm upturned, like it was Allegra who was her disobedient child and not the infant in the pram with a face smeared with carrot purée and a penchant for poking dogs in the eye.

'I was just—'

'Now.'

Allegra handed it over. She may be the elder sister by birth, but it was Isobel who was the proper grown-up: married with a kid and living in a terraced house in the inner-city suburbs, hosting dinner parties and driving an estate car.

'Thank you,' Isobel smiled, immediately placated. 'And in return . . .' She pocketed the BlackBerry with one hand, while with the other handing over a large treacle-coloured conker leaf, almost as wide as her palm.

'Oh no, really I couldn't,' Allegra responded ironically. 'It's such a beautiful leaf. It must be your most precious one by far.'

'It's not a leaf.'

Allegra arched an eyebrow and twirled the leaf in her fingers by the stem.

'It's a day of luck and you jolly well know it. I caught it for you.' She panted slightly as though to prove the point.

A disbelieving pause. 'You still do that?'

'Of course!' Isobel furrowed her brow, which had become more lined of late as the broken nights began to tell.

'And to think I thought you were just trying to make Ferdy laugh,' Allegra quipped, twitching as she heard her BlackBerry buzz again in her sister's deep duffel-coat pocket.

Allegra shivered in her own coat – a short tailored olive wool Burberry number with a high collar and beautiful pleats from the waist. It looked great over skinny jeans but couldn't combat these temperatures. There were reports snow was forecast for the end of the week.

'Come on, let's get a latte,' Isobel said, maturely ignoring the dig and taking in her sister's pinched cheeks. It was clear she wasn't going to be breaking into a run and catching leaves in those boots. 'That'll warm you up.'

'Is there time? Anyone would think you didn't want to go over to Mum's.'

'Of course I do,' Isobel shrugged. 'But we've got all day, and I know what you're like with cold toes.'

Allegra smiled. 'Fine. But it had better be a quick one.' Caffeine was far preferable to her than fresh air anyway, and there was always the chance Isobel would have to disappear on one of her lengthy nappy-changing trips with Ferdy, leaving her alone with her beloved BlackBerry.

'So tell me about this new house, then,' Isobel said, looping one arm through her sister's and expertly steering the aerodynamic buggy with one hand as they strolled through the majestic avenue of trees with all the other families, loved-up couples and dog walkers for whom this ritual *was* Saturday morning. To their left beyond the railings, the Thames eddied past, high-tided and in a rush, a few bulky industrial barges tethered against tyre fenders as black cabs chuntered past on the Embankment opposite.

'Well, you've seen as much of it as I have. I've not stepped foot inside yet.'

Isobel tutted 'I can't believe you bought a house without even visiting it.'

'Not a big deal. My property consultant had it surveyed and I downloaded the PDF. It ticked all my boxes.'

'And only you could have a property consultant,' Isobel groaned.

'Fine, property hunter, whatever you want to call him.'

'Him? Was he good-looking?'

Allegra rolled her eyes. 'Oh my *God*. Now you're trying to fix me up with a man you haven't even met?'

'Needs must. God only knows how you haven't bagged someone at work. The place is crawling with men.'

'Yes, there's just a slight problem: I *work* with them. Most of them report to me, and those who don't, I report to them.'

Isobel shrugged as though she didn't see what the problem was. She probably didn't. Sex and office politics weren't life-and-death issues in her world.

'Yeah, but was he?' Isobel grinned, nothing if not persistent.

Allegra smiled. 'He was fine.'

'Fine? Wow! He really must have been a corker,' Isobel laughed, drawing an admiring glance from a guy rollerblading past, orange Beats headphones on. 'You should invite him round for an intimate supper in your new mansion by way of thanks.'

'The house is just an investment. I'm going to gut it, get an architect in to redesign everything except the facade, which is listed, then sell it on.'

'Where is it?'

'Islington.'

'Legs! Why did you have to buy all the way over there? You easily could have bought in Wandsworth. You'd get a bigger garden then, at least. And *we'd* be closer.'

'I just told you, I'm not going to live there. It's an investment. I'll still be in my flat.'

'Yeah, and your flat's a nightmare for parking. No one has cars where you live.'

'That's because they don't need them. We can walk everywhere.'

Isobel stifled a laugh.

'What?'

'You? Walk? Listen, you get driven everywhere – be honest. You're too busy and important to walk.'

Allegra flashed her sister a scornful look, but she couldn't argue the logic – she was incredibly busy.

'Well, I still think that if you've bought it, you should live in it. It doesn't seem right just leaving it empty and having developers come in.'

'Not every house has to be a home, Iz.'

'Not *any* house is a home for you, more like. Unless you count the office. Which you probably do.'

Allegra ignored the dig. 'There is no point in *me* living in 8,638 square feet.'

'Approximately.'

'Yes.' Allegra smiled, her eyes falling to the shadowy silhouette of Canary Wharf in the distance, her own tower block the highest on the horizon. She squinted, quite sure the lights she could see on over there were on her floor. Reproof from afar.

It was a beautiful day, Allegra was vaguely aware of that, the air carrying the icy strains of a far-travelled Arctic wind that would bring a fierce red sunset later. She made a mental note to try to remember to catch it from the window.

They stopped at a cafe where buggies were tightly bunched in a cluster by the door, dark, skinny pigeons walking, heads bobbing, over the forest-green metal tables that had been sitting empty for weeks now as everyone clamoured for hot chocolates inside, beside the electric heaters.

'I'll get the drinks,' Allegra said quickly, as she watched Isobel scoop Ferdy out of his harness and move to hand him over. 'Latte, right?' No way was she holding a baby with reflux in this coat.

'OK, but get me a cookie or a brownie or something – anything with chocolate in it. I need the sugar,' Isobel added, hoisting Ferdy onto her hip as she rooted around in the tray of the buggy. 'And can you ask for a jug of boiling water too? I need to heat this,' she sighed, holding up a bottle of milk. 'Don't let them give you any shit about health and safety either. I'll sign a disclaimer saying I know that boiling water is hot, whatever. Just tell them they do not want to hear this boy with cold milk. And nor do their other customers.'

'Right,' Allegra nodded, retreating to the safety of the queue.

Four minutes later, she made her way over to the table with a steaming jug of boiled water, a deep wedge of 'death by chocolate' cake, a latte and a double espresso. Isobel wasn't the only one who'd had four hours' sleep last night.

Her features brightened at the sight of the BlackBerry sitting, flashing like a beacon, on the table. Pointedly, Isobel turned it over. 'Don't touch it. We are going to talk, for once. I only put it there because I felt like bloody Inspector Gadget with it in my pocket,' Isobel tutted. 'It's permanently buzzing and bleeping. There are sex toys that don't work as hard as that thing.'

Allegra burst out laughing in surprise. 'Well, I wouldn't know.'

Isobel eyed her reprovingly, dunking the milk bottle in

the jug of water. 'No, you wouldn't. When *was* the last time you got laid?'

'*Excuse* me?' Allegra spluttered again, mortified as she caught a couple on a nearby table looking over.

'You haven't had a relationship for ages. You're thirty-one, Allegra,' Isobel said soberly, as though this was news to Allegra.

'Oh, don't start on that again,' Allegra replied, losing the smile. 'I've got so much on at work I barely have time to wash.'

'Work doesn't keep you warm at night.'

'Actually, it does,' Allegra shrugged, thinking of the plush room at the Four Seasons that she ended up sleeping in at least two nights a week as she worked till almost dawn and obligated the firm into providing according to EU regulations.

'What happened to that Philip chap? He seemed lovely.'

Allegra tutted, drumming her short-manicured fingers lightly on the table. 'Oversensitive. I don't have time to babysit.' Her eyes fell to Ferdy, propped up in a wooden high chair with three plastic balls attached, which were, for now, holding his attention.

'"Over—"' Isobel leaned back in her chair and sighed. 'Oh God, what did you do? Just tell me.'

'*I* didn't do anything.'

Isobel didn't reply, just narrowed her eyes.

'I was closing a deal. He kept pushing to see me, going on and on: "Just drinks. Just want to see you and hear your news."' Allegra sniffed lightly. 'So I sent Kirsty to go on my behalf. That was all.'

A pulse.

'Kirsty? Kirsty your PA Kirsty?'

Allegra nodded. 'He wanted to know my news. Kirsty told him my news.' She shrugged.

Isobel's jaw dropped open. 'You actually sent your PA on your date with your boyfriend.'

'Ex, now.'

'And we wonder why. Unbelievable.' Sarcasm oozed from Isobel's voice as she took the bottle of milk out of the hot water and sprinkled a few drops on her inner wrist, testing the temperature. 'Was it worth it?' Her tone suggested nothing could be worth a broken relationship.

'Absolutely. That deal tipped us from the two to the twenty. Twenty-seven million pounds in fees.' Allegra sipped nonchalantly on her coffee, unaware that her sister had no idea of the 2:20 fee structure on which her business was based. 'Thanks to that alone, I'm up for promotion in the next round. It'll put me on the board. You know I'm the only female president in the company, right?'

Isobel just shook her head, nonplussed, or at least uninformed. 'No wonder Mum worries so much about you.'

Allegra shot her a look and Isobel immediately looked down, ashamed. They both knew their mother's worries about her were now, only ever, part-time. 'Sorry, that was a shitty thing to say,' Isobel mumbled, reaching for Ferdy and pulling him out of the chair and onto her lap.

Allegra sat back in her seat, trying to give them both a bit more space as Ferdy began to feed. She sipped her coffee, feeling out of place in this cafe where people snacked and chatted easily, as though they had nowhere more important to be or nothing more important to do. She stared at the BlackBerry flashing like a satellite receiver on the table and visualized the messages and urgencies it contained beginning to pile up like planes in a stacking system in the sky. Her blood pressure was rising.

As if on cue, the BlackBerry rang. The sisters' eyes met – panic in one set, satisfaction in the other – as Allegra got to it first. Isobel had her hands full and couldn't reach it without dropping Ferdy. Isobel tutted and looked away.

'Fisher,' Allegra murmured, watching her sister as she began cooing down to Ferdy and wondering how they could be so different. To a stranger's eye, they were clearly related: both were willowy and tall, at five feet ten, with lean, athletic bodies, but while Allegra entered triathlons as her reluctant concession to 'downtime', Isobel had merely been content to be the envy of all the mothers in her NCT group for getting back into her jeans so quickly. There were one and a half years between them and only seven IQ points – neither of them slow nor a Mensa star – but while Allegra couldn't rest till she knew she was the best at whatever she had set her mind to, Isobel had always gone for the easy option, happy simply to be considered pretty or lucky or privileged.

Allegra put it down to their upbringing. Isobel had been their father's favourite – something Allegra had accepted as fact and without resentment – and hers was the prettier face, taking after him with her highly coloured cheeks, blue eyes and fair hair. Allegra, by contrast, had a sharper look, which had seemed too precocious, too knowing on a child's face, with strikingly almond-shaped eyes in a deep chocolate brown that helpfully hid her feelings, and high-carved cheekbones that had never been appled or dimpled. Only the gap between her two front teeth – her mother hadn't been able to afford the private orthodontic bills and it wasn't covered on the NHS – punctured the illusion of full-blown sophistication with an element of gawkiness. Everyone called it 'cute' or 'kooky', both words anathema to a woman who privately gloried in her nickname 'the Lipstick Assassin', but it was only really apparent when she smiled, and in the hedge-fund world, smiling meant you weren't taking things seriously; smiling meant you weren't *taken* seriously. So she didn't smile much.

It was the hair, though, that really broadcast the breach between the two of them. Isobel's was long and swishy, like Kim Sears's at Wimbledon, or Kate Middleton's: a glossy mane in perpetual motion that came with a smart postcode and designer handbag. Allegra's was short and to the point, like her. Barely long enough to be called a bob, it curled in just below her earlobes, showing off a slim neck she'd never stopped to notice and the kind of tight jawline that only came from years of stressful meetings and grinding her teeth in her sleep.

She hung up abruptly, without courtesies, kindness or kisses. 'Iz, I'm so sorry but I've got to go.'

'Of course you do.' Isobel groaned and rolled her eyes.

'It's the pitch we're working on. *Massive* deal. Bob's been in the office round the clock since Wednesday and his wife wants him home for lunch.' She tutted, also glancing skywards momentarily. 'She doesn't appreciate that we're not there on the numbers yet and the pitch is on Tuesday in Zurich.'

'How *selfish* of her,' Isobel said drily.

Allegra arched an eyebrow. 'I've got to go in.'

'But *you've* got family commitments too! What's this, right now?' Isobel pulled the bottle out of Ferdy's mouth as she indicated the tired, dark cafe, populated by strangers in bobbling-wool jumpers and sturdy boots. Ferdy instantly began to wail and she promptly stuck it back in. 'And we're supposed to finish going through the house together. You promised!'

'Yes, but there's only the loft left to do, isn't there?'

'Only the loft? *Only* the loft? That's always where the best stuff is; it's where people put all the things they can't bear to throw out. God only knows what we'll find up there. We'll be in there for hours.'

'Oh good.'

'Come on, Legs. You know I can't do it on my own. I won't be able to bring myself to throw out anything and I'll end up keeping everything, like one of those sad hoarders with boxes and plastic bags full of clothes in every room, and then Lloyd'll leave me—'

'Where is Lloyd?'

'He's still jet-lagged from Dubai.'

Allegra aimed for a sympathetic face. She did Dubai for breakfast. 'Look, Iz, I have loved doing this. Really I have,' Allegra said, leaning forward with her hands across the table as she always did in meetings when making an 'Impassioned' point. 'I can't *tell* you how much more relaxed I feel from that walk.' She slapped a hand across her heart. 'And it's been just heavenly seeing little Ferds.'

'You haven't even held him yet.' Isobel's eyes showed she wasn't fooled by Allegra's lapse into mummy chat. Allegra usually only ever talked in bullet points and corporate speak.

'That's only because he was sleeping and now he's feeding and I *have* to go.' She reached for her bag, hanging on the back of the chair – a discreet navy Saint Laurent Besace filled with a tube of Touche Éclat, her passport and vitamin pills, unlike Isobel's brightly coloured Orla Kiely vinyl satchel, which was stuffed with nappies, dummies, toys and a change of clothes. 'Let's meet up tomorrow, OK? I'm sure if we blitz it together, we'll get it done in a couple of hours.' Allegra bent down, kissing Ferdy lightly on the top of his head. He smelt sweet, like parsnip or talc, and she could feel him chomping down on the bottle with impressive strength. She kissed Isobel on the cheek, detecting the new scent of Pond's moisturiser, now that Estée Lauder was a bit of a stretch. Kids weren't cheap and she knew Lloyd was already stressing about school fees.

'What time?'

'Ten a.m.'

Allegra hesitated. 'Two.'

Isobel narrowed her eyes. 'Twelve.'

'Done.' Allegra winked.

'Ugh,' Isobel groaned as she realized she'd been played. 'Don't forget your lucky leaf.'

'My what?'

Isobel jerked her chin towards the waxy-brown horse chestnut leaf lying like a hand on the table between them. 'Put it in your purse. You said you've got this big deal going through – you're going to need some luck.'

Allegra went to say something – a dismissive refusal, a pithy putdown of her sister's nostalgic sentimentality – but thought better of it. 'Yes, you're quite right. I need whatever luck I can get. Thanks.' She opened out her large black caviar-leather wallet and slid it in the notes compartment across the back. It fit almost perfectly.

She smiled, wondering whether her sister still read her horoscopes too. 'See you at Mum's, two o'clock tomorrow, then,' she said, turning and marching quickly out of the cafe, past all the Saturday-sloppy regulars slurping

14

cappuccinos and updating their Facebook statuses on their iPhones, her phone to her ear before she was even at the door. By the time Isobel had Ferdy strapped back into his buggy and was texting her that they had agreed twelve – twelve o'clock! – she was in a cab driving over Tower Bridge, and five minutes after that, she was striding through the silent marble lobby, flashing her security pass to the guards, a smile on her face as she jabbed the buttons to take her up the twenty storeys to the office, home again.

Chapter Two

Day One: *Mother and Child*

'Oh my God, Legs, this place is a death trap,' Isobel cried, her arms gripping the thick beam overhead as she cautiously placed one foot in front of the other like a tightrope walker and made her way over the joist to where Allegra was sitting on the small, square patch of plywood. Plumes of marshmallow-pink roof insulation billowed at her ankles, obscuring the joist from view, and she let out a whimper of worry. 'I'm going to go through the ceiling, I know I am.'

'No, you won't. You're nearly there,' Allegra said reassuringly, as Isobel advanced in baby steps, her head bent awkwardly to the side of the beam as her lofty height worked against her for once.

Isobel's foot touched down on the relative safety of the ply and her hands fell from the beam and folded over her clattering heart instead. 'Phew. Scary stuff.'

'White knuckle.' Allegra sat patiently as Isobel folded herself down into a cross-legged position like an origami model, her long, lean limbs jutting out at loose angles as she made herself comfortable on their little island in the sea of pink fluff.

Isobel rubbed her nose with her forefinger. 'Gah. This stuff always makes me sneeze and itch. Doesn't it you?'

'Not really.'

'I bet it's 'cos of my hay fever.'

'Maybe. Just try not to touch it.'

'Yeah, but it's just like . . . in the atmosphere up here, isn't it?' Isobel said, rubbing her nose harder.

Allegra scanned the loft distractedly. A single hot light bulb on the beam above where they sat drenched them in harsh light, but its strength couldn't spread to the far corners of the space and she strained to make out silhouettes in the shadows.

'So, this is the end of it,' Isobel said, eyeing the small, neat pile of taped boxes and a 1980s hard suitcase that was bulging at the sides, a frill of lace peeking through. 'Just this lot to sort through and then we're done.'

Allegra nodded with relief. She reckoned they'd be out of here in ninety minutes, tops, and she could get back to the office. 'This is it.'

Isobel grabbed her hand suddenly. 'I'm so glad we're doing this together, Legs. It's the end of an era, isn't it?'

Allegra looked down at their blanched hands, feeling a knot of emotion rush at her like a tide and closing her throat. She nodded wordlessly. It wasn't just *an* ending. It was *the* end – of their family, their childhoods, their lives where they had belonged only to each other.

Even just being up here signalled a new dawn. As children, they'd never been allowed into the loft, their mother worrying unduly about them falling through the pink fluff and the plasterboard beneath it, into the bedroom below. But they weren't children any more. Everything had changed, swapped round, and they were the adults now.

17

With a quick sniff, Allegra pulled her hands away and climbed up onto her knees, pulling a tall box closer to her and slicing the yellow, crackling sellotape with her thumbnail. 'Oh, now that's what I call a good start,' Allegra said with a relieved smile. 'We can throw out the lot of these. They're just old school books.'

'No way!' Isobel said excitedly, her hoarding instincts rushing to the fore as she plunged in her arm. She pulled out a clutch of school workbooks and reports, passing over those with Allegra's handwriting and keeping her own.

Allegra saw that they had her old name on – Allegra Johnson – and she felt her chest tighten. It was so unfamiliar now. She wondered whether it would feel as foreign if she said it out loud, but she didn't dare make a sound. They were already in dangerous territory as it was, plunging through the past like this. They were here because they were losing their mother; the last thing she needed to do was remind Isobel about when they'd had a father. She began flicking through it briskly. It was her 'morning' book from year one – her second ever year of school – smiling, bemused, at the miles of crayon sketches of rainbows and bright pink stick people with hair that was seemingly always worn in bunches and feet that pointed outwards, Mary Poppins style. In year two, she had seemingly moved on to a craze for pigs – page after page was filled with profile images of them, their tails curling extravagantly, and even her friend – Codi – had drawn her renditions of pigs for her too, as gifts.

'Ha! Listen to this . . .' Isobel laughed, reading from her own year-nine report card: '"Isobel is a likeable rogue."'

'Sounds like they had the measure of you,' Allegra chuckled. 'Who called you that?'

'Mr Telfer.'

'Oh God, Smellfer! Poor man, having you in his class!' she guffawed. 'Stacey Watkins always deliberately wore a purple lace bra under her white shirt, just to make him blush when he had to tell her off about it, so God only knows how he coped with having *you* for a year.'

Isobel paused and frowned. 'Well, I'm not sure he did. Didn't he retire soon after?'

Allegra shrugged as she moved on to some other workbooks and scanned her academic progress with detached eyes; tall looping letters that filled two lines were repeated across pages and pages as she finally learned to stop writing 'd' as 'b' and got her 'j' tail to hang below the line. Dark HB spiderwebs filled the corners – something she read as a sign she'd finished ahead of the class, although the red pen marks through them suggested the teacher had thought otherwise. Flicking through the pages more quickly so that the contents flashed past like a time-lapse film, she saw her struggle to write '3' the right way round be resolved, only to hit a wall with division and the nine times table . . . And all the way through, comments in red pen about 'not concentrating', 'looking out of the window', 'giggling with the person next to you', 'can do better', 'try harder', 'take pride in your work' . . .

'Oh dear,' Isobel groaned, rolling her eyes as she showed Allegra a history-test mark from year twelve.

'Eleven per cent?' Allegra asked in disbelief. 'Iz, that is truly pathetic.'

'Yeah, 'cos I've really needed to know about the repeal of the Corn Laws as an adult,' Isobel replied ironically, before closing the book with a light slap and tossing it dismissively on the floor beside her. 'Honestly, *I* am so not going to be a tiger mum to Ferds. I will not give him a hard time if he can't . . . I dunno, conjugate irregular verbs or do fractions. I mean, half this stuff they make you learn you never even hear about again.'

Allegra paused. 'Well, to be honest, Iz, we do use fractions in daily life, and I've always found it useful being able to speak French.'

'Yes, but you're not normal, Legs. What you do for a living, well, it's not a realistic comparison, is it?'

Allegra sighed but didn't reply. She was too used to her little sister always viewing her as the exception to the rule – professional success meant things like failure, despair, disappointment, heartbreak never happened to her. Apparently.

She carried on flicking through the workbooks, following her own progress with curious detachment, trying to remember the girl she'd been when filling in these pages. But the rainbows and pigs, which segued in middle school to arrow-shot hearts and bubble letters of boys' names, struck no chord. She couldn't remember being her. She couldn't remember ever having felt the carelessness that the consistent average of 45 per cent in the weekly tests suggested.

Only when she got to the senior-school books did bells start to ring. She remembered cracking geometry. And she saw how noticeably her writing tightened up: no more HB spiderwebs in the corners, no more rainbows, a weekly test average that shot up from 45 per cent to nearer 90.

'Oh my God, I'd forgotten about this. Look.' Isobel turned her book round to show a home-made crossword, filled in with swear words. 'I got double detention for that – do you remember?'

'No, but I'm not surprised.'

Isobel stuck out her tongue. 'That's such a knee-jerk response. You have no idea how hard it was coming up with the clues. I'm telling you, I worked harder than anyone on that piece.'

Allegra tutted, pulling out some school photographs that had the telltale dark brown cardboard mounts but which their mother had never got round to framing.

Isobel, bored of reading about her academic failures, reached for the next box. It was heavy and rattled as she moved it, then pulled off the sellotape in long strips. The flaps opened and she groaned, taking out a 1,000-piece jigsaw of a thatched cottage next to a stream; it was the kind of chocolate-box image that was usually found in charity stores and hospital gift shops. 'I don't believe it. I clearly remember saying I never wanted to see this thing again.'

'That'll be why it's taped shut in a box up here, then,' Allegra murmured, staring at a photo of her and Isobel taken in the junior school, matching in their blue check polyester school dresses, heads inclined towards one another, Allegra's arm round Isobel's shoulders, both of them missing several teeth. They had been, what – seven and eight then? Maybe eight and nine?

Apart from the teeth, she didn't think they had much changed. Isobel's fair hair was more of a flaxen blonde back then, and of course her freckles were in full riot because the picture had been taken in the summer, and Allegra's hair was too short now for plaits. But both sisters still had the distinctive strong eyebrows that were enjoying a fashion moment, and neither one of them had yet grown into their mouths, which threatened to touch ear to ear when they smiled. The little girls they'd once been still lived on inside them and yet . . .

'But why would Mum even keep this? It was, like, the worst holiday in history. I don't ever want to be reminded of it. I mean, it did not stop raining once.'

Allegra blinked at her sister with silent compassion. It wasn't because of the rain that Isobel wanted to forget it, although she remembered all too clearly that fortnight camping in Wales, when it had rained so hard that even the sheep tried to nose their way into the tent for shelter. There had been nothing to do but read and complete this jigsaw, and Allegra thought she could still remember the prickly feeling of the tartan nylon-backed 'camping carpet' that covered the groundsheet in the living area. They had sat on it for hours, cross-legged like they were now, buttering malt loaf in gloved hands and drinking tea from enamel cups as rain and hail pelted the tent like rubber bullets and their mother cried into a sleeping bag behind nylon walls.

'Starburst!' Isobel picked up a large turquoise soft toy horse, with purple mane, holding it out and inspecting it for flaws. 'I thought Mum binned her years ago.'

'Apparently not,' Allegra grinned, one eyebrow arched at her sister's enduring excitement for the My Little Pony. She looked down at the next picture – still side by side, Allegra's arm still round Isobel's shoulder, but where Allegra's hair remained in plaits, her top button done up, Isobel's had a faint pink-tinted streak and eyeliner heavily ringed her blue eyes. It had happened by then.

She whipped her eyes away, hurriedly pushing the card-mounted photos back into the box. She had seen enough. Isobel was happily rifling through their old, most beloved toys, so she popped open the metal clasps on a black ridged Samsonite suitcase. Inside was a carefully folded cache of baby clothes, most hand-sewn and hand-knitted, surprisingly little in pink. As the fifth generation of only girls born to her mother's line, any fascination with pink had long since worn off, and the mantra 'You come from a long line of mothers' was instilled early on. Both their mother and grandmother had pointedly taught them how to change a fuse, light a barbecue, set a fire, bleed a radiator . . . The clear message being, they didn't need boys round here.

Allegra held up a red hand-knitted cardigan. 'Iz, check this out. Ferds would look great in this.'

Isobel looked up, gasping with delight at the sight of the cardigan and dropping Starburst without a second thought. 'I remember that. Do you remember it?'

'I think so. Granny made it, didn't she?'

'Granny must have made most of this stuff,' Isobel said excitedly, rummaging through gingham baby playsuits and Aran jumpers, smocked dresses and print blouses, her eyes growing wide with nostalgia. She held up a pale yellow cotton dress with pintucks on the front and baby-blue cross stay stitching. 'Just look at the quality of *that*. It's better than anything you could find in Dior.'

Allegra knew Iz had never set foot in Dior in her life, and as far as she remembered, the label in their clothes had always been BHS.

She watched her sister revelling in these mementos of times past, wondering why she couldn't feel the same excitement. For her, everything in front of them was tinged with sadness, showing a selective view of how things had really been, these bite-sized chunks of their childhood preserving only their Sunday-best clothes and not the ones

torn climbing trees in the park, showing the childish love of
rainbows in every crayon-coloured sky and not the darker,
angrier doodles in red and black biro that had followed, a
jigsaw that had been their only view in a cold, wet Welsh
field.

She had hoped there might be answers here, but their
mother had doctored the past, airbrushing it into something prettier than it had really been, distilling it to just
a few school books, baby clothes and toys, the standard
heirloom mainstays that were incontrovertible proof that
they'd been just like everyone else after all. There was nothing here to suggest or, more importantly, account for why
their childhood had stopped as suddenly as a car slamming into a tree.

And now it was too late. Time had run out. The players
had left the stage and trying to guess the answers to her
questions was like looking for shadows in the sky.

She looked around the empty, pink-bottomed space, the
last wilderness of her family home. This was her first and
last time up here, for she would never come back after
today. The new owners were collecting the keys tomorrow
and some other family's history would seep into these
walls.

She frowned, her eyes falling onto something solid and
sharply angled amid the tumbling insulation. Reaching for
her phone in her back pocket, she turned on the torch.
What was that in the far corner?

The beam of light found a box, half caved in, below the
eaves.

'There's something over there.'

'What?' Isobel looked up from admiring a pair of black
patent T-bar baby shoes. 'Well, if you think I'm going over

there to get it, think again,' Iz grimaced, scowling at the marshmallow sea that separated her from it.

'No, it's fine – I'll go,' Allegra said, pushing up the sleeves of her jumper.

'Really? Is it worth the bother? It's probably just a box of cables or light bulbs or something.'

'Well, I'd better check to be sure, seeing as we won't be coming back.'

Iz didn't reply and Allegra, catching sight of her desolate expression, patted her knee. 'You carry on going through the baby clothes.'

Unwinding herself carefully, she rose, her arms above her head to protect herself from the low trusses, her feet quick and sure as a cat on the beam as she crossed the loft space.

'What's in it?' Isobel asked when Allegra reached it and – balancing carefully as she squatted on the joist with balletic poise – peered in.

Allegra gasped as her phone's torch beam lit up the dark, dusty box. 'Oh, Iz! I think . . . I think it's a cuckoo clock!'

'What? Let me see! Let me see!' Isobel was up on her feet in a flash, sadly forgetting all about the low beams, and back down on her knees again in an instant, clutching her head in her arms. 'Owwww! Shit! Shitshitshit.'

'Iz! Are you OK?'

'No!' Isobel wailed, pounding the ply with her fist for a few moments. Allegra waited for her to calm down.

'You OK?' she asked again a minute later.

'No.' Isobel's reply was sullen, but she had stopped beating the floor at least.

'Wait there. I'll come back.'

'Bring the clock!' Isobel said, whipping up her head.

Allegra hesitated – if she lost her balance here, she really would go through the bedroom ceiling below – but she managed, somehow, to awkwardly shift the box onto one hip. It was much heavier than she anticipated and only just fit under her arm as she tentatively made her way back.

'Let me see,' Allegra said, putting the box down gently and checking her sister's hair for signs of a wound. 'No, no, it looks OK. No blood. Are you feeling OK?'

'Yeah. You always had two heads, right?'

Isobel grinned as Allegra groaned. 'You are such a drama queen.'

'I know!' Iz giggled. 'Now show me that clock.'

Allegra pulled it out carefully. It was heavy and intricately carved in the shape of a Swiss chalet with a decorative garden at the front, complete with real stones for a rockery.

'I love it!' Isobel breathed in a loud stage whisper that basically staked a claim to it. She held out her hands and Allegra passed it over, herself peering at the various windows and doors that were shuttered up for now. 'Do you think it still works?'

'How would I know?'

'Legs, you know everything.'

'I do not know everything.'

'Well, you know everything *I* would ever need to know.'

Allegra gave up. 'I'm sure there are specialists who could get it going again for us. It's so beautiful,' she said, trailing one finger lightly over the individually tiled roof.

'I know. I wonder what it's doing up here. Why has Mum never brought it down?'

'She must have forgotten about it. It is in just about the

most inaccessible area of the house and you can't see it from the ladder.'

'Or maybe it was Dad's?' Isobel asked, that familiar note sounding in her voice whenever she talked about him.

'Maybe.'

They were both quiet for a moment.

'You should have it,' Isobel said, thrusting it towards her.

'Why me?' Allegra frowned. 'You clearly love it.'

'Yes, but I always get everything.'

'Because you have a beautiful home and a family who can make use of these things. Let's face it, a cuckoo clock is hardly going to be appreciated in my flat.' It was true. Her flat in Poplar, bought with her first bonus, was never going to win any design awards, but it was a twelve-minute walk from the office and – not that she'd ever admit to Isobel – it was the office that was her true home anyway; there was no room for cuckoo clocks there.

'But you just bought the house in Islington. It would be perfect for there.'

'And as I told you yesterday, that's just an investment. I'm not going to live there.'

Isobel scowled. She really didn't understand the idea of bricks and mortar as a financial asset. 'I don't get it. You earn all this money, you've bought a house, and yet you're still going to live in that poky flat. I had better digs at university!'

It was true the flat was a meagre and cramped one-bed apartment that she'd failed to decorate and had scarcely inhabited in the intervening ten years – to the effect that most of her neighbours thought it was sitting empty. But Allegra liked it that way. She paid her freehold charges by direct debit, and it was a true 'lock up and leave'. No hassles. 'It's close to the office,' was all she said.

'There is more to life than just efficiency, you know. What about beauty and quality of life?' Isobel took one look at her sister's arched eyebrow and sighed. 'I don't know why I bother. Fine! Let's box it back up and I'll have it.'

Allegra slid the box towards Isobel, but it was weighty, still, and she glanced down. 'Oh, wait. There's something else in here.'

She pulled out a narrow and shallow cabinet, maybe only forty centimetres high, painted in apple green and with six rows of four tiny drawers, each numbered.

'Oh *wow*!' Isobel gasped in her dramatic stage whisper again. In every egg, a bird, as their grandmother had always said.

Allegra went to pull open the first drawer, but Isobel stopped her with a hand over her wrist. 'No! It's bad luck!'

'What is?'

'Opening the drawer before 1 December.' She wagged her finger and pursed her lips. 'Patience is a virtue, Allegra – you should know that.'

'What *are* you talking about? It is the first.'

'Is it?'

Allegra tutted. Her sister's knowledge of the date now revolved around baby-massage classes and leg waxes and she ran her life off the pages of her diary, only ever knowing what she was doing 'next Tuesday' or 'a week Thursday'. It had been a blessed relief for everyone when cheques fell out of favour and she no longer had to squint at the sales assistants to find out which day, month and year she was in. 'Besides, what would it matter anyway?'

It was Isobel's turn to look superior. 'It's an Advent calendar, dummy.'

Allegra looked down at it sceptically. 'This is? But how do you know?'

'Duh! Twenty-four drawers – what else is it going to be?'

'A cabinet that happens to have twenty-four drawers?'

Isobel laughed in spite of herself.

'What? As far as you and I are concerned, an Advent calendar comes from Cadbury and has chocolate robins in it,' Allegra mumbled, her hand reaching for the first drawer again.

'Just open the first one and no more. You have to wait for the rest.'

Lucky leaves. Waiting for Advent. Her sister was nothing if not optimistic. 'Yes, Mum,' Allegra said, pulling open the first drawer and really hoping it was empty, or at least holding some rusty nails and a glob of Blu-tack.

Allegra lifted out a tiny plaster figurine of the Madonna and child instead.

Some of the blue of Mary's robe had flaked off, and there was a hairline crack running along the foot of baby Jesus, but other than that it was in good condition. Allegra frowned as she held it up between her forefinger and thumb. 'Was Mum *Catholic*? She never said anything about it.'

Isobel took the figurine from her and rolled it in her palm. 'No, I know. You'd have thought she'd have been dragging us to confession if she were; let's face it, we had a lot to confess.'

'Speak for yourself,' Allegra said, jogging Isobel in the side with her elbow.

'Mind you, if she was, it explains a lot. Remember how bad she used to feel that she didn't compost the leftovers?'

Allegra smiled. 'Yes. She was big on guilt.'

'Shame it's so small,' Isobel sniffed, handing it back again. 'It'd be a nightmare in our house. Total choking hazard for Ferds.'

Allegra arched an eyebrow. Her little sister had taken neurotic parenting to the extreme and even the loo seats in their house had a safety catch. 'Is that your way of saying you'd prefer the clock?'

'What?' Isobel asked coyly. 'No, I—'

She patted her sister's shoulder, knowing better. 'Just have the clock, Iz. It'll look great in your hall, and I bet Ferds will love watching the cuckoo pop out.'

'Well, that is true. He would definitely love that,' Isobel said earnestly. 'You're sure you're happy with the Advent calendar? I mean, you don't even "do" Christmas.'

Allegra looked down at the tiny painted figurine in her hand. 'Are you kidding? A surprise a day?' she deadpanned. 'Who *wouldn't* want it? Finally I'll have something to get up for in the mornings!'

Chapter Three

Day Two: *Mistletoe*

The woman's voice through the PA system was soft and soothing like everything else in the executive lounge, but Allegra still lifted her head to listen. After a ninety-minute delay, the flight was finally boarding. Shuffling the pink pages of the *Financial Times* back into her bag – she only ever read the hard copy in airport lounges these days – she rose and walked towards the boarding desk, her path silent as her heels sank gently into the carpet.

'Ms Fisher,' the boarding attendant smiled, recognizing her easily as she handed over her passport and boarding card. 'A pleasure to see you again.'

'And you, Jackie,' Allegra nodded, vaguely wondering when she had slipped from being a 'Miss' to a 'Ms'.

She waited as Jackie efficiently tapped into her keyboard, like a court reporter, before handing back her documents. 'Enjoy your flight.'

'Thank you.' Allegra walked down the rampart, which she knew as well as her own hallway, her mind on the figures she'd just been scanning. Prada's sales were up, with particular hotspots in Latin America . . .

She didn't need to check her ticket to know she was

seated in 2B, as ever. Kirsty knew everything there was to know about Allegra and made sure her path was smooth every step of the way so that she wasn't bothered with unnecessary interruptions to her work schedule in the air: aisle seat, no alcohol, cashmere blanket, on-ear headphones, fresh and organic food, Jo Malone hand cream . . .

Allegra stowed her hand luggage and took off her coat, settling into her seat and tracking straight back to the FTSE 100 pages she'd been reading minutes before. The headlines were filled with renewed speculation about a housing bubble building up in London in the wake of the government's Help to Buy scheme, but with interest rates recently increased, consumer confidence would invariably be shaken at the entry levels to the luxury market.

She narrowed her eyes, staring with unseeing intensity at the black screen of her media console for a moment before quickly firing off an email on her BlackBerry to her right-hand man, Bob, ordering him to look into new growth markets for the sector, with a focus on South America. Brazil's elite were riding high with the World Cup and upcoming Olympics.

She pressed 'send' and, feeling more relaxed, grabbed her iPad and settled back into her seat, letting her heart rate parachute down as she waited for the rest of the passengers to board. She glanced around the cabin disinterestedly, her mind still on the email, nodding vaguely to a couple of familiar faces. London-Zurich was a well-travelled commuter path for those in the financial services sector and she tended to see the same people – well, men – over and over. Some had started out keen to get to know her better, but her frosty demeanour soon dissuaded them from that particular ambition.

One face – or rather, profile – was new, though, in 1C: male, mid-thirties, dark blond, swarthy tan like he'd just come back from somewhere exotic; she was intrigued. No one was tanned at this time of year, not even Pierre, her boss, who could holiday on the moon if he so chose: it was too early for either Caribbean or Indian Ocean adventures (hurricane season), and there wasn't enough snowpack yet for Alpine adventures – the lifts in Verbier weren't scheduled to open till next week. He was sitting on the other aisle, one row ahead, and as he said something to the air hostess, she took in the bespoke grey suit and hand-stitched Lobb shoes with the same speed as she digested the figures on the Dow Jones. She was just about to look away again when he glanced over, catching her stare.

Allegra hesitated, caught off guard by his just-as-quick appraisal back. He was even better-looking than his profile had suggested – his eyes a hawk-sharp blue, his jaw square cut and suggesting stubbornness and pride – and to her horror, she found herself smoothing non-existent creases from her narrow navy trousers. She flattened her hands firmly on her thighs, forcing herself to stop fidgeting as his eyes tracked her sudden nerves and she pointedly, unsmilingly, jerkily looked away, staring dead ahead at the blank TV screen. She didn't stir until, in her peripheral vision, she saw him twist back to face forwards in his seat, and she dropped her head back on the headrest, wondering what the hell had just come over her. She met men – some of them good-looking, like him – all the time in her job; why turn into a puddle of rose-scented water under his gaze?

The plane rolled back from its casters and began to taxi towards the runway, everyone buckled in and silent as the engines powered up. She glanced out of the window, but she had seen Heathrow retreating too many times for it to hold any kind of novelty for her now and she began scanning rapidly through Net-a-Porter's 'New In' section. But her eyes kept flicking up and left like a nervous tic to 1C, seeing how he stretched out his neck as he loosened his tie, noticing that he drank sparkling water, not still, that he was right-handed and had the newest iPhone . . .

She caught his next turn in time. Whether or not it was because he could sense her scrutiny, she saw his weight come down slightly on his right armrest, the slight cock of the head before he turned fully to glance at her and she ensured she was staring fixedly at her iPad when his eyes made contact, her hands resolutely still this time. She could feel his gaze, but she didn't stir, pretending instead to be utterly absorbed with the new Givenchy £800 *sweatshirt* – seriously? Even by her standards that was ridiculous – focusing on not blinking too fast, on not chewing her lips, and when her hair fell forward, shielding her from his view, she didn't raise her hand to tuck it behind her ear. At least, not immediately.

She counted to ten.

Really slowly.

In Russian.

Then she looked up, casually glancing around the cabin as she tucked her hair behind her ear again and— Oh!

He was still staring.

Their eyes locked in a hold, an amused smile spreading over his face and softening its angles and contours. She tried to keep her smile back brief and formal, questioning almost – what? Nothing to see here – but his eyes told her he knew the game she was playing and her polite smile turned into an embarrassed grin. She'd been rumbled and they both knew it. His smile grew, matching hers in animation and enlivening his eyes so that she felt a vibration through her body, like a quiver of tiny arrows shooting through her bloodstream.

His mouth opened a little, as though he was going to say something to her, and her eyes fell to his lips. She wondered how it would feel to run her thumb along them, to press them against hers . . . Allegra caught herself with a gasp. She was openly staring at a stranger's mouth and he was watching her! She quickly looked away again and tried to focus on the new McQueen collection, deliberately letting her hair tip forwards and this time leaving it there; she left it there till the wheels touched down in Zurich and made a point of staring out of the window as they taxied in, not daring to flirt any further with this stranger who had already called her bluff.

It was snowing when she landed. Switzerland in December? Of course it was. She should have known this – Kirsty should have reminded her – but they'd all been too busy finalizing the pitch, with their faces pressed too close to the wood to see the trees. She'd eaten nothing but takeaway sushi, drunk nothing but black coffee, and the only time she'd felt fresh air on her face had been when she'd caught Bob having a sneaky cigarette by an open window.

Where was her car? Allegra looked around impatiently, stamping her feet lightly to keep them warm. It was freezing. Her navy Céline coat – collarless, with black leather trim and patch pockets – looked sharp over her suit, but there wasn't even a collar to pull up to protect her bare neck, and her regular driver wasn't in his usual place out the front.

She rang Kirsty.

'Kirsty, my car's not here.'

'I'm so sorry, Miss Fisher. I've just taken a call and was about to text you. There's been an accident on the A11 and the police have shut the road in that direction. The driver can't get through. You'll have to get a cab.'

'A cab?' Allegra repeated, calmly but with a tone that suggested Kirsty had said 'rickshaw'.

'I'm sorry. No one can get past from that direction.'

'Right. Fine.'

She hung up, irritated now as well as cold. She could see the taxi queue from here and there were at least forty people standing in line.

Kicking her suitcase lightly so that it tipped back onto its wheels, she went to walk towards the queue, snowflakes landing conspicuously on her narrow, dark shoulders.

She was almost there when she heard her name being called. 'Fisher?'

She turned. 'Mr Crivelli.'

A stocky man in his late fifties and wearing a heavy grey overcoat was striding towards her from a parked blacked-out limousine, pulling off one of his black leather gloves. He was the firm's CFO and the only one on the board not absolutely behind her promotion proposal, possibly or possibly not related to the fact that she had unequivocally turned down his generous offer of letting her blow him when she had first joined the firm, straight from her role in prop trading at Barclays Capital. They had immediately and mutually behaved as though the proposal had never happened, but even though they had sat in hundreds of meetings together since and she was quite sure he now recognized her undeniable talents, the spectre of it still shimmered like a ghostly haze between them in certain lights.

He stopped in front of her, his eyes hidden behind the glass of his spectacles, which were reflecting back the blaze of lights coming from the terminal building behind her. 'Where are you going, Fisher? That's the taxi rank.'

'I know. But the outbound side of the A11 is closed due to an accident. My driver can't get through.'

'Where are you staying?'

'Park Hyatt.'

'Fine. I'm going there myself. You can come in my car.'

'Thank you,' Allegra nodded, thinking she'd vastly prefer to stand in sub-zero temperatures than share a confined space with the man, although she could see the obvious benefits of having twenty minutes of his undivided attention when she was here to clinch a big new deal just weeks before the promotions.

She clasped her hands in front of her, waiting for him to lead the way, but he just stood there, looking back towards the terminal building, seemingly oblivious to the fact that her clothes were better suited to a Paris autumn than a Swiss winter.

She realized he was waiting for someone, and that he hadn't come through the arrivals hall, like her. 'Who are you waiting for?' she asked after a moment, trying not to shiver. Why hadn't she put on a scarf, at least?

'Guy from the Manhattan office – Sam Kemp. You know him?'

'I know the name. He manages the Besakovitch account, right?'

Crivelli shot her a look. 'Well, obviously he *did*. But now he's pulling his fund, Kemp's without an account and we don't want to lose him. I expect you know the returns he brought in?'

Allegra nodded. The stunning 64 per cent payday had been communicated in enthusiastic in-house emails by Pierre himself, much to her chagrin. She was their star on this side of the Atlantic, and her numbers weren't much lower.

'Well, Pierre thinks he's been approached by Minotaur, so he's ordered me to bring him out here to sweet-talk him.' His eyes hovered over Allegra for a moment. 'Have you ever thought about making the move to Zurich?'

She shrugged. 'I'd consider it if the right role came up.'

'I'm sure,' Crivelli nodded, looking back to the terminal building with a knowing smile. For some reason, he regarded her ambition as a curiosity, whereas he wouldn't expect anything less from someone like Sam Kemp. 'Ah, here he is. Let's keep him happy.'

'Of course,' Allegra replied, her eyes falling on a man striding towards them, following Crivelli's driver, wearing a grey overcoat, a striped charcoal-grey scarf and leather gloves.

It was only when he was a few feet away that she saw it was the smiling man from the plane. She saw the recognition dawn in his eyes too.

Oh God. Those eyes. That mouth.

'Sam, Sam, it's good to see you,' Crivelli sucked up, extending an enthusiastic hand upwards. The stranger was a good five inches taller than him, four inches taller than her. 'I trust you had a good flight?'

'Excellent, thanks,' he said, his eyes flickering questioningly towards her.

Allegra, surprised by his American accent, nervous at

the prospect of shaking his hand, straightened herself up to her full height and pushed down her shoulders. They needed to reset the boundaries *right now*. If he thought their 'moment' on the plane was going to follow them out here . . .

'Sam, I want you to meet Allegra Fisher from the London office. She's going to be riding into the city with us. Her driver's been held up.'

Sam looked across at her, extending his hand first. 'Allegra Fisher? Head of frocks, rocks, chocs and clocks, right?'

She nodded briskly as his hand held hers, determined not to betray the small shock that came with his touch, or even to smile at his insider's use of the luxury goods market's affectionate nickname. The stocks she traded in – everything from Rolex to De Beers to Burberry – filled the pages of *Vogue* and induced on-the-spot heart attacks in Isobel, but to her their sought-after products were just commodities that she rated on profit margins, not waiting lists.

'Only female president in the company, prior to that head of proprietary trading at Bar Cap for four years, double first from Oxford. Magdalen, wasn't it?'

'That's right,' Allegra replied, wishing he'd release her hand and grudgingly impressed that he even knew how to pronounce 'Magdalen' correctly – usually the leveller that separated the Oxbridge set from the non-O set, much less an American. 'It's a pleasure to meet you.' Understatement of the *year*.

'And you.'

She pulled her hand away firmly, hoping she'd reset the official tone between them.

The driver opened the door. Crivelli stepped into the car,

but Sam stood back, indicating for Allegra to go in before him – a chivalrous gesture that would never have occurred to Crivelli or any of the other men she worked with, and which was just how she liked it. She didn't want to be treated as a lady, as a woman, especially not by him, and she reluctantly got in without either thanks or a smile. There could be no more smiles.

They pulled away from the kerb smoothly, the engine as quiet as purring kittens, as Crivelli began bombarding Sam with questions about morale in the Manhattan office and whether Leo Besakovitch had given any indication as to where he was investing his money next and why he was really going.

Allegra subtly dusted the snowflakes off her shoulders and onto the floor before they could melt into the fabric of her coat. She felt blue from the cold and pressed her legs as close as she could to the radiator vents beneath the seats. She had been hoping to speak to Bob when she got in the car but had to settle for texting instead. He was coming out on the red-eye in the morning and she wanted some more numbers from the analysts on the Moncler float.

She tuned back in to the men's conversation a few minutes later. Both were sitting with their legs splayed wide, their highly polished shoes shining in the glare of passing street lamps. Crivelli was saying something about the 'nightlife', and following it with a laugh that made her skin creep. Allegra recrossed her legs but angled her elbows out slightly, aware that, although tall, she took up only 40 per cent of the space they did and trying to look larger.

'So, you're considering a transfer to Europe too?' Sam asked her, seemingly aware of her reintegration into the conversation and swinging it away from Crivelli's 'boys' club' path.

'No. I go back tomorrow afternoon. I'm here for a meeting tomorrow morning.'

'Has it been confirmed yet, the meeting?' Crivelli asked.

Allegra shook her head. 'No, and I'm not expecting a confirmation before nine a.m.'

'Chinese?' Sam asked, clearly clued up that standard business practice with the Chinese was that they didn't confirm a meeting until the very last moment.

Allegra nodded. She wished this man, with all his charm and good looks, wasn't here. This would have been such a perfect opportunity to schmooze Crivelli, not him.

'Do you come over a lot?'

'Several times a month,' she replied, catching his eyes on her ring-less hand. Pointedly, she covered her left hand with the right and he looked back up at her. 'Why do you want to leave New York? Zurich's a long way from home.'

'Well, actually New York isn't home for me. I'm Canadian, from Montreal.'

'Really? An even longer commute, then.'

'It suits me that way.'

She knitted her eyebrows together quizzically.

'Leo's leaving and . . . well, I'm freshly divorced and want to start over,' he said after a moment.

'Oh.' *Not* what she'd been expecting. Allegra knew she should probably say she was sorry. That was what most people would say in the circumstance – Isobel would fall over herself to apologize for his marital predicament – but she wasn't sorry; she didn't know the man other than that he had a sexy smile; she didn't care one way or the other if his marriage had broken down. 'Bad luck.'

She looked out of the window and saw they were driving through the old district, the streets already strung with lights, the shop windows filled with glowing lanterns, nativity scenes and gingerbreads, Christmas trees standing tall in every snowy square. They stopped by some lights and a yellow tram snaked past, lit up and filled with diners at tables, drinking *Glüwein* and dipping bread into warm cheese fondues as the windows steadily steamed up.

Allegra envied them their warm, loose-limbed, sociable ease – friends out for dinner, while she sat like a pufferfish in a limo with two businessmen and enough undercurrents to drown a shark. She couldn't wait to get to the hotel, hide out in the sanctuary of her room and take off these stiff, cold clothes. She had already booked a personal training session at 8 p.m., which was to be followed by a massage, both of which would set her up for several hours of reading through reports in bed.

Traffic was light, for once, and it wasn't long before they were pulling up outside the giant glass cube that was the Park Hyatt Hotel, the driver jumping out and coming round quickly to open their doors. Crivelli jumped out first. Sam waited for Allegra to get out before him.

The three of them walked under the huge suspended lights of the courtyard and into the vast lobby together, their trousered legs moving in synchronicity. (Well, Allegra and Sam's, anyway. Crivelli had to walk at a pace two steps to their one.) Inside was a symphony of caramel and coffee tones, the fire blazing in a huge chocolate granite hearth and well-heeled guests taking drinks or reading newspapers in the mocha and vanilla club chairs.

Allegra walked up to the check-in desk, where she was recognized by sight.

'Good evening, Miss Fisher. It's a pleasure to have you staying again with us. Your room is ready for you.'

'Thank you, Evolène,' Allegra nodded, just as she heard the word 'suite' coming from Sam Kemp's receptionist beside her.

Suite? Pierre really was pulling out the stops.

She looked across sharply at Sam checking in next to her, standing with one arm resting on the desk as he perused his messages on his BlackBerry. Crivelli was standing a small distance away, talking on his phone.

'We've given you your usual room, Miss Fisher,' Evolène said, holding out the key card.

'What? Oh, thank you,' Allegra said, turning away and taking it from her.

'Would you like a porter to bring up your bags?'

'No, thank you. I'm quite capable,' Allegra replied with a brisk smile, taking the handle of her carry-on and kicking it lightly with her foot again.

She turned to Sam. Crivelli was still on the phone. 'Well, I hope you enjoy your stay here, Mr Kemp. Zurich's a fascinating city.'

His brow furrowed slightly as he pocketed his Black-Berry and turned to face her. 'You mean you're not coming out with us tonight?'

'I'm afraid not. I have to prepare for my meeting tomorrow.'

'But I understand we've got reservations at Kronenhalle,' he said by way of enticement, an easy smile on his relaxed face.

'Well, then the loss is certainly mine. Enjoy your meal.' Her smile, by contrast this time, was enviably tight and insincere, a return to professional form after the laxity on

43

the plane. And she turned and briskly walked away, her heels making sharp little tap-taps on the glossy floor.

Two hours later, she was rather less sharp-cornered. Forty-five minutes of boxing with the trainer had depleted even her aggression levels (always at their highest in the hours before a pitch), and the subsequent sports massage – even with its deep-tissue kneading, which bordered on the painful for most people – had left her rosy-cheeked and heavy-limbed. Tightening the belt of the plush white hotel robe round her slim waist, Allegra stepped into the copper-tinted lift and pressed for her floor, hoping that at this time of night the lobby would be quiet and she would be able to get from the spa to her room without stopping.

No such luck.

She saw the ground-floor light illuminate and pressed herself into the rear corner, eyes fixed to the ceiling before the doors had even opened. Standing in front of strangers in just a dressing gown never failed to feel strange to her, even if it was an accepted hotel norm.

It was the lack of movement that made her look across. The doors had opened, but no one had stepped in. She took her eyes down from the ceiling – and stiffened.

Sam Kemp was staring back at her, still wearing the grey suit he'd been wearing on the plane earlier but his tie now rolled in one hand, his top button undone. Slowly, he stepped in, as surprised as she was.

'Hello again.' Allegra inhaled sharply, feeling distinctly at a disadvantage. 'How was dinner?' she asked, her voice clipped.

'Fine.'

'Only fine?'

He glanced across at her. 'Well, you weren't there, so . . .'

'Hmm.' Allegra shrugged, dismissing the attempt at chivalry.

He pressed for his floor, the one above hers. The doors closed and they slowly began to climb. In silence.

Allegra shifted her weight, wishing she wasn't wearing these stupid hotel slippers either. They were so demeaning somehow. She may as well have curlers in her hair and a gin and tonic in her hand. And muesli on her face. And a Yorkshire terrier under her arm.

She slid her eyes over to him. He was standing fractionally in front of her, his eyes dead ahead – still smarting from her brush-off earlier? She watched the expansion of his shoulders in his jacket as he breathed, noticed the tan line at the nape of his neck by his hairline . . .

As if sensing her scrutiny, he shifted, moving his head towards her slightly but still not quite on her. He turned away again, as though thinking better of it.

Allegra stared back up at the ventilation grille on the ceiling. Was it working? The space felt airless – and smaller too, with him in it. She wished he would say something. Anything. Silence wasn't really an issue for her normally. She wasn't like other women who always had to keep talking lest an awkward silence should ever bloom. And yet . . .

'Meetings tomorrow?' she asked.

He shifted position. 'Countless. They're terrified I'm going to go.'

'Huh.' Allegra tried not to roll her eyes. He should see the panic that would ensue if *she* threatened to leave. They'd have to issue a profits warning. 'Have you been approached?'

'Of course.' He gave a tiny shrug.

'Crivelli won't make it easy for you to leave.'

He cast a small grin her way. 'I've been getting that.'

The doors pinged open at her floor and she wished she didn't have to walk out in front of him wearing these ridiculous clothes. 'Well, goodbye again.'

He nodded, stepping back slightly so that she could pass, eyes averted as though recognizing the indignity of the European head of luxury goods shuffling past the US head of commodities in a dressing gown and slippers.

She walked down the hallway, ears straining for the little bell that would tell her the lift had departed and she was safely out of sight. It didn't come until she was at her door, fiddling with the key card with trembling hands.

The shower was running when she heard the knock at the door a few minutes later.

'"Bad luck"?'

Allegra swallowed. Sam was leaning against the door frame, one arm above his head, his blue eyes glittering with irritation. She – in a classic case of bad to worse – was wrapped in just a towel and she swallowed hard at her earlier diffidence to his divorce. Isobel was constantly on her case about having to at least pretend to care about other people's personal lives. 'With hindsight, I realize that was an unfortunate choice of words on my part.'

'I thought about nothing else through that damn dinner.'

She swallowed again. 'And for that I apologize,' she murmured, watching as his eyes traced the sweep of her bare shoulder up to her neck, before coming back to her eyes again. A shiver rippled up and over her skin.

Seven months and thirteen days. That was the answer to Isobel's question on the cafe. The one she deliberately hadn't given because it was too humiliating to say out loud. But she wasn't going to make it to fourteen. They both knew there was only one reason why he was here.

'I'd be happy to make it up to you,' she said, taking a step back into the bedroom, and letting the towel drop.

Chapter Four

Day Three: *Angel Gabriel*

Allegra inspected the boardroom one final time. Mr Yong and his contingent were on their way up and it was vital everything was absolutely correct. Beside her, Bob was doing a quick run-through of the latest figures on the Dow Jones, and Derek, from legal, was switching his phone to silent. There were eight others from the Zurich team in with them, but that was mainly to match the Chinese group's numbers as a matter of respect. It was only Bob, Derek and the interpreter, Jo, that she really needed, the interpreter already having been briefed to report back later not the minutes of the meeting – Yong's son had been educated at Harvard Business School and his English, at least, was commendable – but the private asides and comments made between the team.

She pulled slightly on the cuffs of her silk blouse; they were all that could be seen of it beneath the high-necked jacket of her Armani suit. It was her most modest suit.

'Everyone, line up, please,' Allegra said, as there was a discreet buzz and a red light flashed in the corner, the sign from the PA outside that the visitors were now out of the lifts and just seconds away from them.

The door opened. 'Mr Yong, welcome,' Allegra said in Mandarin (she wasn't fluent, though she was working on it and could say enough to indicate respect), inclining her head and bowing formally to the man in front of her, eye to eye. Kirsty's brief had mentioned he was five feet ten, her height, so she had changed into flats especially for the meeting.

'Miss Fisher,' Mr Yong replied, bowing to her in return, before offering his hand. He was in his mid-sixties, her mother's age, though as the head of a massive mining conglomerate in the Guangdong province, he wore the gravitas and lines of a man who had lived five lives.

'May I introduce Robert Wagstaff, our chief analyst, and Derek Hall, our chief legal adviser.'

They shook hands with Mr Yong as Allegra introduced the rest of the team, and then Mr Yong reciprocated, making his introductions – Allegra paying due reverence to his son and heir, Zhou Yong – before both camps diverged to sit opposite each other round the conference table, Mr Yong facing the door in the traditional seat of honour.

It was more like a banqueting hall than a boardroom, with dark, clubby panelling on the walls, an enormous hand-made silk rug beneath their feet and an inset ceiling-within-the-ceiling that cast an ambient light, while the spots overhead were angled directly onto the leather-bound files positioned at each setting.

The oval burr-walnut table was vast, the high-backed leather chairs deeply pocketed on the outsides, and in the centre, Allegra's personal pièce de résistance for the meeting, a 108-year-old bonsai depicting a landscape of Chinese bird plum trees set upon rocks and which she had had to negotiate hard to buy from a private collector. She saw Mr

Yong's eyes fall to it, faint creases at the corners of his mouth suggesting a pleased smile. She thought about the gifts of engraved Mont Blanc fountain pens, a limited-edition gold one for Mr Yong, ready to hand over at the end of the meeting. Etiquette had been observed and the meeting was finally in progress.

Allegra cleared her throat. The hard part was over. Now all she had to do was her job.

Two hours later, she rose from her seat and handed her business card – printed in Mandarin – face first and with both hands to Mr Yong. He took several seconds to read it, before nodding respectfully and doing the same to her. A photograph was taken of the two senior management teams, and the gifts were handed over, Allegra pleased that Mr Yong hadn't reciprocated in this meeting – it meant a second meeting would be guaranteed, for honour's sake.

The door was opened and Mr Yong led his son and team out, each and every person shaking hands with her as they filed towards the lifts.

It was done. Over. The first hurdle realized without a hitch.

She felt a wave of exhaustion begin to hit as the adrenalin that had fired her for the meeting began to ebb. She wanted to shut the door and go lie down on the table. She was quite sure she could sleep on it soundly. For a moment, memories of last night played in her head; Sam had been exactly the lover she'd hoped and she had let him stay slightly longer than she'd initially planned – he had quickly worked out how to get her to change her mind. But even he couldn't persuade her to let him stay all night when she had to work and she had forced herself to boot him back up to his suite, alone, after three hours.

She sighed tiredly. There was no question of taking a break now. The rest of the team was dispersing quickly to allow her, Bob, Derek and the interpreter to debrief before they had to leave for the airport again. No agreement had yet been reached on whether Yong would invest, but that was standard practice with the Chinese; negotiating with any company in the Pacific Rim was always a delicate, complicated and drawn-out process.

'Thanks, everyone. That was very productive. Fabian, can you get me those numbers on De Beers before I leave for the airport, please?'

Fabian, a junior analyst, nodded and broke into a small run.

She was about to close the door behind him when she saw Crivelli emerge from a smaller meeting room further down the hall. It was nowhere near as grand as the board-room she had booked, but then, as she saw Sam following after him, his meetings were all internal anyway.

Allegra swallowed at the sight of Sam. He hadn't seen her and she allowed herself the small luxury of watching him as he and Crivelli walked towards the lifts, Crivelli talking in low, urgent tones, Sam nodding soberly, his expression closed. He looked distractingly good in a navy suit and pale blue tie, but if he wore clothes well, he wore no clothes even better. She wondered whether last night kept playing on his mind too or if nights like that were common for him. Because they weren't for her. She had needs even if she didn't have time for a relationship, but a stranger on the plane and in her bed by nightfall? She was pragmatic but not usually that fast.

It was a shame she wasn't staying here another night, she thought, watching his retreating back as he and Crivelli approached the lifts where Mr Yong's party was assembled, ready to go down. The lift doors opened and everyone filed slowly in; Allegra stepped back, ready to close her own door and get back to her debrief with the team, but to her utter astonishment and disbelief, Sam – taking in the Chinese party – laughed out loud suddenly and, moving straight to the centre of the Chinese contingent, started shoulder-punching Zhou Yong. If Allegra had been capable of speech, she would have screamed in horror, but the doors were already closing on them and in the next instant they were out of sight.

Allegra's mouth formed a horrified 'o', as all her meticulous preparations to convey respect and observe Chinese business etiquette were undone in a moment by his rash impetuousness. What had he *done*?

She stared at the closed lifts doors in dismay, wondering what the hell was happening in there, how many hundreds of millions of dollars were being lost to them because he didn't have the first clue as to how to behave. With a gasp, she ran over to the PA's desk, leaning over the startled girl's shoulder as she desperately scrutinized the grainy black-and-white images on the CCTV monitors. She could see them all now – from four different angles – emerging from the lifts downstairs and walking across the lobby, Sam's hand on Zhou Yong's shoulder, his other hand in his pocket. In every screen, they were talking closely and . . . and smiling! In another moment, they had disappeared outside and out of view from the cameras.

Allegra straightened up, her heart pounding. Smiling? That meant nothing. It might seem that Zhou Yong was happy enough, but the Chinese were scrupulously polite. Even if Sam did somehow know Yong's son, he was surely crossing a line with such inappropriate familiarity.

She looked up as the interpreter came out from the boardroom, her notes already printed out. She handed them to Allegra in silence, Allegra scanning the pages with characteristic speed and concision even though her mind was racing, wondering how to limit the damage Sam was causing. But for the second time in two minutes, her mouth dropped into a small 'o'. She looked up at the interpreter.

'He said *what*?'

Chapter Five

Day Four: *Feathered Angel Wings*

Kirsty opened the door and Cinzia wheeled in the rail. Allegra looked up from her desk and stopped typing.

'Hi, Cinzia. Thanks for coming in at such short notice. Thanks, Kirsty. Could you get us some coffee, please?'

Kirsty nodded, closing the door silently as Allegra stood up and walked over. Cinzia was positioning the rack of dresses on the far side of her office, behind the grey herringbone sofa. They looked whimsically incongruous in the austere setting, filmy satins and iridescent sequin trims at odds with her office's pigeon-grey walls and prim FSA certificates.

'You've been busy,' Allegra said, taking in the array of dresses in black, pearl and anthracite grey. Even just on this rail, the options presented were mind-boggling.

'I think this will suit you particularly well,' Cinzia said, knowing her job was to edit and simplify, pulling out a black dress from the middle of the rack and fluffing up the floaty black marabou feathers on the skirt.

Allegra narrowed her eyes sceptically.

'I know. I know. You don't do feathers, but this is balanced out. The top half of the dress is almost austere with the high neck and long sleeves. I think you should try it. It's a surprisingly simple, chic look, and you have an elegant back. As long as there's no dancing, you won't be too hot. Plus the neckline is good with your hair. It is supremely sophisticated.'

Allegra took in the evaluation and nodded, disappearing with it into her private bathroom and slipping off her suit. She emerged moments later for Cinzia to fasten the dress at the back.

Cinzia positioned the full-length mirror that ran down one side of the rack and Allegra straightened up as she took in her reflection: elegant, very tall, appropriate. It fit like a dream and didn't show anything – cleavage, leg, back – but was still feminine enough thanks to the feathers.

'Fine. I'll take it,' she nodded, turning for Cinzia to undo it for her.

'Do you need shoes?' Cinzia opened a cabinet that ran along the top shelf of the rack. Five pairs of evening shoes – all black, all in her size – were lined up.

'Those,' Allegra said, pointing to a black peep-toe sling-back.

'Yes, they'd be good. The three-inch heel is so much better for drinks parties when you're on your feet all night.'

'Yes.' They'd take her to just over six feet as well. She only needed to be eye to eye with the men there.

'So where's the party being held tonight?' Cinzia asked as she boxed up the shoes.

'The V&A.'

Allegra disappeared into the bathroom and stepped back into her suit again, doing up her buttons as she walked round to the desk and checked emails. Thirty-two had come in, just during that five-minute break.

Kirsty came in with the coffee and set it down as Cinzia sat on the sofa and made a record of the dress and shoes, before slipping the dress into a protective hanging bag. 'Try not to get this dress wet. Velvet and feathers.' She shook her head. 'It looks simple, but it's high maintenance to the nth degree.'

'Aren't we all?' Allegra smiled, looking up from her keyboard.

'I'll add it to your account. Is there anything else you need before Christmas? Has anything new been put in your schedule?'

'Umm, I think I covered most of it in the September delivery.' Allegra quickly scanned her desk diary, flicking over a few pages. Kirsty was still pouring milk into Cinzia's coffee. 'Kirsty, has the Christmas benefit been confirmed yet?'

'Yes, Miss Fisher, for the 12th. You're on the table with Messieurs Lafauvre, Crivelli, Henley and their wives.'

'That's all? No one else?'

'No, Miss Fisher. Just the executive committee.'

Allegra allowed herself a small smile. She was on the top table with the boss? Everything was lining up just as she wanted.

'Fine. Then I'm going to need something a little more special for that. Um, black definitely, maybe a little more skin, although nothing too showy, obviously.'

'Long?' Cinzia asked.

'Quite possibly, yes. And a higher heel. Let's go to four.'

'OK,' Cinzia nodded, leaving her coffee untouched on the table. 'I'll bring some things in next week for you to look through.'

'Great. You'll liaise with Kirsty to make sure I'm in the country?'

'Of course.'

Kirsty nodded too, leaning forward to place something on Allegra's desk. 'Here's the photo you wanted framed,' she said quietly, handing over the image of Allegra, Bob, Jo and Derek with Mr Yong and his team, now smartly set in a jet-black Linley frame.

A frown settled on Allegra's features at the sight of it. She had had no word back from the Chinese camp since the incident with Sam in Zurich yesterday and, after a sleepless night, had decided not to interfere, taking the view that his inappropriate behaviour couldn't be considered a reflection on her. Strictly speaking, it hadn't happened under her 'watch', and although she was still fuming about it, she had to assume no news was good news.

'Fine. Send it over to Zurich on the overnight. I'll follow up tomorrow. OK, thanks, both.' And she looked back down at her screen: sixty-six new emails unread. And counting.

The halls of the V&A echoed with the sounds of jollity long before she came to the Dome, where the drinks were being held. In the centre of the vast space was a giant Christmas tree that had been sprayed white, blue lights illuminated the vaulted ceilings, and tall planters overflowed with rowan-berried profusions. In a far corner, a pianist was dwarfed by the proportions of the grand salon, almost lost.

She stood and watched for a moment, her eyes taking in the power DNA of each group of guests, waiters moving between them like skaters on a pond. London was draped

in black and white tonight, women sparkling, men stric-
tured in barathea, and she could almost smell the money in
the air, over the cologne.

The feathers of the skirt shimmied slightly as Allegra
walked, her footsteps light but quick over the floor, as she
approached the closest group; one man, Peter Butler, was
her opposite number at Red Shore, their closest rivals, with
a portfolio within £70 million of theirs.

'Peter,' she smiled, kissing him on each cheek without
actually making physical contact. 'Belinda,' she smiled
again to his wife, repeating the charade and making small
talk about the merits of cockerpoos over Labs in London
and the floppy paddles in the new Discovery 4, before exit-
ing with a regretful smile and moving on to the next group.

She was four groups in when she finally reached her
target, Pierre Lafauvre, founder and chairman of the company and centre of her world. Every night she spent without sleep, every day she spent sequestered from sunlight,
every medical check-up that noted too-high blood pressure
was done willingly in pursuit of his approval. Fifty-two but
looking ten years younger, with salt-and-pepper hair, broad
shoulders and a disarmingly still manner, he had enam-
oured her long before they'd ever met, his business reputation almost mythical on her postgraduate course at LSE,
when he'd been the big ticket at Credit Suisse, before falling
out spectacularly with his bosses over the expenses scandal
– to this day he still maintained the £68,500 bottle of Petrus
had been the clincher for a deal that had netted $486m in
fees – and setting up his own hedge-fund company, PLF,
months later. There was nothing between them romanti-
cally, although she knew people talked. He was her professional icon and mentor – that was all; he had never made a

move on her, but she had sometimes wondered whether he suspected the motives behind Crivelli's resentment towards her, often positioning himself between the two of them as interference. A sort of protector.

His wife was a model, naturally: Allegra's height, Slavic and twenty-three. Someone – Bob? – thought she'd once been an angel for Victoria's Secret, but that was no help to Allegra. She always found it a sufferance having to talk to her; Pasha's English was fine, but her conversational range wasn't and she clearly felt that Allegra's title as president of luxury goods meant they were bonded for life, dooming Allegra to countless evenings discussing Dior's new handbag range and Saint Laurent's unforgiving androgyny.

'Pasha, how lovely to see you. Your dress is beautiful,' Allegra smiled to her, taking in the backless baby-pink number interspersed with crystals and – to Allegra's dismay – marabou feathers.

'Thank you. Elie Saab Couture,' Pasha replied, twisting her narrow hips slightly to make the crystals glitter and the feathers flutter. 'I like yours too. The same, huh?'

Allegra kept smiling, her body rigidly still. She would not flutter. Their dresses were nothing like the same. *They* were nothing like the same. Allegra wasn't in this room on account of the slant of her eyes or the curve of her breasts. She was in here because she deserved to be, because she was every bit as talented and ruthless and disciplined as the men surrounding them in Savile Row conformity. They could all merge as one in their identikit dinner suits, only a slip of coloured lining or change of buttons marking them out, while she stood alone in her black dress, but she was more like them than she was like Pasha – whether they were both bedecked in feathers or not.

'Pierre.' Allegra smiled, visibly relaxing as she met his eyes and almost bursting to tell him about her triumphant first meeting with Yong. Nothing in her world seemed real till he knew about it.

'Allegra,' he nodded, holding his champagne glass by the stem. 'I hear things didn't go according to plan in Zurich.'

She stalled, the smile frozen on her face. 'Excuse me?' Oh God. Sam Kemp. He'd ruined it for her after all. No news was bad news. No news was failure.

She shifted position, stopping the panic from taking hold. 'As far as I'm aware, everything's on track. Yong liked our proposal for the investments, he accepted the gifts with gratitude and thanks, we couriered over the meeting photograph this afternoon, and I'm planning on following up with a phone call requesting the second meeting tomorrow. As far as I'm concerned, it should all be wrapped up and in the bag by this time next week.'

She knew it was foolish to speak so confidently. There were 101 things that could go wrong between now and then. The Chinese were notoriously difficult to pin down to an agreement, and she'd be a fool to think Red Shore and all their other competitors weren't furiously chasing after him too. But she couldn't help herself. This was her big break.

'I have always admired your balls, Allegra,' Pierre said, 'but I don't see how even you can get around this. And I want that account, because then Leo Besakovitch can take his fucking money and go fuck himself.'

Allegra let a beat pass. Besakovitch's money – a $28-billion family trust built on water-sanitation products sold throughout the Third World – had been the start-up fund for Pierre's company, and for nearly a decade they had made each other significantly richer. But the men's once-close relationship had foundered and Besakovitch was pulling his investment a few days before Christmas. Allegra wasn't sure if it was the emotional or financial rupture that had sent Pierre into such paroxysms of rage, but to his mind, success was the best revenge and he had been driving them all even harder since Besakovitch's pull-out announcement three months ago. And it was working – their average returns had increased from 11 per cent to 14 per cent – but Pierre wanted more than just good results on the money they had. He wanted a new big investor, a show pony to restore his pride and put PLF back on top again, and they both knew Yong was the man to do it.

Besakovitch who? Sam Kemp's loss would be her gain, unfortunate but true. It was her contact – a Chinese friend from LSE – who'd tipped her off that Yong was looking to grow his capital outside the Chinese economy for the first time; she was the one who'd spent weeks delicately brokering the meeting, finally managing to secure it in the no-man's-land of Zurich, studying their accounts twenty-four seven and formulating an investment strategy that would promise Yong the returns that would procure his investment and, crucially, bump PLF's returns up from the basic 2 per cent management fee to the 20 per cent of profits payouts.

'I'm sorry, but I don't see what the problem is.'

Pierre's eyes flitted down her quickly – resting fractionally on the feathers – as though the words he was about to say were as surprising to him as to her. 'You are a woman, Allegra.'

'Yes.'

'In the interpreter's report, it clearly states that Yong doesn't feel comfortable negotiating with a woman.'

Allegra's mouth opened, but no sound came out. She didn't know where to begin. She couldn't believe the words had even been articulated. It had been bad enough seeing it on the report, knowing Yong had said it, but for her own boss to put it out there as a 'problem' – it was a discrimination lawsuit waiting to happen, and he knew it.

She closed her mouth again and narrowed her eyes, knowing he wasn't that stupid. Pierre wouldn't bring up this problem without having first configured a solution.

'Well, what do you suggest we do about it, Pierre?'

Pierre looked over her shoulder, jerking his chin up slightly. 'We give Mr Yong what he wants, of course.'

Allegra tilted her head fractionally, glimpsing where he was going to take this, daring him to do it. He and she both knew what the legal position would be on this if he said it. The law would very clearly be on her side.

Someone moved from behind her. 'I believe you and Mr Kemp met in Zurich this week. Trouble with your car, wasn't it?'

But Allegra had stopped listening. She was looking straight into the blue eyes that had last locked with hers on a pillow. What? What was he doing here? She'd never expected to see him again, much less here, standing with her boss.

He smiled and a rush of memories flooded back to her.

She wrenched her gaze away, certain their brief intimacy could be read openly by anyone who happened to look; she couldn't deal with him right now, not when all this . . .

The penny dropped.

She looked back at Pierre in dismay. 'You're not saying

what I think you're saying.' She smiled and forced herself to take a sip of her champagne to hide the spike of anger that was making her hand begin to shake.

Pierre regarded her coolly. 'You probably know Sam was the lead on Leo's pot, but with the fat bastard leaving, Sam's relocating to the London office with immediate effect. By a stroke of luck, he and Yong's son, Zhou, were contemporaries at Harvard Business School. Room-mates, wasn't it?'

'That's right,' Sam nodded, his eyes on Allegra all the while. 'I happened to run into him on our way out of the building the other day.'

'Did you?' Allegra replied, pleading ignorance and ignoring the flicker of heat in his eyes. She looked back at Pierre. 'So your suggestion is that Sam takes on the Yong account and I just . . . fade into the background?' A threatening note sounded in her voice.

'*Au contraire*, Allegra.' He smiled, tackling her barb head on. 'I am proposing that you and Sam work jointly on this account. You are the business lead, devising investment strategy and managing the team; Sam will take the lead on the client-management side of things.'

'How cosy,' Allegra said to Sam. 'Taking your former room-mate out for lunches on the company? You can catch up on old times.'

Sam's expression changed.

Allegra didn't care. She stared at Pierre long and hard, the betrayal arousing in her emotions that never – *never* – assailed her. Quickly, she drained her glass and handed it to a passing waiter. 'Well, on that note, I have to skip off.'

'You have somewhere to be?' Pasha asked, the volatile

undercurrents of the conversation passing her by completely.

Allegra flashed a dazzling, extra-wide smile that radiated a hostility even her toothy gap couldn't assuage. 'Yes, actually. A boxing lesson. It's time for me to beat the shit out of something.'

And with that, she turned on her heel and strode off, furious to know her feathers were flouncing.

'I do love her dress,' she heard Pasha sigh, as the men watched her leave in silence.

She was at the top of the steps outside when Sam caught up with her.

'Allegra, wait!' he called, grabbing her by the elbow and spinning her round with ease. 'Look, I didn't plan it like this.'

'No?'

Her fury was palpable and he raked a hand through his hair, taken aback. 'No. I mean, I admit I wanted to see you again. Making the move to London seemed . . . attractive after the other night.'

Allegra wrenched her elbow from his grip, laughing. 'You moved to London because of me?' The scorn in her voice was scorching.

'Not *just* because of you. London's a lot closer to New York than Zurich . . .' His voice trailed away. It was a flimsy excuse and they both knew it.

She stared at him, classically handsome in black tie, other women staring at him as they passed by on the steps. Why, *why* did it have to be him?

'You think something's going to happen between us, Sam?' she asked, her voice low and shaky. 'Because let me put you straight right now. I was never supposed to see

you again. That was the deal. The other night was just . . .'
She shrugged, not sure she could pull this off. 'Sport. Exercise. A nightcap. A nice way to relax before the pitch.'

But she saw the muscle twitch in his jaw and knew she'd
landed a strike.

'What? You weren't honestly expecting a different out-
come? Did you really think I wouldn't mind you coming in
and stealing from me everything that I've spent months
working on? *I* cultivated the contact, nailed that meeting
down, made the numbers work. But because you're a man,
because you're his friend, you get to come in here and take
all that away from me, and I'm supposed to be *flattered* that
you followed me here?'

She laughed again – a cold, bitter sound that clattered to
the frosted ground like shards of shattered glass – shaking
her head slowly from side to side. 'You just made the biggest mistake of your career, Sam Kemp.'

They both had.

'Allegra—'

'It's Fisher to you,' she said, aggressively pointing a
finger at him, knowing she was overcompensating as she
tried to push him back out of her life – there was no room
for him in it. But he grabbed her by the wrist and the world
contracted in a sudden violent pulse to just the two of them
on the steps, his hand hot on her skin, his eyes burning into
hers. 'We need to be able to work together,' he said quietly,
but there was strain in his voice.

She swallowed. 'No. We don't. What I *need* is for you to
be gone from my life. Gone from this company. Gone from
this country. And I won't stop until you are.'

He stared at her for a long moment, his expression hard-
ening before her. 'That's really how you want to play this?'

'That's how we're already playing this.' And with a sharp tug, she released her wrist and ran down the steps, arm outstretched for a taxi.

Chapter Six

Day Five: *Gold-tipped Pine Cone*

Floral carpets – £3,000 a month and still you couldn't have decent carpets? Her eyes scanned them as she held open the door for a private nurse in a blue tunic who was pushing a gentleman in a wheelchair. He was wearing a tweed jacket and silk cravat at the neck, a bone-handled walking cane between his knees, the knuckles on his hands swollen and white.

'Thank you,' he smiled with a dignified nod as they passed.

'My pleasure,' Allegra murmured, stepping after them into the hall area and wondering where to go. Her mother hadn't been in her flat, and Barry's text (when she had enquired) had told her to find them in the morning room, but she wasn't clued up yet on the layout of the crescent of low-rise red-brick buildings – only that the block her mother's flat was in was opposite the fountain and had an orange front door.

This, though, was the community's hub, and she saw a sign pointing the way to the laundry room. The morning room had to be around here somewhere. She followed at a distance after the gentleman and nurse, hearing the ambient noise level pick up. She rounded a corner and stopped in the doorway of a large octagonal room, taking a few deep breaths as she scanned the activity inside. It was busy, with armchairs positioned in sociable fours and twos, the ones by the fireplace already taken. Some people were sitting alone reading newspapers, others playing board games, yet others engaged in conversations . . .

She looked around for Barry first, as he was the one who stood out here – his ruddy cheeks and bristly brown beard in stark youthful contrast to the wan complexions and bald pates found here in abundance – but it was her mother that she found, sitting in a far corner, the shiny crown of her still head – her once-dark hair grey and slightly wiry now – gleaming under the lights.

It was early evening and condensation had misted the large windows slightly, blurring the landscape, and Allegra knew there would be a slight chill coming from the glass. She picked up a lambswool tartan blanket from one of the empty chairs as she passed.

She stopped just shy of the chair and swallowed, her heart banging like a drum in her chest. 'Hi, Mum.'

Her mother looked up – Allegra thirty-five years from now – her hair plaited loosely and positioned over one shoulder, her raisin-dark eyes so enquiring, so curious.

'Allegra.' The smile, her name . . . Allegra felt the tension inside her slacken.

'How are you, Mum?' she beamed, sinking into the angled chair beside her and automatically opening out the blanket over her mother's legs. 'Where's Barry? Aren't you getting a chill from sitting so close to that window?'

'He's gone to get my cardigan. You fuss too much,' she

said, but her eyes were soft as Allegra tucked the blanket in around her.

'Well, you should be in front of the fire. There was a hard frost last night.'

'Just how I like it. You know I've always loved the cold.'

'Don't I just! I still haven't forgiven you for taking eighteen years to install central heating.'

Her mother chuckled, reaching for Allegra's hand and holding it between both of hers. 'You look pale, darling.'

'I just need to get some more fresh air, that's all. I don't think I've spent even twenty minutes outside this week.'

She refused to dwell on the last of those minutes – out on the steps of the V&A with Sam last night.

'Don't tell me – you're working too hard again.' Julia patted her hand. 'I worry about you.'

'I know you do,' Allegra nodded. 'But please don't. I'm happy, Mum. I'm doing what I love.'

Her mother's eyes roamed her face, a blend of sadness and pride in her eyes. 'So what have you been up to, then?'

'Well, I was in Switzerland earlier this week,' she said brightly. 'Zurich. Only for an overnight stay, but . . .' She shrugged, her voice trailing away. Did all roads lead back to Kemp? 'The lake looked so beautiful with all the lights on it. One of these days I'll actually stay long enough to take a boat out on it.'

'Aren't you skiing soon? I get confused with your comings and goings. Barry's written it down for me, but you're always on a plane somewhere.'

'Yes, I'm going to Verbier over the New Year.'

'With friends?' Her mother's voice lifted.

'Clients.' She saw her mother's expression. 'That I get on

with really well. They're lovely. Almost friends.' She swallowed. 'It'll be fun.'

'When did you last see your sister?'

'Last weekend, actually. We spent Saturday morning together – Isobel and I took Ferdy for a walk in the park.' She didn't want to tell her mother how they'd spent Sunday, closing up their family home for the last time, ridding it of all traces of them.

'Isobel.' Her mother's voice was wistful. 'I haven't seen her lately.'

'Really? She said she was going to come by this morning.'

Julia shook her head. 'But it's lovely that *you're* here. I know how busy you are. What are your plans for this evening?'

She grimaced, already knowing the response she was going to get. 'I've got to go back to the office. I've got some work to do.'

'Allegra! It's seven o'clock. You should be relaxing. You work long enough hours as it is.'

'I know, but . . .' It was pointless trying to explain. 'You're probably right. Maybe I'll go to the gym.'

Julia frowned. 'Have you lost weight, darling?'

Allegra looked down at her narrow thighs. 'No. I don't think so.'

'You look thin.'

'I'm just tired.' Allegra squeezed her mother's hand, touched by the maternal concern that so rarely surfaced these days.

'You need to eat more. You can't afford to be so thin once the snow comes. What if you got left outside?'

Allegra smiled. 'I can assure you I never leave my bag anywhere. My keys are on me at all times.'

'It's never warm enough in the stables, no matter how much straw you've got.'

Allegra fell silent. 'Well . . . I'll try to remember that,' she said. What had it been today? Four minutes, if that? She took a deep breath, trying to pull her mother back, before she drifted too far to reach again. 'Listen, why don't you show me around here? I'd love to see it properly. Isobel said there was a small shop. Perhaps we could get some bits and make supper in your flat.'

Julia looked at her with an unforgiving, hostile stare, a new opacity to her eyes that hadn't been there before. 'You're not coming to my flat,' she hissed ominously. 'Why on earth would I go anywhere with you? I don't know you.'

'Yes, you're right. I'm sorry.' Allegra's voice was quieter.

'Why would you say that? Why would you want me to go outside in these conditions?'

'I don't. I'm sorry. I didn't mean to—'

'Who are you? How did you get in here?' Julia's voice was climbing, her hands beginning to grip the armrests.

'I'm Allegra,' Allegra said quietly, aware of heads beginning to turn, a murmur rustling through the tweeds.

From the corner of her eye, she saw Barry running towards them, Julia's favourite lilac cardigan slung over one burly arm, his rugby-player thighs chafing in his jeans. His eyes met Allegra's in silent communication and she got up out of the chair as he winked and swept past, crouching in front of Julia with kind eyes.

'Come on, Julia. It's time for your rest now. Can you stand for me?' His Welsh accent was lilting, almost like he was singing to her.

71

'Who are you?' she demanded, her fury and aggression switching to him.

'I'm Barry, you know that,' he said in confident tones, a smile that came with double dimples spreading across his face, softening her scowl.

'Have we met?'

'Oh yes,' Barry nodded, immediately beginning to sing the opening lines of 'Delilah' as he got his arm under Julia's and lifted her easily from the chair. It wasn't her body that was weak. 'I just went to get your cardigan for you. You were feeling a bit chilly. See? It's your favourite one. You asked me to get it because you wanted to look nice for your daughter.'

'But I don't have a daughter,' she said, her face turned to him in bafflement as he scrunched up one arm of the cardigan.

'Oh, well then, I must have misheard you – my mistake,' he replied with an easy smile, sliding the sleeves over her arms and shooting Allegra an apologetic look as she remained rooted to the spot. Slowly, he began to wheel her round towards the doors as he picked up the tune again.

'Why's *she* looking at me like that? Who is she?' Julia demanded, never taking her eyes off Allegra as he led her away.

'Come along, Julia, just sing with me,' Barry said cheerfully, their voices retreating.

Allegra watched in silence as her mother took up the lyrics and they disappeared from sight. The muscles in her neck strained from the effort to remain impassive as she registered the silence in the room and all the eyes on her. She thrust her chin in the air as she reached for her bag and made her way quickly from the room. She knew the drill –

experience had taught her not to move a muscle, not to say a word. Nothing would have helped. She couldn't have leaned forward to kiss her goodbye, to put her arms around her in a comforting hug. Julia would have screamed. She would have screamed like she was being murdered and Barry would have had to pull her off like an aggressor, for her mother was no longer her mother; Allegra was no longer her daughter. They were strangers again, and both of them were alone.

'You have to sign this.' Allegra tapped the paperwork on the table as Isobel tried to lose herself in freezing ice-cube trays of courgette purée. 'And I'm not leaving until you do.'

Isobel turned round, a silver spoon in one hand, the green-gunged saucepan in the other. 'I don't understand why we have to rush into this now.'

'This is not rushing.' That wasn't strictly true. Allegra had sped straight here from seeing their mother, finally wielding the paperwork her lawyer had drawn up for them several months ago. 'We've had our heads in the sand for too long now. It's been nearly three years since diagnosis, six since she started having real problems, and the situation is deteriorating badly – you know that. Mum had four minutes' lucidity with me, tops, today. And she had no recollection at all of having seen you this morning.'

Isobel sighed, dropping the spoon into the pan. 'But I thought the whole point of putting her into that flat and having Barry there twenty-four seven was to avoid this – at least for a little while longer.'

'Iz, there is no avoiding this. Barry is an excellent nurse and we're so lucky to have found him—'

'We're so lucky you can afford him, more like.'

Allegra missed a beat. It was true. She had earned good money for a decade, barely dipping into the pot for her work wardrobe or the Poplar flat, and she'd bought the Islington house almost out of embarrassment that she didn't have anything to spend it on. Her long business hours precluded a social life or exotic holidays and she didn't care about 'toys' like cars or boats. It was sad to admit that paying for a live-in nurse to share the flat in the sheltered village with Julia was one of her greatest extravagances. She knew Isobel felt guilty that she couldn't contribute to their mother's care equally, in that way. 'That's irrelevant. All that matters is Barry knows how to make Mum feel relaxed and safe. He makes her laugh like no one else can, and he's the only one who worked out that singing calms her down during an episode. He's brilliant and she's happier than she's been for a long time. But even *with* all that, there is no way back from here. Mum's condition will continue to deteriorate, and the bald truth is, she can't now make the big decisions – be they legal, medical or financial – that need to be made for her own safety and protection. We have to be her voice now in these matters.'

'I know, I know. I just . . .' Isobel sighed again, dumping the pan back on the hob and wiping her hands on her apron as she walked over to where Allegra was sitting and slumped in the chair opposite. 'Well, why do we have to split the power of attorney between us?'

'You mean, why can't *I* do it all?' Allegra asked bluntly.

'No! I mean, isn't it better if just one person does the property and affairs bit, as well as the health and welfare stuff? Won't splitting it up just complicate things?' In the sitting room beyond, they could hear Lloyd cheering as

Chelsea scored a goal against Arsenal. He was supposedly bonding with Ferdy, who – having discovered the freedom that came with crawling – was doing laps of the sitting room before bed.

'Look, I'm out of the country every week. I work round the clock. Sometimes I go into the office on a Saturday in my suit because I've *forgotten* that it's the weekend. If something happened to Mum, medically, and a decision had to be made, can you imagine how awful it would be if I wasn't even in the country? Or contactable? I spend more time on planes than you do in cafes. But you're here. You're an hour down the road if something happens and the doctors need a decision. The property and finances side of things, well, that all works to scheduled hours. I can cover that easily. Legally, under the terms of the lasting power of attorney, we've got to keep Mum's bank account separate to mine, so I've already set up a standing order to her account for . . . well, more than enough to cover all her expenses, put it that way.'

Isobel looked down at the form, a desolate expression on her face. Selling and clearing out the house had been hard enough – it was something that usually happened following a bereavement, and that was how it had felt, emptying their family home of their past. But to become the signatories of their mother's entire life . . . it was like they had become the parents and she the child; it was like losing their mother day after day after day.

'The time has come, Iz. It's the best way to protect Mum now.' She made sure her voice was level. 'She's not coming back.'

Isobel's face crumpled at the words, but they did their

job and she nodded quickly, picking up the black pen and signing her name along the dotted line in a rush.

Allegra picked up the form and blew on the ink to dry it as Isobel got up and marched to the fridge, pulling out a bottle of wine – her preferred coping mechanism. 'When are you going to see her next?'

'Tomorrow, I guess.' Isobel shrugged, splashing the wine carelessly into two large glasses. 'Today was such a wash-out I thought I'd try again.'

Allegra nodded. 'Well, can you take these contracts with you and get Mum to sign? You'll need to get someone to witness it – a professional, so a doctor, accountant, teacher . . .'

Isobel was quiet for a second as she twisted the screw cap back on. 'My friend Sara's a GP.'

'Great. Would she go with you?'

Isobel looked thoughtful. 'RHS Wisley is just down the road from the accommodation. I guess I could treat her to lunch there afterwards.'

'Perfect.'

Isobel nodded, bringing over both glasses and taking a large gulp of wine. They both knew it was anything but.

Isobel slumped back in the chair, her hair falling loose from the ponytail she had scrunched it into at whatever ungodly hour Ferdy had woken this morning. Her skin looked pinched, and her boyfriend jeans were baggier than they were supposed to be.

Allegra watched her little sister. It was only Thursday, but the weekend's carefree high spirits had long since evaporated. 'Listen, why don't you and Lloyd go out tonight? Grab a quick supper somewhere on Northcote Road.'

Isobel raised a disbelieving eyebrow. 'You're kidding, right? Do you have any idea how impossible it would be to find a babysitter at this short notice?'

Allegra shrugged. 'I'm free.'

Isobel frowned. *'You'd* babysit Ferdy?'

'Sure. Why not? You look like you could do with a bit of fun, and I don't have anything else planned.' Her laptop was in her bag. She could work as well from this sofa as her own.

'But don't you want to go out? That's the whole point of being footloose and fancy-free, isn't it? You can go out on a whim.'

'It's fine. I went out last night.'

'Don't tell me, somewhere mega-glamorous as usual. Drinks in Monaco, dinner in Paris?'

Allegra shrugged. 'Cocktails at the V&A.' Isobel's eyes widened, but Allegra didn't want to open up a conversation about any of last night. Pierre and Sam's joint betrayal had run on a loop through her head for twenty-four hours now and she'd barely slept, not remotely fooled by Pierre's assurances. Sam was never just going to be the 'face' of the team for this deal; if Yong didn't want to work with a woman now, he wasn't going to want to work with a woman after they had secured his investment either. And Sam – with Besakovitch off to pastures new – was a fund manager in need of a fund. No, she knew exactly how this was going to play out. She would be marginalized, she would be reporting to Sam, and he would get the job that was rightfully hers. And the question that she couldn't get out of her head was, what was she going to do about it?

She forced a smile. 'Go on. Let's tell Romeo he's taking you out tonight before I can change my mind.'

'Legs, you are the best!' Isobel squealed, hugging her sister delightedly. 'Lloyd!' she cried, running to the knocked-through double reception room where Ferdy was reaching for a lump of smokeless coal, Lloyd oblivious and almost on his haunches on the edge of the sofa as someone took a free kick. Isobel lifted Ferdy clear of the coal scuttle with inches to spare and set him back down on the floor in the farthest corner. 'We're going out. Allegra's offered to babysit.'

Shock, panic and disbelief ran across Lloyd's face in a marble of emotions and Allegra wondered whether he was more concerned about her babysitting their child or him missing the end of the match.

'It's fine,' Allegra smiled, perching on the arm of the sofa. 'If I can manage an eight hundred and seventy-five million pound portfolio, I think I can manage a ten-month-old,' she said drily.

'I'll run his bath!' Isobel hollered, dashing up the stairs.

'That's very decent of you, Allegra,' Lloyd said, talking to her with his eyes still glued to the screen.

'It's the least I can do. Iz looks exhausted,' Allegra said pointedly. 'A night out with you should be just the tonic. It'll be nice for her to get dressed up and feel special again.'

'Uh, right, yes . . . exactly. I'd been thinking along the same lines myself. Something . . . something special.' His voice drifted off as the players entered the goal box.

Allegra rolled her eyes. She had honestly never understood what her sister saw in Lloyd. He was good-looking in that bland, English way, like Nick Clegg: pale skin, symmetrical features, mid-brown hair. Everything neat and tidy, a choirboy grown up. There was nothing alarming about his face – no broken nose or cauliflower ear – but nothing amazing either. But that wasn't what got her antennae twitching – it was the inertia that he gave off; he was always permanently 'exhausted' (even before Ferds) or 'jet-lagged', while poor Iz managed all the broken nights and round-the-clock childcare on top of the shopping, the cleaning, the ironing, the cooking . . . Didn't he remember how special her sister was? Didn't he see how far he'd out-reached himself getting her?

She looked at the screen. Someone in blue was rolling around on the pitch, clutching his leg. She looked away again, already bored. She spent enough time around men talking sport during the week.

Isobel flew back into the room, her colour already improved. 'Right, where's my little man?' she asked brightly, scooping Ferdy out of touching distance of the coal shuttle again. 'Is Daddy taking Mummy out for dinner? Oh yes he is, oh yes he is . . .' she cooed, her voice growing faint as they disappeared up the stairs.

Allegra watched as Lloyd twitched agitatedly, swearing under his breath at the ref and clearly willing the match to hurry up. There were still over forty minutes left on the clock, but Isobel would be ready, and with Ferds down, in twenty.

She watched him in suspicious, disapproving silence as Isobel clattered around upstairs, banging shut wardrobes and chasing after Ferds, who was no doubt crawling on the cream carpets without a nappy. This was the Happy Ever After everyone was sold: the beautiful London house, the gurgling baby, the boyishly handsome husband. Even their black-and-white studio photographs on the shelves per-petuated the myth of familial bliss. But it revealed nothing of the TV on as a substitute for conversation, the crumpled bed linen in the spare room where Lloyd now slept 'so that he's fresh for work', the rigid taking turns of sleeping in at the weekend as they competed for who was the more exhausted . . .

Yes, this was the dream.

Little wonder she didn't want it.

Chapter Seven

Day Six: *Felted Gingerbread Man*

'Bob, where are we on Demontignac?'

Bob lifted a ream of papers, one finger tracking down the centre of a page. 'Up four points since Friday to seventy-eight dollars. It's looking good. We bought at thirty-six dollars, and the analysts are—' He stopped as he saw Allegra narrow her eyes. He knew that look well. 'No?' he asked.

'I keep going over their accounting approach. I don't like the way they're flicking their assets into off balance sheets. It's unsustainable.'

'The analysts are predicting the shares to head towards a hundred dollars.'

'Based on confidence in the overall growing market and lower commercial entry prices for coloured diamonds. But it's the company itself I'm worried about. They don't seem to care what they pay for the infrastructure assets they're acquiring through the unlisted and listed funds. They paid well above the odds in my opinion for the Zimbabwean processing plant. I think they're trading on an inherently unstable platform.'

'So you think we should short?'

She nodded. 'I do.'

Bob hesitated a moment before nodding too. 'OK, then.'

The door opened, but Allegra didn't look up. Catering came in with breakfast on the dot of seven. 'And I've still got concerns about—'

'I hope I'm not interrupting,' an unapologetic voice said, interrupting.

Allegra looked up in irritation as Sam walked into the small conference room. 'I didn't get the memo that the meeting was seven a.m.' His tone was short and unfriendly; they hadn't seen each other since their confrontation on the steps on Wednesday, and she'd heard from Kirsty that he'd been with Pierre all day yesterday. It made her nervous that Pierre was so obviously grooming him for this account.

'Six thirty, actually,' Allegra said, clipped. 'And there is no memo. You just get with the programme.'

Sam's eyes flicked up to hers as he sat himself in the empty chair between her and Bob – in the chairman's seat. A deliberate show of arrogance? 'Well, then I'm afraid you'll have to bring me up to speed on whatever it is that I've missed.'

Allegra didn't reply – she didn't report to him – so Bob did it for her. 'We're selling Demontignac.'

'Why? They're booming, especially after that actress picked up her Emmy wearing one of their necklaces. What was her name?'

Allegra looked at him like he was mad. He was asking *her* the name of an actress? 'They're unstable,' she said dismissively, making a tiny flick of her index finger to indicate for Bob to move on.

But Sam was having none of it. He leaned in on his

elbows. 'You were one of the first in. You bought at, what – low thirties?'

'Thirty-six dollars,' Bob replied for her.

'And they're seventy-eight dollars now,' Sam said, his eyes never leaving her. 'You've already doubled the investment and everybody agrees they're going to continue to climb. They're nowhere near the ceiling yet.'

'In my opinion, they're going to tank,' Allegra said calmly. 'Their business model is flawed. We're getting out. The market may be growing, but the way *they're* operating is unsustainable. Like you say, we've doubled our money. It's time to move on.'

'But—'

'The decision's made, Kemp. It's off the table. If you want to contribute, get here on time.' She looked at him coolly. 'Bob?'

'Uh . . .' Bob scanned his file, nervously pushing his square glasses up his nose. 'Renton.'

'Oh yes, their push into China.' She shook her head again. 'I think it's a value trap. If Prada and Gucci are down '

'You're a China bear?' Sam looked almost amused as he sat back in the chair.

Her eyes appraised him, betraying none of her anger at the way he kept speaking over her. 'You're not? They just defaulted on their bonds payments. They've had the biggest currency sell-off in years, a slide in the equity markets and multiple growth forecasts downgraded.' Her tone suggested he was the fool.

'But commodities are up. Iron ore's well past a hundred and fifty dollars a tonne.'

'Because of panic-buying,' she asserted calmly. 'But as

soon as the cyclones stop and local supply is restored, they'll find themselves with a surplus and it'll drop below the hundred mark.'

He watched her for a moment. 'I couldn't disagree with you more. I think Renton's expansion into Asia is a classic value story – high profit margins, low costs and plans to triple production by next year. And I've heard LVMH are sniffing around them.'

Allegra reached forward for her glass of water and took a sip, taking her time. If they were, that was the first she'd heard of it. She could see Bob stiffen in her peripheral vision. They both knew it was his job to know these things first. 'China is done. The market contracted fifteen per cent last year – partly from brand fatigue, partly thanks to the new government's anti-corruption drive, which isn't going away anytime soon. This year is all about stabilization and keeping prices level, which will mean flat profits yet again.'

'But China still accounts for over a quarter of revenue at Louis Vuitton.'

'Yes, except the Chinese aren't buying it in China. More than sixty per cent of the country's luxury goods are now bought outside of the country. They're going to New York, Paris, London . . .'

Sam shook his head, sitting back in the chair, his hands laced together, fingers pointed into a steeple. 'You're a cata-strophist, Fisher. In the few minutes I've been in here, you've talked about dumping shares in two booming companies.'

Allegra didn't react, even though the way he'd called her by her surname had made her want to wince. It sounded wrong coming from him, even though she had told him to. She wanted him to treat her like a man like all the others, even though he alone in this building was the only one she'd ever been with as a woman. The fact shamed her. Had she known he'd ever be in this building, it would never have happened, but at the time, Zurich had seemed sufficiently far away, his exit from the company all but a guarantee.

'I'm not a catastrophist; I'm a realist. The market has changed. Luxury's splitting into tiers, and the big growth now is in America. It remains the world's number-one luxury consumer market, with "accessible" luxury in particular performing strongly. In addition, Bob's got his team looking at the emerging markets. South America's the new luxe frontier – most notably Mexico – and if we're going to keep a toe in Asia, then it should be Thailand and Vietnam; and India's better insulated against a Chinese flatline.'

'Also we're keeping a close eye on Africa,' Bob interjected. 'It's a niche and pocketed market, but our analysts have identified Nigerians as the fourth largest luxury spenders in the UK, and Zegna, Boss and MAC have all opened in Lagos recently.' He rose from the desk and offered his hand. 'Bob Wagstaff, by the way. We haven't met.'

Sam shook his hand briefly, unimpressed by the joint attack, his eyes straight back to Allegra. 'You're just running scared,' he said, making the colour drain from her face.

She glanced nervously at Bob. Was Sam alluding to them? 'What?'

'You're worried about gravity in the market when the ball's still going up in the air.'

'It's my job to worry. Our investors do very well out of

85

my worry, and Renton's a highly leveraged bet on continued fixed-asset investment growth in China.' Her silver pen ticked irritably between her fingers.

'And I'm telling you, Pierre thinks it's still too early to move.' He shrugged lightly, letting her absorb the insinuation that he had Pierre's ear. 'What are you so frightened of? Surely your success with the Lindover Watches stocks showed you there's still room in the market to turn a buck.'

'Lindover?' She sneered at him. 'What are you talking about? We passed on it.'

'You sure about that? Think again.' He arched an eyebrow, staring at her with a cocksure arrogance that he could just come into her meeting and start calling the shots, undermining her decisions, which were backed up with a ten-year success rate.

She scowled. 'I don't need to.'

'Perhaps you've forgotten.'

'I never forget.'

He stared at her through darkened eyes and she wondered whether they were both remembering the thing that was unforgettable. 'Well, the ledger says differently.'

The ledger? She inhaled shallowly as she realized he'd been checking up on her, going through her past trades, trying to see how she worked. A small smile curved her mouth. He was scoping out the competition, more threatened by her than he'd wanted to show. Maybe she wasn't the only one losing sleep over this after all. He knew he'd have to rely on more than just contacts to keep his job.

'And I clearly recall we discussed and dismissed it. I suggest if you're going to come in and throw your weight around in my meetings, you get your facts straight first.'

His eyes flashed at her put-down, a long moment drawing out between them, with Bob caught in the middle.

'Well,' Sam said finally, checking his watch, 'we'll have to pick this up later.'

How convenient, she thought to herself, sitting back in her chair and watching him. Just as she was beginning to dominate proceedings. 'Why's that?'

He stood up, pulling down his cuffs smartly. 'I'm having brunch with Zhou and his father. I've got a plane to catch.'

'*What?* To where?'

'Paris.'

She stood up abruptly. 'You're not meeting him without me.'

Kemp looked across at her coldly. 'Pierre was clear, Fisher. You take the investment lead. I deal with the client.'

He turned and walked out of the door, Allegra open-mouthed and speechless behind him.

'Well, what a lovely dick-swinging tosser he is,' Bob said, replacing the cover on his iPad.

A smile broke out across her face and she laughed lightly. Bob, as her closest ally, could always be relied on to pull out the right fact or comment at the pertinent moment. 'Isn't he, though?' she asked, her arms crossed. Her eyes narrowed thoughtfully as her fingers began to tap on her arms.

'What are you thinking?' Bob asked, seeing the telltale signs of cunning on her face.

She turned back to him. 'Did it seem to you like he let me take the lead on investment strategy in that meeting?' she asked, her eyes still on the empty doorway.

Bob shook his head.

'No, me neither.' She smiled, her eyes glittering fiercely.

'So then why the hell should I let him take the lead with the client? Yong *owes* me that second meeting; he can't refuse it. It's a matter of honour.'

'Yes, it is,' Bob smiled.

Allegra pressed a button under the desk and a second later Kirsty put her head round the door. 'Kirsty, speak to Sam Kemp's PA. I want to know where he's meeting Zhou for brunch and when. And book me on the next flight to Paris that *isn't* Kemp's flight. If he's Heathrow, I'll go from Stansted or City, so get a driver on standby.'

'Yes, Miss Fisher.'

Allegra pointed at Bob. 'Get me the newest numbers for everything we just discussed in that meeting, including a full report on Mexico. Send it through to the Paris office. They can bike it over to me at the restaurant. My name, but cc Kemp, as the reservation will be in his name.'

'Yes, boss.'

She stopped for a moment. 'And get me the ledgers for his trades on the Besakovitch pot.'

Bob frowned. 'Why do you need those?'

'You heard the man. He's been reading up on me. I think I should return the compliment, don't you? Let's see how his brain works.'

Bob nodded and hurried past with a smile.

'What are you smiling about?' she asked after him as she shuffled her papers.

He stopped and turned, pushing his glasses up his nose again. 'You're great when you get mad.'

Allegra swept from the cab to the doors of the restaurant without pause. Ten fifty-four a.m. It was tight and she had to hope the Yongs were slightly behind time.

It was lucky the driver had known of the restaurant. There were no signs outside to wit and she could have walked past it fifty times without ever knowing what was inside. The facade seemed deliberately obscure – a voluminous wisteria espaliered against white stuccoed walls and covering even the windows, the wide, arched oak doors more like the entrance to a boat shed or wine store than a restaurant.

'Monsieur Kemp, *onze heures*,' she said in perfectly accented French to the concierge, her eyes on the blackened glass of the verre églomisé mirror behind him, trying to spot her brunch companions. The space inside was large, with mossy stone walls and generous spaces between the tables. It had obviously once been a courtyard and was now enclosed by a vaulted lantern roof from which hung modernist white bulbs on long chains, like pearls on a gold necklace. The chairs were a dusty-pink velvet, upholstered chesterfield style, the tables round.

She moved right slightly, looking round a large stone urn of black roses, and saw Sam's bright hair easily. He was sitting with his back to her, alone still, the shape of his shoulders suggesting he was reading his BlackBerry.

'*Ah oui, Kemp. Trois personnes*,' the concierge read back to her from his reservation book.

'*Non, quatre*.' She kept her smile small to make him run all the quicker to put out the extra setting.

The concierge didn't argue. If there was a mistake, the mistake was theirs. '*Mais bien sûr. Voulez-vous me suivre à la table?*'

'*Non, je préfère attendre Monsieur Zhou ici, merci.*'

'*Je vous en prie.*'

The concierge inclined his head and hurried away to

have the extra setting laid. Allegra kept her back to the room, watching the action unfold in the mirror. She observed as Sam's head jerked up as the waiter came to the table to lay down the cutlery and glasses. She saw him stop the waiter, the waiter talking to him in a low voice and then Sam turning, his eyes scanning for the mystery person who had added one to their number. Could he guess it was her? He couldn't see her, not from where he was sitting. The glass of the mirror was too dark and too far away for him to catch her reflection, and as she slid left again, she was obscured by the roses. He could only see her now if he stood and walked over.

A dull clunk outside caught her attention and she turned. Mr Yong was emerging from a limousine, walking towards the restaurant with his head bowed, his son matching his slow stride.

Allegra straightened up as she positioned herself just inside the doorway, giving both father and son a moment to register her presence. She would grant them that courtesy at least.

'Mr Yong, Mr Zhou Yong. It is a pleasure to see you again,' she smiled, bowing her head and forcing them to do the same.

They shook hands, smiling graciously, manners gagging the men from asking what *she* was doing here.

'Mr Kemp and I are honoured that you have agreed to see us again so soon. My colleagues and I felt that the meeting in Zurich was mutually interesting for both parties. I trust your office received the photograph of our meeting, by way of thanks?'

'Indeed,' Mr Yong said, on the back foot that Allegra was here and he, yet again, had no gifts ready to reciprocate hers, something that pleased Allegra immensely; the more indebted he was to her, the better. 'The honour is all ours.'

'Shall we go through? Mr Kemp is waiting for us,' Allegra smiled, leading both men through the restaurant.

Allegra deliberately kept her eyes away from Sam's as she led the two men to the table – she didn't want to give him the satisfaction of being able to land his furious glare on her. Instead, she took off her glossy black ponyskin coat, handing it to the maître d', and tugged the hem of her black peplum-skirted shell top, matched with narrow cigarette trousers (the spare 'work-to-evening' outfit she kept hanging on the back of the door in her office).

It was a more feminine outfit than she ordinarily would have worn for a meeting with Yong. Ordinarily she would have gone to her usual lengths to obscure her gender, or at least negate it as much as she possibly could – high collars, buttoned-up jacket, sober colours, short hair, briefcase-style bags, even flat shoes – but where had that got her on this account? She had delivered the pitch of her life with number guarantees that would make most clients' heads spin off, but it had all come to nothing with them because she was the wrong gender. To all intents and purposes, she was off the account, to be hidden away at her desk making the numbers work while Kemp and his cronies bumped up the expenses account.

Well, not today. Today she was going to face them all down. Honour would force them into sitting with her, returning her good manners, and they could sit face to face with her femininity, the very thing they apparently found so impossible to work with.

She also started smiling a lot, not caring for once about the girlish gap between her teeth – smiling as she let the waiter hold her chair, smiling as the waiter handed her the menu, smiling even as she placed her order.

She could almost see the puzzlement in Sam's expression as he watched this new relaxed Allegra, so different from the one he'd encountered in the conference room in London only hours before, his eyes flitting to her every few seconds, though she didn't look back at him once.

She saw the shiny helmet of a bike courier by the concierge desk and smiled even wider. 'We're so pleased you've been able to meet with us again so soon. We're very excited about Sam joining the team, and I know he was keen to discuss with you a key change that we've decided upon.' Finally, she looked at him, her smile wider than ever, genuine glee in her eyes. 'Do you want to present it Sam, or shall I?'

Sam glared at her. He knew she knew perfectly well he had no file, reports or numbers to hand with which to do the presentation, but he couldn't dissent in front of the client. It would make the PLF team look fractured and disorganized and propel them in the direction of their competitors.

'Why don't you, Allegra, since you led discussions in Switzerland,' he replied, one arm outstretched on the table, his middle finger occasionally tapping the table the only sign of his intense irritation.

He watched suspiciously as the concierge stopped at their table and handed a large brown envelope to Allegra with a nod.

Allegra took it with a smile that could have lit the room. 'OK, then,' she beamed, the papers inside still warm from their run off the printer, as she distributed the reports to the men round the table. 'Sam saw the wisdom of this approach the moment we began going into harder detail on Renton's accounts. You see . . .'

An hour later, they were standing on the pavement, waving off the Yongs through tinted windows.

'Bravo,' Sam murmured as the limo pulled away from the kerb, filling the width of the narrow steel-grey street before turning out of sight. 'That was quite a show.'

Allegra had stopped smiling now the clients were gone. She didn't need to waste her vibrancy and energy and good cheer here. She was unapologetic and triumphant. If they won the account, it would be her strategy they'd be following, not Sam's – regardless of whether she fronted the meetings – and that gave her the ammunition she needed for the promotion. 'Would you have done any different?' she asked, finishing buttoning up her coat.

Sam watched, his face impassive, his body still. Snow was in the air, but he seemed impervious to the arctic temperatures. 'No.'

She gave a small shrug, as if to say, 'There you are, then,' looking down the road for a cab. Her last-minute dash here meant Kirsty hadn't been able to arrange a driver in time. Sam's was standing waiting for him, outside the car, further down the street.

'But you can't sabotage me every time I meet with them. You may have got away with it this time, but if you think I'm going to let you pull that stunt on me again—'

'What? You'll what?' she asked, one eyebrow arched defiantly.

He was quiet again. 'I don't agree with you about pulling out of China, but we have to present a united front.

Zhou told me his father's agreed to a meeting with Red Shore.'

'*What?* Shit!' she tutted angrily, stamping her foot lightly on the ground and looking away.

'We're going to have to come up with something more.'

She looked back at him. 'How can there be more? We're guaranteeing him thirty-six per cent returns!'

'And Red Shore will be going to them with something close to that too. Maybe even better. They're bigger than us.'

'There *isn't* better than what I'm proposing,' she said fiercely. 'I've looked at it from every angle.'

'We need something big, something no one else is on to yet,' Sam said, watching her hair swaying as she moved agitatedly.

'Yeah, well, good luck with that.'

There was a small pause. 'Apparently there's talk of Garrard hooking up with Harry Winston,' he said in a quiet voice.

She whipped round. 'A *merger*?' They were two of the biggest names in the precious jewellery firmament: Garrard had the British pedigree and royal warrant, Harry Winston a Beverly Hills celebrity clientele that was every bit as prestigious, especially in this day and age. 'Why haven't I heard about it?'

He shrugged noncommittally.

'Where did you hear that?' she asked, stepping closer, scrutinizing his face. This was *her* market. She knew every single one of the guys at the US private equity firm that had bought Garrard. She was one of their go-to fund managers. No way was this information in the public domain yet.

He looked up at her through lowered lashes. 'I know someone who knows someone.'

She raised an eyebrow. Was he kidding? She stared at him in confusion. What kind of game was he playing here? What rules did he break? Was *this* how he got his returns? 'I'm sure you don't need me to point out to you that that's illegal,' she murmured, checking no one was within earshot.

'If I acted on it, yes.'

'I can't act on it either!' she hissed furiously. 'You just basically admitted that information is privileged!'

He shrugged. 'It could be what gives us the edge over the others. Don't you want to nail this deal?'

'Of course I do! But not . . . not like that.'

She turned away, but he came and stood behind her.

'What option have you got?' he asked, his voice brushing past her ear, and she suppressed a shiver.

'I'll think of something.'

She saw a taxi come round the corner and held up her arm. It headed towards her.

'Where are you going?' he asked.

She looked back at him. 'Why?'

He shrugged. 'I can give you a lift back to the office if you like. I'm on my way there myself. Thought I'd introduce myself to the Paris team while I'm here.'

More schmoozing. 'No. I'm going shopping.' She wasn't, but it wouldn't hurt to encourage him to underestimate her. After what she'd just heard, she had to get her hands on that report from Bob as soon as possible. At the very least, he was flexible with the industry's governing rules.

'Well, would you like to meet up later? In the interests of

trying to' – he gave a small sigh – 'clear the air, start over, make amends? We could go for dinner.'

The taxi stopped in front of her and she stared at him for a long moment, wishing she'd never been on that damned plane. 'Fine.'

'Great. I'll pick you up from your hotel.'

'No, I'll meet you there.'

'Where?'

'The Ritz. Book a table for eight p.m.'

'OK, then.' He flashed her a smile that belonged on a Diet Coke model and which she refused to return. She slid into the seat and shut the door.

'*Où?*' asked the driver over his shoulder.

'*L'aéroport Charles de Gaulle, tout de suite.*'

Chapter Eight

Day Ten: *Lavender Sachet*

'You can go in now.'

Allegra looked across at the PA – redhead with a designer ponytail and a first in modern languages from Bristol – who was the last line of defence to the inner sanctum.

She stood up and walked briskly across the carpet without a word. Nothing of the outside world permeated the executive suite – the walls were soundproofed, the windows bulletproof, everything around here armoured up, Allegra thought, to deliberately heighten your sense of human vulnerability, of flesh-and-blood fragility, to feel like Daniel as he walked into the lion's den.

She gave a quick tug on the hem of her Saint Laurent jacket – the only armour in her arsenal besides her extraordinary ability to decode numbers – before firmly rapping once on the door and walking in.

Pierre was sitting behind his desk at the far end of the room. He didn't look up as she entered, continuing to write whatever he was writing, but she wasn't fazed. They had had these state-of-the-nation chats many times before and they were like old warhorses hoofing the ground before they went into battle.

'Pierre,' she said in greeting, crossing the cherry-wood floor that was so highly polished she half wondered whether he used it to look up his PA's skirt.

'Allegra,' Pierre continued, still writing. 'A drink?'

'No, thank you.' She stood beside the chair on the opposite side of the desk to his, waiting to be told to sit, her eyes admiring the intensity on his face as he wrote.

After another minute or so, he threw – actually threw – the pen across the desk in front of him and looked up. His smile was cold. Her heart flipped a beat.

'I think we do need a drink,' he said, getting up and pouring them each a brandy, even though it was only four in the afternoon. He handed one to her. 'Take a seat.'

She did as instructed, watching as he walked towards the long, tall windows that afforded commanding views over the Wharf and back towards London proper. His silhouette was as sharply cut as the London skyline. Like her, he was a triathlon freak, and his PB was only eighteen minutes faster than hers – they had even run together on several occasions – and they had spent many evenings alone in his office, the last ones to leave, discussing carbon-fibre bikes and skinsuits.

But it wasn't his fitness or success or drive that she respected most. It was his intellect – a cool, rational brain that she could predict and understand, and which silenced the braggadocio of the look-at-me traders. It had brought him a personal fortune of £7 billion, homes on almost every continent in the world (had he wanted a ski lodge in Antarctica, he could have had one there too), a model wife (third) and, better than any of that put together, a reputation as a City goliath that saw CEOs of FTSE 100s stand even when he entered a ballroom.

Allegra watched in silence as he turned back to her, his eyes appraising her for a long moment before he wandered back to his desk. She tracked him like she was watching through the scope on a rifle, never blinking, not moving a muscle lest that be enough to lose him from view. She realized she was cold.

She hadn't seen him since she'd stormed out of the V&A, but Pierre wasn't delicate about high tempers; in fact, he actively encouraged passions in his employees. But she'd promised to bag the Yong deal within the week and her follow-up calls to Yong's office yesterday and today had been politely brushed off with the unsurprising news that Mr Yong was away travelling.

She couldn't ask Sam Kemp either, assuming that he'd tell her even if he knew. Not after the stunt she'd pulled . . . He had flown from Paris straight back to New York, apparently to wind up his affairs there and formally hand over to his successor, but Kirsty hadn't been able to find out when he was due back and Allegra hadn't pushed it for once – she didn't want to rely on him in any way or for anything.

There was a strong knock on the door and it opened.

'Pierre.'

Allegra felt her sinews tighten. Christ, talk of the devil.

'Come in, Kemp. We've been waiting for you.'

Allegra didn't stir as she heard Sam's tread over the floor, saw his frame fill her peripheral vision to the left: navy suit, navy tie, black shoes . . . She refused to imagine him sitting alone at the table in the Ritz. She refused to wonder how long he had waited before realizing she wasn't going to arrive.

Pierre poured him a drink and handed it over. 'The two of you seem to be having trouble clinching the Yong deal.'

'I wasn't aware that I was even allowed to clinch the deal,' Allegra said quickly, determined to get in first. 'Aren't I supposed to be back office on this now?'

'You didn't sound very back office in Paris,' Pierre replied with cold, knowing eyes.

Allegra straightened her back. News of her 'heist' had got back to him, then.

'Chinese etiquette dictated a return meeting and offering of gifts. By turning up unannounced, I was trying to obligate him into acting,' she said simply.

'Well, it didn't work, did it?' Pierre replied, unimpressed. 'Far from it. In fact, it seems to me that you've pushed him into the arms of our competitors. Thanks to Kemp's "in" with the son, we know that the Yongs had dinner with Peter Butler and his fucking cronies at Red Shore in Berlin last night.'

'There's no way they can compete with our strategy,' Allegra said confidently, determined to sound unafraid. 'It's Teflon-plated.'

'Really? Because not everybody is of the same opinion as you on China. Shares in Demontignac are up to ninety-one dollars. You just lost us forty-two million pounds by bottling last week.'

Allegra thrust up her chin. 'I didn't bottle. They're going to tank. Their business model isn't—'

'Stable? Thank you, I've read your report,' Pierre said dismissively, looking across at Sam. 'Did you agree with her decision?'

'No. It was a unilateral decision by Fisher. The first I knew of it was when she hijacked the meeting in Paris.' His voice was cold, unemotional, the brandy glass held languidly in one hand as he slouched to her military bearing. 'I'm not convinced we'll get anything like the same numbers going in at the low end of the market in the States, but there's precious little we can do about it now. We can't change our minds on it *again*. They'll think we don't know what the fuck we're doing. If they bite, then we can change the investments further down the road. They won't care so much about a U-turn when they see the P&Ls.'

Allegra was finding it hard to hear him over the sound of her own blood rushing through her head. Panic was beginning to flood her thoughts.

'What's the son said to you?'

'Zhou?' Sam shrugged. 'He's trying to sway his father in our favour, but he says his father won't make a decision until 18 December.'

'What?' Pierre thundered so loudly that Allegra almost shattered the glass in her hand. 'But Besakovitch is out on the 19th. The 18th is too fucking tight.'

'I know, but Yong's been advised that's the most auspicious date,' Sam said calmly. 'You know the Chinese.'

'Fuck auspicious!' Pierre shouted. 'He's got eight hundred and ninety million pounds that I want locked up.'

'I know and I'm doing everything I can. I saw Zhou in New York yesterday. He's on our side.'

Allegra felt her muscles tense to learn of a meeting that had happened without her there, without even her knowledge. How many others had there been, Sam hooking up with his old room-mate, while she was stonewalled by his office?

'On our side, or yanking our chain?'

'We'll get him, I promise.'

'Promises mean fuck all. *She* made me a promise last week and here we are, no further on!' Pierre drained the brandy, slamming the glass down on the desk. Allegra tried not to flinch, tried not to do anything that brought attention to the fact that she was a *she* and not – crucially – a *he*.

It wasn't the first time in her life that she'd failed on that score and the rush of anger helped her find her voice – strident and clear. 'Pierre, I'm going to look at the proposal again. Maybe we are too biased to the long side. Maybe you're right about China. I can take a fresh look. The markets are low volatility at the moment, trending upwards . . .' She shrugged, not believing in the words she was saying, but willing to say anything to buy time. 'Maybe I've been too market neutral. If Red Shore is coming in with something edgier, if Yong wants us to turn up the risk? We can do that. Just give me the word. I can go hardcore on this.'

Sam flashed a look across at her and she saw from his expression that he, too, was thinking about his non-legit tip in Paris.

Pierre stared coldly at her, then at Sam. 'Well, *one* of you has to do something. Leverage contacts, Kemp? Grow a fucking pair, Fisher? Because if Yong signs with Red Shore just because . . .' He groaned. 'Christ, if he signs with them because red is considered *lucky* . . . !' He was almost yelling.

'That won't happen, Pierre.' Allegra's voice was cool by comparison. She liked it when Pierre began throwing his toys out of the pram. It made her feel calmer and look more in control.

'It had better not. The rewards are great – I'm telling you that now.' His black eyes flicked between the pair of them.

'Whichever one of you seals this deal, you'll be in the office next door to here the following day. But if you don't and Yong fucks us over' – he sniffed – 'I'm not carrying dead weight.'

'Got it,' Allegra said, standing up adroitly, placing the untouched brandy on the desk.

Pierre stared at her. 'Not thirsty, Fisher?' he asked.

Allegra blinked, before picking it up and downing the shot in one, ignoring the burn in her throat. Sam stood up, his glass already empty, and nodded stiffly at Pierre.

The two of them marched towards the door and the safety of the outer sanctum.

The door had no sooner closed than Sam whirled round and was in her face. 'I gave up my career, my *life*, in New York, for this shit? Last week, Minotaur was offering me US CFO and here I am, two hours off the plane and already being threatened with the sack, because of you!'

'Not because of me,' Allegra hissed. '*I* didn't ask you to come here. If you can't close the deal, it's nobody's fault but yours. I mean, aren't you supposed to have been the one to stop Besakovitch from pulling out in the first place? He was your client. What is it with you? You just can't quite pull it off. You've got every advantage going – daddy's boy in your pocket, friends with—' She stopped speaking abruptly. The accusation couldn't be said out loud.

He snorted derisively. 'I hope you've updated your LinkedIn page, Fisher. You're going to need *your* contacts.'

'You're the one he told to leverage contacts,' she snapped back. 'It seems to be all you're good for.'

'Miss Fisher?'

Allegra turned in surprise, unaware of anyone else

around them, unaware that Kirsty had been standing anxiously beside her for several moments now. 'I'm sorry, I have an urgent message for you.'

Allegra paled. 'Is it my mother?'

'No.'

'Then can't you see I'm in the middle of something?' Allegra snapped.

'I'm sorry, it's very important. A sergeant called from the Swiss Police.' Kirsty's eyes slid to Sam, who was listening to every word, his eyes still blazing, jaw twitching. 'He says it's a personal matter, Miss Fisher.'

'I sincerely doubt that. There's no reason whatsoever that they should be calling me – unless they've found the ski pole I lost in Verbier last year.' She allowed herself a wry smile.

Kirsty was unmoved. She was paid well to remain unmoved at all times. 'He's quite sure it's you he needs to speak to. He confirmed your personal details with me. You have to contact him immediately.'

'Did he say what it was about?'

Kirsty looked awkward. 'Identifying remains, Miss Fisher.'

'Remains?' Allegra frowned.

'Of your grandmother. I'm afraid it was hard to hear: the connection was bad. He said something about a hut found in the snow and human remains?'

'No. That doesn't make sense.' Allegra shook her head firmly. 'My father's mother is alive and well in Bristol, and my maternal grandmother died in 2001. Ring him back. Tell him there's been a mistake.'

'I can't, Miss Fisher. Sergeant Annen says he will only

talk to you because you've got power of attorney. I've left the number on your desk.'

What? Allegra watched her go. The lasting power of attorney? So this was to do with her mother, then?

'Well,' Sam said, watching the confusion cloud her face and beginning to walk away. 'It sounds like you're going to be busy for a while.'

She blinked, returning her attention to him, staring at his expensively tailored back. 'It's a misunderstanding, Kemp. This changes nothing.'

'Yeah. Good luck with that,' he muttered, out of sight, but never, it seemed, out of mind.

'Sergeant Annen, please.' Allegra rubbed her face in her hands, tipping her chair back as she turned to face London in its night guise. It had been a long day, scrutinizing screens and reports till the numbers had begun to swim before her eyes, and she'd completely forgotten about this inconvenience, hijacked by Bob and a meeting with the new chief exec at Burberry as she'd arrived back on her own floor.

Kicking off her shoes, she put her feet up on the window-sill. Her hamstrings felt tight from too many hours sitting hunched and she felt an urge to get out of there and pound the streets. She loved running through London at night, moving sleekly from one pool of light to the next along the Embankment, her arms and legs moving rhythmically as her mind – for once – was unfettered and could drift on a meaningless stream of consciousness.

She wanted to feel the cold shock of the bitter night air in her lungs, to push her body and not just her mind, but she couldn't. She needed to redraft the numbers; tonight, no doubt, was going to be spent in the Four Seasons and she'd have to ask Kirsty to reschedule Thursday's weekly report to the ex co for next Tuesday so she could get this new proposal done.

The blue light was flashing on her phone – a signal she had a text – and she mindlessly picked it up, frowning to see she in fact had sixteen texts. All from Barry.

'Annen speaking.'

She sat up with a jolt as she remembered the other phone at her ear.

'Oh, yes, uh . . . Sergeant Annen? This is Allegra Fisher calling from London. You called my office earlier today.'

'Miss Fisher. Yes. I was expecting your call this afternoon.' His accent was slight, the irritation in his voice carrying over fluently.

'It's been a busy day, Sergeant. How can I help you?'

'We've been trying to contact your mother, Julia Fisher. I've been told you have power of attorney for her.'

Her eyes fluttered down to her mobile screen and Barry's numerous texts. Annen's name appeared on them all. What was this about? 'That's correct. I have LPA for her business and legal affairs. My sister has LPA for her health and welfare. Is it me you need to speak to?' She felt slightly ashamed for trying to pass the buck on to her sister, but what was the bet Isobel had had a dramatically less shitty day than her?

'Then it is you I need to speak to.'

She sighed. 'Go on.'

'I regret to inform you that we believe we have found the remains of your grandmother Valentina Fischer.'

'OK, if I can just stop you there,' she said briskly, pleased to get to the nub quickly. 'There's been a mistake. I've never heard of anyone called Valentina in our family. My paternal grandmother is still alive – her name is Patricia Johnson – and my maternal grandmother was called Anya.'

There was a silence and she heard the sound of papers being shuffled in the background. 'According to the birth reports, Anya was Valentina's sister. Valentina Fisher, born September 1930. Sister to Anya Fisher, born 1934, deceased 2001. Next of kin Julia Fisher, date of birth 23 February 1948, currently residing Buttersmere, Hampshire, UK.'

Allegra was silent. Her mother's date of birth. Her grandmother's name. 'Well, as I said, my grandmother was Anya Fisher. I've never heard of a sister called Valentina.'

'It is believed she died in an avalanche in January 1951.'

'Well, my mother would have been not quite three then, so that explains why she knows nothing about her aunt dying in an avalanche in . . . Where did you say it happened again?'

'I didn't. It was in Zermatt.'

'Well, I don't understand what any of my family would even have been doing over there in the 1950s. This doesn't make sense to me.'

'It doesn't make sense to anyone right now, Miss Fisher. That's why we need your mother to provide us with a DNA sample. Assuming that the records are correct, she is the closest living relative to Valentina Fisher.'

'No, I'm sorry. My mother isn't well enough to help you with that. She's very fragile. Alzheimer's.'

The word had a blunt force to it that she knew from experience stopped most conversations in their tracks. Sure enough, he paused. 'I'm sorry to hear that. But it's a painless procedure – an oral swab, a couple of hairs and some nail clippings.'

'Absolutely not. She wouldn't understand what was happening. I'm sorry but my answer is no.'

'Miss Fisher, please understand we cannot sign off on the case without it. It is a live police investigation, and until the remains are formally identified, there can be no burial. It will remain an open enquiry and all the paperwork tells us that this woman was your grandmother.'

'And I've already told you, my grandmother was Anya Fisher. We buried her when I was eighteen.'

'Then you'll agree there's a discrepancy here that doesn't add up and we have even more questions to answer than we initially thought. If your mother isn't well enough to help us, then we have to ask you, as her daughter and her LPA, to help us instead.'

'You want *me* to supply a DNA sample?'

'You are the next closest living relative. It is close enough.'

Allegra sighed irritably. If it meant they'd leave her mother in peace . . . 'What do I have to do?' she asked with a truculent tone.

'I can send over the necessary papers authorizing a DNA test to be done at your local police station tomorrow. It won't take more than a few minutes.'

Oh, this was just excellent. 'Fine. Do you have my email?'

'Yes, I liaised with your secretary earlier. I'll send everything through within the hour.'

They hung up briskly, Allegra staring unseeing at the back of her door, her emergency day-to-evening outfit already dry-cleaned and hanging in its usual place. Beneath her hands, papers and reports were growing cold. She needed to get back to work.

Instead, she picked up the phone and dialled a number.

'Hey, it's me. You free to talk for a minute?'

'Oh yeah, it's the best time of day, this. Ferdy's down. Lloyd's out with clients.' Isobel's voice was relaxed and Allegra guessed she was on her 'restorative' glass of wine by now. 'What's up?'

'I just had a really odd phone call from a police officer in Switzerland.'

'Eh? Switzerland?'

'Mmm. Have you ever heard of a great-aunt called Valentina?'

There was a short pause. Allegra thought she was thinking, but then heard her sister's lips smacking together and realized she was taking a sip of wine. 'No, never. Why?'

'Apparently, her remains have been found in Zermatt.'

'Eeew! What do you mean by "remains"?'

'I'm not really sure. Bones? She disappeared in 1951 apparently. An avalanche.'

'Grim.'

'Yes.' Allegra was quiet for a moment. 'I've got to give them a DNA sample so that they can confirm the identity.'

'Huh. Well, I've never heard of any great-aunt. I'm certain Mum said Granny was an only child, and that's not the kind of thing you get wrong.'

Allegra stared at her short, filed-square nails, glossy with a natural lacquer. 'How was Mum when you saw her this week?'

Isobel's voice flattened. 'Oh, well . . . so-so. We had a reasonably good spell yesterday. Enough to get the LPAs verified, at least.'

Allegra rolled her eyes. Didn't she know it! The paper-work had barely gone through and already she was embroiled in a bureaucratic fiasco.

'Oh, hang on a minute, wait . . . You're not thinking of asking Mum about any of this, are you?' Isobel said in a panic. 'Because that is the last thing she needs. Long-lost dead rellies turning up out of the woodwork.'

'Snow.'

'Whatever.'

'No. You're right. There's no point in bothering her with this. Not yet, anyway. We'll see what the results reveal first. It's bound to be a mistake. One typo and they start barking up the wrong tree.'

'Mmm.' Isobel had always been easily placated by her sister's calm authority.

They lapsed into an easy lull.

'Are you still in the office?' Isobel asked, hearing the silence at Allegra's end. The TV was on at Isobel's, and Allegra was sure she could hear Ferds gurgling over the baby monitor.

'Of course.'

'You could come here for supper if you like. Lloyd's out late tonight, and I've got enough stir-fry for two.'

Allegra smiled, imagining the warm glow of Isobel's kitchen, a bottle of red open on the table. She looked up at the almost fluorescent glare of the office lights – conducive to keeping everyone awake at their desks. 'Thanks, but I've got some catching up to do. One project's being a bit tricky.'

'Sure.' The resignation in Isobel's voice suggested she hadn't really expected any other answer.

'Look, I'll speak to you soon, OK?'

'Yup.'

Allegra hung up, spinning in her chair and standing, pressing her forehead to the cold of the glass. She was too high up to see the people below in the darkness, but she could feel the gravitational pull of them, a tide of office workers leaching away to their homes for a few hours' respite before beginning the same cycle again tomorrow. Where would she go, right now, even if she could? To the house in her name that stood empty and dark on an Islington street, like an abandoned dog with not even a collar round his neck to show he belonged to anyone? To sit beside her mother, alone in a community full of strangers but kept company by a choir-singing, rugby-playing Welshman and the past in her head? Would she call the friends she never called? Search for the man she hadn't yet met?

She knew she would do nothing. This was the only life she knew – the only home, the only lover she had. She turned away from the window and returned to her desk, her back to the rest of the world.

Chapter Nine

Day Eleven: *Metal Hoop*

Allegra knocked lightly on the orange door, not realizing she was holding her breath as she listened for the sound of footsteps on the other side. She looked at the plush eucalyptus wreath and its deep red holly berries twisted between the leaves, which she'd brought with her. Would it clash? she worried, holding up the wreath to get a sense of the colours together, just as the door was opened and Barry's face was framed by the leaves so that he looked like a jolly Caesar.

'Ho, ho,' he chuckled, planting his hands on his hips and doing his best Santa impression.

'I thought this might look cheery,' she said, holding it out to him, aware of the single, somewhat straggly strand of blue tinsel Blu-tacked to the communal hall wall.

'Amazing,' Barry beamed, the word bouncing like a rubber ball in his accent, and standing back to let her pass. 'We're getting well into the festive spirit here. We made a start on the Christmas cards this morning,' he said, stepping into the small kitchen and retrieving a tack and hammer from a drawer.

A 'but' hung in the air.

'But?' she enquired, looking nervously down the short hall. There appeared to be no movement inside. Where was her mother? Sleeping?

'Well, it's not a great day today, so she had a nap and we've been listening to carols and having a sing-song ever since. We'll try again tomorrow.'

'Oh.' Allegra looked at him with gratitude and bafflement. She couldn't fathom the selflessness required to care for another human being who wasn't your own flesh and blood. How many nights was his sleep disturbed by her mother trying to hide Monopoly money under the mattress? How often did she abuse him – verbally, if not physically? Allegra didn't suppose her mother's feeble swings registered on his rugby-honed physique. What impelled him to dedicate his own precious days to caring for someone who didn't remember him half the time, who would refuse on a whim to eat his meals and felt no social compulsion to be 'nice'?

'Where is she now?' Her voice was low, as though she was scared of being overheard.

'In the lounge. You go through. I'll just put this on the door and then pop next door to Judy's.'

'Judy?'

'Yes, at number eighteen.' He paused, wrinkling his nose. 'We'd talked about afternoon tea and a game of cards, but I'll put her off till tomorrow, all things considered an' all.'

'OK.' Allegra watched as Barry shut the door gently behind him and a tapping began on the other side. Slowly, she stepped through the hall and into the living room. It wasn't large, the ceilings not high, but it was warm and bright with tulip-printed wallpaper and sandy-coloured carpets and a beige chenille two-seater sofa with matching armchair. A small plastic Christmas tree had been set up on one of the side tables in the corner, with multicoloured fairy lights and a gold star at the top, a red paper tablecloth wrapped round the base. Allegra noticed a trio of cardboard angels arranged on the mantelpiece of the electric fireplace in among a couple of cards showing robins and Victorian carol-singing scenes.

Her heart lifted at the sight of them, for they were proof that there were still other people in her mother's life besides her, Iz and Barry.

And of course, there were all the photographs taken of Barry with Julia – out on walks, beside the sea, picnicking in the park – the all-important visual standbys that reassured her she knew him, the proof that she could trust him, when the confusion crowded in.

It took a moment for her eyes to find her mother. She appeared to occupy so little space these days and she was so still that it seemed easy to miss her sitting on the armchair, her gaze on the circular rug, but her mind clearly many years in the past.

'Hi, Mum.'

Her mother looked up at her, startled by her voice. 'Who are you?' Her tone was wary but calm.

Allegra swallowed. Oh God. 'I'm Allegra. Barry . . . Barry sent me through,' she smiled, her eyes doing their usual, wonderful job of hiding her emotions. 'May I sit down?' She pointed to the sofa.

After a moment or so, Julia shrugged. 'What did you say your name was?' she asked, visibly leaning away from her.

'Allegra.'

'I like that name. I'm Julia Fisher.' She held out a trembling hand.

Allegra stared at it for a moment – the hand that had smoothed her hair as she was tucked into bed at night, the hand that had held hers on the first day to school, the hand that had stroked her cheek with pride when she'd got her offer letter from Oxford – before taking it in her own, holding in check the impulse to squeeze it, to rub the skin with her thumb.

The touch was fleeting, painful.

'Have you heard it's snowing in the Midlands?' Julia asked, turning her head left and looking out across the landscaped gardens. It was dusk and the light had an ultraviolet quality to it, a final burst of pigmentation as night and day rushed at each other in a clash of colour prisms before darkness finally, inevitably, won out.

'Is it? I haven't caught up with the weather forecast lately.'

'I had to send my girls to school in their thermals today. They put up such a fuss.' Julia shook her head solemnly.

'Really?' Allegra asked politely, remembering how her sister had always taken them off in the loos the second they arrived. 'I imagine Isobel didn't want to wear double tights.'

Julia clicked her tongue against the roof of her mouth, but a smile enlivened her eyes. 'Oh, she's a madam, that one, always wanting to look right. She'd rather be fashionable than warm.'

'Hmm,' Allegra nodded, remembering the morning battles well.

Julia looked at her. 'You've met my daughter?'

Allegra blinked. What did she say? 'Yes, both of them, actually.'

'When?'

Allegra hesitated, trying to find a way through the lie. 'At their school. I'm a teacher there.'

'Is that why you're here?' Julia's face clouded. 'Has something happened?'

'No, not at all,' Allegra replied quickly. 'Everything's fine. I . . . I just dropped by to say how well they're doing. I thought you'd like to know.'

Julia relaxed again, a proud smile smoothing her features. 'Oh yes. They're such bright girls. Allegra, she's so dedicated. Strives so hard all the time. I think she thinks . . .' Julia's voice trailed off.

'Mu—' She caught herself. 'Mrs Fisher?'

Julia looked at her, eyes clouded with emotions she couldn't understand, memories she couldn't filter. 'It wasn't her fault. I keep telling her that, but she doesn't believe me.'

'She does. I'm sure she does,' Allegra said, reaching forward and clasping her mother's hand urgently. 'And she's fine. She just loves you very much. She wants to make you proud.'

'I keep seeing her face that night. The church was lit by candles. She looked so beautiful. So full of hope. She thought she could . . . could stop it.'

Allegra watched, angst-ridden as she saw her mother's lips tremble, glassy tears dropping one after the other down her thread-veined cheeks. 'Mrs Fisher, I came here today to tell you how happy Allegra is. She told me today at break-time. She's thriving; she loves you so much. Everything she does is for you.'

Julia turned her face towards her, her eyes wandering over Allegra's face, and for a moment, just a moment, Allegra thought she saw recognition gather behind her eyes. But it was like the sun peeping out from the clouds on a windy day, gone before it had even registered.

'Thank you, Miss . . . I'm sorry, I don't know your name.'

It was bad today. She didn't remember the introduction. 'Call me Valentina.' She didn't know why she said it. She hadn't known she was going to say it. Maybe she just wanted to get a knee-jerk response – her mother wasn't 'here' today; she was locked in the past again. But there was no response. No ripple of enlightenment, no crack of understanding.

'Valentina . . . That's a pretty name.'

'Thank you.' Allegra swallowed back her disappointment.

Somewhere in the hallway, she heard a door close and then footsteps and she knew Barry would come bounding round the corner like an Old English sheepdog, too big and messy for this place, which was all about low-maintenance ease and wipe-clean tidiness.

Sure enough, the strains of 'Bread of Heaven' drifted into the flat, and a minute later, he was standing in front of them, his hazel eyes twinkling as he held out a saucer with some home-made sugar-dusted mince pies. 'Judy thought we might like some of these,' he said. 'Shall I pop the kettle on and we can treat ourselves?' The tiny shrug of his shoulders afterwards indicated he was more excited by the prospect than anyone.

'Uh, I'm afraid I have to get back,' Allegra said, her voice thin and flat.

Barry took in her dampened demeanour immediately

'To your own family?' Julia asked.

Allegra nodded. 'Yes, that's right.'

'Enjoy it. They grow up so quickly. I can hardly believe

my girls are getting so big. They'll be taller than me soon.'

'Yes,' Allegra nodded, trying to smile as she stood with her mother. She had been five inches taller than her by the time she was thirteen.

'I'll walk you to the door,' Julia said, leading the way. 'It was so good of you to come.'

'My pleasure.' Allegra's voice was subdued.

Julia led her through the tiny vestibule and to the front door. The wreath on it looked so large and deep, like a plump velvet cushion, it diminished somehow the plain fire door it decorated, having been designed for the Farrow & Ball-painted panelled Victorian doors of the smarter London postcodes and obscuring slightly the brass number '16'. Allegra frowned, pushing the leaves down a little with her finger. Would it confuse her mother if she couldn't see the numbers clearly? Should she have bought the smaller size?

'Well, goodbye.' Julia held out her hand again and Allegra took it, her hand limper now than her mother's.

'Goodbye.' She saw Barry, behind her mother, gesticulating wildly with his hands.

'I'll call you,' he mouthed.

Allegra walked briskly up the corridor, aware the orange door hadn't clicked shut yet and wondering if her mother was watching her go, realizing . . .

'Allegra! Isobel!' Her mother's voice.

She turned with a start, but hope fled as suddenly as it had come as she saw her standing by the fire stairs and calling up into the void: 'Girls! Supper's on the table!'

Allegra slapped a hand to her mouth, tears that were never permitted to swell spilling out in defiance of her will as she watched her mother waiting for ghosts. She turned quickly and pushed through the doors that led into the garden, huge sobs heaving her shoulders as she ran towards the car park. She fumbled in her pockets for the keys, desperate to hide in the blackness of the car park.

'Allegra?'

Barry's voice – melodic though it was – was like a bucket of cold water upon her, shocking her into sense and her hands automatically wiped away the tears, drying her face in an instant. 'Hi, B-Barry.'

'Oh, poppet,' he said, his head tipped to one side as he took in her distress.

'Sh-sh-she didn't remember me,' she gasped as his arms wrapped around her, making the tears come properly again. Resistance was futile with his bear hugs and she let her head loll heavily against his chest, the smell of Lynx assailing her, the sound of his big heart a dependable plod beneath her ear.

A few minutes passed before she recovered enough to pull away with a gulp and a smile, embarrassed that he was having to take care of her as well as her mum.

'Sorry, sorry,' she hiccupped. 'It's a bad day for all the Fisher women clearly.'

'You are perfectly entitled to have shitty days. It's a shitty thing you're going through.'

She nodded, staring down at the ground and dabbing her eyes with the backs of her hands.

He patted her shoulder. 'I only wanted to check that policeman had got hold of you? In Switzerland?'

She sniffed, looking back up at him. 'You mean Sergeant Annen?'

'Yes, that's him. I know you're busy, but he was a royal pain in the arse and I couldn't have him pestering your mother like that. It was doing more harm than good, him going over the same point again and again about that woman they found.'

'You mean he actually spoke to Mum about it?' She remembered how the name Valentina had elicited no response whatsoever.

'No. I never put him through to her, but he was very persistent and I was worried she might pick up in my absence.' Barry flicked his fingers distractedly. 'I know you've only just submitted the LPAs for registration and all, but—'

'No, no. It's fine, Barry. It's definitely better I deal with it.'

'That's what I thought.' He patted her shoulder. 'I should get back or she'll eat my mince pie and we'll have a falling-out, she and I,' he chuckled, turning to leave.

'Of course.'

He noticed the plastic carrier bag in her hand for the first time. 'Is that something you wanted me to give her for you?'

Allegra peered in at the little motley collection of knick-knacks she had scooped from some of the opened drawers of the Advent calendar: the figurine of the Madonna and child, a sprig of dried, beribboned mistletoe, a carved wooden Angel Gabriel, a gold-tipped pine cone, feathered angel wings and a felted gingerbread man.

She held the bag out towards him. 'They're just some Christmas decorations Iz and I found when clearing out the house. They're pretty old, but I just thought Mum might like to have them around her – you know, to help make the new flat feel like home.'

'That's a cracking idea. I'll put them in her bedroom so

she can see them before going to sleep and when she wakes up,' Barry smiled. 'But are you sure you don't want them?'

She shook her head quickly. 'No. I don't do Christmas.'

'What? Not even a Christmas tree?'

She blinked at him as more tears threatened. 'It's always a really busy time for me, work-wise.'

'Of course,' he nodded, but she thought he looked sad. 'Well, listen, I'd better get back or that mince pie will be lost to me forever, and I don't want to have to arm-wrestle your ma again,' he said with a wink, breaking into a run back across the gardens, thighs chafing, the carrier bag swinging wildly in his grip.

She watched him go.

Nurse Barry, an unlikely hero, but the only one they had.

Chapter Ten

Day Twelve: *Tin Trumpet*

Cinzia was already sitting outside her office when she walked in, Kirsty jumping up as Allegra shrugged off her coat and swapped it for the bunch of messages on Post-its in Kirsty's hands. The DNA test hadn't taken long, but even an hour out of her schedule created a logjam.

'Hi, Cinzia. Sorry to keep you waiting.' Her eyebrow arched with satisfaction as she saw how many of the messages were from Sam Kemp. He wasn't the only one who could conduct meetings in secret and she had spent most of the day holed up in the Mayfair office with Bob, revising and redrafting their investment strategy into something a lot bolder. Garrard's name hadn't come into the discussions once. She wouldn't stoop to his level.

'And this is the report you were waiting for,' Kirsty said quietly, handing over a thick file of trades. Allegra glanced at it: Kemp's work for the Leo Besakovitch pot.

'Great, thanks. Just some coffees, please, and then you can head off.'

Kirsty nodded gratefully. It was only 6.30 p.m., but the Christmas benefit was the company's biggest event of the year and everyone – even cool-headed, sensible girls like her PA – liked to have proper time to get ready. 'Uh, you should know Mr Kemp's been very anxious to get hold of you this afternoon, Miss Fisher.'

Allegra glanced at her unflappable PA; she understood Kirsty's understatement well enough to know that meant he'd been hitting the roof. 'I see that,' was all Allegra murmured, with a cool smile, as she strode into her office, dropping the Post-its into the waste-paper basket as she passed. 'Come in, Cinzia,' she said, noting with a small stab of alarm that her personal shopper had only a single bag hanging over her arm, and one large carrier.

Allegra walked to the desk, throwing her report file behind her desk and quickly bringing up the Dow Jones, FTSE and her emails on the trio of large screens, even though she'd been replying to others in the taxi from Duke Street.

She looked up, a businesslike smile on her face. 'So, what have you got for me?'

Cinzia unzipped the hanging bag. 'Give this a chance.'

Allegra straightened up, already cautious. Any dress that came with a warning . . .

Cinzia pulled a long, strapless, black guipure lace dress from the bag. Allegra's eyes slid from it to Cinzia. 'And . . . ?'

'That's all I had for your brief. I'm sorry. We had an unexpected visit from the Qatari royal family. Our stock was almost cleared out in a day and I had to hide this, as it was. The only other thing I had that was remotely suitable in your size was a gold mesh thigh-high.'

Allegra pulled a horrified face and walked over to the sofa. Her hand reached out for the fabric.

'I'm sorry, Allegra. I know you think lace isn't appropriate for business functions, but it's long and the cut is modest by contrast. Plus I think the shape will really work for you.'

Kirsty came in with the coffees, her eyes widening with surprise as she saw the dress in Cinzia's hands. 'Mmmm,' Allegra said, echoing her thoughts. 'See you later.'

'Trust me. Just try it on.'

Allegra took a sip of the coffee, feeling her shoulders drop from her ears a little as the warmth revived her tired body. 'Well, I guess I'd better,' Allegra said, walking towards the private bathroom.

She shut the door and leaned against it for a moment, bitterly wishing she could, for once, go home to curl up on the sofa. Last night's disastrous visit to her mother had left her unable to sleep again, and after a day of number-crunching – and the Yongs still infuriatingly uncontactable – the thought of pushing her feet into a pair of heels was almost more than she could bear.

She slipped out of her suit and stepped into the dress. It almost stood on its own thanks to the boning that ran down the front and side seams, and she had to inch it up slowly over even her lean hips. She pulled it up over her bust, tipping her head admiringly as she saw the scoop of the neckline, which somehow managed to plunge from under her arms without creating acres of cleavage. It was lined with a champagne silk lace that gave the appearance of nudity beneath – she would have preferred black, but on the plus side, at least it wasn't red.

She bobbed her hair lightly with her hands, annoyed that she had let the day run away from her, but there wasn't time to get it done now – the party started in under an hour, and she still had her make-up to do. She opened the door and walked back into the office.

Cinzia's face broke into a delighted smile as she saw her client. 'I knew it!'

'Well, it fits, at least. Just. Can you zip me in?'

She held the sides of the dress together at the back, elbows out, as Cinzia walked round her, checking the fit.

'You look incredible,' Cinzia said, beginning to inch up the zip.

'I don't know.' Allegra bit her lip, staring at the clock on the wall and wondering whether she could get back to her flat, change and over to the party in time. What did she have in her wardrobe that would work for tonight? 'I think it's too . . . much for a work event.' It was the kind of dress models wore to red-carpet events. How was this going to go down at a party in the finance sector?

'Just because you work in a man's world doesn't mean you need to look like—'

The door burst open and both women looked up in astonishment.

Sam Kemp was standing in the middle of the room, fury in his eyes. 'Where the hell were y—' His voice cut out like a shorted fuse as he took in the sight of her, half dressed, overdressed by the sofa. 'Kirsty's not at her desk,' he said, as if by way of explanation for arriving unannounced.

Allegra jerked her chin in the air, mortified to have been caught like this – as if she was 'dressing up' like all the women huddled into the loos. 'What do you want?' She hadn't seen him since their spat on the executive floor, when Pierre had pitted them against each other in the clearest of terms, and she scanned his face for signs that he had edged ahead of her, leveraged his contact as required to get that signature on the dotted line. Because if that happened . . .

'Where the fuck were you in the ex co meeting?'

'What?' Allegra's blood ran cold. 'What are you talking about? I postponed it. It's been rearranged for Tuesday afternoon.'

'No. It just happened. And I've just sat through a grilling from Pierre and Crivelli with absolutely no numbers support. Is that your idea of . . . what? A joke? One-upmanship?'

'Don't be ridiculous.'

'*I'm* ridiculous? We're supposed to be working this thing together. Instead, you're keeping me out of the loop, not cc-ing me on the reports, and if I come by here, you're in fucking off-site meetings that I've been told nothing about.'

'Ha! You want to talk about meetings happening without your knowledge? What about you and Zhou hooking up in New York and God knows how many other times? Don't think I don't know that it's you telling him to get his office to blank my calls.'

Sam stared back at her, shaking his head disgustedly. 'I've never made any secret of my friendship with Zhou; I've got Pierre's express instruction to use it to our advantage. But you . . . playing cat and mouse and then throwing me to the sharks like that—'

'I did no such thing,' she said angrily, pulling away from Cinzia, the dress still unzipped and gaping at the back as she clamped her elbows to her waist to keep it up and strode over to her desk. Sam followed after as she entered her passcode and brought up her diary on the screen. 'See? I clearly . . .' Her voice faded away. She clearly hadn't. She'd been so focused on moving the numbers, on finding new growth as she pushed through the long night hours, that it had completely slipped her mind to actually get Kirsty to rearrange the meeting at which she would present them. 'Oh *shit*.'

She turned back to Sam, the whites of her eyes clearly visible as she immediately took in the ramifications of her oversight.

He gave a contemptuous laugh. 'You think I'm buying this act? You think you're going to convince me it was accidental? We may not have to like each other, Fisher, and I sure as hell don't know what your problem is, but if you want a war, you've got one. I don't give a shit if you get thrown out on your ass, but keep up your games and we're *both* going to get fired. Pierre's on the fucking warpath. He wants your head on a plate, and after the stunt you pulled today, I'll goddam serve you up to him myself.' He marched back to the door, his eyes flicking up and down her lightly. 'And don't think looking like *that's* going to save you.'

Allegra stared at the door as it slammed shut behind him, feeling light-headed. Several minutes passed in stunned silence before she remembered Cinzia standing there, discreet and silent as a maid. She smiled wanly. 'Sorry about that, Cinzia . . . Uh, it's been a tough day.'

'I see that,' Cinzia replied in a low voice, watching her with quiet concern. 'You're sure you have to go to this thing tonight?'

Allegra shook her head, staring up at the ceiling to ward away the first tears threatening to prickle her eyes. 'Trust me – if I thought there was any way to get out of it . . .'

'He was tough on you.'

Allegra shrugged. 'I dropped him in it with the executive committee. I'd be livid too if the tables were turned.'

'But anyone can make a mistake.'

'Not me. Not here. My head is constantly above the parapet. There's no margin for error.'

'You mean because you are a woman?'

Their eyes met. 'That's how it is. I'm visible at all times.'

Cinzia looked down at the dress, frowning as she took in its dramatic silhouette. 'I'm so sorry. I didn't realize. I've let you down.'

'How?'

'Well, that dress . . .' Cinzia gestured one forlorn hand at her. 'It may as well come with its own spotlight.'

The company had gone to town this year, taking over the penthouse of the Gherkin, and she had been able to see the pink lights through the latticed glass as far away as Whitechapel in her taxi. Stepping out of the lift, she half wondered whether she needed a passport – or at least a heavier coat: tons of landscaped fake snow and a herd of reindeer harnessed to a sleigh were arranged in the entrance as the warm-up act.

In the cloakrooms, she didn't want to shrug off the black velvet coat that had kept the statement dress a well-hidden secret up till now and she kept it on as she touched up her make-up; but she couldn't stay swaddled and hidden forever. She shivered slightly as her bare skin came into contact with the cooler temperature, quelling the burst of panic that shot through her as she took in the mathematical proportions of her own hip-to-waist ratio – courtesy of the dress's firm but lightweight boning – and the paleness of her skin against the heavy black lace. But the coat had to stay off and she had to go out there.

With a toss of her head, she walked out into the crowds

and for a moment, as she felt herself swallowed up, wondered whether she'd been blowing the problem out of proportion. Why should anyone even notice her? Hemlines were up, cleavages were out, skin was orange, and eyes were on stalks, a light, flirty atmosphere pervading the room in readiness for the night's later promises. Last year's party had led to a pregnancy, a long-term, not-so-discreet affair and one marriage break-up. (*She'd* got a promotion on the back of impressing Pierre over dinner with her views on euro-zone monetary-policy makers being behind the curve on deflation.) The vodka luge – this year carved as an Alpine downhill race jump – stood menacingly at the bar. As the cause of most of the carnage, it had a lot to answer for.

Moving slowly through the throng, she noticed a crowd was gathered around a tall man in a dandy coat with Byronic hair who had a way with scissors. Allegra walked slowly past, staring with rare interest as he snipped quickly at a sheet of black paper in his hands, his eyes all the while on Vicky from accounts as he traced her profile – face and hair – into a perfect miniature cameo.

She went up to the bar and ordered a cucumber martini. It never bothered her, walking into a room alone; she had done it hundreds of times and refused to think that sanctuary lay in another person. This dress, though . . . She sensed, though couldn't quite catch, the stares coming her way. Not that she needed to. She was senior in rank to every male in the room bar five – Pierre, his CFO, his CEO, his soon-to-retire COO and Sam Kemp – and she knew none of the other eighty or so would be foolish enough to think that the Christmas party was a warrant to make a pass.

The bartender handed her the drink – made to perfection – and she walked towards the glittering view pressed up against the windows. London looked bedecked in diamonds, the Thames a ribbon of silk rippling behind the buildings at their feet. She pressed a hand to the cold glass, staring down into the anonymity of the city night, as she always did at the office. Same view, different angle. Same woman, different dress.

She ran the pads of her fingers over her thumb before smoothing a hand over her hip, ironing out wrinkles that weren't there, and she realized that – for once – she *was* nervous standing here alone. She didn't feel as invincible as usual. The repeated loss of her mother was rubbing her emotions raw, and with today's cock-up visible on everyone's radar, she needed someone to hide behind. She actually wished she'd brought a date. She never bothered with them since Philip had got in the way at an event a few years back, wanting to talk to her about a winter-sun trip to Mauritius instead of allowing her to talk to the then head of futures. It was precisely because of the plus-ones thinking they were there on a *date* that made her prefer going on her own. But Iz would have bolstered her spirits, sparked her courage like she always did. Then again, the thought of exposing her sister to the brutality of the industry she operated in : . . . Allegra shook her head and took a sip of her drink.

It was a moment before she detected the heat, the buzz, around her, the quiet, quick snipping as tiny triangles of jet paper fluttered by her feet like black butterflies.

She looked back, but the scissoring artist stopped her with the slightest shake of his head. She couldn't change angle.

'I don't want my cameo done, thank you,' she said quietly – although not moving out of respect.

'Nearly done,' he replied, his eyes never leaving her, his fingers never hesitating. She felt as drawn by his mere scrutiny as if he'd laid her on a sheet and traced round her with a felt-tip. He was bringing attention onto her for all the wrong reasons and Allegra's eyes flicked warily over the faces watching her, all of them intrigued by the sight of her bare shoulders, her feminine silhouette in the hourglass dress . . . The scissor man didn't know she was the most senior-ranking woman in the room, one deal away from making the board. She was just another woman in a pretty dress to him, and she hated it. Without even trying to, he had made her feel lost and disempowered. She could be the keynote speaker at a conference of 500 CEOs, but to have the office juniors looking at her, appraising her as a woman . . .

'That's enough,' she said, breaking the hold suddenly, at the exact moment he said: 'There.'

He smiled and held out the mini masterpiece – for it was exquisite – a four-inch rendering of her entire silhouette, not just her profile, and she saw with private eyes that he had caught the tiny bump at the bridge of her nose, the small kick of her hair that showed she should have had it done tonight, the 'noggins' at her wrist that she'd inherited from her father. He hadn't missed a thing and she briskly nodded her thanks, wondering what else he could see.

She moved off into the crowd again, knowing she needed to get involved, to start making small talk, but it was always a trial for her if a party wasn't about networking or winning deals. Socializing, connecting on a more personal level left her mute and she didn't need a psychoanalyst to explain why *that* was.

Across the room, she saw Pierre talking to the Collateral Management team, one hand resting lightly on Pasha's hip.

Allegra turned away, knowing the crowd she instinctively chose to stand apart from would be her only protection tonight – until dinner at least; there'd be no escape then. Her eyes met those of Kevin Lam, a quantitative analyst, and she saw the ambition light up in his face as he realized this was his moment to make an impression.

A waiter stopped in front of her, seeing her glass was empty. 'Another martini, Miss Fisher?'

Allegra nodded. 'And get rid of this, will you, please?' she asked, sliding her miniature cameo onto the tray, just as Lam's polished shoes stepped into her peripheral vision.

'Of course.'

The waiter headed for the bar as Allegra steeled herself for Lam's assault. She was used to the quants trying to outdo her with their 'mathletics', but it was the syrupy conversation that accompanied it that really sapped her spirit. She didn't notice the waiter stop by two of the only men in the room in bespoke dinner suits, his head inclined as one of them placed an order. Nor did she see the other reach out his arm and discreetly lift the cameo off the tray, sliding it into his inner jacket pocket like it was a business card he intended to keep.

Chapter Eleven

The master of ceremonies had already announced dinner and most people were gathered round the tables, holding on to the backs of chairs as they talked with the animation that immediately preceded full-blown drunkenness. Allegra hadn't moved in over an hour from her shadowy spot by the bar. She and Lam had decamped there after they mutually decided the waiters weren't refreshing their drinks often enough, but in truth, she felt safer there. Bob, the only person in the building she remotely counted as a personal acquaintance and actively wanted to speak to, was standing too conspicuously on the dance floor, which was already flashing pink, red and blue squares. Several times she had seen Pierre scouting the room, and while she couldn't be sure he was looking for her, per se, Kemp's words earlier had left her with a bad feeling even five martinis couldn't shift.

'It looks like we'd better take our seats,' Lam said reluctantly, noticing that everybody was now sitting and that Pierre would shortly be getting up to make his annual Christmas toast. 'Would you like me to escort you to your table?'

'Why not?' she replied, seeing his chivalry for what it was – face-time with the senior management committee –

and admiring it. Most of the ambition she encountered wasn't gloved in gallantry. Tonight was a rare treat.

They walked over the floor in silence, Allegra caring less about the stares, which were more brazen now. Lam didn't dare to place his hand on the small of her back, instead walking stiffly like a wind-up soldier beside her. Her dress had a split in it, at least allowing her to walk at a sensible stride, instead of tottering about in pigeon steps, although it did also mean everyone in the team was afforded a flash of her legs.

'It is Pasha, Pierre's wife?' Lam asked nervously.

'Yes. But I suggest you address her as Mrs Lafauvre.'

'Right, yes, of course,' he nodded, and Allegra wondered whether his palms were sweating. 'And the blonde lady beside her?'

Allegra frowned. She didn't have a clue as to her identity, although she was facing away from them, showing only glossy hair, which had been blow-dried to fall down her back in enchanting waves. Allegra scanned the table quickly, wondering whose wife she was. Not Crivelli's, she knew that. Not Pasha. Definitely not Bernadette Henley, the outgoing COO's wife, who was one of the few women who still believed in the allure of a blue rinse in her couture.

They stopped at the table, Allegra resting her hand lightly on the back of a chair. 'Hello, everybody.'

Pierre, on the opposite side of the table, sat back in his seat and folded his arms at the sight of her. His black eyes were cold and merciless. 'Allegra! I've been wondering where you were.' Sarcasm tainted his welcome and bled it of any friendliness.

Allegra smiled, the five martinis doing a fine job of

hiding the sickness she felt. 'I've been engrossed in conversation with Kevin Lam, one of our quants.'

'How unlike you, Allegra, to fraternize with people who can't help your career.' The ambient temperature round the table dropped by ten degrees.

'Isn't that the point of the Christmas party? For everyone to mingle and connect?' she smiled, showing off her girlish gap for once. 'Besides, I think Lam probably *can* help my career. He'd make me look very good in meetings. He's been riveting me with his thoughts on Apple's iWatch. Very interesting, *very* interesting. We need to hold on to this one,' she smiled, patting Lam's shoulder lightly as though she and Pierre were of the same mind.

Lam nodded as though he was meeting an emperor. 'It's a pleasure, Monsieur Lafauvre.'

Pierre, not fooled for a minute by her routine, nodded back disinterestedly – an acknowledgement and dismissal in one – his eyes coming straight back to Allegra and running a swift up-down of her in the dress. Allegra pretended not to notice, quickly making introductions to Lam of the rest of the executive committee and their wives.

She got to the blonde.

'We haven't met. I'm Allegra Fisher, president of luxury goods, and this is Kevin Lam, one of our star analysts.'

'Tilly Bathurst. I'm Sam's date.'

'Sam? Sam Kemp?' He was on this table? Allegra's eyes scanned the place settings. Three were still sitting empty – hers, of course, but two others. Two? She counted again, but the place settings came to the same even number, and if Tilly was Sam's date, then who was the other place for?

'That's right.' Tilly's eyes were wide and clear in a pale blue that had been brought out by some expert blending of grey shadow on her lids. Her make-up had been applied immaculately, coming over as lighter than it really was, and she looked elegant but appropriate in a black mousse-line silk dress that only worked on a flawless figure. For once, Allegra felt like the overdone, gauche girl – like Jessica Rabbit to Goldilocks – and she wished she'd stopped at one and a half martinis. She felt a little . . . de trop by comparison. Tilly was the woman all the other women in the room wanted to be, even though she had introduced herself merely as someone's date, and Allegra could see – without needing Sam even to be there – what a striking couple they'd make.

But Allegra didn't care about that, or, rather, she refused to. That wasn't her currency or what she traded in. She looked down and stared at her own hands gripping the chair back, only one thing whirling through her mind: when had *he* been invited onto this table? Only yesterday Kirsty had confirmed the attendees for her. It must have happened this afternoon, after the meeting.

Her eyes briefly met Pierre's, and she wasn't surprised to find his still on her. He was like a cat pinning a mouse by its tail, watching her squirm, and she knew exactly what it meant: the Queen is dead; long live the King.

'So where is Sam?' she asked Tilly, turning away quickly, refusing to show either her hurt or fear even as the foundations of her world began to shake and crack.

'He's somewhere around here,' Tilly smiled, her pretty eyes eagerly scanning the room for her date. 'He had to take a call.'

Lam cleared his throat and Allegra glanced back at him. He indicated discreetly to a spare place at the table and she realized he thought he was doing her an enormous favour by becoming her plus-one.

Tilly straightened up excitedly. 'Oh, here he is!'

Allegra straightened up too, but she refused to turn round; Sam's arrival didn't prompt the same happiness in her as it did Tilly. Quite the opposite, in fact.

Tilly's chair scraped back and Allegra heard Kemp's voice. 'And this is Tilly Bathurst, my date.'

'Your girlfriend?' a man asked.

Her head jerked up at that. That accent – the trace of American with something fuller, she'd heard it before.

'My . . . uh . . .' Sam hesitated.

Allegra turned.

Zhou Yong – he who had been so unreachable, so internationally unavailable – was standing not two feet away from her. And Sam was standing beside *him*, one hand resting proprietorially on his friend's shoulder.

Allegra looked straight back at Pierre, who was beginning to rise from his seat, understanding slowly dawning on his features. She watched his eyes brighten like hot coals as he walked round the table to greet them, a personal welcome from one power player to another, Sam rewarded with a warm back slap. He was in the club now.

It was another few minutes before she was even introduced. First the other members of the board had to make their acquaintance, then their wives, before finally . . . her.

'It is good to see you again, Mr Zhou Yong.' She bowed her head – although not as low as she once would have – before offering her hand.

'Miss Fisher! I scarcely would have recognized you.'

She hesitated fractionally before nodding, unsure whether he had intended to insult or compliment her. This dress, of course, made no apology for her gender, unlike her Armani suits.

'*Two* dates, Sam?' she muttered under her breath as Pierre and Zhou exchanged formalities. 'You are a busy boy.'

'Well, I was told I could absolutely rely on you not to bring one,' Sam said in an equally unfriendly voice as Tilly came and stood closer to him, her hand finding his and her slim fingers intertwining like ivy.

Allegra looked away. All around them, the guests at the other tables had begun pulling crackers, and many were already squeezing paper crowns on their heads. Lam was nowhere to be seen. The sight of Zhou had clearly overpowered even his ambition.

'Shall we sit? The chef's ready to serve,' Pierre said, ushering everyone back into their seats. Allegra walked round the table, looking for her name, hoping she wouldn't be beside Pierre, hoping she would be beside Zhou Yong.

She was right on one count at least – with Crivelli to her left and Henley to her right, she was in no-man's-land, beached between an imminent retiree and a man who'd been gunning for her dismissal for years . . . She slumped back in her chair as the almost-elderly men either side of her shook their napkins onto their laps and Tilly brightly led an open-table conversation about the lights on Regent Street.

A waiter almost immediately set down a plate of mackerel tartar in front of Allegra and she turned her head to speak in her ear.

'Bring me a cucumber martini on your way back,' she said quietly. Why the hell not? Pierre's message was subtle but clear enough. It was game over for her. Kemp had won.

It didn't matter that he'd looked a fool in the meeting earlier today (even that was better than not being there at all); he'd brought the prize catch out of the river and into the infinity pool. Contacts, not numbers, were going to swing this.

She tilted her head, trying to look interested as Pasha joined in the discussion – had she ever seen Red Square at Christmas? Magical! *Magical!* – but it took everything she had just to set her facial muscles to neutral. She was out. Her world was falling apart as everyone laughed and partied around her, and it felt like only the dress was holding her together.

The waiter came back with her drink within minutes. She picked up her fork and looked at her plate, not sure she could force down the food. Her throat felt constricted and her dress too tight over her ribs, making her feel like she couldn't take a breath . . . She took a sip of the martini instead, making no attempt at small talk with the men either side of her. There was no point; she felt spent.

Tilly was still sparkling like crystal, delicately spearing her mackerel as she vied for Sam's eye.

'Zurich was special, wasn't it?'

It wasn't so much the question Allegra heard as the silence that followed and it was a few moments before Allegra realized all eyes were upon her.

'I'm sorry, what?'

Zhou smiled back at her. 'I think it must be the reflection of the lights on the water.'

She wondered if she had missed another drift of the conversation but smiled wanly anyway. 'Uh, yes. Right . . . the water.'

'Everyone says Paris is the ultimate Christmas city, on

account of the bridges, I suppose, but give me Alpine splendour any day. It's the purity of it that I love. Probably because clean air isn't something we get much of in Beijing.'

Allegra tried to climb back out of her head again. 'Of course, yes. Someone told me they actually televise the sunrise now.'

'Sadly true.'

She fell quiet, but he continued to smile at her, so that she felt obliged to continue the conversation. 'And are you, uh . . . in Beijing much of the time?'

'I used to travel a lot more,' Zhou replied with a smile. 'I was based in the States until recently, but my father is getting older now and he's preparing me to take over the running of the companies. I'm having to spend more and more time there.'

'Meaning you don't get to see your old friends so much,' Sam said, patting Zhou on the shoulder matily, a smile on his lips but none in his eyes as he shot a warning glance at her. There was only one person who could claim Zhou as theirs.

She fell quiet again. What could she do? Zhou was Kemp's pet tonight and Pierre knew it.

'Well, Zurich's beautiful, I grant you,' Bernadette Henley interjected, clearly pleased for the opportunity to cut in. 'And Paris too, of course, but for Christmas opulence it has to be Vienna.'

'No, Frankfurt! The markets there are to be seen to be believed!' Crivelli's wife added. 'I do all my Christmas shopping there.'

'Yes, but Red Square, Zhou,' Pasha exclaimed with impressive focus and little tact as she leaned in to the guest of honour with a winning smile. Had Pierre instructed his wife to flirt with the star client? It didn't seem likely. He had looked as surprised as any of them to see Zhou attending a staff party. 'I mean, you've been there, I take it?'

Zhou, who had been watching Allegra impassively, turned back politely to Pasha, sitting on his right. 'Of course. Who hasn't?'

It was the cue everyone needed to break up the conversation into smaller clusters and allow everyone to eat again.

'So are you taking the Richemont team to Verbier again for New Year's Eve?' Henley asked her, making a fuss of cutting a tomato.

'That's the plan.' She kept her eyes away from Pierre, in case he was listening in. She didn't need to see the rebuke in his eyes, the correction that she wouldn't be going on the company's time or expense account. Not now.

'Well, I must say it's awfully good of you to continually give up your New Year's Eves like that. Every year you do it.'

She shrugged. 'It suits me fine. And I like skiing.'

'But don't you ever want to ring in the new year with loved ones?'

'I'm not sentimental. It's just another day to me.'

'I suppose you're right. I mean, it's not like it's Christmas, is it?'

'It honestly wouldn't matter if it was.'

Crivelli's wife interrupted, clearly shocked. 'What? But why ever not?'

Allegra just shrugged. She was under no obligation to

explain herself to this woman, and frankly, she found Mrs Crivelli's overreaction tiresome and bourgeois.

'Well, my dear, all I can say is you must be doing it wrong!' she laughed, her voice like the tinkle of a bell.

'Did I hear you say you like skiing?' Zhou asked, across the table again.

Allegra looked up, surprised to find he was directing his question at her. 'Sorry?'

'Skiing?'

'Uh . . . yes.'

'Me too.'

'Oh.' She nodded, vaguely wondering why he was showing so much interest in her suddenly. Her calls to his father's office had clearly been returned to Sam and not her. He had sat opposite her in meetings in Zurich and Paris when she had thrown her best at him and his father, and he had shown nothing but blank politeness. And in coming as Sam's guest to this, he had effectively stamped her death warrant. So why was he now trying to engage her on Christmas lights and skiing holidays?

'Sam was telling me about how stunning Montreal is at this time of year,' Tilly said. 'Has anyone else been there at Christmas? I'd love to see it.'

Allegra bet she would! Her eyes slid hatefully towards Sam again and she was surprised to find his already on her.

He looked away quickly.

'We always spend Christmas at our chalet in Zermatt,' Zhou continued, his eyes on Allegra as he ignored Tilly's question. 'Have you ever been there?'

There was a polite silence as everyone waited for her to

answer. They couldn't possibly begin to guess at the reasons why she might now be tied to that very place.

'No. I usually go to Verbier.'

'It's beautiful. You must go.'

'Well,' she said with a tense smile, 'I'm sure I will at some point.'

There was a short pause as Zhou laced his fingers into a steeple, pressing his forefingers together. He looked thoughtful and it made her nervous.

'Of course, we could always guarantee it.'

Allegra simply blinked. What?

'Well, you've just been saying how you go to Verbier with clients over New Year. You should come to Zermatt with us, next week.'

Us?

'My parents don't arrive till the 18th, so we'd have fun till then at least.'

He laughed and everyone joined in – including Pierre, excluding Sam. And excluding her, because all she could think was, Define 'fun'.

Zhou leaned in closer over the table. 'Listen, I'm going out on Saturday,' he said keenly, his dark eyes sparkling. He seemed so much younger and freer outside of his father's sphere. 'And I always host a Christmas party. I would like you to come for that, next week. I am very aware of my family's debt to you.'

Allegra inhaled sharply and slumped back in her chair. There it was – the reason for his sudden interest. She stared at him, disappointed and angry, hardly able to believe this was his way of repaying the debt. She wanted him to sign a contract, not invite her to a party! He just thought he could buy her off cheaply because she was a woman?

'Well, that's very kind, but I assure you your family is in no way indebted to me,' she said in a tight voice.

Lie. Lie. Lie. They both knew it. Her hand on the table balled into a fist.

'I've already asked Sam to come, so he will be there too,' Zhou said, misunderstanding her reluctance. 'It'll be the PLF team on tour!'

It was another joke, but Allegra simply shrugged, her expression opaque. She wasn't going to let him buy her off with a sodding party invitation, even though she could see Pierre shifting in his chair as the pendulum of fortune began to swing her way again, and Sam was staring between her and his friend with an expression fast approaching panic.

'I love skiing,' Pasha smiled, her mackerel tartar all but untouched before her. 'But Pierre always teases me because I have a phobia of button lifts.'

The comment was met with bafflement. 'Well' – Crivelli's wife cleared her throat diplomatically – 'lots of people hate the Pomas.'

'I would be grateful if you would stay with us as guest of honour at our chalet,' Zhou continued, as though Pasha hadn't said anything at all, as though Allegra's silence was some sort of bargaining tactic, driving up the offer from party invitation to house guest.

Allegra looked away at the left-field offer. It still wasn't enough. The deal was what she wanted and she wouldn't settle for being fobbed off with anything less. 'Well, that's incredibly kind, Mr Yong, but under the circumstances, I don't think it would be appropriate,' she demurred.

There was a momentary hesitation before Zhou acquiesced, but it was clear from his expression that he had taken offence. She saw Pierre see it too and his expression changed dramatically as he glowered at her across the table.

'Of course. I understand,' Zhou nodded tersely.

She had turned down flat the company's new cash cow and she watched in frozen silence as Sam leaned over and whispered something in Pierre's ear, Pierre's scowl deepening and his eyes settling on her with chilling coldness, moving over her bare shoulders and cleavage with consideration.

She stared back in rising nausea. She had not only turned down but also offended their key new client, but she would not accept his invitation. Inviting her to a party didn't let his family off the hook for all the work she had done on their pitch – she either won or lost on merit. She didn't inhabit the grey areas of flirting with clients, and being bought off with perks was no consolation.

Low chatter gradually started up around them again, the wives discussing their Christmas arrangements, and Allegra tried to eat. Her phone buzzed softly in her bag and she pulled it out discreetly to read it.

Stay in his house. Stay in his bed. Do what the fuck it takes to nail this deal down.

Allegra's mouth dropped open as she read the text once, then again, her eyes slowly rising to meet Pierre's. He was pretending to listen to something Henley was saying – at least his posture suggested it – but very slowly, he swivelled his eyes to meet hers. Disbelief trammelled through her that her boss, her mentor, would sell her out like this. He had been the one to see Crivelli's prejudice for what it was; he had been the one to promote her through the ranks as she endured evenings sitting at dimly lit tables as girls in thongs gyrated on her colleagues' laps beside her; he had been the one who saw that she worked harder, for longer just to be on level pegging with the boys. That he could be ordering her to do this . . . That he'd even written it down. She had a sexual discrimination claim against him all wrapped up on her lap. And yet he didn't care. That was how badly he wanted this? He was prepared to sell her down the river and destroy a relationship that had been built over six years? Tears pricked at her eyes and she bit her lip to hold them in check.

'Allegra looks incredible tonight, doesn't she?' Sam asked suddenly, making the rest of the table – women – fall silent. 'I mean *really* stunning. Don't you think, Zhou?'

Zhou looked startled by Sam's sudden pronouncement. 'Absolutely,' he replied politely.

'I guess it must be strange for you seeing her looking so . . . I don't know, womanly, seductive. I mean, whenever you've met before, she's been dressed pretty much the same as me.'

A titter rippled round the table.

Zhou's eyes settled on her. 'I guess so, yes.'

'But, you see, Allegra is a very controlled person. I guess she has to be, working with animals like me and . . . this lot.' Cue a self-deprecating laugh as he gestured vaguely to the rest of the room, where drinking games were starting in earnest and there was already a queue at the luge. 'And I think that makes it hard for her sometimes to relinquish that control. I don't think she meant to come across as so . . . dismissive of your generous offer. Obviously she is used to entertaining clients all the time, and I think she's probably just not used to being the one entertained. Isn't that right, Allegra? But I know better than most how much work she's put into this pitch and a skiing break in Zermatt is the very least she deserves.'

Allegra's eyes met his across the table. Bastard. Bastard! He knew exactly what he was doing.

'And after all, even the aloof Allegra Fisher has been known to make the exception to her rule and mix business with pleasure *occasionally.*'

The fork dropped from her hand and clattered noisily on the plate. She couldn't believe he'd said it. She saw the corners of the men's mouths lift in smirks at the clear insinuation and a knot of anger tightened in her stomach. To reduce her to . . . She looked around at her dining companions. Half the faces round the table were the ones she saw more than any other in her life and yet none were her friends – none were even her allies – and it had never been more apparent than now.

Her eyes settled on Pierre, his directive still flashing on her phone, his betrayal still warm, and she realized he had never cared about her or her career. She had been useful to him only for as long as she had made him money.

She looked away, aware of all eyes on her, as she strained for dignity.

Pierre coughed lightly. 'You know, Sam's right, Allegra. You've been working very hard recently, too hard. Take a few days off and join him and Mr Yong,' Pierre said with a casual wave of his hand as he sat back in his chair. 'My treat.'

'Sadly, my diary won't allow that . . . Christmas rush.' She shrugged.

A beat passed.

'Allegra, I'll *personally* make sure your schedule is cleared for you.' His icy eyes made the unspoken point – do this or go.

Another beat.

'No.' Somewhere, it had become a battle of wills, and her words could have been sung by angels, such were the stunned expressions that greeted them. Even Zhou's poker face slipped. 'I have other commitments.'

'Such as?'

She looked down at the napkin in her lap and realized her hands were wringing it. The sound of blood rushing in her ears had drowned out the background music and all she could see was one exit strategy from this.

'Allegra?' he pushed, his tone more forceful this time. 'What else could you possibly have to do?'

Her eyes met his. 'I'll be looking for a new job, Pierre.'

One by one, like a domino course set into motion, jaws dropped open as her words hit like punches.

'What?'

She smiled as she rose from the table. Pride was still hers. He hadn't got the satisfaction of firing her; she hadn't let him demean her. This was always going to have happened: she'd been on the way out anyway. She'd known it the second he'd put Sam on the team, on this table; she'd known it the very second he'd greeted her tonight. She couldn't have stopped it, only delayed it – she realized that now with utmost clarity.

She looked across at Sam – the antagonist in all of this – but he was staring into his wine glass with sudden interest. He didn't even look up as she pushed back her chair, although Tilly shot her an apologetic, timorous smile, seemingly feeling entitled to communicate on his behalf.

Without a word, she walked across the dance floor, her shoulders back and chin high as every set of eyes in the room settled upon her in immediate curiosity. Her imperious, undulating shadow was cast four ways on the dance floor by the revolving glitterballs and she almost wanted to laugh, Cinzia's words coming back to her as more of a prophesy than apology: this dress really did come with its own spotlight.

Chapter Twelve

Day Thirteen: *Sprig of Dried White Flowers*

The intention had been to sleep till noon, but it was impossible to sleep through the almost constant buzzing of voicemails on her phone as people – Bob? Kirsty? HR? Financial journalist? – tried to get hold of her. And besides, who was she kidding? She'd never managed to sleep late, even as a student. In fact, it was on the bucket list Isobel had once drawn up for her – she would learn to sleep into double figures, along with learning the lyrics to 'I Will Survive', playing Candy Crush at least once and watching daytime TV.

But not today. The relaxing buzz from five and a half martinis had segued overnight into an antsy agitation and she'd woken up as usual on the dot of five, rolling from side to side in bed, her legs thrashing and her heart pounding. Even after sitting up and staring at the wall for twenty minutes, she hadn't quite been able to believe she had actually done what she feared she'd done, until she'd found her laptop and logged on.

Password denied.

Only then did she realize it was official. She'd quit, pulled the plug on an orbiting career that was on the brink of going stratospheric, turned her back on everything she had ever wanted just as it was in her grasp, that final reach just fractionally, fatally, too far.

The phone kept flashing even though it lay silently beside her bed now, the voicemail filled with messages she couldn't bear to listen to – she didn't want sympathy or pity. The shortcoming hadn't been *hers*. She had simply jumped before she was pushed: Zhou's play, Sam's ambition, Pierre's greed and that dress had collided spectacularly and this was merely the fallout.

She kicked the duvet onto the floor in a fit of rage. Well, she may have no job, but she was going to do very well, financially, out of this. Pierre's text on her phone would be all she needed to force him into a very hefty settlement payout. She wasn't the only one who'd be waking up with a bad taste in their mouth this morning. Oh no! Even the glory of landing an investor like Zhou was going to be scant compensation for the PR havoc she was going to wreak on PLF's reputation.

She paced the small flat, repeatedly boiling the kettle but never quite remembering to fill her teacup, her mind overloaded, her concentration destroyed as she replayed over and over being cornered like a rat at that table, steely calm alternating with white-hot anger and shooting through her veins like flames. She couldn't settle, couldn't rest. She didn't know what to do. Without the office to go to, her day had no shape, her life no purpose. Everything she knew and believed in had gone, pulled away from her like a dusty rug, the courage from last night's martinis fully ebbed away so that only a bleak desolation remained.

She was screwed.

She could demand back her job. Threaten to go public

with the text. If the *FT* ran the contents of that text on the front page, PLF's shares would nosedive.

But . . .

But . . .

Blackmail was beneath her.

And a discrimination case would hit the deadlines. It would destroy Pierre's reputation, but her name would be blackened too. That was how it worked. No one likes a tattletale. She'd never work in the City again.

There had to be another way . . .

She looked for the answer on the pavements, running hard in the cold frost, her lungs screaming as she raced past the muffled office workers all striding in the opposite direction to her. She ran past St Paul's, scaring the pigeons off the steps as her feet slapped the ground, her hands held in fists, her arms pumping like pistons, fury and despair the fuels that drove her forward as last night's faces swam in front of her eyes – Pierre's shark-like eyes, Sam's contempt, the smirk on Crivelli's mouth, Tilly's perfect make-up . . .

She was at the end of Isobel's road before she realized where she was – her feet on autopilot and bringing her back to her sister, the only person in the world who might possibly comprehend the magnitude of her actions – that there was nothing else outside of her career, that she was nothing outside of her career.

Her hand was up, ready to knock, when the front door opened suddenly and Lloyd – on the other side of the threshold – jumped back in alarm.

'*Jee*-zus, Legs! What the hell are you doing here?' he cried, dropping his briefcase and slapping a hand across his heart, his words indistinct behind a cranberry-red cashmere scarf that he had wound round the lower part of his face like a muffler. The collar of his grey coat was turned up, his hands were gloved in sheepskin mittens, and he was wearing a peculiarly ignominious trapper hat for the brisk walk to the Tube. 'It's six thirty in the bloody morning.'

'I've got the day off,' she replied, panting hard, with her hands on her thighs, thinking quickly. 'Thought I'd spend it with Iz and Ferds.'

'You? Have a day off? Pull the other one!' he laughed, quickly tugging off the mittens and pocketing them in his coat.

'Yeah, I have. For, uh . . .' She blanked. What did people do if they didn't work? 'For Christmas shopping, that's it.'

'Oh.' Lloyd pulled a face. He supposed even she had to do that. 'Well, they're still asleep.'

She rolled her eyes. 'Yeah, but you know me — I never can sleep in. I'll just make a cup of tea and wait, shall I,' she said rhetorically, rubbing her hands and blowing little white plumes into the air. It was freezing out here, she realized for the first time.

'You'd better get out of the cold,' Lloyd said, frowning at her thin – albeit thermal – running layers, her ankles bare and only three-quarter-length running tights on beneath her shorts.

'Thanks,' she said, dipping past him into the warmth of the hall. Now he was on the step and she was inside the house. With a smile, she picked up his briefcase and handed it to him – a strange role reversal that left Lloyd even more confused.

'Uh, right, well, see you later, then,' he said, looking unsure whether he should peck her on the cheek too.

But she made the decision for him. 'Yep. Have a good

day,' she said briskly, closing the door on him. She pulled off her trainers and padded quietly down the dog-leg hall into her sister's kitchen, feeling soothed already.

Her sister's house conformed to all the usual South London stereotypes that seemed to matter – granite surfaces, the entire range of Jo Malone scented candles, a sludgy-grey palette and the ubiquitous black-and-white family portraits on the walls – but it somehow never looked like the neighbours' kitchens. It was never tidy, for a start – cookbooks towered perilously on buckling shelves, piles of paperwork mushroomed like fungi on the island, and the tea towels were always stained, even after a boil wash. But then, that was why Allegra loved it here. She could almost guarantee there would be a tub of hummus and an orange Le Creuset of spaghetti bolognese in the fridge, a bag of Cadbury's giant buttons secured with an elastic band in the fruit bowl and a half-drunk bottle of cava with a spoon in the top.

It was perfect in its imperfection and the closest thing she had to a home.

Making a pot of tea – taking care to shut the kitchen door to stop the sound of the kettle boiling from travelling upstairs and waking Ferdy – she settled down on the charcoal-grey sofa in the far corner and turned on the TV, flicking straight to BBC News 24.

The first rush of anger was gone and emotional and physical exhaustion were beginning to hit. By the time Isobel descended the stairs an hour later, Ferdy on her hip and yawning, Allegra was curled up on the sofa, fast asleep, her hand still holding on to her phone.

*

'There you are!' Isobel grumbled, as Allegra pocketed her phone and pushed her way through the crowds to where her sister was standing, grim-faced, as she rummaged through a sale bin of French baby clothes. Ferdy, who was strapped to her back in one of those curious baby backpacks, was delighted by the melee around him and kept pulling other women's hair if they got too close. 'I want your thoughts on this.'

Isobel held up a delicate baby-blue and ivory silk sailor romper suit, complete with flapping collar – more like a mini cape – at the back.

'No, I'm not sure you do,' Allegra replied.

Isobel sighed dramatically. 'Not funny. I need something for Ferdy to wear on Christmas Day.'

'And have you met your son? Let's just take a moment to consider the facts. He is the child who eats like a cow, having to spit up his meal at least once before finally committing to digestion.'

Isobel snorted with laughter. 'He's not that bad.'

'Iz, you are blinded by love, but I am telling you now, no sailor who ever sailed the high seas could do to that costume what Ferdy will do to it. Navy. Navy is your friend. Go for something navy.'

'But this has got seventy per cent off.' Isobel pulled a pained expression.

'Which should give you some indication of just how many other people knew it was a bad idea too.' She patted her sister's arm.

Isobel tutted. 'I hate shopping with you. It's like shopping with Lloyd. Everything has to be *practical*. What's wrong with wanting to celebrate my beautiful boy? One day, he'll be too big for me to dress and it'll be dirty jeans and hoodies all the way.' But she took one look at Allegra's expression and let the fey sailor costume drop back into the bin.

'Close one, buddy,' Allegra said to her little nephew, stroking his cheek as he kicked his legs in reply.

'You're unusually acerbic today.'

'Thank you.'

Isobel regarded her sister suspiciously. 'Why are you really here? I usually have to get the lowdown on Kirsty's divorce before she'll book me in to see you.'

Allegra looked surprised. 'Kirsty was married?'

Isobel groaned. 'Ugh, God! How can you not know that? She's been your PA for almost five years!'

There was a short silence. 'Well . . . the office isn't the place to discuss personal matters,' Allegra mumbled finally.

Isobel just rolled her eyes and they moved away from the sale bins, wandering slowly over the packed shopping floor. Slowly was all they could manage. It was lunchtime and all the local office workers had emptied out of their buildings to try to get ahead on their Christmas shopping before the weekend began and it was fast becoming hard to move. Carols were being piped through the speakers everywhere, and at every escalator, a stall had been set up with freshly baked gingerbread and mulled wine. Isobel nimbly sidestepped a double buggy with sleeping twins inside.

'*Not* for boys, Iz,' Allegra said, taking a pair of 'cute' striped tights out of her sister's hands.

'I don't know why you're knocking my taste so much today,' Isobel said, as Allegra silently pulled her away from the velvet duffel coats too. 'You look really good in *my* clothes. Much better than in your own.'

'Thanks.' Allegra looked down at the clothes Isobel had lent her: boyfriend jeans that hung comfortably on her hips, chequered Vans skate shoes, an oversized tweed jacket and a grey marl sweatshirt with red sequinned lips on the front. Isobel had told her she looked 'on trend', but to Allegra's mind, she looked like an overdrawn student and she had seen the way the security guard's eyes had narrowed slightly on their way in.

'Again, that was not intended as a compliment.'

A woman stampeding towards the hallowed shoe department caught Allegra's arm with her bag, the hard corner jabbing against her, but the woman didn't stop, apologize or turn round, and within ten seconds she'd disappeared again, swallowed up by the crowds.

Ferdy began kicking his legs and wriggling in the backpack – tired now of being constrained and a grizzly look brewing on his chubby pink face. Isobel bounced softly on the spot, trying to soothe him, completely unaware of how conspicuous she looked, 'boinging' in the middle of Selfridges. 'All I'm saying is you should respect my opinion a bit more. I know you're a maths genius who actually knows what a derivative is, but when it comes to clothes, I know what I'm talking about: *my* clothes make you look five years younger than you are; *your* clothes make you look twenty years older than you are.'

Allegra refrained from rolling her eyes – there was no point in explaining that a boardroom was one of the few places left on earth where women didn't want to look younger than they were.

Another woman – also in a half-run – trod painfully on her toe, although at least she had the courtesy to apologize over her shoulder. Allegra turned on the spot, irritated and fast losing her patience. She could use her elbows as weapons along with the best of them, but she didn't have the reserves for shops as warzones today. She saw the illuminated sign and grabbed Isobel by the arm. 'Come on. This way.'

'What? Where are we going?'

'I can't do this. Ferdy's getting upset, and life is too short to spend it being knocked over by strangers.'

'But I haven't bought anything for Mum yet,' Isobel complained, still walking with a peculiar bounce to pacify Ferdy, who was nonetheless escalating to full-on tears, as Allegra pressed the button for the lift and the doors pinged open. 'And Lloyd's desperate for a jacket. I have to go down to menswear,' she protested as Allegra pressed to go up. 'What are you *doing*?'

Ten seconds later, the doors slid open to reveal a perfumed suite with bronze walls, tulip-wood floors and dip-dyed silk rugs. Books were clustered in coloured groupings on shelves, and heaps of powder-pink flowers were arranged in bowls on low tables. At one end was a bar, and at the other, a library, the sisters' reflections echoed back to them from numerous mirrored surfaces.

Isobel's mouth fell open and even Ferdy – distracted by the sudden calm – stopped crying. Momentarily, anyway. 'Where the hell are we? Is this someone's *house*?' Isobel whispered, just in case it was.

Allegra shook her head as they stepped out. She forgot her sister's expensive tastes always had to be filtered through Zara first. A woman in a skinny black suit and studded heels, with a fluoro-orange necklace at her throat, came towards them. She was smiling, but there was hesitancy in her demeanour. Was it their clothes, the bawling baby . . . ?

'Hello. May I help you?'

'I hope so, but I'm afraid we don't have an appointment,' Allegra replied briskly, her hands fishing in her pockets for the credit card she'd had the presence of mind to slip into her running shorts before leaving/escaping the flat this morning. Her voice was thin and lifeless, and she knew she sounded snappy.

'Ah. Well, I'm sorry—'

Allegra silently handed over her black Amex card with a knowing look. Regardless of whether the inevitable 'sorry' was down to the clothes or the bawling baby or both, she knew exactly how to trade here. 'We need to get our Christmas shopping sorted, you see, and my nephew here is hungry. He needs . . .' She turned back to Isobel. 'What does he need?'

'Um, like, maybe a finger sandwich or a banana?' Isobel offered weakly, intimidated by the elegant decor and drawing up damage-limitation plans in her head. He was, after all, the child who ate like he had more than one stomach. She started bouncing on her toes as discreetly as she could in an effort to placate Ferdy, who was beginning to grizzle again.

'Can you do that?' Allegra asked, looking back at the consultant, her hands clasped in front of her in an authoritative but relaxed stance.

'You couldn't have timed it better,' the woman replied. 'All our consultants are booked today, but we have *just* had a cancellation. Would you like to take a seat on the sofas and I'll arrange for some refreshments to be sent up to you?'

'Thank you.'

Allegra led the way round a glass shelving unit to a drawing-room area with turquoise lamps and plump sofas studded with jewel-like velvet cushions. It felt like a 1950s film set, like *An Affair to Remember*, or a Doris Day–Rock Hudson collaboration.

Isobel sank gratefully onto one of the sofas, jumping straight back up again as the boy terror began to holler with renewed relish in her ear. Isobel planted her feet wide and dropped into some frantic pliés.

'Should we let him go free?' Allegra asked, imagining the personal shopper's strangled expression when she encountered *this* scenario. God, did her sister have *any* idea . . . ?

'What? Here? Are you mad?' Isobel hissed, dropping particularly deeply. 'Have you seen how much glass is in this room? Even if he doesn't break anything, just imagine the *smears.*'

Allegra pulled a face. 'Oh yes. The smears.'

The woman came back. 'All ordered,' she said, her voice trailing away as she watched Isobel rising and falling with rhythmic determination. Recovering herself, she stopped staring and sat daintily on the sofa opposite. 'So, I'm Tanya,' she smiled, her hands fluttering over her chest to reinforce the point.

'Allegra Fisher, Isobel Watson and Ferdy,' Allegra said.

'Would you prefer to go into one of the consulting suites? It's more private in there, and there are changing areas too?'

'We're not buying for ourselves, so we don't need to try things on,' Allegra said. 'And frankly, I'm not sure any of us want to be locked in a confined space with him when he's this hungry.'

'Oh yes. Quite.' Tanya looked across at Ferdy in alarm, before opening her iPad and quickly taking some personal details from Allegra to find her account. 'So then, what is it you're looking for today?' Tanya asked, directing the question to Allegra, the bearer of the black card.

'My sister needs a jacket for her husband.'

'Something khaki – you know, military style – but nothing too . . . tricksy,' Isobel said, going into freestyle as she started doing side lunges. Ferdy seemed a lot happier with that lateral motion – maybe because it brought him to within swiping distance of the lamps. 'No braiding or badges. No hood.'

'I know *exactly* what you're after,' Tanya said confidently, her head moving left and right to maintain eye contact.

'And it must have lots of pockets – you know, like big enough to get a nappy in.'

'Oh, uh . . .'

Isobel gave her a desperate look, realizing she'd lost their connection. 'Do you have kids?'

Tanya shook her head.

'No,' Isobel sighed, feeling ridiculous and misunderstood.

'Um, what size is he, your husband?'

'Medium.'

'Do you happen to have a photo of him?'

'Totally,' Isobel said, stopping the lunges and immediately beginning to scan the photos on her phone for the most flattering picture. Lloyd wasn't, in Allegra's opinion, very photogenic and seemed to have a special skill of blinking at the exact point the shutter closed. Ferdy began to munter again and Isobel resumed quick heel raises.

Please, not star jumps, Allegra thought to herself, her

arms and legs crossed. 'While Isobel's doing that, we need something for our mother too. We were thinking maybe . . .' Allegra automatically looked to Isobel for help – she was the designated present-buyer in the family – but she was engrossed in their photos from Turkey and trying to find one that didn't make Lloyd's tummy look too big. 'Well, she feels the cold, so maybe something in cashmere or sheepskin.'

'Does she enjoy going on walks? Is she a gardener?'

'She enjoys walking in the garden,' Allegra said more quietly, aware she was making her mother sound like a Victorian lady of leisure.

'How old is she?'

'Sixty-six.' Too young to be where she was.

'I see. And her colouring, build . . . ?'

'Grey hair, dark brown eyes, medium height, slim build. Classic style – roll-neck jumpers and twinsets, pastel colours. A regular fourteen now.'

'OK, good. Well, I can think of a fair few things that you may like.'

'Here's one!' Isobel cried, leaping enthusiastically over to the sofa where Tanya was sitting. Lloyd was scrambling, bare-chested, over some rocks, and from the angle all you could really see of him were his shoulders and arms (he must have been holding his tummy in), but his eyes looked nice.

'Oh, he's so handsome!' Tanya said, bonding with Isobel, the less fearsome sister. 'I have just the thing for him.' She looked back at Allegra. 'And is that everything on your list?'

Allegra turned to her sister. 'Do you need some stocking-fillers?'

'Legs!' Isobel wailed, throwing her arms up behind her and trying to cover Ferdy's ears.

'Iz, he's ten months old. I don't think Santa's secret is out *just* yet.'

Tanya laughed confidingly and rose. 'Strictly speaking, we don't cover childrenswear or toys up here, but let me see what I can do. I've ordered the refreshments to be brought up to you, so they should be here any moment. My colleague Mary is in the adjoining suite, so if you need anything at all while I'm gone, please do knock. She's in the blue suite, just there.'

She pointed to a closed door with a number '8' on it. 'And there are plenty of magazines at your disposal. Our iPads are set to our designers' collections if you're interested.'

'Ooooh yes,' Isobel said interestedly, leaning forward to retrieve one from a low table, so that Ferdy almost slid out of the backpack head first.

'Whoa!' Allegra cried, lunging forward to stop him as Tanya looked on, open-mouthed in horror. 'Steady there, buster.' She helped right him, his bawls growing louder by the minute – almost jumping back as she saw that his nose needed a wipe. 'Oh, uh, Iz . . . his . . . his nose,' she grimaced. 'Gross.'

'OK, so then . . . I'll . . .' Tanya called over the noise, gesturing that she was going to the lifts and clearly concerned about leaving the trio unattended.

'Great. Just great,' Isobel muttered, pulling a stiff hanky from her jeans back pocket and trying to catch hold of Ferdy's head behind her own, but he was reaching a new crescendo. 'Dammit, we can't afford to wait for lunch to come up. Can you check in my bag? There's a carton of milk and a bottle in there.'

The noise was growing so loud that Allegra was beginning to feel disoriented and panicky, and she handed it over with trembling hands.

Isobel expertly decanted the contents into a small empty bottle and shook it vigorously like it was a fancy cocktail. Then she sank onto the nearest sofa cushion. 'Quick! Get him out of this contraption for me. We're going to get thrown out if he keeps this up.'

It was true – they were. Even unlimited credit came with some provisos. If all these other suites were occupied . . .

Allegra fiddled with the straps and hoisted the distressed child clear, trying to make sure his foot didn't connect with Isobel's head. 'Here, just let me give it to him. You must have tinnitus from him screaming next to your ear like that.'

Allegra leaned back as far as she dared and, grabbing the bottle, settled back with Ferdy in her arms, his little hands patting the sides rhythmically as he immediately began to glug. His eyes closed as he drank and both women revelled in the sudden, loud peace, just as a door – door 8 – opened and a stern-looking woman stepped out.

'Tanya?' she asked, grim-faced and tight-lipped.

Isobel stopped flicking through American *Vogue* and turned on her seat to face her. 'Tanya's gone down to the shop floor,' she said brightly. 'She said she wouldn't be long.'

The woman looked at Isobel as though surprised she had responded, before catching sight of Ferdy hungrily drinking the milk. It was clear he was – or had been – the source of her displeasure. 'I see. Thank you.' And she disappeared into room 8 again.

Isobel turned back and pulled a face. 'Oops. She looked pissed off.'

'Maybe this wasn't one of my better ideas,' Allegra murmured, looking down at Ferdy, who – now clean-faced and silent – had the cheek to look angelic. 'They're trying to sell thousands of pounds' worth of clothes and Ferdy here's on a one-man mission to blow the walls down.'

'He'll be OK now,' Isobel said, gazing at her son adoringly for a moment, before quickly picking up one of the iPads. 'I wonder if they've got Isabel Marant on here.'

Somewhere down the corridor could be heard the sound of a fire door being opened and, shortly afterwards, footsteps on the wooden floor. Allegra looked up as two assistants set down trays – one piled high with cloud-soft finger sandwiches, chopped fruit, juice and a strawberry mousse, and on the other, some olives, crisps and two fizzing glasses of champagne.

Both sisters eyed the glasses hungrily. If ever champagne had been earned, shopping in Selfridges two Fridays before Christmas with a teething, hungry baby in tow qualified them for a free flute.

'Cheers!' Isobel beamed, handing Allegra her glass, and they each took a sip, but Allegra didn't warm to the taste. Her body wasn't receptive to more alcohol so soon after the martinis, and besides, what did she have to celebrate?

Her mind wandered back to the night before as a silent but insistent buzz in her pocket made her stiffen suddenly, and she awkwardly shifted position, trying to free her phone from her jeans. Ferdy didn't protest. His tummy was filling nicely and so long as nothing came between him and the milk, peace was assured. She clicked on the screen and, seeing the name on it, instantly pocketed the phone again with a scowl, just as door 8 opened once more and the grumpy woman who'd been looking for Tanya emerged. She walked past Isobel and Allegra like they weren't there, even though Isobel – who was mid-bite of a sandwich – had politely half turned in her seat. Allegra's eyes followed the woman as she marched officiously across the floor – her arms laden with black and red ski kit – towards a desk in the next section. Setting down the clothes on a nearby chair, she began typing away at the keyboard, frowning as she peered at the screen, all the while looking very important.

A man came out of room 8, buttoning the jacket on his suit and glancing across at them as he briskly walked towards the saleswoman. He stopped abruptly.

'Fisher? What the hell are *you* doing here?'

Isobel's eyes widened at hearing her sister being referred to by her surname.

It took Allegra a couple of moments to respond. 'Isn't it obvious?' she replied lightly, lifting Ferdy in her arms slightly. Sometimes her ability to mask her shock/upset/ fear/hurt (delete as appropriate) amazed even her. Sam took in the high tea, the scattered magazines, Allegra's uncharacteristic clothes, the feeding baby in her arms.

He frowned. 'Not really, no.'

Allegra didn't reply and simply looked back down at Ferdy, not trusting her voice to carry off an insouciance she didn't feel. The brutality of last night's events rushed back at her with fresh power and she felt the adrenalin spike into her muscles. Everything had, after all, ignited because of him – what he'd whispered to Pierre, what he'd said to Zhou. If he'd never brought Zhou to the damned party . . .

If he'd never moved to London . . . If he'd never been on that plane . . . in that lift . . .

'I tried calling you all night!' he said, stepping closer, his eyes moving warily to Isobel before resting on Allegra again.

'And, funnily enough, I was sleeping.'

'I doubt that.'

Her eyes snapped to his and immediately away again.

'You could have returned my calls.'

'Could I? Why? What is it I owe you exactly?' Her tone had hardened, flecks of venom glistening in her words. 'You got what you wanted.'

He was quiet for a few beats and Allegra stared down into Ferdy's deep blue eyes, which were wide and fixed upon her like she was the sun in his sky.

'I need to see your last report, what you were working on with Bob this week. We'll need it for the new pitch.'

What? Her head whipped up again. *That* was his only concern?

'Fuck. You,' she said with ominous quiet.

Isobel's jaw dropped down. She didn't like bad language to be used in front of Ferds, but something – call it survival instinct – told her now wasn't the time to bring it up.

Behind her, Allegra heard the gentle ping of the lift doors, Sam's eyes raising up as he saw Tanya heading towards them.

'Enjoy your ski trip,' she said with withering sarcasm. 'At least you'll look the part.' Her eyes flickered towards the matron ringing up his clothes by the desk as Tanya rounded the corner with a small wheeled trolley, already impressively stacked with polythene-gloved clothes, and

Allegra thought she must have run around the designer floors like it was a supermarket sweep.

'Ladies . . .' Tanya said, smiling first politely at Sam, then more brightly as she took in the finer details of his face. But Sam didn't notice. He was too busy staring at Allegra, who, in turn, was again suddenly engrossed in watching Ferdy feed.

'It's OK,' Allegra smiled, looking up at her. 'He was just leaving.'

Tanya's face fell as Sam walked off, the tension in his shoulders clear even from behind. She recovered quickly, pushing the rack of clothes towards the sisters, but Isobel wasn't interested in jackets for Lloyd right now.

'Who the hell was *that*?' Isobel hissed, getting up and collapsing on the same sofa as her sister.

'A creep I used to work with.'

'He called you Fisher.'

Allegra looked at her sister and shook her head lightly. If *that* shocked her . . . 'Yes.' She looked down at her nephew feeding peacefully in her arms. The milk seemed to have made him sleepy.

Isobel carried on staring at her. 'Well, he may be a creep, but he's a gorgeous creep. You can see that, right?'

Allegra didn't dignify the comment with a response.

'You're sure you couldn't just . . . overlook the creep bit?'

'Oh, are you kidding me?' Allegra snapped. 'Were you just sitting here or not? Which bit of mutual contempt didn't you get?'

Isobel frowned quizzically, falling so far back in the cushions that she was practically horizontal. But she knew better than to say another word.

Chapter Thirteen

Traffic was heavy along Park Lane, thanks to roadworks outside the Grosvenor, and their taxi driver seemed to be lacking in festive spirit as he cussed at every motorist, biker and cyclist who tried to get past. Isobel didn't notice. She was far too busy peering into all the bags bundled by their feet – admiring over and again the bounty of gifts that Allegra had bought without even glancing at the price tags. With the Christmas shopping sorted and Ferdy sleeping, Allegra should have felt relaxed, but instead she was digging her nails into the palms of her hand, feeling perilously close to tears.

Her phone buzzed again and she pulled it out of her pocket with a frown.

'Aren't you going to answer that?' Isobel asked, watching her sister's expression harden.

Allegra glanced up at her. 'No.'

'Your phone's been going off all day.'

'My phone is always going off,' Allegra murmured, not wanting to be drawn into a conversation about it. As much as she'd tried to downplay the shock of bumping into Sam in Selfridges, the truth was, it had undone her resolve to stay calm and it was harder now to pretend she was fine.

She was not fine.

'Yeah, but even by your standards . . .' Isobel said, sitting up and taking a better look at her sister, as if seeing for the first time how pale she looked. 'What's going on? Why aren't you *answering* your calls? Why are you even sitting here in a cab with me on a Friday afternoon?'

But Allegra ignored her concern, slipping the phone back into her pocket and looking out of the window. They had stopped outside the Porsche showroom, and inside, a man in a dark suit was lightly running a hand over the flank of a 911 S.

Isobel, getting the hint, picked up a copy of the *Evening Standard* that a previous passenger had left on the seat and began flicking through it. Allegra had no doubt she'd be looking for the horoscopes.

A group of Japanese tourists were crossing the road from the Dorchester towards Hyde Park, and the taxi hit the glorious heights of third gear as the traffic began to flow again, past the roadworks.

'Well, this is interesting,' Isobel murmured after a moment. 'Supposedly a certain individual is trying to get my attention. Hmm, wonder who that could be?' she said wryly, throwing a glance at her sleeping child, before continuing to read. 'But the problem is, "Changes in circumstance have thrown existing arrangements into disarray. Others are unsure how to handle the chaos." They're hoping I'll know what to do but are too shy to ask. Ha! I don't know any shy people.'

'I can't believe you still read these things. What's wrong with you? Lucky leaves, horoscopes . . . You'll tell me you believe in ghosts next.'

'You mean you don't?' Isobel gasped, before a crafty smile escaped her.

Allegra looked down the length of Piccadilly as they rounded Hyde Park Corner. The Ritz was lit up like a birthday cake in the lilac dusk, giant illuminated stars straddling the road as red double-deckers shuffled beneath and cold pedestrians competitively thrust gloved hands in the air to hail cabs.

'Now you . . . Capricorn,' Isobel continued. 'Ah, *you* . . . Well, "Usually planning ahead is wise. While certain matters need to be organized, you're urged to ensure those arrangements are flexible. That way, you'll have no problem adjusting to the sudden but ultimately worthwhile changes triggered by Jupiter's powerful aspect to Pluto."' Isobel looked across at her sister. 'Oh yes, I've often said it – never mess with Jupiter's aspect to Pluto.'

Allegra arched an eyebrow. 'Honestly, I despair,' she said as her phone rang again. She pulled it out from her pocket. Her expression changed as she looked at the screen and she pressed 'accept'. 'Hello? . . What? But how? . . . I see,' Allegra murmured, glancing back at Isobel. 'Yes, I understand . . . Um, I don't know yet. I'll need to think about that. Can I get back to you on it? . . . I see. Yes . . . Not at all . . . OK, thank you . . . Yes, goodbye.' She pressed 'end call', biting her lip pensively.

'Who was that?' Isobel asked distractedly, flicking further back to the sports pages. Chelsea's fortunes would dictate how good her weekend was going to be.

'That was the Swiss Police. They've got the results back on the DNA test.'

Isobel's eyes widened. 'Oh. That was quick!'

Allegra shrugged. 'Electronic age.'

'What'd they say?'

'It's a positive. Valentina definitely was our grand-mother. Mum's mum.'

'*What?*' Isobel leaned back against the leather seat. 'But *how?*'

Allegra knew Isobel didn't really need an answer to that and they were both quiet for a bit, trying to let the news settle.

'Well, do we have to tell Mum?'

Allegra shrugged. 'I don't know. We should ask Barry, see what he thinks.'

'Yeah, good idea. Good idea.' Isobel nodded thought-fully, but an anxious expression had settled over her previously happy-go-lucky features.

The cab started moving again, the driver changing lanes suddenly and almost taking out a biker weaving through the traffic on the inside lane. 'He also asked what we wanted to do about the remains. You know, whether we wanted to have them couriered over here or—'

'Couriered over? How do you courier a body? Oh God, I feel sick.'

Allegra patted her arm lightly. 'Don't get in a tizz. I'll deal with it.'

'I know, but . . .' She took a deep breath. 'Where is she?'

'Zermatt still.'

'Oh great. Really accessible,' Isobel grumbled. 'So how have you left it?'

'I said I'd call him back. It'll be fine.'

'How can it be fine that Granny lied to Mum all her life about being her mother?'

'I'm sure . . . I'm sure she had a good reason. Granny loved Mum. And us. There'll be a reason.'

Isobel looked back down to the newspaper on her lap,

but her jaw had begun to jut. They were travelling over Albert Bridge now and Allegra looked up at the lights strung along the tension cables that, she always thought, looked like harp strings.

'Oh my God!'

Allegra looked back in alarm at her sister's sharp tone. 'What?'

'You were *fired*?' Isobel cried in disbelief as she continued to read.

'*What?*' Allegra echoed, snatching the paper from her sister's hands.

Her own image stared back at her, taken – she remembered – at an annual conference in Singapore last year when she and the other keynote speakers lined up on the steps of the building. She was the only woman, of course, her black Armani trouser suit and sharply bobbed hair doing a fine job of minimizing the fact.

Her eyes scanned the text quickly, alert to anything libellous. If they said they'd sacked her, she could have them on that as well as the discrimination charge. But there was nothing. Only 'sudden departure . . . internal dissatisfaction . . . exciting new phase . . . Sam Kemp . . .'

She put the newspaper down, her hands shaking, her sister waiting.

'I was not fired,' she said finally. 'I quit.'

'*Why? When?*'

Allegra swallowed. 'Last night. For reasons that are far too boring to discuss.'

'Uh, I don't think so! Tell me, now.'

'Honestly, it's just politics. It'll get sorted. I'm hiring a lawyer to deal with it all. It's open and shut.'

As if checking that it still was, she found her phone and

scrolled back through her texts quickly. Pierre's crude –
illegal – demand blinked back at her in black and white.
She pocketed the phone quickly, not even wanting to look
at it.

'So that's why you came round this morning,' Isobel
murmured, reaching out a hand and laying it softly on
Allegra's arm.

Allegra looked quickly out of the window. 'I just couldn't
sleep that well. I went for a run and . . .' She shrugged, her
voice was close to cracking. 'Well, I was at yours before I
even knew it.'

'You poor thing.'

Allegra looked back sharply. She didn't want pity, or
sympathy – it suggested she had lost. 'I'm fine. It's just
tedious.'

But Isobel wouldn't be thrown off the scent this time. 'It
is not tedious. It is upsetting and stressful and scary. Your
job is your world.'

'There'll be others.' But the strain of the lie was too much
for her voice this time and it fractured, a sudden sob erupting from the void, and Allegra pushed her fingers to the
bridge of her nose to stop the tears that were threatening.
She took a few deep breaths.

Isobel stayed quiet, the concern etching deeper into her
face. 'Is it anything to do with that bloke we saw?' she
asked quietly.

'Yes.'

'I thought so.' Isobel rubbed her arm soothingly.

The taxi was turning onto Clapham Common now, a
light mist hovering above the expanse of frozen ground as
wrapped-up joggers ended their day as she'd begun.

'You'll stay for dinner, right?' Isobel asked.

'Thanks,' Allegra nodded. 'That'd be good.' The last thing she could think about right now was food, what to make or how to cook it. Worse, being alone. For once, she really didn't want that.

A few minutes later, they were outside Isobel's house, heaving the shopping bags from the cab, the cold air like a slap on Ferdy's face and waking him from his sleep. Allegra paid, not bothering to get a receipt, and the three of them jostled their way into the narrow, inviting Victorian terrace.

'You know, I've got an idea,' Isobel said as she walked straight through to the kitchen, over to a cupboard and lifted down two wine glasses, an action as reflexive to her as breathing. 'Lloyd's parents are coming down tomorrow for the week. They're spending Christmas with his sister this year, so they want some time with Ferds beforehand.'

'That'll be nice,' Allegra said limply.

Isobel rolled her eyes as she grabbed an opened bottle of cava from the fridge, a spoon dangling in the top. 'For Ferds maybe. Diane still hasn't forgiven me for not going with the tiles she liked in the bathroom.'

'Oh.'

Isobel took a deep breath as she poured the wine. 'So, why don't we go out to Zermatt, just you and me? Seeing the authorities face to face would mean we could get everything settled more quickly with this mystery grandmother of ours.'

Allegra shot her a look.

'What?' Isobel held her hands up innocently. '*And* it would give you a break. You need to get away for a bit; it's always easier to get perspective when you're not at home in the thick of it.'

'What about Lloyd?'

Isobel shrugged. 'He'll be fine; he doesn't get enough time with either his parents or his child. It would be good for him to hold the fort for a bit; it would only be for three or four days.' She bit her lip as she handed Allegra a glass. 'And of course if there was time for a run or two, then I'd have no problem with that.'

Allegra couldn't help but crack a smile. Isobel was a ski *demon*. 'I bet you wouldn't.'

'So is that a yes?' Isobel asked, holding her drink, as if poised for a toast.

Allegra hesitated. She needed to instruct a lawyer and crack on with things here, pick up the phone to the head-hunters and try to get her career back on track. It was the worst possible time to take off on a whim and go skiing. Not to mention the two people she disliked most in the world were going to be there too. How big was Zermatt anyway? Could she feasibly avoid them? At the question, she remembered the time when she'd been separated from her friends on the university ski trip to Val d'Isere and, even knowing their distinctive ski kits, she hadn't been able to find them just on the one mountain. Zermatt, she thought – from a brief Google when she'd been on the phone to Annen – had three. That would be big enough to hide in, surely? It wasn't like she knew what either Zhou or Sam would be wearing on the slopes and with helmets and goggles on, everyone was incognito anyway. She could be skiing next to Rihanna and not know it.

Besides, Isobel had a point. This was the most efficient way of getting the whole sorry mess cleaned up and she had some time on her hands, for once. They had phones where she was going, and this revelation, as Isobel said, of a brand-new grandmother raised more questions than the DNA test answered. If they were going to have any chance of presenting this news to their mother, they needed the full facts.

She looked at her sister's hopeful smile and raised her glass in a toast too. 'Yes. Yes, it is. Why the hell not?'

Chapter Fourteen

Day Fourteen: *Nesting Dolls*

Zermatt was ready for them. All of them. Skiers and snow-boarders disgorged from the cog-wheel train from Visp, spilling out into the square in their hundreds and making well-practised beelines for the waiting non-motorized taxis that were scarcely larger than tuna tins and emitted whines, not fumes. Beside them, looking overscaled and old school by comparison, stood the regal carriages of the Mont Cervin Palace hotel, the glossy horses that pulled them standing patiently, occasionally pawing the ground as the drivers, wrapped in heavy coats, lifted trunks and suitcases onto the roofs.

Isobel, who was trying to take charge so that Allegra could 'rest', was insistent upon leading the journey, and as she rummaged in her bag for the town map, Allegra stood beside the town's snow-dusted Christmas tree, soaking it all in. It was only eleven days till Christmas and the first week of the winter peak season – the pistes were pristine, the restaurants and boutiques fully stocked for the festive onslaught – and the sense of anticipation, of unleashed energy, lent a crackle to the air as snowflakes hurriedly tumbled to earth.

She watched the taxis – skis sticking out from the external racks – begin to creep up the steep hills on caterpillar tracks as Isobel finally found the map in her jacket pocket; she listened to the charming jingle of the bells on the horses' reins, ever so politely telling people to get out of the way, while Isobel turned the map the right way round, looking up moments later with a concentrated confusion. 'I think it's this way,' she said finally, pointing left.

'Just follow me,' Allegra sighed, losing patience and heading right.

'But—' Isobel protested, wrestling with the release mechanism on the handle of her wheelie bag.

'It's south, sixth right off the Bahnhofstrasse.'

'Oh.' Navigation had never been Isobel's strong point. 'It's because I'm starving. You know I can't think on an empty stomach.'

'We'll drop our bags and change, then get lunch.' Allegra gave a quick smile to soften her bossiness as she realized she was dictating the schedule and hijacking Isobel's mothering intentions. Besides, it wasn't hunger that had left Isobel dazed and confused, it was exhaustion. Allegra was well used to packing with only a moment's notice – she even had a ski bag at home, ready-packed – and she'd bought the business-class flights on her air miles within minutes. But whilst she had gone online to look for accommodation, a glass of wine in her hand, Isobel had had to crawl into her loft to find her ski gear that had been boxed up for the best part of eight years and then write a detailed itinerary for Lloyd and her parents-in-law about Ferdy's meals, sleep times, predilection for coal and his busy social diary. It had kept her up till midnight and Allegra hadn't fully appreciated her sister's ability to manage the complex logistics of Ferdy's life.

They walked through the main street, their bags bulging with ski kit behind them, both their heads turning left and right, Isobel trying to spot the best pharmacy and deals on Moncler, Allegra looking for the correct turn-off.

Zermatt was exactly as she'd expected it to be. Unable to break with her usual habit of research, research, research, she had memorized the piste and town maps on the flight over so that even without seeing it, she knew the river must run alongside the next block to their left, that the old town was dead ahead, the heliport was behind them to the right . . .

They walked slowly past shop windows where 20,000-Swiss-franc designer watches sat next to chocolate-rendered mini Matterhorns, and bundles of so-chic cashmere jumpers sat cheek by jowl beside novelty marmots. Christmas lights were strung up above the streets, deep (empty) flowerboxes hung at every window, snow was piled like marshmallow toppings on every roof, and festivity hung in the air like perfume.

The street was teeming with people as skiers trudged the pavements in their distinctive rocking gaits, the bindings on their boots clumped with snow from their last run, their skis swung over their shoulders like rifles. She saw a group of hung-over snowboarders – their trousers worn low and antlers on their helmets – grabbing a snack lunch with hot chocolates and crêpes on their way to the slopes; she peered in at the shoppers clustered in the coffee houses with bags at their feet and their hands round *vin chauds*. God, she loved being in the mountains. Sometimes she felt they were the only place she was truly relaxed.

Turning right opposite the Mont Cervin Palace – impossible to miss on account of the wall of light pouring down six storeys from the balconied windows – they found themselves in a narrow side street of rough-hewn stone buildings and Isobel redeemed herself by finding the apartment first. With cold hands, she entered the combination code they'd been given by the owner, took the key from the deposit box and fell into the lobby to escape from the cold, carrying their bags up a narrow turning staircase.

'I knew it!' Isobel gasped as she unlocked the door and they saw the apartment they had found last night on their frantic internet search for somewhere to stay. With the Christmas season officially under way and such strong early snowfall, everywhere was booked solid, and even this they only had for four nights until Thursday, changeover day.

Allegra walked through the flat, appraising it with cool interest: limed oak streaked with grey tones, a creaky knotholed floor, red nappa-leather sofa, cowhide rugs on the floors, glossy burnt-orange units in the kitchen, solid-oak shutters with heart cut-outs, box beds in the bedrooms. It was a contemporary fusion of traditional craftsmanship and urban design, and Isobel was in raptures. Wandsworth it wasn't.

'I love it! I love it, I love it and I want to live here,' she gasped, twirling on the spot and running her hand over the twisted, warped wood walls.

'You can – for a bit,' Allegra called, carrying the bags through to the back. 'Which bedroom do you want?'

'You choose,' Isobel insisted, running after her. 'This is your break.'

'Iz, you're the one who has a tiny baby and who hasn't slept for nearly a year.'

'*I* am fine. It's you who needs to catch a breath.'

'*I* am fine,' Allegra echoed back. 'We are here primarily to get everything sorted for Mum, not for a spa break.'

'So then we're both fine.'

'I guess we are.'

'Fine.' Isobel put her hands on her hips and stared across at her sister. Isobel's eyes widened.

Allegra sighed. 'I am *not* getting into a staring competition with you,' she said, picking up her bag and walking into the smaller bedroom. 'I'll take this room. It looks nice and dark.'

Isobel chuckled, considering that a victory, as she took her bag into the room opposite.

Allegra put her bag on the bed and unzipped it. Clothes sprung out like a jack-in-the-box and she pulled them out, refolding everything carefully in the wardrobe. From the clatter coming across the tiny hall, she could hear Isobel doing the same, although it sounded more like she was catapulting them.

She lifted out the small wooden Advent calendar at the bottom of the bag, protectively wrapped in her pyjamas. As scathing as she'd been in the loft about the novelty of a surprise a day, she had been amazed at how much – and how quickly – she'd come to enjoy the little ritual of peering in a drawer. It was really the only thing that varied in her day, along with choosing her lingerie sets, but also the sprinkling of festive *objets* on her dressing table – as tiny as they were – was the closest she'd allow herself to get to Christmas decorations. After all, what use was a wreath on her front door when it faced onto brown nylon carpets in the communal hall? A sprig of mistletoe hung in the sitting-room doorway would only alarm the cleaner, and dragging a Christmas tree up three flights of stairs would almost certainly mean it would be bald by the time she got it there.

But this . . . It had been so early when they'd left for the airport this morning that she hadn't thought to open today's drawer, and she settled on the bed, wondering what she'd find.

She opened the drawer; inside was a matryoshka nesting doll, except that it wasn't painted in the traditional Russian style but Swiss – with hair in plaits, aproned skirt and a cropped trimmed jacket. The outer doll wasn't large by any means, fitting easily in the palm of her hand, and she smiled as she twisted it open to reveal the smaller one inside, and then the smaller one inside that . . . The smallest one of all was no bigger than a dog's tooth and she squinted in amazement at the detailed paintwork on it. Five dolls all fitting into each other, just like her own family. *A long line of mothers . . .*

'We're getting changed and going straight out, yes?' Isobel called five minutes later, having 'spoken' to Ferdy and Lloyd on the phone.

'Yes,' Allegra replied, restacking the five dolls inside each other and placing them back inside the number-14 drawer. She put the cabinet on her bedside table and undressed, changing into her skinny black stirrup trousers and pulling on her ski socks.

She wandered over to the window as she belted her ivory Moncler jacket, her eyes falling on the brooding mountains that ringed the town like the walls of an amphitheatre, the snow clouds stretched low between them like a false ceiling. It felt strange being in Zermatt, knowing as she did now that her grandmother had died here. It made her feel odd. She had never been to this town before, but already she knew it by heart. She was a stranger and yet, supposedly, she was home.

They forgot to eat. Once the clouds were below them, the edges of the world were crisp, the Alpine peaks like jagged shards trying to puncture the taut billow of the blush-pink sky, and they skied for hours, grabbing every passing chairlift to 'just try' another run before the light went.

They had learned to ski as children, each other's best companion in ski school and then, in their teenage years, looking out for one another as they pushed into back-country and the world of off-pisting. Isobel had always been the more naturally gifted of them on skis. Moguls and ice had never bothered her and she had always teased Allegra about the time she'd come down a treacherous red on her bottom. But things had changed since then – Allegra had long since learned that it wasn't fear that was the most terrifying emotion – and they were well matched, echoing each other's moves like twins as they curled left and right in poetic silence.

'What do you think – Chez Vrony or Findlerhof for scoff?' Isobel asked, her cheeks rosy, her eyes bright with the exhilaration that comes from the double punch of hard exercise and unfettered freedom. She was standing beside a worn wooden post, its arrows pointing in numerous directions, the universal sign of a crossed knife and fork suddenly a beloved motif.

'Oh God, yes, either. My thighs are on fire. I've been on glycogen for the past hour.'

'Why can't you just say you're starving, like most normal

people?' Isobel laughed, pushing her poles into the ground and sliding gently down the narrow track that was pointing towards the restaurants.

They stopped a couple of hundred metres later, where a confluence of skis and poles heralded a popular stopping point, and jammed theirs in the snow with them, walking carefully along a hard-packed path that had become icy from traffic.

A tiny hamlet of dark, almost blackened huts were clustered together, and as they rounded the corner of one, they stopped in their tracks, enormous smiles growing on their faces. The number of European languages drifting over a bleached terrace was as cosmopolitan as an ambassador's drinks reception, as free-riding snowboarders in baggy neons shared space with euro princesses in fur-trimmed Bogner and St Barts bobble hats. They were all starting their après-ski up the mountain now that the lifts had stopped for the day. (The run back into town was a respectable blue back to the funicular.) And who could blame them for not wanting to leave? Sheepskin and reindeer hides blanketed the wooden chairs; deep sleigh-shaped benches lined up deck-side to overlook the plunging valley and were softened with more throws and rugs so that they were almost like outdoor beds. From where they were standing, Allegra could only see legs outstretched from them, heavy-booted feet resting on the veranda, lolling hands holding foamy beers and the tops of heads with hair mussed up from helmets.

'Um . . . busy much?' Isobel said rhetorically. All the tables were taken and a huge standing crowd had swelled at one end of the deck as music started pumping.

'It'll be quieter inside. Let's try for a table in there,' Allegra suggested sensibly.

They crossed the terrace, Isobel beaming back at every interested stare that came her way. 'Still got it,' she whispered delightedly under her breath to her sister, who was far more concerned with finding somewhere to sit.

Inside was no better. Damn.

A beautiful girl in tight black ski pants and carrying some menus stopped by them in the doorway. 'You want only drinks, yes?' she asked, although it came across as more of an instruction than a question.

'No, to eat, please,' Allegra said, her eyes still scanning the various dark nooks inside. Did anyone look like they were preparing to leave, at least?

The waitress sucked her teeth. 'We are very full—'

'But we haven't had lunch,' Isobel said quickly, as though this fact would sway whether or not the waitress would find them a table.

'I'm sorry. The kitchens, they are open for another five minutes, but there is no room. All the tables are taken.'

Allegra sighed irritably. It looked like she was just going to have to put up with a bit more thigh burn until they could get into town.

'They can sit with us!'

The three women looked to their left in surprise. A guy – he could only be mid-twenties – was twisted on one of the benches at the edge of the deck and leaning towards them with a bright smile. His helmet was still on, the chin strap unclasped, his goggles pushed back on top. His accented English suggested he was either Swiss or French. 'We got room for another two.'

The waitress looked back at them and shrugged. 'It's probably the only way if you want to eat.'

Allegra wasn't so sure.

'Great!' Isobel exclaimed, instantly pulling off her helmet so that her long hair billowed, and walking over.

'Uh . . .' Allegra looked back at the waitress. 'Well . . .'

The waitress held out some menus. 'You want to see?'

She shook her head with a sigh. 'No, we'll just take the chef's specials each, a bottle of your best sauvignon blanc and another round of whatever it is that they're all drinking.'

'Sure.'

Allegra wandered over to the table, pulling off her own helmet and gloves. Isobel was already seated, sandwiched between two boarders, and it appeared the only other space for her, on the opposite side, was also in the middle. A gaggle of grins stared back at her. 'Hey,' they all nodded in chorus.

'Hi.' She felt tongue-tied and awkward. She didn't want to sit with a bunch of complete strangers while she ate.

'Take a seat,' the guy who had called them over originally said, indicating to the empty space beside him. He had deep brown eyes and a quite beautiful smile that seemed to be highlighted by the thick stubble surrounding it.

Allegra hesitated. 'You're very kind to have offered us some room on your table, but we don't need to interrupt you. We're more than happy to sit at the end.'

'Are you kidding?' he asked with a flirtatious smile. 'You just made us the most popular guys in here. The least we can do is give you the best seats.'

Allegra arched her eyebrows at the compliment, trying

to make eye contact with her sister, who, harbouring no reservations whatsoever about joining a bunch of total strangers, was studiously avoiding her gaze. Allegra bit her lip, feeling her confidence flee and her usual social awkwardness return. If she couldn't talk shop, she had very little to offer – the downside of spending nineteen hours a day in the office.

'What is your name?' the guy asked as she delicately stepped over the bench seat and sat down. 'I am Maxime. Max.'

'Allegra.'

'Allegra,' the guys all echoed approvingly, imbuing the word with melodic overtones that came so naturally to the Continental languages but was flattened in the English tongue.

'Eeess-o-bel and Aaaa-leg-raa,' Max echoed as though committing them to memory. 'This is Brice' – the strawberry-blond guy with green eyes sitting on Isobel's left grinned – 'Fabien' – the olive-skinned guy in an orange jacket on Isobel's right nodded – 'and Jacques.' The man to her left with wind-burnt cheeks smiled.

'It gets crazy here, no?' Jacques said, just as the waitress came over with everyone's fresh drinks.

The men looked momentarily puzzled as the beers were set down before them.

'It's to say thank you,' Allegra said quickly, as she poured the wine and handed Isobel her glass.

'Man!' Fabien laughed, raising his with a flourish. 'To new friends, uh?'

Isobel met Allegra's eyes finally as their glasses were all raised in a convivial toast and Allegra looked back sternly.

She had seen that look on her sister's face before, many years ago.

'So how did you find the snow today?' Brice asked Isobel.

'White and fluffy,' she said, and they all laughed.

'Your first time in Zermatt?' Fabien asked her, leaning in towards the table and forcing Isobel to twist in his direction instead.

'That's right. Our first day, in fact. We only got here this afternoon.'

Allegra watched with practised patience. Men had always fought over her sister. She idly wondered at what point Isobel was going to announce she was married with a kid, but she saw her sister had kept her silk liner gloves on – obscuring her rings – and knew it wouldn't be for a while yet. Isobel thrived on male attention.

'Where are you from?' Max was watching her.

'Oh. Uh . . . London.'

He nodded as if he'd already guessed the answer.

'You?' she asked back, taking a sip of her wine.

'Lyon.'

'I've never been there.'

'That's really saying something. Legs has been everywhere,' Isobel said, cutting in as the waitress brought over a basket of fresh bread. 'She goes to Switzerland, like, twice a week and does things like have breakfast in Rome, lunch in Paris—'

'My sister's exaggerating,' Allegra said quickly.

'You are jet set?' Max asked, his eyes taking in her sleek, expensive clothes and the discreet yet flawless diamond studs at her ears.

'Not in the least. I travel for work. It's very boring.'

'What are you, then?'

Isobel giggled at his error as she tore apart a small roll. 'She's a hedgie.'

The Frenchmen looked confused. 'Hedgie?'

'Like a banker. Only richer.'

'Iz!' Allegra snapped. She looked back at Max and forced a smile. 'I work in financial services.'

Max nodded as he lifted his beer, his eyes steady and dark.

'What about you?' she asked, deciding to pass on the bread.

'I am . . . how you say . . . ?' He shut his eyes, trying to find the word, and Allegra noticed how his lashes splayed on his cheeks, like a young child's. He really couldn't be more than twenty-four, twenty-five, she decided. He opened them again and caught her staring. 'I shape the gardens.'

'Oh, you're a landscaper?' she clarified. 'So you spend your days trying to tame all this?'

'This can never be tamed,' he said, sitting back, one arm stretched along the veranda railing behind them and staring into the view. 'I know that every time I ride the mountains.'

She noticed the view behind them suddenly – her focus had been more on table-bagging and carb-loading when they'd arrived – and she twisted in her seat too.

'Oh wow,' she murmured, looking down into the steep-sided wooded valley. Zermatt was hidden from view, the clouds below them here sifting snow over the streets down there, but the trees were heavily laden with powder, their fronds sagging beneath the weight. She looked up and saw the Matterhorn closer than ever, its jagged peak so familiar to her already. It almost felt like she could reach across and touch it. How could she not have noticed it before now?

'Beautiful, *non*?'

She nodded. Had Isobel noticed it? She went to point it out to her.

'Like you.'

Allegra looked quickly back at Max, not sure she'd heard correctly. His voice had been low, like he wanted no one else to hear, like he barely wanted her to hear.

'What? It is just a fact,' he laughed quietly, seeing her expression. 'You must know it, surely?'

She closed her mouth again, not sure what to say, but sure her cheeks were burning. She grabbed a piece of bread after all and made a play of breaking it apart.

Max watched her.

The waitress arrived with their food, setting down the plates before gathering up the empties. 'Any more?'

The boys looked at the sisters.

'What do you say? We owe you a drink now,' Brice smiled at Isobel.

'Really, it's fi—'Allegra began to demur.

'Fab!' Isobel cried, making Fabien jump to attention.

'Yes?' he asked.

'No, I meant . . .'

Jacques, Max and Isobel all laughed.

Brice grinned up at the waitress. 'More beers, please.'

Chapter Fifteen

It was dark before they slid back into town – using the torches on their phones to light the way – and Zermatt looked even prettier in its night garb. The peaks of the Savoyard roofs were picked out with fairy lights, creating a miniature Alpine rendition of the Manhattan skyline, and the snow glowed golden beneath the street lamps. Another few inches had fallen just in the time they'd been on the mountain and it was getting heavier, in-filling the footprints that tracked back and forth between chalets and bars.

The boys had rented lockers down by the Sunnegga funicular and they locked the girls' skis in with theirs for safe keeping for the night. Allegra had picked up strains of excited plans to ski together tomorrow, but the details eluded her. She and Max had been locked in conversation for over two hours, head to head, glass to glass, and she had long since stopped keeping track of the number of beers they'd had.

She leaned against the wall, watching as they all changed out of their ski boots. 'We should go, Iz,' she sighed, beginning to feel her bed beckoning. They'd been up at five thirty that morning.

'What? No!' Fabien, Jacques and Brice cried. 'You have to

come dancing with us. You can't come to Zermatt and not go to the Broken Bar.'

Allegra wanted to reply that actually they could. They weren't twenty-four any more. One of them was a happily married mother-of-one, and the other was more used to socializing with bald men in bespoke suits than moshing in a sweat pit with a bunch of handsome, cocky French snowboarders. But her voice didn't work and it felt really nice to rest her head against the wall.

Maxime came up to her, resting his head against the wall too, his face just a centimetre from hers. 'You must dance with me, Allegra.'

She opened her eyes and looked back at him. Their posture felt surprisingly intimate given that they were standing up, clothed and not even touching. 'And how am I supposed to dance in ski boots, Max?' she asked, one eyebrow arched in amusement and wondering what it would be like to kiss him.

'You are not. Wait and see,' he smiled.

Allegra frowned, puzzled. 'But I can't even walk in my boots now. I'm too tired,' she pouted.

'You don't have to,' he said, with simple confidence.

The others came over to them, Isobel having linked arms with Brice.

'You are ready?' Fabien asked.

'Have you told them you're married yet?' Allegra asked her sister. She had taken her gloves off now, at least, but was everyone too drunk to have noticed, or did they just not care?

Isobel rolled her eyes furiously. 'Oh, for God's sake, Legs! It's not a secret! I'm not doing anything wrong. We're just having fun. Fun! Remember that?'

Allegra stuck her tongue out at her in reply, making the boys laugh at least.

'Come on, then. We go to the Broken Bar,' Fabien said, heading towards the bridge over the river and the main street.

'You are ready?' Max asked her.

Allegra hesitated as she watched Isobel and Brice walk off. It wasn't like she could leave her sister alone with them all, lovely as they were. She shrugged – and then shrieked, for in the following moment, Maxime scooped her off her feet and began carrying her after the others.

'Max!' she cried, half protesting, half laughing as he continued apace.

'You dance with me,' he said, looking down at her. 'Only then will I let you go.'

He carried her the whole way – switching to a piggyback halfway there – and they pushed through the doors of the Hotel Post with her head on his shoulder, her ski boots creating painful bruises on his outer thighs that he didn't complain about once.

'You see?' he exclaimed, setting her down gently. 'No problem.'

'Where are the others?' she asked, looking around them. They were in a dimly lit lobby, with a pub through a set of doors to their right and a staircase leading down ahead of them. The walls had been painted a matt slate grey, with split logs set into recesses as design features and a fire leaping silently behind a glass screen. But it was the only thing that was silent. The muffled beat of music could be heard – and felt – beneath their feet.

'Come,' Max said, taking her by the hand and leading her down the stairs. With every step down, the volume

levels increased, the temperatures rose, and she saw coloured lights flickering on the walls before they turned a
corner.

'Welcome to the Broken Bar,' Max shouted, holding out
his arms and introducing a . . . heaving, sweating mosh pit.
It was set down in the catacombs of the building, with low
arched ceilings and thick support pillars that seemed to
be propping up many of the guests as well. Everywhere
she looked, twenty-something ski bunnies were downing
shots, dancing with their arms in the air, having a great
time. At the far end was a small stage with a couple dancing on it.

Allegra burst out laughing. 'I can't go in there!' she
shouted, trying to be heard over the music.

'Why not?' Maxime leaned in closer to her, trying to
hear.

'I'm way too old!' she shouted again, just as Jacques
waved at them from a small bar area and started coming
over with some drinks.

'Allegra, how old are you?'

'Too old for you, Maxime!' She gasped and popped her
hand over her mouth with surprised eyes. She hadn't
meant to say that out loud.

'I have twenty-three years.'

'Oh God!' she half shrieked, half laughed, even more
mortified. It was even worse than she'd thought!

'Age is not a number. It is a feeling,' Max said, squeezing
her arm.

'Only a Frenchman could get away with saying that,' she
sighed, just as Jacques reached them and gave them each a
bright orange drink.

'We are over here,' he said, pointing with his finger, and

Allegra saw her sister, Brice and Fabien huddled round a table, looking at something on Isobel's phone. Allegra breathed an inward sigh of relief. Isobel was as drunk as she was now and was no doubt showing them photos of Ferdy, from birth. If Brice had had any lingering amorous intentions towards her sister, that would kill them off once and for all.

She took a sip of the drink. 'What is this?' she asked, taking a bigger sip. It felt refreshing after all the beers, and she was conscious of getting beer breath.

'Aperol, Prosecco and soda. You have had it before?' Jacques asked.

'No,' she shrugged, taking another sip. 'But I like it.'

They wandered over to the others. Maxime was openly keeping his hand on the small of her back now and she didn't feel impelled to remove it. It turned out Isobel wasn't showing pictures of Ferdy after all; she was showing the boys her stats from the MyTracks apps they had used to record the distance, speed and altitude of their runs earlier, but Allegra couldn't be bothered to care about that either. She felt very unbothered for once and she liked it.

They all drank quickly, each buying a round, so that within half an hour, Allegra had forgotten she was still in her ski boots and started trying to dance. It was actually rather useful having kept them on, and both she and Isobel got the giggles, swaying backwards, forwards and to the side at alarming angles, without their feet ever lifting off the ground.

'Oh my God, these are the perfect drunk-dancing shoes,' Isobel cried, leaning so far forward that Brice almost dropped his glass trying to catch her, even though her feet remained as planted to the floor as if they'd been set in concrete.

But Allegra wanted to move properly. The alcohol had hit her bloodstream, sloughing off her post-beer lull, and she wanted to dance harder. The music sounded so good; moving felt so good; being fall-down drunk felt so good.

All the anger and frustration that she had been so effective at hiding, even from her sister – *especially* from her sister, her best friend in the world – came out now as she shook her head like a teenage thrash-metal fan, her arms punching the air with force, shouting the lyrics to the songs at the top of her voice. Why had she never realized how good it felt to let go, to properly lose control? After years of hiding her every emotion behind an impassive, unflappable mask of professionalism, it felt amazing to not give a damn. No one here knew who she was; no one here cared.

She reached down to release the bindings on her boots. She wanted at least to loosen them so that she could get some degree of movement in the ankles, but Maxime bent down and unclipped them for her – and then some. She felt him pull the tongue of the boot forward and press gently behind her knee to get her to bend it.

'I can't dance in my socks,' she protested as he lifted up her leg. 'Someone will break my toe if they stand on my foot!'

'Just trust me,' he grinned up to her.

Allegra, being unusually unbothered, did. He took off her boots and then, as he had only an hour earlier, scooped her off her feet again – albeit less steadily; he'd drunk a lot too.

'Max!' she laughed as he pushed through the crowd with her. 'Put me down. Everyone's looking!'

But he simply smiled in reply, breaking into a couple of surprise spins that made people cheer, before depositing her on her bottom on a huge barrel. She realized it was the small stage she'd seen on the way in and she put her hands down on it for a moment, waiting for her spinning head to catch up with her still body.

'Now get up there and dance,' he said.

'What? No way!' she laughed, one hand on each cheek with sudden embarrassment.

He leaned forward, placing his hands over hers. 'It is the only way to be free of me,' he said, his eyes dancing. 'Don't you remember?'

A moment contracted between them – the one that had been coming all night.

'Well . . . what if I don't want to be free of you?' she said back, a flirtatious smile on her lips.

Maxime stepped towards her, parting her knees to get closer, his hands sliding up her thighs. Sitting on the barrel, she was the same height as him and she closed her eyes as he leaned in, his lips touching hers with a softness that was at odds with the throbbing music and pulsating crowd. She let the kiss ride the rest of the song, her arms trailing languidly over his shoulders as she stopped caring about whether anyone was watching.

Beyoncé started up and he pulled back, his eyes weighted upon her.

'Now dance for me.'

Allegra blinked back at him. Folding her legs in, she slowly stood up, feeling the beat of the music vibrating beneath her feet through the barrel, feeling her body begin to sway, her eyes to close. Max was right. Age was a feeling. She was thirty-one years old and most of the time she behaved like she was twenty years older than that. But not now, not here. She was drunk, yes, but for once she felt how she thought she probably was supposed to feel: sexy, wanted, desired, needed, uninhibited, wild, young, free—

'Miss Fisher?'

Her eyes flew open, panic bolting through her body like bullets as she scanned the crowd for the source of the voice. Who . . . ? Who . . . ? She didn't have to look far.

Zhou Yong was standing not five metres away, a tray of drinks in his hand.

'What a surprise seeing you here.'

Allegra couldn't reply. How could this have happened? What were the chances of running into him like this? Him, of all people! She would have given everything she owned for it to be *anyone* but him.

'We weren't sure if it was you or not.'

We?

Her eyes lifted behind him and caught sight of the familiar silhouette that was always in her peripheral vision, always in her mind. Sam stared back at her with a black expression.

Correction. Almost anyone.

Chapter Sixteen

Day Fifteen: *Jointed Teddy Bear*

'Nuh.'

Her hand flailed blindly out to the side, swatting at the sound that had jerked her out of a motionless oblivion. It stopped. Her arm dropped down again, the hand limp, limbs heavy.

But it had been enough.

What . . . ? Where . . . ?

Her mind was beginning to buzz, trying to establish the basic facts of the semi-conscious moment. Where was she? The light seemed to be coming from the wrong side of the bed. She always woke up on her left, but that usually meant the sun was on her back. Not her face. But she was on her left. Wasn't she? Left. Opposite to her right. Her writing hand. Wait, where was it?

Her brainwaves were starting to spike. She usually slept beneath a duvet, but . . . One hand patted the bed . . . There was no duvet here. There was . . . Her hand continued patting, but lack of contact with anything except the mattress forced a frown and one eye to open.

Too much. The eye shut again, as if in pain. The light hurt and one hand found its way to her face, providing shelter. She tucked her legs up closer to her chest, tightening like a bud.

What day was it, then? Meeting . . . ? Daily . . . 6.30 a.m. with Bob . . .

It came to her then, last night's events rushing at her like a torrent of white water, drenching her as selective memories came back in vivid technicolour: her dancing on the barrel, Max kissing her, Sam and Zhou's faces . . .

Her eyes flew open and she sat up in a swift, ill-advised motion, her vision catching up a second later as her hands patted her body for evidence of . . . She frowned. She was alone and still fully clothed. Still wearing yesterday's ski kit.

She had slept in her ski kit? Her mouth dropped open in dismay at the sight of her stirrup trousers twisted up round her ankles, her jacket unbelted and unzipped, but still on. No wonder she hadn't missed the duvet.

She groaned, dropping her head into her hands as the shock of being upright tagged onto her body's to-do list, along with breathing, not vomiting . . . Her mind was more beleaguered than her body, though, as she struggled to assemble the facts first. What had happened with Max? How had she got home? Had she walked back in her ski boots? Had she left them behind? Had Max carried her home again? Why hadn't he stayed? Or had he, but then left?

But no, no, if he'd stayed, she wouldn't still be in her clothes . . .

Her phone was on the bed beside her, Pierre's controversial final text to her open on the display. She frowned. Why had she been looking at that?

A sickening thought came to her, and with fumbling

fingers, she scrolled through her outbox. Please no, please no . . . Say she hadn't been so off her head that she'd lost that inhibition too. Her discrimination case against Pierre would be completely undermined if she'd texted him back . . .

But there was nothing there.

She collapsed back on the pillow. Probably her fingers hadn't been dextrous enough to send a text last night.

She groaned again. Oh God, how much had she had to drink?

'Iz?' she croaked, lifting her head slightly, but the door was shut and she didn't have enough power to raise her voice.

She dropped her head again, feeling like the whole world was against her. After another minute, she slowly swung her legs off the bed and stood up, holding on to the headboard for a moment, before walking to the door and opening it. Isobel's door was closed and Allegra hesitated for a moment, as the blur of last night's events swirled around her sister's antics too. Brice . . . ?

Knocking on the door once, she opened it. Isobel was lying face down on top of the bed, her hair over her face, also wearing her ski kit. But she was alone. Crucially, she was alone.

'Iz? You OK?' Allegra asked, one hand going to her temple as her cracked voice hurt her head.

A grunt was all that came back in reply, but she was breathing at least.

Allegra shut the door again and walked back to her bedroom – holding on to the walls for support – to run a shower. She stood under the hot water until it ran cold, letting it pummel her stiff muscles, the steam opening up her blood vessels and giving the toxins an escape route.

It helped a little, but she needed food and she and Isobel hadn't shopped yet.

Ignoring her ski kit, which she left in an ignominious heap on the bedroom floor – she needed to draw a line between yesterday and today – she pulled on her black jeans, red Nordic jumper and Sorel snow boots, and left a note for Isobel on the kitchen table. Closing the door softly behind her, she descended the creaky stairs, pulling on her bobble hat and ski gloves, and belting up her jacket with shaky hands.

The cold air, as it hit her face, felt like a shot of Alka-Seltzer and she inhaled deeply as she leaned against the wall for a few seconds. She was clean, fresh and she hadn't been sick yet. She was doing well. She hadn't drunk like that since . . . Actually, she'd never drunk like that. Not at sixth-form college, not at university, and when entertaining clients, she famously never drank more than two martinis.

Heavy snow had fallen overnight and hers were the first footsteps to break through the new cover; her and Isobel's tracks from last night had been completely obscured. She walked slowly down the narrow street, stopping as she emerged on the Bahnhofstrasse. It was nearly ten o'clock and most people were already on the slopes – Max and Brice too? – but the street was still crowded nonetheless with locals and non-skiing visitors soaking up the chocolate-box Christmas scene.

She stopped outside the Bogner boutique and watched the dynamic, extreme skiing films running on loop on the TV screens in the windows. They wouldn't be skiing today. She sincerely doubted Isobel would even get out of bed today.

She wandered on, stopping at a hole-in-the-wall crêperie, and minutes later was leaning against a thick stone windowsill, tucking into a deep, crunchy liege waffle and wiping maple syrup off her chin with a paper napkin.

Her physical recovery was coming in pigeon steps, but her mind was still tormented by the blanks from last night, and Zhou and Sam's faces kept flashing in front of her eyes. Zhou's shock, Sam's disgust . . .

Her head dropped again. What had she done? In just a few minutes she had undone a professional reputation that had been a decade in the making. She may have stopped short of drunk-texting Pierre, but she had given Kemp all the ammunition he needed to smear her reputation and undermine her. She might be gone from PLF and he might have won the Yong deal, but he had to be worried that she was more dangerous to him now that she would be working against them. And it was all the more reason for him to play dirty.

She blinked and started walking again, trying to push the thoughts away. Denial. That had been her strategy till now, three days of turning away from the facts – shopping, skiing, getting drunk – as she tried to outpace the shock. But she couldn't lose any more time. She knew how Pierre operated; he'd already 'managed' the news of her departure to the press, and once Kemp reported back that he'd seen her last night . . . She had to start retaking control.

She had yet to listen to a single message on her phone and the inbox had been full for over twenty-four hours now. She put it to her ear as she walked, her lower lip trembling as Bob and Kirsty apparently tag-teamed in trying to get hold of her, Kirsty's ice-cool composure slipping as she ended: 'I really hope you're OK.' Lots of colleagues – Kevin Lam included – had offered their condolences and words of support, keeping in her good books just in case she should choose to take people with her; after all, it wasn't like morale had been high at PLF lately.

Her feet stopped as she came to Kemp's voice on there too. 'Fisher? Kemp. We need to talk. Call me back.'

She remembered his words in Selfridges, demanding her undelivered final proposal, and anger and contempt blasted through her body, more toxic than last night's alcohol. She felt the ground beneath her drop a little and put her hands out for balance, but she was in the middle of the street and she stumbled. A church with shallow, wide steps was opposite and she walked over, collapsing onto the steps with a sob – her head in her hands as she wondered yet again how her life had imploded so spectacularly, so unfairly.

Bells started ringing out from the tower above her as the double oak doors opened and a steady stream of people filed out, all closing their coats and pulling on gloves as they emerged into the sub-freezing temperatures, their minds and souls cleansed for another week.

She sat on the steps until her bottom went numb – jeans were scant protection – and wondered whether Isobel was up yet.

As she rose to standing, her body felt stiff and aged, and she gave an embarrassed smile as a man in a cassock stepped out, closing the doors to, a spritz of incense wafting out onto the street. It would be eighteen years this Christmas since she had set foot in a church. Christmas Eve in fact.

She turned to leave, just as the heavy door was pushed open again and the priest's head popped out.

'*Möchten Sie kommen?*' he smiled.

'I'm sorry? I don't understand.'

'English?'

She nodded.

'Would you like to come in?'

'Oh no, no,' she said, taking a step down, away. 'I'm fine, thanks.'

He took a step out. 'Are you sure? You look cold – and like you could do with someone to talk to.'

She blinked at him, tears threatening. The hangover was leaving her feeling stripped of a layer of skin and she wasn't sure that she could pull off her usual hiding act today. 'I'm not . . . Catholic.'

He shrugged lightly. 'We don't need to read the small print.'

She shook her head again, finding it hard to meet his eye.

'It is up to you, of course. I'm making coffee. Please come in if you would like.'

He smiled kindly before he left, and she stared at the tight grain on the wooden door as it closed behind him. It had none of the elaborate embellishments she associated with the Catholic Church – it was just a plain, cat-slide-roofed building with an arched portico sheltering the doors – although she supposed that at this altitude, things were designed to endure rather than look pretty. And besides, how could anything man-made compare to the granite cathedrals of the mountains surrounding them on all sides here?

Not sure why she was doing it – the lure of a hot coffee, perhaps? – she pulled on the handle and peered inside, only to be surprised by the unexpected majesty within:

soaring hollowed-out ceilings, an ornate gilded altar and pastel-painted frescoes that were in juxtaposition to the pristine whitewash, light suffusing the nave from deep windows.

She walked slowly down the aisle, her boots almost silent on the ancient stone floor, her eyes moving side to side towards the shadows as though expecting an ambush. She couldn't see the priest, although she could hear the sound of a kettle billowing steam from a room off to the side, and she sank heavily onto one of the wooden pews, her gaze fixed on a stained-glass window that depicted Mary and the baby Jesus.

Her eyes skipped lightly around the room, taking in baroque golden crosses and gold-embroidered linens. It was a moment before she noticed the priest coming towards her, two steaming mugs in his hands.

He looked pleased to see her.

'Are we allowed to drink in here?' she asked with a worried expression, as he handed one over and sat beside her on the pew.

'Well, technically, I'm the boss, so . . .' he smiled.

She took it with a grateful smile, almost sighing with pleasure as the heat thawed her hands. Coffee was *exactly* what she needed.

'Your English is very good,' she said after a moment.

'Thank you. I studied in Cambridge for seven years.'

'Oh.'

They fell silent, his eyes ahead on the ornate stained-glass windows in a kind of peaceful contemplation. Allegra tried to steal a proper look at him – tall and thin, with black wire-rimmed glasses, she guessed he was in his early forties.

She stared down into her coffee, wondering why she had come in here. She never talked. Her entire adult life had been an exercise in not talking. Doing, that was her thing. Doing achieved far more than talking ever could.

'I am Father Merete, by the way,' he said, watching her.

'Allegra. Allegra Fisher.'

'Fisher?'

The way he said it – as though it was remarkable or rare in some way – made her turn. 'Yes.'

He hesitated. 'I don't suppose you are related to Valentina Fisher?'

Her jaw dropped open. 'How on earth do you know that?'

'It has been in all the papers about the woman they found on the mountain. A local sensation.'

'Really?'

He nodded, clearly assuming she knew more about it than he.

'Apparently she was my grandmother,' Allegra said after a minute, resentment in her voice.

'I'm sorry for your loss.' The way he said it suggested he was. He sounded sincere, but then she thought he must have to deliver that line a lot in his work.

'Thank you, but I didn't know her, so . . .' Her voice trailed away. It felt strange being comforted about the loss of someone she'd never even heard of until this week, much less ever known.

'Still. It's a tragic loss of a woman who, by all accounts, was a central figure in the community. I understand she was only twenty-one when she died, and yet she is very much remembered in the town, even after all these years.'

Allegra's eyes scanned his face. 'Do you know much about what happened?'

'Only what has been in the newspapers, although some of my older parishioners have lit candles for her these past few weeks – they knew her personally.'

'Do they know any background on what happened?'

Father Merete shook his head. 'They seem to be as confused now as they were then. They don't understand why she went out to the hut in such violent weather and snow conditions.'

'What are these huts? Shepherd huts?'

Father Merete looked taken aback by her ignorance. 'You don't know about your family?'

She shook her head. 'Until last week, I thought my family hailed from Sheen in London. I never heard anything that suggested we had Swiss relatives.'

But as the words left her mouth, the cuckoo clock she'd found in the loft with Isobel popped into her head. It was one of Switzerland's most iconic exports and even depicted a Swiss chalet. Just a coincidence?

'Well, maybe it is not my place to tell you,' Father Merete hesitated, reading the conflict in her face.

'But I don't know who else can. My mother's family are all dead, and my mother is an only child. Please, Father. I'd be grateful for anything you could tell me. If everything the police are telling me is true, I know less than anyone about my own history. I need somewhere to start in trying to understand it all.'

He nodded. 'Well, as I have been led to understand, your family, the Engelbergs, owned one of the largest dairy farms in the valley.'

'Dairy? You mean cows?'

'No, goats. Long before tourism ever came to Zermatt, this was a farming community, and your family had some of the biggest and best pastures here. Your ancestors would have spent eight months of the year living up on the slopes as the animals grazed, and the mountain huts were their home during the warm months. But no one ever stayed in them when the snow came. They were too vulnerable to avalanche, and the temperatures get so low you would freeze to death. And Valentina, having been born and raised into farming life, would have known that.'

Allegra frowned. 'And no explanation was ever given for why she was up there?'

'According to her husband, they had had dinner together. He went out to check on the animals before they went to bed, and when he came back, she had gone. Disappeared.'

'Just like that?'

Father Merete shrugged. 'Apparently so.'

'But people don't just disappear from their own homes,' she argued. 'Surely the police didn't accept that story. Didn't they look into the possibility of foul play?'

Father Merete smiled. 'You have to understand they were different times back then. We didn't have the resources we have now, and the conditions in which Valentina died, they're classified as a once-in-a-hundred-years phenomenon. The January of 1951 was one of the most catastrophic events in Swiss history – over a thousand avalanches in a three-day period. When she wasn't found in the town, the only other conclusion that could be drawn was that she was on the mountains, and everyone knew there was no way she could have survived.'

Allegra nodded, staring up again at the intricate stained-glass windows. Her eyes settled on Mary.

'How likely is it that she'd have been Catholic?'

But she already knew the answer. The Advent calendar had been found alongside the cuckoo clock. And the fig-urine of the Madonna and child had been in one of the very first drawers.

'Almost certain. Even now over eighty per cent of the villagers are Catholic.'

She nodded, the mug quickly growing cool between her hands.

Father Merete twisted slightly so that he was angled more towards her. 'Have your family had any thoughts yet, about the burial arrangements?'

She looked back at him. 'That's the thing. There isn't a body to bury, as such. Just . . .'

He leaned in, saving her from having to say the words. 'I understand. We often receive the remains of people who have died on the mountains.'

They were quiet again.

'Is cremation . . . ? Is it an option? For Catholics, I mean.'

'The Catholic Church does not object to it, and I agree it would seem the best solution in this situation.'

Allegra looked down at her hands. 'It's hard to know what to do – what's right, I mean. My sister and I have come out here to take her remains back to England with us, but now that I'm here and I see the . . . scope of life here, the beauty and scale of the mountains . . .' She swallowed again, wishing she could be more eloquent, but her mind was a mess. 'This was the only life Valentina would have known. It doesn't seem right somehow to bring her back to *London*. And the mountain was her final resting place after all. I'm beginning to feel we shouldn't take her away from here.'

The priest was quiet for a moment. 'She was your mother's mother, you say?'

'Yes, but I'm here on my mother's behalf. She isn't well enough to do it herself. I'm her legal advocate.'

'So your mother is in England now?'

'Yes.'

'And what does she think? Perhaps it would be a comfort to her to have her mother's remains in England with her, especially after so many years missing.'

Allegra's eyes met his. 'She doesn't know.'

'She doesn't know that her mother's body has been found?'

Allegra inhaled deeply. 'My mother is in the advanced stages of Alzheimer's, Father. She is easily upset and confused. Very often, she believes she is a child and that her mother is still alive.'

He was respectfully quiet for a moment. 'I'm so sorry. It is a sad situation that I see too frequently. Do her doctors believe she should not be told?'

'If Alzheimer's was all there was to it, then they said there was a chance we could tell her; sometimes she seems perfectly well.' She sighed. 'But there is more to it. Long before she fell sick, my mother buried her mother, thirteen years ago in England.'

Father Merete straightened up. 'I don't understand.'

Allegra took a deep breath, wondering where to start when she didn't have all the answers herself. 'Well, according to the police, the woman who raised my mother wasn't her mother at all, but her aunt, Anya. Valentina and Anya were sisters.'

She watched Father Merete's frown deepen.

'All of this has only to come to light because I had to provide DNA samples to the police for them to confirm identity of the remains. And when it proved that Valentina was my maternal grandmother, it also proved that my mother's entire life had been a lie.'

Father Merete was silent for a few moments, deep in thought. 'You said your mother's family were all dead, but what about your grandfather? Surely he can enlighten you?'

Allegra shrugged. 'He died when my mother was a toddler.' She saw his expression. 'What?'

'You are sure about that?'

'Well, yes, of course . . . That's what I was told. It's what Mum always said, and she was obviously repeating what Granny had said to *her*. There was never any reason to . . .' She swallowed.

No. There never had been any reason to question the stories she had been fed about her mother's family. The lies had always been on her father's side, but a DNA test and a phone call had changed all that, wrecking the foundations of her world and casting her most beloved people as liars.

She looked at him with sudden nervousness. 'He's not dead?'

'Let me show you something.'

He rose and she followed him into an antechamber where an oak refectory table sat in the middle of the room, bedecked with a purple and gold embroidered runner and a baroque golden cross.

He lifted a huge black tome from a sideboard and carried it over to the table.

'Our parish records,' he said, placing one hand over it.

The leather was cracked and stippled beneath his hand, the gold lettering – spelling something she didn't understand – all but faded. 'Every birth, baptism and marriage is recorded in here from the last two hundred years.'

'Really?' she asked in astonishment.

He nodded, opening the book with care and laying the cover flat. 'Now, we know Valentina died in January 1951, so . . .' Slowly, he slid his fingers into some pages towards the back third of the book and peered down.

'That's 1894,' he murmured, withdrawing his fingers and moving down a half-inch. 'And . . . 1943. Right, yes.' He opened the pages wider, using both hands to lay the front two-thirds flat. 'OK . . .'

She watched as his eyes scanned the decorative calligraphy, his finger moving lightly over the pages as he repeated Valentina's name under his breath.

'Ah yes,' he said after a while. 'Valentina Engelberg. Married 3 October 1946 to Lars Fischer.'

'Lars Fischer,' Allegra repeated slowly, immediately clocking the difference in spelling of their surname. Her breath caught. Was that it? The typo she and Isobel had been hoping for? The proof that this woman, Valentina, belonged to a different family of Fishers, one with a 'c' in their name, and not hers after all? The DNA test said otherwise but there was always a chance it was wrong – contaminated, flawed . . . And she'd never heard the name Lars being used by her grandmother, Anya. Not once.

'Now, if we look here . . .' He closed the book and brought over another, almost identical book. 'This contains the deaths and burials records,' Father Merete said, carefully laying the book open. 'You said your mother was told her father died when she was a toddler?'

'Yes. Uh, I think she said she was three.'

'And your mother was born in which year?'

'On 23 February 1948.' Her brain automatically – habitually – did the maths. If Annen and the DNA test and these records were correct, if her grandmother's family *had* owned pastures here, if her grandmother *had* died here in 1951, then in all likelihood her mother, who had been born three years earlier, would have been born here too, surely? Was she really supposed to believe her mother was Swiss and had never once mentioned it?

'So then if she was three, her father would have died in 1951 as well.' Father Merete found the 1951 entries and opened the book fully, stepping back slightly so that she could look through the names herself.

'Lars Fischer,' she mumbled over and over, her finger drawing an invisible line down the page as her eye took in every name . . . but not his. 'He's not there,' she said finally, frowning.

'No.'

'So then maybe he moved and died outside of Zermatt? He wanted to set up a new life for himself after his wife died.'

'Possibly,' Father Merete nodded. 'Or maybe he hasn't died at all.'

'But . . .' Allegra's mouth opened, even though no further words followed. She didn't want to say the words out loud because each one would dismantle the memory of the grandmother who'd been her world. The one who'd got her through it all.

'You should know there is a Lars Fischer in my congregation.'

Allegra blinked at him, her brain automatically rejecting the idea, her head shaking side to side.

'He is in his late eighties now. He usually attends service every week.'

Usually? She looked back at him. 'But not recently?'

Father Merete raised his eyebrows. 'He hasn't been to church for a few weeks now. Not since the news broke that Valentina had been found.'

Allegra looked at him, still resisting what he was trying to tell her: that their grandfather was alive and not just alive, but here. She had a typo on her side and she wasn't going to give it up without a fight. There was still a chance she could disprove the priest's and the policeman's and the scientist's version of the truth and go back to believing in her grandmother's. Anya's. 'There's just one more thing I'd like to see,' she said, masking her defiance with a smile and knowing exactly how she could prove they'd all got the wrong family. She was a Fisher, no 'c'. Period.

Chapter Seventeen

'You're up!' Allegra exclaimed in astonishment as she fell through the door.

'Up' was a loose term. Isobel was actually lying flat out on the red leather sofa, her legs dangling over one arm, her ski kit still on.

'Ugh! Don't shout!' Isobel winced painfully, staring back at her with rheumy eyes. 'Where have you been?' she asked, trying to sit up but only managing a feeble half sit-up before collapsing back down again. 'God, I can't believe you went out without me.'

'You were comatose.'

'So?'

'I did you a favour letting you sleep it off. I thought you might appreciate being allowed to sleep in for once.'

There was a short silence. 'I don't suppose you got any milk, did you?'

'As if I'd let you go more than twelve hours without a cup of tea,' Allegra said, rolling her eyes and plonking a blue carrier bag on the kitchen table, triumphantly pulling out a box of teabags, milk, biscuits, bread and jam. 'I suppose you need some digestive sandwiches too, am I right?' she asked, opening the packet of McVitie's and quickly spreading two with butter and jam before pushing them together.

'Oh my God, I haven't had one of those for years!' Isobel exclaimed excitedly, grabbing a clutch of cushions and tentatively propping herself up with them as Allegra handed over the plate. 'Mum always made these when we were sick.'

Allegra didn't say anything as she filled the kettle. Isobel ate wholesome, home-cooked family meals these days, but Allegra – if she wasn't in a restaurant and she was home alone? More often than not, this was her dinner.

'Mmm!' Isobel said appreciatively as she took a bite, spraying herself with crumbs and brushing them onto the floor. 'Tch, I can't believe I slept in my clothes,' she muttered. 'I haven't done that for years.'

Allegra didn't reply. She'd never done that.

'It was a good night, though, wasn't it?' Isobel grinned, looking up at her sister with wicked eyes. 'You and Max were getting along nicely.'

'He's OK,' Allegra mumbled, reaching for some cups.

'Good kisser?'

'Don't really remember,' Allegra lied, pretending to search for teaspoons.

'No, me neither,' Isobel said in a puzzled voice.

'What?' Allegra spun round. 'You *kissed* one of them? Iz! You're—'

'Relax! Don't have a cow! Jeez. I just meant I don't remember much about *last night*. I obviously can't handle my drink as well these days.'

'Oh.'

The kettle boiled and she poured their cups of tea.

'It's annoying that you're looking so perky and being as efficient as usual,' Isobel grumbled, watching as her sister set them down on the coffee table. 'I can hardly even move.'

Allegra arched an eyebrow sympathetically. 'Well, I've been up for a few hours now. And I've eaten. Here, drink some of this.' She pushed the cup towards her.

Isobel sighed and swung her legs round to the floor. Using her hands to push against, she sat up, her head lolling heavily like a rag doll's. 'Ugh. I'm dying.'

'You'll be fine,' Allegra grinned, tucking her legs in and watching her sister closely, wondering whether she was physically strong enough right now to handle the news she had to tell her.

A few minutes passed as Isobel slurped her tea like a Labrador, finally looking sidelong at her, an apologetic expression in her eyes. 'We should ski.'

'We can't ski,' Allegra replied, shaking her head so that her hair was mussed up on the cushions. 'Our bodies won't work today. We broke them.'

'Legs, you have to ski . . . I said we'd ski.'

'To who? Who did you say that to?' Allegra asked suspiciously.

'Bri—'

'No! No! Stop right there,' Allegra demanded, holding up a hand and closing her eyes. 'I think they've done quite enough damage for one ski trip, don't you?' she asked, gesturing at their battle-weary bodies, even though the worst of the damage couldn't be seen. Her hangover – brutal as it was – still couldn't compete against the annihilation of her professional reputation. Fresh misery washed over the rest of the week's hurts like lemon juice on a paper cut, and her hand flew to her face, pinching the bridge of her nose. There was too much to absorb right now. She inhaled slowly.

'Well . . . we kind of have to. He's got my phone.' Isobel's voice was quiet.

Allegra's hand dropped. 'What?'

'I gave it to him last night as insurance that we'd race the Infinity today.'

The Infinity? A buzz in the back of her brain became a drone. She remembered hearing about it last night, vaguely registered excited plans, phone calls being made . . .

'Why would you do that?' Allegra asked, her voice three octaves higher than usual.

'Because he wanted to see me again and I'd drunk a barrel of beer by then.'

'But you are married *with a child*. He knows that! What are both of you playing at?'

Isobel tutted and rolled her eyes. 'Legs, I haven't done anything wrong. I am allowed to talk to other men, you know. Being a wife doesn't mean I've become a nun, and being a mother doesn't mean I stop being a woman. It's just some light-hearted fun.'

'You are blurring the boundaries and you know it,' Allegra pushed back, jabbing her finger towards her sister. 'You do not need their validation. Why do you always need to have men fall in love with you?'

But she instantly regretted asking the question. They both knew why.

'You weren't so angelic yourself last night,' Isobel said sulkily.

'*I* am single. I can do whatever I like.'

Isobel glared back at her resentfully, but she didn't argue further.

A minute passed and Isobel lightly drummed her fingers on the sofa. 'Well, I still need to get back my phone.'

*

Above the clouds again, it was a beautiful day. Allegra had always thought this must be the best part of being a pilot. It didn't matter what was happening on terra firma, above the clouds the sun was always shining, and she closed her eyes as the sun pulsed gently, trying to pink up her pallid complexion.

The queues for the gondolas had been huge, the two of them shuffling forward, inches at a time in the heaving mass of mountain joyriders, and it had taken over an hour to get to the summit of Klein Matterhorn and to the start of the race, where Brice, Max and the others were supposedly lining up.

It could have taken far longer, she knew. She could have not found her ski boots kicked under the bed (and now obscured by the displaced duvet), and Isobel could have forgotten in exactly which locker Brice had stored their skis, helmets and poles. But some things, at least, were going their way.

'Ugh, I'm still starving,' Isobel wailed dramatically, finding a woeful lack of cafes at the top of the lift station and dropping her hands onto her knees.

'It's a wonder you're not a Ten-Ton Tessie,' Allegra joked, fishing a tatty 'emergency' toffee from her jacket pocket. 'Sorry, best I can do,' she shrugged.

'Ace!' Isobel said with wide eyes, chewing so furiously the bobble on her hat bobbed as she looked around for the Frenchmen. Allegra scuffed the snow with the toes of her boots, trying not to make eye contact with anyone. She didn't want to see Max again. She had offered to buy Isobel a new phone to avoid precisely this, but Isobel had immediately started listing all the once-in-a-lifetime photos of Ferds on the SIM card . . .

'Oh, I can see them over there,' Isobel said, handing over her skis and disappearing into the crowd.

Well, then, if they were all over there . . . Allegra thought, deliberately turning to face the opposite direction. Hundreds of people were milling about, all wearing numbered bibs as people with clipboards tried to herd everyone into groups, and they seemed to encompass every age group, from families with very young children, breakfast still stuck to their cheeks, to university ski trips, to retirees with tans.

Allegra watched as a young boy and girl thumb-wrestled, their hands clasped in a death grip. She smiled wryly as a boarder jump-walked past – his board still strapped to one foot – wearing a onesie and a rooster hat. She looked on as two off-pisters skied off the chairlift, wordlessly bypassing the congregated crowd and disappearing over the top and across the border into Italy.

'Hi.'

She looked up. Max was standing beside her, his arms draped over his board, which he'd jammed into the ground like a resting post.

'Hi.' Dammit.

He looked younger today, his cheeks already flushed beneath his dense stubble, his eyes bright from a full morning of runs – how was that possible? She and Isobel had been *destroyed* all morning – and it made her wonder whether she looked older in the bright light of day.

'How are you this morning?' An easy smile spread on his lips, and were it not for what he had cost her, she would have found herself smiling back too. But she didn't. He came at too high a price. And he was twenty-three.

'Fine.' She remembered how his lips had felt on hers and she felt ridiculous now. 'You?'

He just nodded, his eyes doing all the talking for him. Over his shoulder, she could see Isobel's yellow and navy bobble hat wobbling like it was on a stick as she chatted to the others, clearly with none of the inhibitions of her older sister.

'That guy last night . . .' he began with a quizzical expression.

'He's a client,' she said quickly.

Max smiled, as though he didn't quite believe her. 'Well, it's a shame,' he said after a moment. 'You looked so happy until he showed up.'

'Oh.' She wasn't sure what to say. 'Well, my work is . . . isolating.'

'Isolating,' he echoed, and she wondered whether he understood the word.

'Lonely.'

Now he did. 'You are younger than you think, Legs.' The sound of her nickname, wrapped in his accent, made her blush, though it was what he had called her all night. She remembered that at least. 'You are freer than you feel. And you are definitely sexier than you know.'

His hand had found hers, but she couldn't hold his gaze. The light out here was too pure to hide in; what had seemed possible in a dimly lit bar couldn't stand up to scrutiny out here.

A man with a young boy stopped beside them to ask Max something, and Allegra stepped back, self-consciously tucking her hair behind her ears.

Max turned back to her, taking in the distance she had put between them. His mouth opened, as though he was going to say something, but a whistle was blown and officials began hurriedly herding the last bibbed stragglers to the taped areas.

'It is time to go. Where are you racing?' he asked, throwing his board on the ground and bending down to strap in one boot.

'Oh, we're not. We only came up here so that Iz could get her phone.'

Max straightened up, a quizzical expression on his face.

Allegra saw Isobel running towards her with a bright smile – her hangover seemed miraculously cured by the altitude – just as Max leaned in to her. She turned back at the movement and found his face mere inches from hers.

He smiled, their eyes locked. *'Joyeux Noël*, Legs. It was fun.' And he kissed her on the corner of her mouth.

'Bye.' Allegra watched him walk-jump off to where the others were gathering together in the front group, sliding easily along the snow with steady grace.

'Last night's attraction still going strong, is it?' Isobel smiled, handing her a bib.

'Don't be ridiculous. He's twenty-three.' She looked at the bib in her hand. 'And what is this? I hope you don't think we're competing?'

'Of course we are! I told you that. Brice entered us all last night.'

'No!' Allegra wailed. 'You said we were just coming up here to get your phone.'

'Oh, you didn't believe that. I know you didn't,' Isobel said, smartly clicking her boots into her skis. 'Listen, there's only one way to kick this hangover in the arse and that's by flying down a twenty-two-hundred-metre drop in twenty kilometres.' Isobel grinned. 'Who knows, maybe today will be the day you finally beat me.'

'Ha, ha,' Allegra said drily, joshing her with an elbow.

She pulled on the bib and followed in Isobel's tracks to the first of the holding areas. What else was she going to do?

'Hang on, don't we need to go to the back?' Allegra asked as they joined everybody readying themselves at the line.

'No, the back's for people who are doing the race just for fun,' Isobel replied, fiddling with the strap on her goggles.

Just for fun? Allegra looked across at her. 'So then what's the middle?'

Isobel paused in thought. 'People who are racing to beat their personal bests, I think.'

'And up here?' she asked slowly.

Isobel smiled, adjusting the pole straps round her wrists. 'Those racing to win.' She winked, before turning her attention to the man with the whistle, her weight poised over her poles.

Allegra saw the French boys in the front row, their baggy gear at distinct odds with some hardcore types who were chesting the start ribbon in skintight racing suits. They were all laughing at something Jacques had said, looking young again from here. A medley of images from last night played through her head again, but they clearly had no such remonstrations, no regrets. Last night was already today's chip wrappings to them. It was another day, another mountain, another bar . . . another girl.

The whistle blew, the tape flickered, and they were off. Allegra felt the ground slip away beneath her skis and the wind pick up with her pace. She angled her hips, felt the edge of the skis carve the snow, a rhythm begin to form, some clarity begin to push through the fog of her hangover. Moguls had formed over the course of the morning runs, but her body, which had been so wooden and stiff all morning, bounced easily over them and she was past them in a few minutes, easing into quick, short turns as she found her rhythm on the smoother, steeper slope.

She could see Isobel a hundred metres ahead, in the leading pack. Her skiing had a balletic quality to it that combined with an almost reckless love of speed and she was only just behind the French boys, who were whooping all the way down the mountain, huge arcs of snow spraying left and right like fountains of water as they angled their bodies with athletic ease.

Allegra was fast, but she couldn't keep up with them, and as they began to pull further away, everything retracted from her – last night, Valentina, her mother, her lost job – until all that was pin-sharp was the fifty metres of snow immediately ahead of her, her eyes tracking the fall line as it changed every moment, the peak of the run higher and higher above her as she swooped down the piste with heady freedom.

She was so caught up in her own head, in her own moment, on her own mountain, that when another skier passed, cutting aggressively in front of her and only just avoiding clipping the tips of her skis, she almost wiped out. The near-miss threw her off her rhythm, making her heart pound erratically as her body tried to correct from the shock, and she almost lost her balance, one leg flying high in the air, poles waving about like it was a comedy skit.

She recovered, just, but anger quickly replaced adrenalin as she scanned the skiers ahead, trying to determine which one it had been. It was almost impossible to tell. Everyone was hunched down in a racing position, helmets and goggles on, plumes of powder dusting the air and reducing visibility.

But she had a clue. One of them was in red and black kit, and she'd seen it when it still had the price tags attached.

Tucking herself down, her eyes trained on his back like a sniper's gun, she stretched out her turns, flattening her line as near to a vertical drop as she dared. Gaining quickly as he almost punched the ground with his poles, she sped past him again with a defiant 'Ha!', leaving him behind her.

Allegra didn't dare to look back. She'd never been frightened of speed, but she'd never gone this fast before either and she felt like a cello string turned to breaking point – too much one way and she'd snap, too little and she'd fall slack. She was already over halfway down the run, a route she didn't know and had never skied before, and though her eyes were sharp on the snow ahead, she couldn't get her mind off the skier behind. The sun was behind her and his shadow criss-crossed hers constantly, like they were duelling, everyone else forgotten.

They moved into the trees, the light changing and the wind dropping. Everything became more lucid there and that was when she heard it again – the sudden slicing sound, just feet away, it seemed, too close. She couldn't help herself – she had to look to see exactly what the margin was between them and she glanced up on the next turn, the fibres in her muscles flinching at the sight of the silent skier just metres behind, his eyes tracked not on the snow but on her.

The indulgence cost her. The momentary glance was all it took to take a bit of pace off her speed and in the next instant he was past her, his triumphant smile just a blur as his greater weight gave him the momentum to ease past.

She made her turns tighter and shorter still, as brief as she dared without finishing the rest of this run on a straight downward trajectory, but it was no good. Ability, ambition and determination couldn't help her here. Plain and simple physics were going to be the deciding factor in this. The gap between them was growing and he began to pull away, even though she matched his tracks. Life felt like it was on fast forward and zoom all at once as she tried to close the gap, her thighs burning, her breath coming faster than it did during her boxing classes.

They turned off the end of the piste and onto a road that led back into town, the final stretch. Its gradient was fairly shallow, but it was narrow and icy, and the speed at which they were both travelling meant they flew along like it was a luge, both of them tucked tight as they tried to minimize their wind resistance on the straight home run. She could gain on him here . . .

They were just about at the roof level of the chalets now, and she tucked herself smaller still. She could do this; she could still take him. She knew she could. If she could just—

They ran out of slope. This mountain wasn't big enough for the two of them. The road had levelled off and she almost collided with him as she slid to an abrupt stop, the parking equivalent of a handbrake turn. Showering him with snow was scant consolation, though, and he had the nerve to be standing with his goggles pushed up and clicking off his skis, as though he'd been standing there for hours.

He stared down at her with cold contempt and she blinked back at him, her breath coming hard, tears pricking her eyes behind her goggles, which she would not – under any circumstance now – take off.

'Hey, Legs!' Isobel shouted, waving her pole to catch her attention. 'Over here!'

Allegra glanced across, but it was all it took to break the spell. When she looked back, Sam had turned and was already walking off.

Chapter Eighteen

'I miss my baby,' Isobel said in a quiet moan, watching as a toddler was pulled through the snow on a sledge by his father. They were walking back through the town, skis stowed in lockers, and Isobel was keen to top up her Christmas shopping. The Infinity race had been high-octane fun, but once the excitement and adrenalin had ebbed, they had been left even more exhausted than before and had only managed a few snoozy blues before calling it quits for the day.

'Of course you do,' Allegra said, looping her arm through her sister's and squeezing it. 'It's only natural. But he's with his grandparents, remember, and Lloyd's around in the evenings. I bet he's being spoilt rotten. It's probably ice cream and chocolate for breakfast, lunch and dinner.'

'Oh God, don't say that. He's a nightmare at letting me clean his teeth. I'm sure he'll have fillings before he's two.'

Allegra chuckled. How could this neurosis come from the same woman who'd just – according to her ski app – clocked a top speed of 103 kilometres an hour on the downhill? 'Iz, he'll be fine.'

A carriage slid past, the horses' hooves picking high out of the snow, the driver's face almost obscured by the thick grey collar of his coat, the tinkle of jingling bells like a soundtrack to Christmas.

The town was busy again. The weather had closed in on the upper slopes throughout the course of the afternoon, forcing some of the lifts to stop, and all but the most hardened skiers had come back down.

'Come on, let's get a hot chocolate. Your nose has gone all red from the cold.'

'It has not!' Isobel gasped, immediately covering it with her other gloved hand.

Allegra laughed. Her sister was so vain. 'Besides, there's something I want to tell you,' she said, steering them towards a cafe on the opposite corner.

She waited for the inevitable pestering as Isobel's curiosity was piqued, needing to know *now*. She had never been one for delayed gratification.

But there was nothing.

Turning, she saw Isobel wasn't behind her but peering in the window of the gift shop next door, hands round her face as she tried to get a better view of something inside.

'What are you looking at?' she called from the cafe door.

'There's an amazing nativity set here, Legs. Come and see.'

'I don't want to come and see. I want to thaw out.'

'But I really want to get one for Ferds.'

'Why?'

'What do you mean, why? It's the Christmas Story.'

'Right. Because that was always forefront in your mind when you woke me at dawn every Christmas Day for fifteen years.'

Isobel stuck out her tongue. 'You might hate Christmas, but we need a nativity set now we've got a child. Not having a nativity set is like not having a Christmas tree or not having turkey or—'

Allegra sighed. Her sister didn't have a religious bone in her body and yet she wanted to recreate a biblical scene in her sitting room? 'Fine! You get that. I'll order the drinks and meet you in here.'

Isobel squealed with excitement and darted inside, as though Allegra was her mother and had given her permission to buy sweets at the corner shop.

Allegra ordered two foamy hot chocolates and a strudel for them to share, and found a table for them by the steamed-up windows. It was busy in there, clearly a sort of happy hour for the coffee shops as tired skiers and shoppers alike converged for a well-earned rest.

Absently, she wiped the window with her hand, looking out onto the street like she was peering through a gap in the clouds. Her silent combat with Kemp earlier had left her shaken. She still couldn't recall anything of last night after she'd clocked him behind Zhou, but she remembered his hostility – then and today – at finding her here in Zermatt and it rattled her. What did *he* have to be so angry about? She was the one who'd lost the war!

Isobel joined her minutes later, an enormous cardboard box in her arms.

'Oh my good God!' Allegra burst out laughing. 'Is that it? It's almost to scale, surely.'

'It's uh-mazing!' Isobel beamed, sitting down opposite, her eyes shining. 'You should see the stuff they've got in there. All hand-made wooden toys and decorations. The girl told me her dad and grandfather still make it all themselves.'

'Yeah, right. They say that to justify putting the prices up another thirty per cent. I bet you find a "Made in China" label underneath.'

'You are *so* cynical. Honestly, I pity you. Pity you,' she echoed with a superior smile.

'And obviously you've factored in the cost of getting that back on the plane. You may as well buy another seat for what they're going to charge you.'

Isobel's smile disappeared, panic moulding her mouth into a small 'o'. 'Lloyd'll kill me.'

'Oh, it's fine. I was only teasing!' Allegra smiled, rolling her eyes and patting her sister on the hand. 'I'll cover it.'

'No, but—'

'No, no buts. Just forget about it. You'd better let me see it, though. I assume it comes with a free donkey?'

Isobel grinned, putting the box on the floor and pulling in her chair. 'I'll show you back at the apartment. They wrapped all the pieces individually and it's a bit crowded in here. Besides, I want to hear what your news is,' she said, taking such a big slurp of her drink that she ended up with a chocolatey moustache.

'Oh, so you *did* hear me . . . Right . . . Good.'

'Sounds ominous,' Isobel said with a frown.

'Uh, no. No, not ominous . . .' Allegra cleared her throat. 'Actually, it's sort of good news.'

Isobel frowned harder. 'Now I'm really worried. Spit it out.'

Allegra took a deep breath. 'I found out this morning that . . . Valentina's husband, and therefore our, uh . . . grandfather . . . He's alive.' She cleared her throat again.

'Say what?' Isobel murmured after an age.

'He's not dead. Never has been.'

Isobel blinked. 'And how exactly did you find out that?'

'I ended up – slightly accidentally, actually – in the local church this morning. Turned out the priest knew quite a lot about her. It's been in the local papers apparently. People have been going in and lighting candles for her. He even checked the parish records for me and showed me their marriage entry. And Mum's birth.' She had denied it for as long as she could but their mother's birth record, right here in Zermatt, had been the final proof that Annen had the right family, anchoring once and for all the fact that Valentina was their grandmother, and Anya had lied.

Isobel's eyes widened. 'Mum was born here?'

'Mm-hmm. And our family – the Engelbergs – had one of the largest goat farms in the valley.'

'Oh jeez, I don't believe it. Peasant stock after all. Lloyd will never let me live this down.' She dropped her head in her hands dramatically.

Allegra squeezed her hand. 'That's not the main point I'm trying to make, Iz. Contrary to what Granny told us, Mum's dad never died when Mum was little. He's still alive and living here.'

'Here? *Here*?' Isobel spluttered.

Allegra nodded, pulling out the piece of paper the priest had written on for her. 'That's his address. He's about six minutes away.'

Isobel withdrew, sitting back in the chair, shaking her head slightly from side to side, every bit as stubborn as her sister. 'How can you know what he's saying is true? He's a stranger. How can he know more about our own family than we do?'

'Because he's a priest, Iz. And because I saw the entries with my own eyes.' She reached her hands out towards her sister's, over the table. 'Hey, we've got a grandfather. This

is a good thing.' She smiled more strongly, hoping she was doing a passable job of looking happy about it. 'Hell, it's a great thing! Poor Ferds is the first boy born into the family in five generations. Frankly, he could do with a bit of male company!'

Isobel had to crack a small smile at that, and her posture loosened a little. 'I guess,' she said quietly. But Allegra knew she was thinking about their granny, wondering about the lies she had told and why. What could have happened that she had written him out, erased him altogether from their family history? It felt almost as though him being dead wasn't enough. 'So what now?'

'I think we should go and see him. It's crazy not to, when we're already here and, well . . . he's Mum's father! We have a responsibility to at least talk to him and let him know that he's got a family.'

'But I don't understand how he can't know already.' Isobel frowned. 'I mean, if Mum's his daughter, what did he think had happened to her? Do you think Granny told him *Mum* was dead? It doesn't make sense. Why would he have lost his daughter and not known what had happened to her? What was Granny bloody well *doing*?'

Allegra sighed wearily. She had just as many questions jumping around in her own head. 'I've got no idea. I guess we'll only find out by asking him.'

'What, now?'

'No, not now. I think we both need a bit of time to just . . . absorb the news. And anyway, we should go to the police station first. We need to collect Valentina's personal effects, and we also need to sign off on transfer of her remains.' She pulled a nervous expression. 'Oh, and that's the other thing that happened this morning.'

'What? What other thing? Jeez, I thought you just went out to get milk!'

'Yes, well . . .' Allegra took another deep breath. She'd been wise not to do this in the throes of their hangovers. 'I think we should organize a cremation and memorial service for Valentina here.'

Isobel stared at her for a moment. 'But what about Mum? The whole point of coming out here was to bring Valentina back with us and have more time to decide what to do about telling Mum.'

Allegra shook her head. 'I know, but . . . the more I think about it, the more it seems wrong to take her away from the only place she ever knew. There are people here who still remember her. The priest said people have been coming in and—'

'Lighting candles for her. Yes, yes, you said,' Isobel said distractedly, staring at her nails.

'He also gave me the details of a highly regarded crematorium and said he'd be able to conduct a service for her on Thursday before we go back. It'll be tight but it was the best he could do.'

Isobel's eyes flicked up to her.

'If you agree, of course.'

'Yeah, right. Like I could ever win an argument against you,' Isobel sighed.

'We need to be united on this, Iz. Mum would want us to do what was best. She'll never know her own mother now, and she may never even know of her, but don't you think that after all these years of being lost on the mountain, Mum would want her to be put to rest in the only place she ever called home?'

'I guess so.'

They were both quiet for a few minutes, lost in their own thoughts as the cafe hummed with excitable conversations.

'Come on, if we go to the police station now, we can get it over and done with. Then we can go back to the apartment and flop,' Allegra said, trying to muster the energy in herself as much as in her sister.

They scraped back their chairs and shrugged on their jackets.

'What do you fancy for dinner tonight?' Isobel asked, heaving the box into her arms, unaware she looked like Poirot with her chocolate moustache.

'You tell me. I'm happy to cook,' Allegra said, holding open the door for Isobel to step through.

'You, cook? Aren't you the same person who, when I wanted toast at your place once, rang San Lorenzo and got them to deliver it?'

Allegra looked sheepish. Once, she'd done that. Once. And only because she didn't have any bread. Or a toaster.

'Let's just go out. I'd feel a lot safer.'

Allegra frowned as she glimpsed the tail end of a smile on her sister's face. 'Hey!'

His voice didn't fit his face. On the phone, Sergeant Annen had sounded twenty stone and like he feasted on buffalo for breakfast, so it was something of a surprise for Allegra to be led to an office where a man who looked like he hadn't started shaving yet was waiting for her and her sister. He had very round eyes that bulged slightly – overactive thyroid perhaps? – and fine, straight hair that immediately fell back over his forehead every time he pushed it away, and a certain springy energy to his movements.

'Miss Fisher?' he said, coming round from his desk but not sure which of them to shake by the hand.

'Sergeant Annen,' Allegra said in reply, shaking his hand. 'This is my sister, Isobel Watson.'

'Mrs Watson,' Annen said, shaking Isobel's hand too. 'Thank you for making the trip. Please, take a seat.'

'Thank you.'

Allegra looked slowly around the office. A few posters – no-smoking, drugs campaigns – were Blu-tacked to the walls, a few framed photographs of police officers standing in line like in a school photograph, gently fading from years of sitting in a sunny spot.

'I hope you don't mind that I asked for you to be shown in here. I wanted to thank you personally for your cooperation. We treat every unexplained death with the same respect and diligence, regardless of whether the deceased has been dead a day or . . .' He shrugged. 'Well, over sixty years.'

'That's reassuring to hear,' Allegra said, crossing her legs, her back straight and her hands laced loosely in her lap. Out of the corner of her eyes, she saw Isobel follow suit. 'And has our grandmother's death now been explained?'

Annen hesitated. 'Not entirely.'

Allegra frowned.

'While the deceased's identity has now been confirmed, thanks to your help, there are still some questions we don't have answers to.'

'Such as why she went up to the hut during the storms, you mean?'

He nodded. 'Exactly. I'm afraid we have yet to discount the possibility of foul play.'

Isobel whipped round to look at Allegra, but Allegra forced herself to stay still.

'You don't believe her husband's account of events?'

'Well, we haven't been able to *disprove* his account of what happened that night, but there's never been anything to suggest he's telling us anything other than the truth.'

'So then who do you suspect?'

Annen blinked at her. 'One line of our enquiry is looking into the motives and actions of the victim's sister.'

'*Granny?*' Isobel burst out. 'But you can't be serious. She was ... She was totally the kindest, gentlest, most loving woman ever. There's no way she ... There's just no way she would have hurt her own sister.'

Annen's eyes slid between the two sisters sitting before him.

'But I understand she never mentioned having a sister to you or your mother?'

Allegra shook her head, determined to stay calm, even though anxiety was beginning to make her feel light-headed. 'No.'

'And did she ever mention her husband?'

'He died of tuberculosis when Mummy was three,' Isobel said firmly.

'Anya's husband?' Annen clarified, looking more grave.

'That's right.'

'Well, I'm sorry to say that was a lie. Her husband, Lars Fischer, is still living in this town. He was even the mayor for a few years.'

'Sorry, wait—' Allegra said, leaning forward. 'There's a mistake. Lars Fischer was Valentina's husband, not Granny's. Anya's, I mean.'

Annen hesitated. 'According to town records, he was married to them both, Miss Fisher.'

Time halted its path. 'What?'

Annen picked up a pen and began absently twiddling it in his fingers. 'Valentina died in January 1951. Lars, her widower, married Anya Engelberg in March 1952.'

'But . . .' No words would come; thoughts couldn't form. Granny had married her own sister's husband?

She turned slowly to look at Isobel, who was herself ashen, her mouth agape.

'In addition,' Annen continued, with a note of apology in his voice, 'Anya left her husband in 1953. She disappeared, taking her niece and stepdaughter – your mother – with her. No one in the town ever knew where she went.'

Allegra turned away, wanting to cover her ears with her hands, to get up out of this chair and leave this room and forget every single last detail of this conversation. Denial. Denial.

'You're trying to tell us Granny stole our mother and took her away from her only true parent and left the country with her?' Isobel asked, trying to inject a laugh into the comment, to make it sound ridiculous, unbelievable, but her voice was tremulous and rising.

Annen looked across at her with regret and nodded. 'Lars Fischer was never able to trace her.'

Because she had left the country.

The room fell silent as the sergeant allowed them to process the revelation.

'Does anyone know why she left her husband?' Allegra asked after a while, rallying. 'Was he . . . I don't know, was he a drinker, a gambler, a womanizer? Did he use his fists? Because Granny wasn't . . . As my sister said, she was a kind and gentle woman, devoted to our mother. What you're telling us doesn't tally with the woman we knew.'

'I'm sure it doesn't. But with respect, you only ever knew her as children – and after she had got away with it.' He coughed lightly. 'And the gossip in the town at the time Valentina disappeared alleged that Anya had been secretly in love with her brother-in-law for years.'

'Gossip? Is that what she's to be judged on?' Allegra asked stiffly.

'It isn't fact, I know, but as you might imagine, there's precious little paperwork to go on, and it helps us build up a picture of motive. With two of the three players involved now dead, it is even more difficult to get to the truth, but none of us can dispute the simple fact that she lied to you all.'

Allegra looked away, sickened by what she was hearing. She didn't know what to believe, who to trust. Her grand mother had been her rock, the only person who had held *her* together when she'd been everyone's else glue after their lives had been so spectacularly blown apart eighteen years earlier.

She looked back at him with renewed focus, her brain quick to spot a contradiction. 'Well, why would she have left him if she'd been secretly in love with him for years? She'd married him for heaven's sake. She got him.'

'Jealousy can be hard to live with, Miss Fisher. And Valentina made for a beautiful ghost.'

Allegra glanced across at Isobel – her head was resting in the cradle of her hand, her complexion waxy – and wished she'd come here alone. She should never have involved her in this. Isobel wasn't renowned for handling shocks like this well.

'Is there anything else we need to discuss, or can we go?' Allegra asked, grabbing her sister's hand and squeezing it hard.

Annen looked surprised by her sudden change in tone. 'No. I just wanted to appraise you of the ongoing investigation.' He rose from his chair. 'Are you staying in Zermatt long?'

'A few more days,' Allegra said, rising too. Isobel followed after like a child. 'We're arranging a private memorial service for Valentina later this week, so . . .'

Annen nodded. 'Has the transfer for custody of the remains been completed?'

Allegra blanched at the terminology. 'Yes. That's why we came. We signed the paperwork just now.'

'Good.'

'Where do we collect the possessions that were found with her?' Allegra asked, holding Isobel lightly by the elbow as she came to stand by her. Her sister looked like she was going to keel over. 'The policeman at the desk said they're not stored here.'

'That's right. They're with the SLF,' Annen said, hurriedly scribbling a name and address on a piece of paper. 'I shall tell Connor to expect you.'

'What's the SLF?' Allegra asked, merely glancing at it before zipping it safely in her pocket.

'The Swiss Federal Institute for Snow and Avalanche Research. Better known as the Swiss Anti Avalanche Agency.'

'Oh.'

Annen held out his hand. 'I'm sorry to be the bearer of such bad news. I know this information must be very difficult to accept.'

He didn't know the half of it. He couldn't possibly understand that his revelations hadn't gained them a grandmother; he'd lost them one.

Allegra shrugged, shaking his hand with extra firmness. 'Nothing surprises me, Sergeant,' she said briskly. 'My sister and I know better than to have any faith in anyone but each other.'

And linking Isobel's arm through hers, she led her sister through the police station and away from the sergeant, who stared after them with pity growing in his eyes.

Chapter Nineteen

'I like the Angel Gabriel best. Check him out – he's got cheeks like Barry.' Isobel held up the wooden angel with a tipsy giggle. 'Angel Barry.'

Allegra took it, chuckling lightly. The nativity scene Isobel had all but snatched from the gift shop's window was now recreated on the coffee table before them. A large stable had been detailed with traditional Swiss motifs in the woodwork, and the nativity figures were all crafted from wood, but the baby Jesus lay in a manger with a real straw base and soft leather whip-stitched blanket, the kings were robed in beautiful velvet cloaks, the sheep had genuine fleeces ... The quality and craftsmanship were undeniable. She studied the angel more closely, sure she'd seen it before.

'I agree you were right to get this. It's beautiful. Something he'll have forever.'

'Yeah,' Isobel beamed, falling back to her prostrate position on the sofa again. 'Just so long as we don't eat till March and I hide the Visa statement from Lloyd, it'll be fine.'

Allegra looked up. 'Listen, why don't I give this to Ferds for his Christmas present?'

'Uh-uh. No.' Isobel shook her head firmly.

'Why not? I haven't got him anything yet and it would do me a massive favour not to have to worry about it.'

'Legs,' Isobel said sternly, 'I know exactly what you're doing.'

'What am I doing? I need to get Ferds a present and you've just bought a present. Just let me give him that and you can get him something else.'

The two sisters blinked at each other before Isobel scrambled off the sofa and threw her arms around Allegra's neck. 'I don't know what I'd do without you,' she mumbled into her hair. 'You're the best.'

'No, I'm just living in terror of you,' Allegra replied. 'I'll never forget your face when I gave him that Steiff bear. Even now, there are still times I wake up in the night in a cold sweat.'

Isobel shot her an earnest look. 'Legs, those tag thingies in the ear are such a choking hazard.'

'Iz, those bears are highly collectable, and Steiff have been making them for over a hundred years. I think they know what they're doing.'

Isobel went back to the sofa with a laugh. 'Yeah, well, I don't take chances where my little man's concerned,' she said, falling back on the sofa once more and stretching out languidly, her hand finding the glass of Bordeaux safely stashed next to the sofa.

They lapsed into quiet again, only an incomprehensible soap on TV providing any soundtrack to the little apartment. Isobel began flicking through the channels as Allegra settled into reading the papers.

'You know, I just don't believe a word of it,' Isobel mumbled five minutes later, draining the glass.

'Of course not,' Allegra said, resting her iPad on her bent

knees and looking over at her sister as she opened a second bottle. 'There's no way Granny would have done any of what he said. It's all going to turn out to be just a tragic accident.'

'Yeah,' Isobel agreed, but Allegra knew she'd be back on it again in a few minutes. They had been stuck on the same loop ever since leaving the police station, Isobel refuting the allegations against their grandmother, then finishing a glass of wine; refuting the allegations . . .

Isobel stuck out her arm, frantically waving the remote around as she tried to change channels. 'God, there must be something in English,' she muttered, briefly stopping on some prank home-videos show. 'I swear I saw that on *You've Been Framed.*'

Allegra's eyes flicked back up, just in time to see a man in trunks dive-bombing onto a frozen-solid pool. 'They just syndicate the material internationally, I expect. Cheap programme-making.'

She went back to her iPad as Isobel flicked through another few channels, before her arm dropped suddenly and she twisted back on the sofa to look at Allegra again. 'I mean, the whole bloody notion of it is completely preposterous! What they're saying Granny did, that's like *me* dying, *you* hooking up with Lloyd afterwards and then doing a runner to *America* a year later and bringing up *Ferds* to think *you* were his mum!'

Allegra dropped the iPad back down again. 'Exactly. It's completely unbelievable. And that's what reassures me it'll all be OK, Iz. Somewhere along the line, they've got one vital fact wrong.' She knew it wasn't the typo – not now she'd seen the marriage record of Lars and Anya for herself. The Fischer family with a 'c' was her family. 'It only takes one mistake to skew an entirely innocent turn of events into something more sinister. We just have to keep reminding ourselves that we both knew Granny and we know she wasn't capable of that.'

'Yeah, exactly,' Isobel said, nodding vehemently, her eyes fixed on Allegra.

Allegra tried to smile reassuringly, hoping she was hiding the doubt that was drifting like a solitary black storm cloud in her mind. Because how *did* they explain away that their grandmother had married her sister's husband? That was fact, noted not just in the parish records but also the civic registers. And what possible justification could she have had for taking a child away from its father? If her explanation was so innocent, why had she kept it a secret from their mother all these years?

She smiled a bit wider, and Isobel – placated, for the next few minutes anyway – twisted back again on her sofa. Allegra took another sip of her wine and returned to flicking the virtual pages of the *FT*. It soothed her to absorb herself in the machinations of big business. There was a safety in numbers she could always rely on – she understood how to smell panic, the first top notes of confidence – and she found comfort in the rhythms of the markets. She knew how this game was played, at least.

Her eyes scanned the business pages: 'Unemployment Levels in the US Stuck at 6.7%'; 'FD of Tesco Resigns Hours Before Results Due'; 'Pharmaceutical Giants' $40bn Merger Talks'; 'Hedge Fund Makes £6bn Profit in Q4.'

She stopped flicking and double-clicked on the last headline, her hand flying to her mouth as she saw Pierre's photo. Tucking her knees closer to her chest, she began reading avidly. It was essentially a profile piece on Pierre's return to prominence – PLF was now third in the market and officially the same size as the world's largest commercial bank, the Industrial and Commercial Bank of China, running a fund of close to $40 billion. Kemp was profusely name-dropped, but that wasn't what kicked the breath out of her. It was the timing of this.

A $6-billion profit in one quarter was a great result and certainly higher than she had been anticipating – although she knew their returns for the first three quarters of the financial year were well above the industry average – but the fourth quarter didn't close for another two weeks, and under the rules set out by the US Securities and Exchange Commission, they didn't need to file their F13 records for another forty-five days after that. So why was he jumping the gun, more than six weeks early?

She stared into the unblinking eyes that had once looked upon her kindly, admiringly, and thought she could guess. He was getting the report in before Besakovitch's money was withdrawn. This number would be half a billion smaller next week, but it wouldn't be officially reported until May next year, giving him plenty of time to get Yong's business in and signed on the dotted line. This was a siren call to the Chinese businessman. Pierre had a new dream team, a star fund manager to manage their assets. How could he possibly ignore numbers like these?

How could anyone? Because this was also a message – to her, to Leo Besakovitch, that he didn't need either one of them. Pierre hadn't just closed the door behind them both, he'd locked it too.

'Legs?'

'Huh?' She looked up. Isobel was leaning back at a contorted angle, her head tipped so that she was staring at her upside down. 'You OK?'

'Yes, of course. I'm fine. Why?'

'You've just been reading that with your hands over your mouth like you were going to scream.'

Allegra realized her hands were still at her mouth and dropped them down. 'I'm absolutely fine. Just . . . getting caught up with work stuff, as usual.'

'But you're not working at the moment.'

'That's just fine print. I've already had six offers left on my phone and I've not even spoken to anyone yet.'

'So then why don't you speak to them?'

'Because I want a break before I go back,' she said. It was only a half-lie. She felt like a lioness who'd been attacked by her own pride and had retreated for her own safety, but there was also unfinished business here. She had a lawsuit all wrapped up on her phone, she had job offers stored in her voicemail, and yet she wasn't using any of it. She wasn't acting, wasn't *moving*. And that in itself was odd.

Perpetual motion had always been her game plan – never stopping long enough to place both feet on the ground lest she should become planted, always hopping instead from project to project, team to team, like a frog on lily pads, determined not to get her feet wet – because to get wet would be to drown.

Every day she was out of the market, she knew her old life was beginning to pull away from her like an ocean liner – moving in a slow, strong, sure steady line, unable to swerve back and scoop her from the seas. But there was only one person who could do that and she had to keep the door open for him – because he would come back for her; of that she was certain.

They'd been a team, the two of them. She knew him better than any of them – better, even, than his wife. She was the one he'd come to find late at night, a bottle of whisky and two glasses in his hand, knowing she'd still be in her office, talking through his worries with her as she sat and listened and understood. Just like she understood that it hadn't been *her* Pierre that night. He'd acted out of character, urged on by Kemp and a desperate, reckless bravado in front of Zhou. He was hurt by his old friend Leo's desertion and was trying to restore some pride. She knew all that. Of course she knew all that. She could even forgive it, because she knew he would be regretting it. So she'd keep waiting, just a little longer . . .

It wasn't *him* she blamed.

She frowned, remembering something . . .

She got up from the sofa and walked into the kitchen, stirring the soup that was bubbling quietly on the stove. 'D'you need anything?' she called over.

'Have we got any of those crisps left?'

Allegra emptied the bag into a bowl and brought it over.

'I was just saying *Notting Hill*'s on. Fancy it?' Isobel asked. 'I mean, I know we've seen it a million times, but' – she shrugged – 'it's this or CNN.'

'Is it in English? Because I don't think I could bear to hear Hugh Grant dubbed into German.'

Isobel laughed out loud at the thought. 'Ha! I almost hope it is. That would be so funny!'

'Fire away. I'll just be a sec.' And she disappeared into the bedroom, pulling from her suitcase the report Bob had compiled on Kemp's activity on the Besakovitch fund. How could she have forgotten all about it? Holding it behind her back as she returned to the sitting room, and then hiding it from Isobel's view behind a cushion, she curled up on the sofa and began to read. And learn.

Chapter Twenty

Day Sixteen: *Miniature Rocking Cradle with
Whip-stitched Goatskin Blanket*

'Are you sure this is right?' Isobel asked, clutching at a wall
as she skidded on some ice. The backstreet they were walking down was no wider than an alley, here in the Hinterdorf
area, or the Old Town part, of Zermatt, and though they
were only two roads away from the Bahnhofstrasse, the
splashy, sumptuous boutiques and hotels couldn't have
been further removed from the old rickety-looking wooden
buildings along here, which were almost blackened from
standing up to over three hundred Swiss winters. Some of
the huts were only one room wide, most were balanced
precariously off the ground on stone mushroom pillars,
pretty whittled balconies protruded from chunky stone
walls, and black-out shutters were boarded over the windows.

Allegra frowned in agreement. This couldn't be right.
She pulled the piece of paper from her pocket and read
Annen's notes again: *Connor Mayhew, SLF, Schweinestall,
Hinterdorfstrasse*. She looked around her with an expression
of disbelief. It seemed hard to believe that the Zermatt
branch of the Institute for Snow and Avalanche Research –

which had showed a modernist HQ in Davos when she'd Googled it last night – was going to be found somewhere down here. And yet they were in the right street . . .

'Well, according to this it is,' she said with a sigh, folding it back in her pocket. 'Let's keep going.'

They continued onwards, tired after a morning's hard skiing on Gornergrat in which they had each tried to break the hundred kilometres an hour reading on their MyTracks apps (Isobel had managed it; Allegra had 'failed', at ninety-seven kilometres an hour) and taking tiny pigeon steps in their boots. The snow had become hard-packed beneath the taxis' caterpillar tracks here, forcing them to clutch at walls for support as they peered up at each door, looking for a number or name.

But even when Isobel found it, she didn't believe it. Set high on slate stilts with a stepladder up to it that was nothing more than a tree trunk with notches carved in alternate fashion up either side, the hut was about as far from an official agency building as you could imagine. It was only ten feet wide or so, with no windows at the front, and a shallow slate ledge only just protruded in front of the door to create some sort of standing area.

'*Really?* I've seen more official-looking barns,' Isobel said sceptically.

Allegra stopped at the bottom of the ladder and stared up. 'Schweinestall' could be clearly seen etched into a small wooden plaque beside the door. There was no mistake – they were at the address Annen had given them.

Carefully, Allegra climbed up the steps. The shelf on which she had to stand was not more than a foot wide, and having knocked twice, she stood with her hands on the door, weight forward, like she was trying to push it down.

'Be careful!' Isobel said anxiously, ever the health-and-safety officer.

The door opened after a minute.

'*Ja?*' A stern face stared back at her, almost nose to nose.

Allegra dropped her hands quickly, resisting the impulse to step back. To do so would be to fall seven feet.

'Connor Mayhew? Allegra Fisher.'

Nothing.

'Sergeant Annen gave me your details. He said he'd call ahead to let you know to expect us?'

Mayhew frowned back at her – his default resting face, she imagined. Soft and cuddly he wasn't. He looked like a man who had wandered into town after a year of living with wolves, although his wind-burnt, tanned skin picked out his eyes, and his hair seemed to suit him grey. In his mid- to late forties, she guessed, he had a long, rectangular face and tightly drawn mouth, a wiry build and greying stubble that was on its last day before it graduated to a beard. He was also exceptionally tall, even to her, and wore the unselfconscious clothing of someone for whom the kit was chosen on technical merits, not aesthetic – orange down jacket, a pair of yellow soft-shell ski trousers that were grubby on the knee, navy thermal roll neck. This, then, was the man who had brought her grandmother down from the mountain.

'Valentina Fischer?' she prompted, watching the recognition finally dawn in his eyes at the name and wishing they could do this inside, off the ledge.

'Oh. Yes.' He paused, stepping back into the room. 'Come in.'

'My sister is with me too. Isobel Watson.' Allegra motioned down towards her, but Connor simply signalled disinterestedly for them both to enter. With a surprised shrug – unused to being invisible – Isobel scampered up the ladder.

Inside, the hut had low ceilings, with a vertiginous spiral staircase rising at the back and rows of shelves with wooden boxes on them lining the walls. Both women trod carefully, their eyes roaming up, down, all around, their feet automatically checking for weak spots beneath their treads, but everything felt solid and quiet. And warm. Connor had walked to the far corner and was crouched in front of a tiny stove, thick gauntlet gloves on as he pushed a split log into the tentative fire. The flames instantly leaped like Hades' hounds and he shut the door, looking back at them both with sharp eyes. 'Do you have ID?'

'ID?' Isobel repeated.

'I must see proof that you are who you say you are.'

'Oh, yes.' They both reached inside the zipped pockets of their coats and pulled out their passports.

Connor looked at them, matching the photos to the women standing before him. 'Fine.' He held them back out for them, his tone fractionally more friendly. 'I have to ask. We get all sorts trying to claim things from here. Trophy-hunters.'

'Really?' Allegra grimaced. Who could possibly want the personal items of people who had perished on the mountain?

He walked over to a small, square wooden table in the far corner and began flicking through the pages of a hardback ledger. 'Was she your grandmother?' he asked over his shoulder, running one finger down the pages until he found what he was looking for. 'GXC41220,' he murmured, immediately walking over to some boxes on the right-hand wall.

Isobel shrugged. 'Apparently.' A resentful tone hardened her voice and Allegra knew – and understood – her sister felt a growing antipathy towards this woman whose sudden appearance in their lives had thrown their love for their known grandmother, history and their memories into jeopardy.

Allegra's eyes wandered the room. It was so surprising in here, like a rustic Tardis. The stove was flickering quietly, and she noticed a small black kettle sitting on the top. There was a large rocking chair in front of it, with a tweed wool blanket thrown over the back, and in the opposite corner behind the stairs, the small wooden table with a couple of chairs. As well as the book he'd just looked at, there were some papers and a rucksack on it, and a thermos sat beside a small foil-wrapped parcel of what Allegra guessed to be sandwiches. Oil lamps hung from hooks on the overhead beams.

'Did people actually live in these houses?' she asked, subtly trying to peer up the stairs. What was up there?

'Some of us still do,' Connor replied with a chilly tone, glancing back at her.

'Sorry. I didn't mean to . . . It's charming. Just not what I was expecting,' Allegra said, as Isobel jabbed her in the ribs.

'Davos is our headquarters. This is just a regional field office. There's only me and two others in our team, and our "office" – if you want to call it that – is on site up the mountain. We don't need more than this in town. Besides, there is a limited supply of office space in Zermatt, as you might expect. Seemingly the council only wants super-chalets developed here.'

'What are you doing up there? On the mountain, I mean.'

'We investigate avalanche dynamics at the test site. We are developing an avalanche detection system that can deliver information concerning avalanche activity in a specific terrain to safety authorities. That means setting off controlled explosions and assessing how and where the snow comes down.'

'So you're an avalanche expert, then,' Allegra said drily.

'Yes.' He said the word with a certain reluctance and she guessed the irony of the situation that had brought them together wasn't lost on either of them. 'Ah, got it,' he muttered, pulling down a box and checking the number written on the side.

He stared down at it for a moment, his back to them both, and Allegra sensed his manner change slightly.

He turned. 'So this is it. Your grandmother's box.' He held it out to them. Allegra glanced over at Isobel in astonishment. It was tiny, not ten centimetres by ten centimetres.

Allegra took it, stared down at it: the hard proof that had forced a seismic lateral shift in their genealogy, the scissors that had simply and silently cut through the tight knot of stories and memories that had wound and bound and knotted around them. There it was, sitting innocuously in a cardboard box that fit in the palm of her hand.

Slowly, Isobel reached for it. 'That's *it*?'

Allegra spoke up quickly, embarrassed the man would think they were avaricious, the so-called trophy-hunters after all. 'And are all these boxes filled with . . . last possessions like this?' she asked quietly, her eyes on the shelves behind him.

He paused. 'Yes. Mostly it's just artefacts like a camera

or old boots that have been lost by hikers, but we archive it all in case they can be traced to a missing person on our files. The seasonal movement of the snowpack and ice melt means objects can sometimes travel of their own accord down the mountain, a distance away from where they were lost.'

'Are there many people missing?'

'Officially two hundred and eighty people in the Valais region since 1926.'

Two hundred and seventy-nine now, then. 'And how often do you find the . . . bodies?'

'More and more regularly. The glaciers are retreating at an unprecedented rate. The Ober Gabelhorn glacier, on the opposite side of the valley to where we found your grandmother, shrank by almost three hundred metres last year.' He shook his head. 'The mountains keep many secrets and for a long time. But not forever. We always find out in the end.'

Allegra nodded, her eyes sliding over to the teeny-tiny box in her sister's palm, thinking about how it wasn't just the mountains that had kept a secret – her family had too.

Isobel continued staring at the small box. 'I don't know why I thought it would be bigger,' she murmured. 'I thought there would be something . . . dramatic. Something substantial that would explain it all, you know?' She looked up at Allegra.

'I know. Me too,' Allegra nodded, rubbing her arm lightly.

Connor's eyes slid between the two women as their disappointment grew. 'You need to sign a release form.'

He pulled a sheet of paper from a box file on the shelf and, finding a pen, wrote the case number and Valentina's name in the blanks. He pointed for Allegra to scribble her signature on the dotted lines so that the contract would be fulfilled, the brief business between them ended: a mouth swab, a signature and now a stranger's last known possessions were theirs. A woman they'd never heard of, much less met, had become their responsibility.

'OK, then,' he said, pushing the biro lid back on and indicating they could take the box away. 'It's all yours.'

Allegra had to stop herself from replying with a sarcastic 'Really? *All* of it?' Instead she said: 'Can I ask you something?'

Connor looked back up at her.

'You found her, right?'

He hesitated for a moment. 'Yes.'

She swallowed. 'What did it look like, the hut?'

He held out his arms, indicating the room they were standing in. 'Not much different to this. But just one room, one window. It was a lot smaller.'

'Smaller,' she echoed, imagining the walls in here closer, the ceiling lower. Less space, less security, the sound of a mountain falling down upon them . . . 'It must have been pretty much destroyed, then, by the impact.'

He fell still. 'Strangely, no. Not like you would have thought. It had been wedged into a crevasse, so one wall was completely smashed against the rock; the others were at broken angles but still up. We think it must have surfed the snow to have remained so intact.'

'Surfed?'

'Like this one, the hut was built on stone pillars to protect from snow in the winter and also to keep vermin from entering. We think it must have been in the run-off zone of the avalanche, when it would have been losing volume and power, but there was still enough force to lift the hut and carry it the distance to the crevasse.'

She tried to visualize the mountain hut skimming the froth of an avalanche, a young woman helpless inside. She tried to imagine the terror Valentina must have felt as the hut 'surfed' with her in it, not knowing where she was going, unable to see what was coming next . . . The sensation of falling as the hut left the slopes . . . the terrible noise as the wall cracked and splintered, the sudden stop and silence of the stone. Those had been the final moments of her mother's mother?

'Why . . . why has it taken so long to find her? Surely people searched? They must have had search parties looking for her? Someone must have realized the hut had *gone*?'

'Yes. But over the three-day window that she disappeared, there were over a thousand avalanches. Hundreds perished; many were never found. It was impossible to send out rescue parties in the immediate aftermath – conditions were too unstable and dangerous. And afterwards, the devastation was so great, the snowpack so deep . . .' He held out his hands in a helpless gesture. 'And when the spring melts occurred, in this instance the hut had been swept away from where it had been standing. It wasn't actually far from the original spot, but there was no way of knowing where it had been moved; most people just assumed it had been destroyed altogether by the force of the snow.'

She looked away, nodding, the full horror of her grandmother's death becoming more real, more tragic, with every revelation. 'So how did she die, then, if the hut itself wasn't destroyed?'

'We think suffocation. Her left tibia was broken, but the

hut was swept into a gully and the entire void would have filled with snow. The force of it would have been as hard as concrete. It was unsurvivable. The snow cover was so hard-packed it never melted, even in the summer months. That was why it wasn't found.'

Allegra saw the anomaly immediately. 'So then how did you discover it if the snow didn't melt?'

He tried to supress a sigh and Allegra became aware she was coming across as an interrogator, trying to trip him up almost, machine-gunning questions at him that must be as difficult for him to answer as they were for her to hear. 'As I mentioned, the glacier is retreating, which means more and more meltwater is rushing through the gully, and that erodes the snow there. It was enough to expose some of the tiles on the roof and I spotted it from a path.'

'When was this?'

'In September, near the Ober Gabelhorn glacier.'

Isobel had had enough. 'Come on, Legs, let's just go.'

But Allegra shook her head. She had to know every-thing; she had to understand – even if these facts made a liar of her grandmother and revealed her as a monster. Because the truth, no matter how brutal, was always easier to bear than lies.

'One more thing. What was it you actually found in there? Her body, I mean . . .' She swallowed.

He seemed to understand what she wanted to know. 'We found a skeleton.'

Isobel juddered like she'd been pushed and Allegra's arm instinctively shot around her like a safety rope. Isobel was right. It was time to go.

Only . . .

'A skeleton? *A skeleton?*' Isobel repeated fiercely, a telling crack in her voice. 'So then how did you come to tally up an anonymous heap of bones with *our family*? None of us had ever even heard about her. There was no proof she was anything to do with us till Legs had to do the DNA test. What right did you have to drag us into this? We already had a granny – the best!'

Huge, hot tears rolled down her cheeks, but her eyes were ablaze and Connor looked at the floor awkwardly.

'It was because of this,' he said, flipping open the paper file and pulling a photograph from it of a small cowbell with a faded red leather strap looped to it. 'Valentina' could be seen inscribed in the grain of the leather. 'We found this round the wrist bone; when we checked the name against local records, a Valentina Fischer was recorded as missing in January 1951.'

It was useless trying to push Valentina away from them. No matter what they said, no matter how they protested their grandmother's innocence, all the records, all the facts pointed to Valentina being theirs too. Allegra curled her arm around her sister's shoulders and herded her out, pushing the box in her pocket so that they could use their hands to get back down the rudimentary steps.

Ten minutes later, they were sitting in the coffee shop, nursing hot chocolates and staring at the little box on the table between them. It was relatively quiet in there, compared to the heave of yesterday's visit, and neither one of them was saying very much. The gruesome details of Valentina's death couldn't help but arouse sympathy in them for her plight, but at the same time, every gesture of acceptance towards Valentina eroded their history with Anya. They were caught between two women – two sisters – two histories that were insupportable to each other, because as much as their hearts lay with the grandmother they had known and loved, how could they ignore the facts, which were telling them a woman had died in terrifying circumstances, far too young and leaving behind a child – their mother?

'I guess we have to open it sooner or later,' Allegra said, one finger poking the box lightly.

'S'pose,' Isobel said, pointedly looking out of the window and showing that it wouldn't be her who did it.

Taking the butter knife, Allegra slit through the packing tape and opened up the flaps, peering in. She pulled out a short, two-inch stub of red candle, the wax tears still clinging to it; she placed it on the table in silence, meeting Isobel's angry eyes with apology. Besides it, she placed the miniature cowbell, with the red leather strap that had appraised the police of her identity in the first place. The leather itself was badly perished, cracked and stained with tidemarks, but 'Valentina' was still clearly visible when held up to the window and light speckled in through the punchmarks.

Looking in again, Allegra frowned, this time pulling out two rings. One had a yellow-gold band with three diamonds set along it. The other was incredibly plain, the metal very dark and dull, with no stone or embellishment at all. It bellied out like a signet ring, but there was no crest or insignia on it.

'That's it,' Allegra murmured, setting them down on the table beside the cowbell and candle.

'Huh, don't fancy yours much,' Isobel muttered, picking up the diamond ring, her eyes briefly meeting Allegra's with a flash of devilry.

Allegra grinned, grateful for the light relief. 'It's not

much to speak of, is it?' she said, picking up the dark ring. She slipped it on her right ring finger. A perfect fit. 'A candle, a bell and two rings.'

'Maybe the other stuff rotted in the snow. Her clothes and stuff.'

'Yes.'

'If it was just a shepherd's hut, there probably wasn't much in there anyway.'

'No, you're right,' Allegra agreed. 'She must have been wearing these when she died.' She held up the ring on her finger and gestured towards the one Isobel was holding.

'I guess so. That bloke just now said she had the bell on her wrist too. Does it still work?'

She lifted the bell from the table and shook it lightly. Nothing happened and she turned it upside down. 'Huh. Rusted solid. It won't work.'

'It can probably be treated with WD-40 or something. It's a pretty thing.'

But Isobel had already lost interest in the cowbell. 'They're really different, aren't they?' she said, indicating the rings.

'Hmmm?'

She held up the diamond ring by the base. 'This one seems pretty flashy, but didn't you say they were goat farmers? You wouldn't have thought a goat farmer could afford that.'

Allegra considered for a moment. 'No, but Father Merete did say the farm was one of the largest in the valley. They may have been asset rich.' She shrugged. 'Or maybe it was a family ring, passed down through the generations.'

'So what about your one, then? That's totally the other end of the scale.'

Allegra laughed lightly. 'Oh, I see! We've already decided on dividing up the spoils, have we?'

Isobel looked mortified. 'No, I didn't mean—'

'Iz, I'm just joking.' She took a sip of her hot chocolate. 'Try it on, though. Does it fit?'

'It needs a good clean,' Isobel said, sliding the diamond ring on her right ring finger too. 'Wow. We must have been similar builds?'

'Unlikely. Mum's only five foot five.'

'Yeah, but Dad's hardly a giant.'

'Five eleven is tall enough,' Allegra argued, slightly reluctantly as she realized it meant she was on 'his side' for once.

Isobel shrugged. 'It could've skipped a generation, that's all I'm saying.'

'Well, we can always ask.' Allegra's eyes flitted meaning-fully up to Isobel's. 'When do you think we should introduce ourselves to . . . you know, her husband?'

'Do we have to?' Isobel sat back in her seat, arms folded across her chest. 'I mean, haven't we heard enough? What are we going to find out next? That Mum had seven brothers and sisters and they all died in the plague or were attacked by the goats? I mean, isn't it enough to know that Granny had a sister and we're going to bury her here in her own town?' Her hands fanned out beseechingly.

Allegra reached her hand forward and grasped Isobel's fingertips. 'You know it's not – not when it means Granny's sister was actually Mum's mum. And not now we know Mum's dad is still alive. We have to know what happened – for Mum's sake.'

Isobel dropped her head. 'Ugh, God, I know. I just . . .'

'I know. But the sooner we get this done, the better. The

truth is never as bad as the scenarios running through your head.'

Isobel scraped back her chair. 'That's because you lack imagination, Legs. Trust me, what's going on up here right now?' She knocked her temple with her knuckles. 'It's like Halloween in lederhosen.'

'Really?' Allegra chuckled, rising too and leaving a tip on the table. 'That's one powerful image you've just conjured.'

'Oh yeah.' Isobel grinned, swinging her arm out, ready for Allegra to loop hers through. 'Why be calm when melodramatics will do?'

Chapter Twenty-One

It felt odd walking to the home of a grandfather who'd been dead their whole lives, and they both fell into a nervous quiet as they rounded the street the priest's note told them he lived on.

Questions, too many, were running through Allegra's head. How should she tell him who they were? He was an elderly man – would he cope with the shock of being suddenly presented with the daughters of the child he'd lost over sixty years ago? And how much should they tell him about her mother? Would it distress him unduly to let him know the extent of her decline?

Their feet took them soundlessly past the historic, blackened, elevated stadels that had been so bewildering to them only a few hours ago, but they had experienced for themselves now their one-room, windowless humility, their rustic simplicity that had weathered the very worst of the Alpine elements and still endured. These huts were basic, yes, but they had an integrity and substance to them that had to be respected. This was simply how life had been in an isolated farming community sixty years ago and before. She would make no such faux-pas about the huts with her grandfather as she had with Connor. This was the life her grandparents had known and into which her mother had been born, and it was as much a part of her heritage as the Edwardian semi they had grown up in, in Sheen.

She knew what to expect: Connor's base had been an insight into just how compact and confined their grand-father's home would be – she remembered the lanterns hanging from hooks (no electricity), the black kettle on the stove (no central heating), the hay-barn ladder to the upper level and a bed that must surely – given the dimensions of the roof – be just a mattress on the floor (no en suite) . . .

They had arrived. 'Chalet Gundersbach' was carved into a plaque on a high wooden gate – a smart wooden gate – that even they couldn't see over.

'Oh,' Allegra said in surprise, staring at the intercom system like she had never seen one before.

Isobel pressed the button. It was a long time before anyone answered.

'*Ja?*' It was a woman's voice, fairly young-sounding.

'H-hello?'

There was a pause. 'Yes?'

'We've come to see Lars Fischer.'

'Do you have an appointment?'

Isobel whipped round to look at Allegra, her nose wrinkled. An *appointment*? 'Sorry, no.'

'Then he is busy. Goodb—'

'Wait! . . . Uh . . .' Isobel cleared her throat. 'It's impor-tant. It's about Valentina.'

There was another long pause, so long Allegra began to wonder if the woman had gone away.

'Hello?' Isobel repeated.

A sudden click released the latch on the gate and it eased open fractionally. Allegra stepped through, expecting to find a small garden. She had noticed some of the larger properties had them, but this wasn't a garden; it was a path – an extremely long one with split logs painstakingly arranged against the walls on the left, metre-high glass lanterns spaced every five metres, filled with church candles, on the right.

'What the . . . ?' Isobel spluttered. 'It's like a bloody Anouska Hempel hotel.'

They walked briskly, their frowns growing as they took in the espaliered fruit trees – bare for now – and Isobel crouched down at one of the lanterns, pointing out a silver hallmark with wide eyes. The path was on an incline, and as it turned sharply left, they came face to face with another door, which was on the latch.

It led into a lift.

'This is bloody weird,' Isobel muttered, pressing the 'up' button.

The woman had sounded very officious, Allegra realized. 'It must be a care home.'

'Yeah? Well, then, can I come and live here too, please?'

Allegra smiled, but she was as flummoxed as Isobel. Exactly how big did their farm have to be for a goat farmer to afford this?

'Oh! What do you think we should call him?' Isobel asked suddenly, just as the lift arrived at the floor and the door opened. A woman in her fifties with short blonde hair and tight jeans was waiting for them, no smile.

'What did you say your name was?' she asked.

Allegra straightened up to her full, imposing height – at least five inches taller than the woman. Her mother had instilled in her a deep dislike for bad manners. 'We didn't. It's Allegra and Isobel.'

Her eyes moved between the two sisters, but her voice

was less strident, her eyes seeming to catch repeatedly on Allegra. 'Allegra and Isobel . . . ?'

The woman wanted a surname, but to say it would be to tell the story before they were even in the same room as their grandfather. 'Does it matter?' she asked. 'If you could just tell him it's about—'

'Valentina.'

The man's voice wasn't strong, not any more. It tremored at the edges like a frayed hem, but the sound still resonated with a bass timbre that Allegra instinctively understood had once filled rooms, silenced enemies, won women. The white-haired, moustached man in the wheelchair was weak now in body, but not in spirit, and as he stared at her across the lobby, she knew this was no care home. This man had power and wealth – the Rolex Daytona and handmade shoes told her that.

'I would have recognized you anywhere,' he said, his eyes surveying her like she was a painting – or a ghost. 'You are just like her. Your hair, your height . . . her nose too. Hands—' He stopped, as though out of breath.

The blonde walked over to him. A private nurse, then? 'Lars?'

But he flicked the joystick on the left arm of the wheelchair and revolved away from her. 'Bettina, bring us drinks in the lounge,' he said curtly. 'Young ladies, follow me.'

Allegra and Isobel glanced across at the nurse, who had straightened up as though he had slapped her. Striding past them both without making eye contact, she muttered: 'You can hang your jackets on the pegs by the door.'

'Well, she's a peach,' Isobel said under her breath, doing as she had been told, her eyes casing the large square hall. It was a melange of blond pines, older in style than the contemporary vogue for woven green oaks, but still deluxe with antique rugs scattered over the floors and some antique wooden skis and snow shoes fixed to the walls. A console table, opposite to where they were standing, was the only furniture in the space, with two gold, red and white Japanese lamps at either end and some framed black-and-white photographs on the surface. But it was the woman in an oil portrait hanging above that caught her eye – and Allegra's too.

'Holy crap!' she whispered under her breath, her head turning quickly between the woman in the painting and her sister: fearless blue eyes that looked haughtily, almost defiantly, at the artist, long black hair that fell past her shoulders, pinned with pink and red flowers like a corona, berry-stained lips that seemed on the cusp of parting as though about to laugh, smirk, scold . . . 'That is creepy! If it wasn't for the eyes, she could be you. In fancy dress, I mean.'

Allegra shot her an unamused look. She was too shocked by the resemblance herself to be able to laugh yet. She was too shocked by all of this. This chalet, the first sight of their grandfather . . . the first image of Valentina . . . But she had to agree – were it not for their eyes, she and Valentina would have made a matching pair.

'Come on,' she said with another nervous glance at the painting, following after where Lars had passed through a large arched door into a lavish room with panelled walls and an imposing fireplace. Deep red and green velvet sofas with bullion fringe were plumped high with tapestried scatter cushions, and a cuckoo clock ticked quietly on one wall. Lars was lowering himself into a fireside club chair, holding on to the arms for support.

Both women hesitated behind the sofa, not sure whether to offer to help, seemingly paralysed by indecision and nerves.

'You are my granddaughters,' he said with a puff of effort, looking down as he placed a carved walking cane, which he had used to get from the wheelchair to the club chair, against the side table next to him.

'Yes.'

He looked up at them both expectantly, seeming surprised to see them still halfway back across the room. 'Come, come,' he motioned. 'I am as deaf as a table and so blind I can hardly see my own feet.'

Allegra cracked a tiny smile, grateful for his humour, though she knew he was just joking. There was nothing wrong with his eyesight, as he had proved in the hall. Hers, though . . . It was only now they were close that she was able to take in the finer details herself. The shock and distance in the hall had been too great to absorb the minutiae, but now she saw the swelling in his hands and guessed at arthritis; she saw the broken veins on his cheeks, which were full coloured, and guessed at a love of fine wines; she saw the beak-like angle of his nose, which wasn't hers or Isobel's or their mother's – from his side of the family, then. She looked for herself in him, but it was hard to tell in such intense circumstances. Maybe his hair, before it had turned white?

They walked forwards, taking small steps and both feeling like nervous children, as they settled themselves on the sofa to his left, facing the fire.

His eyes never left them. 'What are your names?'

'I am Allegra,' Allegra said. 'And this is Isobel.'

'You are the elder.' His eyes were on her and she nodded.

'Yes. I'm thirty-one, and Isobel's twenty-nine, nearly thirty.'

'You are the protector, the strong one.'

Allegra glanced at Isobel. 'N-no. I wouldn't say that. Iz is incredibly strong and determined. Most of the time she ends up looking after me as well as her son.'

Lars looked at Isobel, his hands so clawed from the swelling they seemed to grip the armrests. 'You have a family of your own?'

She nodded. 'One boy. His name's Ferdy. He'll be one in February.'

Lars's mouth opened, but no sound came, his blue eyes watery and red-rimmed, still staring at the two of them too intently.

Isobel smiled awkwardly under the scrutiny, crossing and recrossing her legs, and Allegra knew her sister was biting down the impulse to get up and run out of here.

Lars, appearing to sense her discomfort, looked away and blinked for a long moment. 'I am sorry if I am staring at you both. It is a shock to me, you understand.'

'Of course.'

The blonde woman came in, silent as the snow, with a tray of coffee and biscuits, and they all fell quiet as she set it down on the table between them. They watched as she took her time pouring the coffee into the cups, putting one on the table beside Lars before offering Allegra hers while still holding the handle herself. Allegra shot her a mutinous look as the too-hot cup singed her fingertips before she could turn it round.

The blonde woman began poking the fire, throwing on another log, and Allegra wondered what to say next. Lars seemed defiantly silent in the nurse's company.

Isobel filled the silence for her. 'You speak very good English.' A note of suspicion tinged the words.

A half-smile played on his lips. 'In this town? It is necessary now. We are international.'

'You have a beautiful home,' Allegra said, before Isobel could say more.

'Thank you. I built it myself, 1954. Everyone thinks I am too old, of course, to stay here, but this is my home and I will draw my last breath within its walls.' He stared fiercely at the blonde woman – as though she were one of the 'everyone' – as she set down the poker on the hearth and exited the room again as silently as she had entered.

'Well, they can hardly blame you for feeling that,' Allegra murmured. 'I think I would feel the same. Wouldn't you, Iz?'

Isobel gave a polite shrug. The memory of their mother bitterly resisting being moved out of their family home – her tears and desperate pleas – was still far too fresh in both their minds.

'You love your home too,' he said to Allegra, his eyes on her again.

Allegra nodded, to be polite, but she wasn't sure where home was – certainly not the flat in Poplar, which was still little more than student digs, certainly not the house in Islington, which was a financial investment and nothing more, and certainly not the orange-doored flat that protected her mother. Isobel's maybe – when Lloyd was at work or out with the boys and it was just her and Iz and Ferds?

He cocked his head to the side slightly, regarding her with an inscrutable expression, and she wondered whether it was her he saw or Valentina. 'Tell me about your mother.'

Allegra straightened her spine a little. It never got easier saying the words out loud; the guilt was as bad now as it had been then. 'The best mother we could have ever asked for. Intensely loving and protective. She always did her best for us.'

Lars stiffened, picking up the past tense immediately, his mind clearly still pin-sharp. 'She's dead?' His voice trembled.

'No! No. I'm sorry. I didn't mean to make you think—'

'So she is here?' The urgency in his voice betrayed the emotion behind the question. 'She has come to bury her mother?'

Allegra shook her head. 'She doesn't know about any of this. She has Alzheimer's . . .' She hesitated. Did that translate? But she saw his face change and knew he understood. She fell quiet, understanding the impact of her words: within minutes of bringing hope of reuniting him with his daughter, she was pulling it away again like a child playing a cruel trick.

His expression folded inwards, growing smaller. 'What . . . ? When did it start?'

'Six years ago. It was early onset.' Allegra rubbed her lips together at the memories — her mother's sudden violence when she couldn't find the jam in the fridge, only for it to turn up in the dishwasher, her overnight clumsiness that saw cups of tea dropped straight to the ground as she missed the table by clear gaps, her excitable chatter in a girlish voice that harked from the past . . . 'We kept her at home as long as we could. I tried moving back in with her, but I travel a lot and work long hours and just couldn't be around enough. We tried a care home, but she was so devastated about being put in there.' Allegra exhaled, trying to steady her breath. It made her angry even now, when she remembered the call from the police saying she had escaped from the home and had been seen walking on the motorway slip road. 'She's in an assisted-living complex now, with her own nurse.'

Lars was quiet for a long moment as he looked into the flames of the fire. 'It isn't right that she should be so young . . .' His words trailed away, but his hand tightened round the arm of the chair.

'Please don't be distressed. In her own way, she's happy. Her nurse is the very best, and she herself isn't aware of the confusion most of the time. It's me and Iz who . . .' She cleared her throat. 'Well, we're the ones who have to adapt. Very often she doesn't know who we are and we . . . you know, just have to accept it as part of the disease. But at least she's not frightened herself. That would be worse.'

'You are too young to lose your mother in this way.'

She was quiet for a moment, staring down at her hands. 'There's never a right time, though, is there?' She realized their loss was mutual – they had all lost Julia too young, Isobel, Allegra and Lars.

'What about her husband?'

'Excuse me?' The question was like a bullet that she hadn't seen coming and she glanced across at Isobel, who looked like she'd taken the hit. 'Her husband,' Lars said, his eyes narrowing as he took in her reaction. 'Your father.'

'He . . . he left a long time ago.' Allegra clasped her hands together over one knee, the knuckles blanching.

His expression fell. 'When your mother fell ill?'

'Before then,' she nodded crisply, her voice suddenly distant and formal. 'He has another family.'

'And you have no contact with him,' Lars said, more as

a statement of fact as his eyes darted left and right, reading her and Isobel's body language.

'That's right.' Her chin was beginning to push up in the air, a habit from childhood when she'd thought that to tip her head back would be to force the tears back down. Gravity on her side.

He turned to the fire again, as though aware of the fragility of the ice he was walking on. 'She has suffered too much, my daughter.'

'No,' Allegra said quickly, too quickly. 'We were happy. We *are* happy. We didn't need him anyway. We had each other – me, Iz and Mum.' Her fingers found Isobel's and interlinked with them. 'Didn't we, Iz?'

Isobel looked up at her and Allegra saw the hollowness of her lie reflected in her sister's eyes. Yes, they had had each other, but they had been fatally diminished by his desertion, like a tree that had been too brutally lopped – still alive but no longer able to grow.

'And we had Granny too.' Isobel's voice rang out cold and steely and strong.

The blood drained from Lars's face. 'Who?'

'Granny.' Defiance clung to the word.

Allegra trod more softly. 'She means Anya. We grew up believing she was our grandmother.'

'Anya said she was . . . your grandmother?' Every word aged him.

Allegra nodded, watching him closely. The truth was somewhere in this room with them. 'Mum doesn't know yet that Valentina was her mother. We only discovered it ourselves last week, when the police traced us in England.'

'England.' A sound came deep from inside Lars's chest,

an expression coming into his eyes that would have seemed dangerous on a younger man.

'You didn't know that was where she went?' Allegra asked, her eyes scrutinizing his every move.

Lars shook his head.

'When we got the phone call, it was the first time we'd even heard Valentina's name. No one had ever mentioned her before—'

'Or you,' Isobel said, interrupting again, her every word a pushback against the new truth that made a liar of the only grandmother she had ever known and loved. 'We were told you had died when Mum was a toddler.'

He looked back at her, disbelief slackening his muscles. 'Anya said all that?'

Isobel paused, a look of regret on her features, and Allegra knew that she felt it too: caught between histories that had been lived out long before either of their first breaths.

Allegra looked back at the old man, who seemed to be withering under every word that told him he'd been forgotten, killed off, dispossessed . . . 'If we'd known you were still alive . . .' she began, but she ran out of words, not quite sure what *to* say next – for what would they have done? Visited? Stayed with the man Anya had left? Reunited the father with his adult child?

She watched as he lifted his head, stretching his neck like a dog, so that the skin stretched tight against his frame once more. Was he, like her, trying to make the tears drop back too? Was this something they shared? A small genetic quirk that carried over the generations, even through sixty years' isolation from one another?

'Why did she leave here?' Her words were careful.

'Here', not 'you'. Without accusation, without judgement . . .

The words tiptoed across the space between them, trying to build a bridge that spanned those lost years, reconnecting them all again. Only answers could heal the rift, and there was still time – just.

Lars rocked gently in the chair, his eyes far away, his mind in a distant land, and for a long time, he didn't even try to speak.

'She was jealous,' he said finally. 'Valentina was the love of my life; there was no hiding it. I could not! She was the kind of woman who breaks a man with her beauty, her passions. She was strong, not of her time, and certainly she did not belong to the farming life. Every man wanted her, the richest, the strongest, the married . . .' His eyes lit up faintly as the reflected flames leaped higher. 'Why she ever chose me . . . She was dazzling. No dress was beautiful until she wore it, no joke was funny till she laughed at it.' He looked back at Allegra with the eyes of a young man. 'Are you loved like that?'

She swallowed. How many people were? 'No.'

'That surprises me. You are beautiful like her and clever too, I can tell.'

She smiled weakly, not sure what to say, embarrassed that all his attention was on her. Did Isobel see that he looked at her and saw ghosts?

'Women like you don't know the power you have over men. I was a – how would you say? – vigorous man in my youth. Handsome, strong, ambitious. I knew I had to excel for her, be even more than what I was born to be. And I tried. I wanted to be the man she deserved. But when she died, my world was broken, as well as my heart.' He shook his head, his fingers blanched as he clawed the armrests. 'Poor, sweet Giulia. I was no father to her. I could not feed myself, could not eat . . . so when Anya moved in to help . . .' He fell quiet, drawing his lips together like a threaded purse. 'It seemed logical after a while that we should marry. She and Giulia were close, and, well . . . Valentina had always teased me about Anya's infatuation with me . . . I couldn't love her in the way that I had Valentina, but I thought we could be happy enough.' He shrugged again, a helpless gesture. 'I was wrong. She didn't want to live her life as second best.'

'*That's* why she took your daughter?' Isobel said, accusation in every word, as though the fault was his.

He looked at her. 'Yes.'

Isobel's mouth dropped open. She hadn't expected him to concur. 'How could you just let her get away with it?'

'Because it was the best thing for Giulia.'

'To be raised on a *lie*?' Her voice was growing shrill, a sure sign that she was on the way to losing it.

'To be raised by a woman who loved her. Farming is a hard life. I spent most of the year out of the town, on the pastures with the herd. How could I do that alone with a child? It was my livelihood, the only way I knew to make money to survive.'

'But how could you survive losing the woman you loved *and* your child?'

He didn't reply, but picked up his coffee with hands that trembled slightly, and Allegra discreetly put her hand on Isobel's arm – a plea for caution.

But to no avail.

'Well, you're obviously not a farmer now,' Isobel said drily, gesturing to the decorous chalet.

'No, that is true. When the tourism began, I sold the farm and developed some properties. Even became town mayor for a while.' He cleared his throat. 'And I know what you are thinking – I had money by then, yes, but it was too late. Even if I had known where Anya and Giulia were living, I had no way of knowing whether Anya had remarried, had children . . . I would be a stranger to my own child. All I could be certain of was that Giulia was safe with her. Anya loved her as much as any real mother loves her child.'

They were all quiet, only the crackle of the fire between them.

'She never remarried,' Allegra said quietly, trying to mitigate her sister's harsh scorn. In protecting their grandmother, Isobel was attacking him. Couldn't she see he had clearly suffered enough? The man looked broken by their news. 'And she did love our mother, very much. They were extremely close.'

A spark flew from the fire, landing on the granite hearth, and he watched as it sizzled, twisted and extinguished before them, but Allegra couldn't take her eyes from him: the poor man who had become rich, the loved man who had been forgotten, the father who had ended up alone. What had their grandmother done?

She sat forward slightly on the seat, clasping her hands around her half-full cup. 'I've spoken to Father Merete. He's agreed to conduct a private memorial for Valentina on Thursday.' Isobel gave a small gasp beside her, but Allegra just kept her eyes on him. 'Will you come?'

'What are you doing?' Isobel whispered furiously.

'He's Valentina's widower. He deserves to be there.'

Allegra kept her voice to as low a murmur as she could manage.

'And Granny's too, remember. He married them both, or have you forgotten that?'

'You heard him. He was trying to build another family for Mum.'

Isobel rolled her eyes and sat back furiously in the cushions, making her feelings perfectly plain.

Allegra turned back to Lars with an embarrassed smile. 'Please.'

He looked back at her with reddened eyes, gratitude on his face. 'It is the goodbye I have both dreaded and longed for . . . Thank you, I will be there.'

Allegra smiled, feeling something inside her strengthen. They had been right to come here – Isobel would see that when she had had time to cool off. 'We should go,' she murmured, setting her cup down on the tray and smoothing non-existent wrinkles from her trousers.

Isobel followed with impolite haste.

'Wait.' He beckoned Allegra over to him, taking her hand in his – which were marbled hot and cold – and looking up at her gratefully. 'Will you come back tomorrow? We can talk some more. There is so much still to be said. I am an old and lonely man. I want to know my family before I die.'

'Of course we'll come,' she smiled, making sure to include Isobel in the invitation. 'This time tomorrow?'

He released her hand with a satisfied sigh, falling back in the chair as though a cushion that had propped him up had been suddenly whipped away.

The nurse appeared at the door. Had she been listening in? Her timing was too perfect.

Allegra and Isobel followed her out to the front door, collecting their jackets from the pegs and shrugging them on in silence as Bettina held the lift doors open. Allegra stepped in after Isobel, turning and staring back into the hall with a growing giddy delight. She watched as the doors closed on the expensive portrait of a woman who, with every new fact, seemed to be explaining Allegra to herself. She had always been the black sheep in the family – too dark, too stubborn, too proud, too awkward compared to her mother and sister's fair-haired sensitivity and easy smiles. She'd never had a feel for those softer social skills that came so easily to Isobel. She'd never had a knack for making people laugh or holding a room as she told a story. Allegra dealt only in logic, black-and-white facts, mathematical reasoning, abstract concepts with immutable rules. To Allegra, something was either right or wrong, good or bad, and even as a thirteen-year-old girl she'd known, standing on the grass, that her father wasn't supposed to be having a picnic with that family.

She had often wondered how different things might have been if it had been Isobel, and not her, in the park that day when she saw them all together for the first time and realized the truth. Would Isobel have been able to make him stay? Certainly, she'd always thought so. He had chosen the wrong daughter to save them. But at last she had found her people. If she was her grandmother's image, she was also her grandfather's pupil. The parallels between them were obvious: like her, Lars had achieved great success; like her, Lars had endured devastating personal loss; like her, Lars needed a family again. Isobel had her own, her mother had her past, but Allegra was every bit as alone as the old man in a chalet who had been written out of their history because of a broken heart.

They stepped back out into the snow, both casting around the elegant entrance with new eyes. A goat farmer? A care home? Ha! Isobel's shoulders were stiff, but Allegra had to bite back a smile as they walked briskly towards the street. Finally, her own ambition was understood. For the first time in her life, finally *she* made sense.

Chapter Twenty-Two

'We need a drink,' Allegra said, catching up with Isobel. She had been walking a half-stride ahead the whole way up the side street.

'No. I just want to go home.'

'Even more reason why we need a drink. Come on. There's a pub just over there,' she said, pointing to the Brown Cow and bullishly leading Isobel by the arm.

It was falling dark now. Their back-to-back 'meetings' had eaten through the afternoon, and the snow glowed with a blue tint as the sky lit up in an ultraviolet haze.

They pushed through the doors and Allegra quickly ordered some *génépy* as Isobel grabbed a leather sofa by the windows overlooking the street.

'Well . . . cheers,' Allegra said, holding up her glass.

Isobel stared at her moodily. 'What on earth is there to celebrate?'

'We're not celebrating. We're just having a drink. It's what people do, isn't it?' Allegra said, quickly taking a sip.

Isobel scowled. 'You are totally celebrating.'

Allegra sighed. 'Well, it's not every day you meet your only grandfather. You can't deny it's . . . exciting.'

'Oh, I can and I will!' Isobel said huffily. 'How dare he

say all those things about Granny when she isn't here to defend herself!'

'But he didn't say anything bad about her. In fact, I thought he was very measured. It sounds like he was a wreck after Valentina died and he obviously genuinely believed Mum was better off with her – whatever it may have cost *him*.'

'Oh, come on, Legs! You honestly buy that?'

'Why wouldn't I?' Allegra protested. 'Iz, the simple fact is, Granny *did* take off with her sister's child and she kept that fact a secret all her life. Now, I know she loved Mum as much as we do, but her silence is damning, however you look at it. I think Lars's account of things is very . . . generous under the circumstances.'

'You're just riding high because he clearly preferred you. You look like Valentina, and I look like Granny, and if you ask me, it seems his affections for them have transferred to us.'

'*That* is ridiculous. I am simply trying to find some sort of positive from all of this. We can't change what happened. It's nothing to do with either one of us. But, Iz' – she twisted position on the chair so that their legs were angled together – 'we've met Mum's dad! Imagine telling her that. Imagine telling her that he's still alive.'

'Yeah,' Isobel said crossly. 'Just imagine telling her that. Barry would have a stroke coping with the fallout.'

'That's not fair.'

'No. None of this is. We've spent all afternoon being bombarded with one bombshell after another and I feel like someone's just beaten me up.' She slumped further down the seat. 'I knew it was a bad idea.'

Allegra dropped her head back on the sofa, feeling her

temporary euphoria ebb away. It was too exhausting staying positive. Besides, Isobel was right – telling their mother
about Lars came with as many, if not more risks attached as
telling her about Valentina. She threw her arm over her
head and closed her eyes, wishing they hadn't come here,
wishing they were back in the apartment and she was running a hot, foamy bath.

Isobel glanced across at her, biting her lip anxiously.
'Gah, I'm sorry, Legs! Ignore me. I'm being a bitch!' Isobel
winced, remorsefully laying her head on her sister's shoulder. 'I'm not as resilient as you. I never cope well with
change.'

'No, you're right.' Allegra sighed after a while. 'I'm the
one getting carried away with fantasy scenarios that can
never happen. I guess I'm just so desperate for something
to go right for a change . . . It's been a bad couple of weeks,
that's all.'

Isobel rested her chin on Allegra's shoulder, looking up
at her guiltily. 'Come on, let's have another drink. We
should get wasted.'

Allegra looked at her sister from the corner of her eye.
'That's always your answer.'

'I know – because it works,' Isobel said with a wink, getting up and heading towards the bar.

Allegra watched her go, hoping it was true what they
said about hair of the dog. She'd never tried it herself –
ordinarily she never did 'drunk', much less two nights on
the trot – but she was thirty-one years old and this was a
new first for her.

A commotion outside travelled to her ear and she rolled
her head to the side to look out of the window. A herd of
people – lots of whom were children and all of whom were

dressed in full kit with skis over their shoulders – were following after a Father Christmas figure who was walking with a brisk, distinctly athletic gait and had clearly been padded out with pillows. He too had skis over one shoulder, and over the other, a filled hessian sack.

She glanced at her watch. Seven thirty. The last lifts had closed three hours ago . . .

Her eyes widened. 'Oh, Iz! Stop!'

Isobel turned round, clearly mid-flow with the barman, as Allegra wove her way past the other drinkers towards her, both their jackets in her hands.

'Iz, there's night skiing on Klein Matterhorn,' Allegra grinned as she pushed her arms through her ski jacket and handed Isobel hers. 'Come on! They've got a Father Christmas leading everyone down. We always said we'd do it, but we never have.'

'But . . .' Isobel looked at the barman, who was holding a bottle mid-air. 'Hold that thought! We'll be back later.'

And with a laugh, the two of them burst through the doors like a gale.

Blue snow, purple shadows, a sky cut from jet paper that had been pierced with pinpricks as silvery light from far-away worlds shone through the holes. As the glittering lights of the town receded behind them, somewhere in the darkness, owls hunted in the silence, the gondola's bubble-shaped shadow passing over tightly tucked blankets of virgin snow, the larches and conifers looking sugar-sifted, their fronds drooping like moustaches.

At the top, the scene wasn't so unadulterated. There were at least a hundred people up there, half of them under ten and jostling to have their photo taken with Father

Christmas while their parents enjoyed a quick glass of *Glühwein* before their night ski. A St Bernard was lying on a rug, too, placidly keeping his muzzle to the ground as children leaned against him and tried to rattle the beer barrel on his collar.

Allegra and Isobel gave them all a wide berth. Isobel wasn't 'on duty' tonight and she instantly began shaking her arms out and doing side bends to warm up.

They took the first run slowly, slicing through the crisp night air with relaxed ease to find their ski legs again and judge the effect of the *génépy* on them. But on the second and third, they started to speed up, Isobel making Allegra laugh as she did all the tricks she'd mastered so easily as a child – skiing crouched down on her ankles, skiing backwards, making a jump out of every bump, positioning her poles like antlers on her helmet . . .

Allegra felt free again, up here – free from the split loyalties between her new family and old, which was beginning to threaten to divide her and Iz; free from the anxiety about when Pierre would make his next move.

'D'you know, I think we might squeeze in two more runs before they close the lifts. You're a lot faster than you used to be.' Isobel joshed her lightly as they relaxed momentarily in the bubble on the way back up.

'Gee, thanks. High praise indeed.' Allegra rolled her eyes, just as the doors slid open and they got up again, pulling their skis from the racks. 'Did it ever occur to you that I could take you now? We're not kids any more. I've skied more times than you've made Ferds hot dinners.'

'That's actually not saying much,' Isobel laughed. 'I only weaned him a few months ago.'

Allegra laughed too, clipping her skis on and pulling her goggles down off her helmet.

It had quietened down now that Father Christmas had led the children back onto the slope, and even the St Bernard was on his way back to his kennel in town. The temperatures were plummeting beneath the clear skies and the snow was quickly becoming icy.

'Come on, then. Let's race.' Allegra arched an eyebrow at her sister.

'Yeah?'

'Why not? It's good visibility, and the runs are almost empty. It's as good a time as any.'

'You're just saying that because you've had a bit of Dutch courage,' Isobel grinned. 'Go on, then. Do you want a head start?'

'Bitch,' Allegra couldn't help but laugh as they positioned themselves level. 'You ready?'

'Born ready.'

They pushed off, both coiled tight with competitive energy as they carved the snow with elongated S-bends, neither one wanting to lose time to turns, to take off the pace. Isobel was bent forward in a racing position, her body low, poles horizontal, but Allegra had been right – years of regular skiing had brought her almost level pegging with her naturally gifted sister, and as the angle of the slope steepened and they headed into the trees, she began to pull ahead.

Exhilaration from the familiar feeling of winning began to course through Allegra's veins as her sister's lean profile disappeared behind her. She had never once beaten her on the snow. Not ever. Not in ski-school competitions when the battle for gold was invariably between the two of them, and not when Isobel had tagged onto her university ski trip and promptly ensnared all the boys with her Heidi-esque cool-girl plaits and tricks wizardry in the snow park, which even they couldn't match.

She was fully ahead now, a clear distance between them, so that Isobel's progress was too far behind to be heard. 'Hey, Iz! Eat my snow!' she whooped, waving one pole in the air jubilantly as she eased into a few languid turns, showing off her advantage.

There was no reply.

'Iz?' she called behind her again.

Nothing.

Swooping to a sharp stop, she looked back up the slope with pink-cheeked breathlessness. 'Hey—' she began, her smile fading as she stared up the empty white expanse, unsettled only by her tracks.

'Iz? Iz!' She twisted, turning one way then the other, trying to find her sister in the trees that bordered the piste, but the globes that lit the run couldn't permeate the thick vegetation and nothing but silence came back to her. Her breath started coming quickly as panic rose.

Think, Allegra, think, she told herself, quelling the urge to scream. Her sister wasn't on the piste – that much she could see. So then she had to have gone into the trees. She must have found what she thought was a quicker line down. She was an expert off-pister. She could probably weave through the trees quicker than Allegra could bomb down a bashed run. She was probably at the bottom already!

Allegra looked downhill. She was maybe six minutes away from the foot.

On the other hand . . .

She looked up again. What if she'd fallen?

Checking her watch, she saw there was only four minutes till they closed the gondola for the night. At least if she stayed on the run, she could find her.

Slowly, she began sidestepping up the slope. It was steep – roughly fifty degrees, she estimated – but if she could make out her and Isobel's tracks before they'd diverged, she could follow her sister's route down.

Even moving as quickly as she could, she made slow progress, struggling to get an edge into the icy snow and slipping down five metres for every ten she gained.

'Iz!' she shouted, over and over, her breath coming hard, when over the ridge she suddenly saw a couple of figures coming down the run.

'Stop!' she shouted, waving her poles to get their attention. They both saw her, but misunderstood and the first one skied on to draw level with her. 'No! Stay there! Stop!' she screamed louder, pushing her hands in front of her to stop the other one from continuing down. 'Stay there!'

The skier now beside her held his hand up too and his friend further up came to an abrupt stop, sending a shower of snow onto the nearby trees.

'Oh God, thank you for stopping!' she cried, leaning on her poles, her thighs burning. 'It's my sister. She—'

'*Allegra?*' The skier pushed back his goggles and she found herself staring at the astonished face of Zhou Yong.

For once, she was glad to see him. 'Oh, thank God!'

He reached an arm out in concern. 'What's happened?'

'It's . . . it's my sister. She's disappeared. We were racing down here and I went in front, but when I called back, there was no reply. So I turned round and . . . she'd just gone.'

'Has she got her mobile on her?'

'Mobile!' she said with a gasp. Why hadn't she thought of that? Rummaging in her pocket with fumbling, clumsy hands, she pulled her phone out and quickly dialled the number.

It rang . . . and rang.

'She's not picking up,' she said with frightened eyes.

'It's OK. Let's just think. She must have gone in the trees, right?'

'That's what I thought. She's a brilliant skier. She'd be able to cut through them really quickly. And she'd do anything to beat me.'

'But you don't know which side she took?'

Allegra shook her head.

'That's OK. That's fine,' Zhou said, soothingly, clearly trying to keep her calm.

'What's going on?' the other skier called down to them.

Allegra heard the accent and knew who it was, although any reasonable process of elimination would have brought that conclusion too.

Zhou got out his phone and called Sam instead of shouting back. 'It's Allegra's sister . . . Yeah. She thinks she's gone into the trees, but she's not picking up her phone . . . Yeah, OK.'

He disconnected. 'Sam's going to take the left side. He says it meets up with the piste about a hundred metres down. We're to go down to the bottom together and meet him there, check she's not already waiting for you.'

'If she is, I'll kill her,' Allegra said with gritted teeth and a tremor in her voice.

'If she's not and Sam doesn't find her, we'll get the

authorities to send out some skidoos. It'll be fine. We'll find her.'

'OK,' she nodded, so grateful to have someone else taking charge. Her mind felt such a jumble at the thought of something happening to Iz.

'Come on, let's get down.'

'She'll be down there. I know she will,' Allegra murmured to herself as she wrapped her pole straps round her wrists again. 'She'll wonder what I'm making such a fuss about. I always call her our health-and-safety officer. It really winds her up, you know, because she's so precious about her little boy . . . I'll never hear the end of this . . .'

She knew she was rambling, but she couldn't stop, and Zhou didn't try to stop her. They pushed off, taking the rest of the run slowly, peering into the trees all the way as Allegra berated herself, lips moving, for ever having suggested the race in the first place. What had been *wrong* with her? What had she been thinking, trying to beat her sister at the only thing she had ever bested in?

It was alarmingly quiet at the bottom, with almost no one around – just a bus half full of skiers waiting to take the last stragglers back to the centre of town. Isobel wasn't in it – Allegra personally checked – and she still wasn't answering her phone.

'Anything from Sam?' she asked, walking back to him, worry beginning to deepen on her features again.

'He's not picking up – but that's probably a good thing,' he said quickly. 'It means he's skiing and can't hear his phone. Don't worry – if your sister's up there, Sam's the man to find her. He's disgustingly good.'

'Maybe we should tell the authorities. Look, they've

closed the lift now. They'll all be going soon and she'll be left up there . . .' Her voice had risen an octave.

Zhou reached into his pocket and took out a hip flask. 'Here – take a sip. It's whisky. It'll help with the shock.'

Allegra did as she was told. And then some, taking three large gulps.

'He'll either be down in a minute or he'll ring,' Zhou said, staring into the trees. 'Let's just hold our nerve for a little while longer.'

'OK, OK,' Allegra murmured, stamping her feet to stay warm and staring back up the run with grim desperation.

The minutes dragged past, Allegra glancing back at Zhou with increasing frequency. 'Where is he? He should be here by now.'

'He will be.' But the situation was looking worse by the minute.

'Look!' she gasped, pointing as several figures appeared like black dots on the piste. But there were too many of them – four, five.

'No, I think it's the last of the staff coming down,' Zhou said, a note of despondency even in his voice.

'Right, that's it!' Allegra said. 'We're reporting this now. My sister's still up there and everyone's going home for the ni—'

Just then the headlights of a skidoo crested the drop and shone down the run, highlighting the skiers ahead and gaining on them.

'Oh God, they found her!' she whispered, her hands folding over her heart as the figures advanced rapidly towards them. 'She's been hurt.'

'I can see Sam,' Zhou said, evident relief in his voice as distinguishing colours became visible.

Allegra saw the red and black kit too and she ran towards him as he slid to a stop and clicked out of his skis. 'Where was she? What happened?' she demanded.

Sam pushed his goggles back up onto his helmet and looked down at her. 'She's OK. Just twisted her knee, I think. But you were right – she took a fall in the trees. I managed to get her down to the piste just as the organizers were going past. She's—'

'Oh God, Iz!' Allegra said, rushing over as the skidoo drew level. 'You gave me a bloody heart attack!'

'Sorry,' Iz grimaced, looking sheepish.

'No, no, I'm just so glad you're OK,' Allegra said, throwing her arms around her neck. She pulled back and looked at the driver. 'Thank you so much for bringing her down.'

He shrugged, looking not quite so pleased as Allegra. 'We could not leave her there, obviously. Although it was foolish for her to have gone off-piste *in the dark*.'

He shot a look at Isobel and Allegra suspected she'd already had a serious telling-off. 'What do I owe you? How can I settle up?'

The driver went to reply, but Zhou interrupted. 'Allegra, the most important thing right now is to get your sister warm and have a doctor look at her knee. My driver's just over there. Sam will help her into the car. Let me deal with this.' He put a gentle hand on her arm.

'But—'

'No buts. Just help Sam.'

Allegra nodded obediently again, so grateful for Zhou's calm authority. She grabbed Isobel's skis and poles from the skidoo and tried to catch up with them. Isobel had slung her arm around his shoulder and was groaning with discomfort as he helped her hop her way over to the Yong 'limo' – one of the town's caterpillar-tracked taxis, but with blacked-out windows.

Isobel took one look at it and twisted back to her sister with a grin. 'Cool!' she beamed.

'Home, sweet home.'

Allegra looked across at Zhou as he motioned for her to exit the taxi first. It was clear he had a sense of humour. The chalet was many things – opulent, overscaled, no doubt overpriced – but sweet it wasn't. She waited as he followed after her. The roof line was etched out against the silky sky with pinprick white lights, but it seemed almost laughable to her that the chalet's silhouette needed to be picked out at all – the entire frontage of the chalet had been built in glass and plumes of golden light radiated from the building like atmospheric gold.

Unlike a lot of the other chalets, where the approach was from above, this one had its own private funicular hidden behind a reinforced door and Isobel winked at her as Sam helped her hop to the lift. Clearly the rich couldn't be expected to climb stairs.

'How are you feeling?' Zhou asked Isobel, as the men graciously settled her on the bench seat, taking care of her skis and poles for her.

'Better, actually,' Isobel nodded, perking up with every passing moment. 'Thanks *so* much for helping me out, Sam. I don't know what I'd have done if you hadn't been passing.' Isobel looked up at him with big doe eyes, which Allegra had seen put to use many times before.

'Well, it was Allegra who—'

'I know,' Isobel sighed happily. 'She's a doll. So protective.'

Sam's eyes met Allegra's briefly, but they both looked away just as quickly, and she wondered whether he too was remembering what had happened the last time they'd shared a lift. It all seemed so long ago now, but it had been barely over a fortnight . . .

The doors opened onto a vaulted hall of knotty, almost marled oaks that had variegated tones of caramel, blond, grey and ash streaking along the boards like waves. Overhead, chunky oak beams crossed the ceiling, more like decorative lattice-work than structural pinnings, and discreetly positioned low-lit halogen spots created almost as artistic an effect on the walls as the priceless works of art they were illuminating. A life-size black-bronze sculpture of a snow leopard was set on a jet mantel and she couldn't help but brush her fingers over it as they passed.

'Allegra, Isobel, this is Martin, the chef, and his wife, Estelle, our housekeeper. Any problems, she'll get them sorted for you.'

'Hi!' Isobel said excitedly, hopping past with Sam's help again, as Allegra nodded in silence to the smiling couple standing in the doorway of the kitchen and wearing matching all-black trousers and shirts. They followed Zhou into the drawing room.

It was double height, but here the roof was glass – let the sky come to them! – as well as the walls, and the overall effect of three huge ivory sofas draped with white fur throws and a giant white sheepskin rug on the floor, whose pile came up to their ankles, was of a captured snowdrift. Overhead, a trio of cylindrical crystal chandeliers dangled from the rafters, throwing out a flattering dappled light. On every console – mainly red lacquered and no doubt priceless artefacts from Imperial China – were pictures of the family: Mr Yong standing stiffly in front of a mine; Mr and Mrs Yong standing next to Indian steel magnate Lakshmi Mittal and his wife, Usha, in formal dress; Zhou wearing his Harvard colours and standing in the same guarded pose his father favoured – his arms hanging, hands flat against his thighs, military fashion – as people in the background could be seen grabbing hands and back-slapping each other.

A limestone chimney had a fire set and already lit behind a glass panel, and outside on the veranda, she could see teak loungers draped with reindeer hides. She walked to the window as though magnetically drawn. The view over Zermatt from here was superb – the brooding silhouette of the Matterhorn was framed almost perfectly by the gabled windows, the peak of the mountain seemingly nestling within the peak of the glass, and Zermatt lay between their two points, sprinkled before and below them like an earth-bound galaxy. This was how billionaires played.

'Come and lie down here,' Zhou said, rearranging some cushions as Sam helped lower Isobel onto the plush sofa. 'How does that feel?'

'Fine,' she grinned, her eyes practically popping out of her head at the sight of the sumptuous chalet.

'The doctor's already on his way,' Zhou said, hovering over her anxiously and clearly wondering what else he could do. 'I'd offer you a drink, but I think until the doctor's assessed you . . .'

'Oh, totally. Listen – that view? That alone is healing. I can feel my leg getting better already.'

Zhou laughed, almost shyly, and Allegra looked at him as though seeing him for the first time. She had never considered him as anything other than a client, his father's son, one of the signatories of a fund that would enable her to invest and trade and analyse and play all the games that made up how she passed her days. He had just been a suit and formal manners in his father's company. (Although, hadn't she too?) Here, though, she saw he was kind, considerate, gracious and sweet. He was modest and understated – nothing in his clothes or demeanour gave away his billionaire status – and apparently in possession of a good sense of humour. He was good-looking too – with flawless skin and a light bone structure, his chin square but relieved by finely carved cheekbones when he smiled – which he seemed to do a lot.

Sam had taken off his jacket and was prowling by the windows in his black ski pants and a thermal top that seemed to trace every muscle – at least, it did under the lights.

Isobel caught Allegra's eyes and, jerking her thumb towards his turned back, mouthed: 'Bloody hell! Phwoar!'

Allegra glanced at Zhou, hoping he hadn't seen her sister's indiscretion, but from the trace of a smile on his lips knew he had.

She rolled her eyes, hoping he wouldn't think she shared her sister's wildly misguided opinion, but Zhou just smiled more openly. 'So, where are you staying?'

'Down by the Mont Cervin. Off one of the backstreets.'

'It's a really cute apartment,' Isobel said. 'I mean, nothing like this, but . . .'

Allegra shot her sister another look, wishing she'd stop fawning over the Yongs' place.

'It's such a surprise seeing you here. I mean, you said you'd never been here before and yet . . .' Zhou had the grace to look apologetic, remembering the fallout from the conversation.

'Here we are, yes.'

'Can I ask what . . . ?'

'Personal business,' Allegra said quickly. Sam had stopped pacing at the window and was listening in, and she wondered whether he remembered Kirsty delivering Sergeant Annen's message outside Pierre's office.

'Oh, I see,' Zhou said, too discreet to press further, and Allegra had no intention of elaborating. They didn't need to know the details of—

'We just found out our grandmother's from here,' Isobel piped up from her resplendent position on the sofa. 'She's dead though!'

'Iz!'

'Allegra?' Isobel retorted with an innocent look, knowing full well she was overstepping her sister's boundaries. 'What? It's not like it's a secret. It's in all the papers here.'

'Ugh!' Allegra said, throwing her arms in the air and beginning to pace too. Did her sister have no comprehension of when something was personal?

Sam waded in to the discussion. Of course he did.

'What happened?' he asked her, perching on the arm at the far end of the sofa.

'She disappeared in a snowstorm sixty years ago. It was a really famous tragedy apparently. Anyway, she died in an avalanche and they only just found her in this tiny little mountain hut.'

'Oh . . .' Sam and Zhou's eyes swept over to Allegra, but she had turned away and was pretending to look out across Zermatt.

'Mr Yong, the doctor is here,' an unfamiliar female voice said.

'Thanks, Estelle,' Zhou replied, Allegra turning to find him shaking the hand of a grey-haired man in a long grey overcoat. 'Dr Baden, this is my friend Isobel.'

Isobel visibly grew two inches at the words.

'She hurt her knee skiing this evening.'

'I see. Well, let's take a look, shall we?'

'We'll give you some privacy,' Zhou said, motioning for Allegra and Sam to leave with him.

'But—'

'She'll be fine,' Zhou smiled, beckoning her away from the sofa. 'Let's get a drink while we wait. And if you'd at least take off your coat, I'd personally feel a lot more relaxed.'

He shot her another of the easy smiles that she found so disarming and Allegra looked down at herself, unaware that she'd even left it on. It wasn't like they were staying.

'I'm going to shower and change,' Sam mumbled, disappearing with laidback familiarity into the chalet.

Zhou led Allegra into a smaller room at the back of the chalet – the study. The walls were lined with copper silk chinoiserie panels, and a fire was already flickering quietly, as though it had been awaiting their presence.

'Here,' he said, handing her a brandy.

She frowned, remembering the glass of *génépy* in the pub, the *Glüwein* on the piste, the whisky in his hip flask . . .

'I'm sorry to hear about your grandmother,' he said, perching on the edge of a vast partner's desk as she ambled vaguely around the room.

'Thanks,' she murmured.

'Will you be staying in Zermatt long?'

'Only until the memorial service on Thursday.'

'I see.' They were silent. 'And have you managed to get much skiing in?'

'Some. We've had to have a lot of meetings to finalize all the paperwork.'

'Yes. I can imagine.'

There was a small silence again.

'Listen, I—' he began.

'Really, there's no need,' she said quickly, already knowing what he was going to say.

'Please. I *want* to apologize. Things seemed to be . . .' He cleared his throat and she thought he looked embarrassed. 'They seemed to be taken out of context. I never wanted you to feel that '

'Really, it's fine. I'm a woman operating in a man's world. It's not the first time it's happened and I doubt it'll be the last.'

'No, I'm sure,' he said after a moment. 'I know it isn't easy being in the minority, especially in the circles we operate in.'

Her eyes flicked over to him. What did he know about it? How could this Harvard-educated son of a billionaire have any idea of the discrimination she encountered on a daily basis for daring to be not just a woman in a man's world, but a woman at the top of a man's world? He just smiled and nodded his glass towards her.

'But seeing as you're here now, I guess that means you can come to the party after all. It's tomorrow night.'

Allegra sighed. *Seriously?* Didn't he see there was absolutely no point at all in her going to his party now she wasn't even employed? Any debt his family had accrued with her was redundant. She couldn't use it for professional gain, and the deal was all but guaranteed to go to PLF, if it hadn't already. Surely Zhou's father waiting until the 18th was just a formality?

'Mr Yong—'

'Zhou.'

His correction made her feel foolish for addressing him so formally when he could only be a couple of years older than her. 'Zhou, you're very kind, but it's not really the time for me to be going to parties right now. My sister and I have to focus on getting our family affairs sorted at the moment.' It was a more diplomatic refusal than the one at the Christmas benefit, at least.

'Of course. I understand,' he agreed, lapsing into silence as he stared into his glass. 'Look, to be honest, I just wanted to give you a last opportunity to make a final bid before my father makes his decision.'

She blinked. 'I'm sorry, what?'

'My father is coming out here tomorrow evening and will be making his announcement on the 18th. I really think you should be here. You brought us to PLF's door, and if my father awards the contract to them, it should be you taking the credit.'

Allegra stiffened. 'OK, two things: one, I've quit, so PLF is no longer my problem, nor am I theirs; secondly, your father has made his feelings about dealing with a woman perfectly clear. Sam's the face of the team now.'

'Sam is too close a friend for my father to see him objectively. It is not necessarily a benefit for PLF to have Sam doing the negotiations. Maybe Pierre doesn't realize that?'

She was too female, and Sam was too friendly? 'Your father is a very complicated man, Zhou,' she said archly.

'He is old guard, yes. It's hard to persuade him some-times to accept new ways – especially in our dealings with the West – but I have done it before and I can do it now. Allegra, yours was the best pitch.'

'But I'm not going back to PLF.' Her lip trembled as she remembered Pierre's text. How could he have said those things to her?

'Then win the deal for your new employers,' he said easily. 'You must be speaking to people already.'

She didn't reply. Red Shore had left six messages now. They were the biggest in the market. It made perfect sense for her to return their call . . .

'And Sam told me you have a new proposal that you never presented to the board and won't give him.'

'That's right,' she said defiantly. 'Why should I? He's benefitting enough from my work. I don't owe any of them anything.'

'I completely agree. And if you've put together some-thing even better than before, frankly the deal could be awarded to you *personally*. You could pretty much demand a board seat wherever you wanted . . . Or set up on your own like your mentor did . . . We both know that under the right manager, this could be a starter fund. My father might be open to that.'

She looked at him in bewilderment – it was like he had tapped into all her innermost dreams. 'Why are you doing this? Sam's your friend. He trusts you.'

'This is business, Allegra. We're talking about eighty hundred and ninety million pounds. It's about who's best for the job.'

She stared at him, adrenalin beginning to make her hands shake. It was too much to take in – the deal, not just revived but offered up as a golden hello? Her own company . . .

'So your father's coming tomorrow evening?'

'Yes, he's flying in for the party.'

Zhou narrowed his eyes, his voice low and cajoling. 'Come on, Allegra. We both know you're not a quitter. The bid doesn't stop here.'

A knock at the door made them both turn.

'Mr Yong, Dr Baden is just leaving,' Estelle said.

'Ah, right,' Zhou said, motioning for Allegra to lead the way.

'It's a knee strain, quite nasty,' the doctor said, meeting them in the hallway. '*Possibly* there's some damage to the anterior cruciate ligament, but we won't be able to tell until the swelling starts to go down. She'll need to have an MRI scan at some point. In the meantime, I've stabilized it and applied a knee cuff with cooler, but she really mustn't move for the next forty-eight hours. And the leg should be kept elevated at all times. I've given her a prescription for some strong painkillers too.'

'Thank you so much, Dr Baden,' Allegra said, shaking his hand. 'Let me give you my contact details for your invoice.'

'No, Allegra, it's fine,' Zhou said quietly, patting her shoulder as he walked past. 'Dr Baden works on retainer for our family. It's all covered.'

'Oh.' That was the second time he'd paid for her this evening. Little by little he was wriggling out of the debt his family owed her.

She watched for a moment while the two men talked in lowered voices by the front door as Dr Baden shrugged on his coat. Then she hurried back into the sitting room, where

Isobel was lying with her leg elevated on a pile of cushions, taking photos of the chalet on her phone.

'Iz! What the hell are you doing?' Allegra hissed, breaking into a run, snatching the phone off her and instantly deleting them.

'Hey! I wanted to show Lloyd. I just rang him, told him what's going on. He said he wanted to see this place.'

'Iz, this is their private home. You can't start sharing it around with people.'

Isobel pouted. 'Lloyd is not "people".'

'No, I know *that*, but what if he shares it with someone at work and then they share it with someone else?' She could well imagine Lloyd showing off.

Isobel gave a little sigh but didn't protest further.

'How are you feeling?' Allegra asked, sitting herself on the edge of the sofa.

'A bit idiotic, to be honest.'

'You gave me such a fright.'

'I'm sorry. Really I am. I just . . . slightly lost it. I couldn't believe you were beating me.'

Allegra smiled. 'I'd never have beaten you to the bottom. We both know that! I just had a lucky streak for a bit, that was all.'

Isobel's eyes moved onto someone behind her and her smile brightened. 'Ah, my hero!' Her voice lowered to a – for once – scarcely audible whisper. 'Christ, he's gorgeous. Are you blind or what?'

Allegra got up from the sofa, staring with ill-concealed disdain at Sam. He had changed into jeans and a camel-coloured Nordic jumper, his hair still wet, and it was true he did look depressingly good. But she didn't give a damn about that. Any gratitude she had felt towards him earlier for rescuing Iz had been replaced once more by her usual contempt – she would never forgive him for what he had made Pierre do, and Zhou had just handed her the perfect opportunity for revenge . . .

Zhou came back into the room. 'Well, that's all sorted, then.'

'What is?'

'Dr Baden has said Isobel mustn't be moved, so Estelle's just preparing the guest suites for you both.'

'What? No!' Allegra cried, at the exact moment Isobel exclaimed: 'Great!'

'It's no problem, and frankly, some female company would be a welcome boost. There are far too many men in this house. I'm not sure I can cope with any more arm-wrestling.'

Allegra watched in panic as he walked to the low pock-eted ottoman in the middle of the room and pulled a bottle of champagne from the ice bucket.

'Zhou, we couldn't possibly impinge on your hospitality any more than we already have,' she said, walking towards him there. 'Our apartment isn't even ten minutes away. If we can just call a cab, we'll be out of your hair in no time and Isobel can rest up there. I'm sure it won't matter for her leg to be down for a few minutes.'

Zhou looked up at her. 'On the contrary, Dr Baden was adamant that for the best chance of recovery, her leg must be elevated, quote, at all times, unquote.'

'This is silly,' she half laughed, just as the cork popped softly and Zhou began to pour.

A young girl, dressed all in black like Estelle, came over to Allegra. 'May I take your coat for you, Miss Fisher?'

'Legs, it's important we do everything right,' Isobel said

behind her. 'The doctor said this is the "acute healing phase", and I do think I'd be happier taking a more . . . conservative approach, for these first two days at least.'

Allegra looked down at Isobel crossly, knowing full well her sister just wanted to stay in the chalet.

'Zhou,' she heard Sam protest, but Zhou was already holding out a glass of champagne to her. She looked over at Sam and saw the same resistance in his expression as hers. They couldn't even share a mountain. How the hell were they supposed to share a chalet?

'It's just a couple of days, Allegra,' Zhou shrugged, a conspiratorial look in his eye reminding her his father was back tomorrow. 'Where's the harm?'

Her and Sam Kemp living together under one roof? She knew exactly where the harm was – but she handed her jacket over anyway.

Chapter Twenty-Three

Her bedroom was vast: cerulean hand-painted walls with a bed covered in ivory cashmere and mother-of-pearl furniture. As for Isobel's room across the hall, upholstered as it was in baby-blue velvet with coral accents, Allegra was quite seriously concerned her sister might never leave.

She smiled politely as Zhou pointed everything out to her, while Sam and Isobel chatted upstairs. The very thought of it made her wince. What were they talking about? She knew well enough that it would be no idle chatter on either's part – Sam would be asking targeted questions about her; Iz would be finding out his romantic history.

'Mine and my family's rooms are on the top floor, but Kemp's room is next to yours, Massi's is opposite, and—'

'Uh, wait,' she said. 'Who's Massi?'

Zhou smiled again; it made him look ten years younger. 'Nothing to do with work – don't worry. He's another friend from Harvard. He was meeting up with a business contact for a drink this evening, but he should be back any minute. You'll like him. This week is all about having some fun before my parents arrive.'

Allegra looked at him in surprise. Coming from someone as controlled as him, the comment was fabulously indiscreet, but whether he had intended it to be or not, he carried on with the tour without missing a beat and she was left feeling more confused than ever by this strange blurring of the professional and personal boundaries between them. 'And just through this door here is the hammam and massage room,' he said, opening a door wide enough for her to glimpse an all-marble room with bench seats built into the wall and an arched ceiling. 'There's a selection of new, tags-on swimwear in the cupboard to the left there. Heidi Klein, is it?' he said in anticipation of her protest that she hadn't brought anything suitable.

'And across here,' he said, crossing the hall, 'are the pool and gym.' He opened one of a set of double oak doors onto a glittering turquoise pool with a teardrop chandelier hanging not five feet above the water and a mammoth screen filling the entire wall at the far end. 'Anything you want to watch, basically . . .' he murmured.

'Right,' she replied slowly, even though they both knew she wasn't going to be lying on a lilo watching *Celebrity Big Brother*.

They stepped back into the lift and moments later returned to the sitting room.

'Will everything be to my satisfaction, sis?' Isobel enquired in a lofty tone that made Zhou smile.

'I think we can safely say so, yes,' Allegra replied sardonically, while trying to detect from Kemp's body language alone what might have been said about her. But he simply sat on the opposite sofa to Isobel, one ankle slung over the opposite knee, his arm outstretched along the back, giving nothing away.

A little silence erupted and Allegra felt aware of Isobel

and Zhou's eyes moving between her and Sam. Her sister, she expected no better from – Sam was a man with a pulse – but Zhou . . . Had Sam told him about them?

The sound of sudden laughter made them both sit straighter in their seats as a man whom Allegra deduced had to be Massi sauntered in. He stopped dead in his tracks at the sight of the two sisters, still in their ski clothes – Estelle had despatched one of the chalet girls to pack up their things and bring them over from the apartment for them – being entertained.

'Massi, we've been waiting for you,' Zhou said. 'I want you to meet Allegra and Isobel Fisher. Allegra and Isobel, this is Massimo Bianchi.'

Allegra rose politely from her seat to shake his hand – Isobel clearly couldn't – but Massi crossed the room in three strides, planting his hands on Allegra's hips and holding her in front of him with an open-mouthed look of delight. 'My God!' he said with a lusciously thick, creamy Italian accent. 'She is so beautiful!'

Zhou sighed and gave her an apologetic shrug. 'Passionate temperament.'

'Uh . . . uh . . . a pleasure . . . Oh!' Allegra said, trying to shake his hand, but Massi, still with his hands on her hips, began to propel her round on the spot, like she was on a revolving pedestal.

'Beauty . . . classical beauty,' he pronounced. 'The bones, the height . . . Even, see how she stands . . .' Massi proclaimed.

'I *would* stand,' Isobel said, almost in protest, from her spot on the sofa, 'but I'm under doctor's orders not to.'

Massi, kissing the back of Allegra's hand with a crafty

wink, went to join her. 'Ah, you are Rose Red to your sis-ter's Snow White.'

Isobel preened happily. 'Pleased to meet you, Massi. But I'm afraid Zhou got my name wrong. I'm Isobel Watson. I'm married, but Allegra's single.'

'You are married? That I understand,' Massi tutted. 'But her? Single? I do not.'

'I know, right? It does my head in. Hundreds of men are in love with her, but she ignores them all. She will not get down off that shelf.'

'No,' Massi breathed sympathetically, looking back at Allegra. 'You are on the shelf?'

'Legs is totally on the shelf.'

Allegra closed her eyes in despair. Had her sister really just called her by her private, family nickname in front of her former colleague and client?

She opened her eyes and shot a glare in her sister's direction. 'Actually, I love the shelf. I want the shelf. The shelf is my favourite place to be,' Allegra said with a warn-ing note in her voice that only Isobel could hear. How on earth could she have made Allegra's marital status the topic of conversation within a minute and a half of talk-ing?

'Can you believe that?' Isobel asked, looking over at Sam, politely keeping him included in the conversation.

'Yes,' Sam said tersely, no hint of a smile, from his spot across the room.

Isobel arched one eyebrow interestedly and Allegra knew she wanted to probe further, but she was saved by Massi. Sort of.

'So you are models, yes?' Massi asked, making Isobel give a silent scream of delight.

Massi's face broke into a genuinely satisfied smile at the sight of Isobel's excitement. His hair was worn long over the ears and neck, crazy curls springing like spaniels' ears as he talked and flopping over his eyes, a small gold hoop in his ear winking at her sporadically. His features were rounded and soft, still retaining an impression of his boyhood self, and even as he spoke, his mouth stayed turned upwards in a smile.

'Have you locked the doors?' he mock-whispered to Zhou behind a cupped hand. 'Fast – lock the doors. I'll keep them talking. They never must leave.'

'You're crazy,' Isobel laughed. 'Like I'm going anywhere!'

Oh God, Allegra groaned inwardly. Peas in a pod.

'Damn, she is cute,' Massi grinned, spinning out the word like it was elasticated. He turned back to Allegra and she paused, her champagne flute frozen in mid-air as he shone the spotlight back on her. 'Thank God you are here.'

Allegra's eyes jumped from Massi to Sam to Zhou and back to Massi again. 'Why?'

'Terrible company, both of them. *He*' – he pointed to Sam with a sneer – 'has been in foul temper since we arrived, and *he*' – he pointed to Zhou – 'is unpressed about his parents coming back tomorrow night and clipping his wings.'

Allegra smiled at the way he pronounced 'clipping' as 'cleeping', but wondered what Sam had to be so miserable about. He was the new golden boy. He'd taken away from her everything she'd ever worked for. Wasn't that enough for him?

She tried to imagine his face two days from now, when he realized she'd stolen the deal from under his nose.

'Well, I won't be *de*pressed tomorrow night at the party,' Zhou said, sitting back in his armchair as one of the chalet girls came round with a plate of canapés. 'Oh, Clarice, can you tell Martin we'll eat on our laps tonight? To keep Isobel company.'

Allegra's phone buzzed. She pulled it from her trouser pocket and frowned as she saw Barry's number. She glanced at Isobel quickly and mouthed his name. 'Uh, sorry, I have to take this. If you'll just excuse me . . .' she murmured, hurrying from the room, Isobel's eyes on her back all the way.

'Barry?' she said, hoping she'd get good reception in the hall, but the walls were too thick – his voice warped and broken – and she quickly ran downstairs and out onto the terrace off her bedroom. 'Hello? . . . Oh, that's better! Is everything OK?'

'Hello, Legs,' his voice swam down the line. 'There's nothing to worry about. I was just calling in to see how everything's going out there.'

She sighed. 'Well, it was going fine until an hour ago, but Iz has just hurt her knee, so she's going to be laid up for a couple of days.'

'No!'

'Yes. I don't think it's serious, though. She's certainly in excellent spirits.' Understatement of the year.

'Oh good. And how about all the meetings?'

'So-so.'

'Oh, that doesn't sound too encouraging.'

'No, it is. We're finding out a lot. It's just that half the time it's things we'd rather not know.'

'Oh, Allegra.'

Upstairs, a whoop of laughter erupted, making her look

up, and she could just make out Massi's loping silhouette through the huge windows. 'We met Mum's dad today.'

There was a short silence. 'But I thought he died,' he said in a puzzled tone.

'So did we.'

'Oh! So what's he like, then?'

'Lovely, really. Bloody old, obviously, but sharp as a tack, and he's successful too. He wanted to know all about Mum and us. We're seeing him again tomorrow.'

'Oh, that's nice,' Barry said soothingly. 'I'm glad it went well.'

'Yes, me too. I was really in two minds about meeting him, but it was the right thing to do.' She swallowed, feeling nervous about asking the question that was already hanging from her lips. 'What chance do you think there is of telling Mum about him?'

There was a small silence. 'Well, if you'd asked me last week, I'd have said none. The move here really unsettled her, but she's been sleeping so much better since you put those Christmas decorations in her bedroom.'

'Christmas decorations?' Allegra echoed, puzzled.

'Yes, you know – the little wooden angel, the Mary with baby Jesus and whatnot.'

'Oh, those! They're just from an Advent calendar we found in the loft. I thought they might brighten the room up a bit for her.'

'Well, she loves that one of the Mary. She kisses it every night before she goes to sleep.'

'*Does* she?' The news thrilled her.

Barry chuckled. 'And she keeps saying the angel looks like me. I don't know whether to be complimented or offended. You should see the cheeks on that thing.'

Allegra laughed, delighted by the comedy echo. Hadn't she and Isobel said exactly the same about the one in Isobel's nativity set?

'Anyway, she says she remembers it from when she was little. It really seems to have struck a chord with her, I have to say. She's been talking non-stop about her childhood ever since.'

'What kinds of things?' Allegra felt her heart beating a little faster. 'Does she remember anything of her life here?'

'Who can say? It's all a bit of a muddle most of the time, but it's just snippets, you know. Little details here and there, like when her mam changed her hair from dark to blonde. And she was telling me this morning about a blue dress that had daisies embroidered on the chest and that she was only allowed to wear on Sundays, her favourite apparently. Do you remember when everyone had a Sunday best? Nobody does that any more.'

But Allegra wasn't listening. Her mother would have been four when she left Switzerland for the UK, too young to remember details like a Sunday-best dress surely? It must have been a memory from when she was older and living in England. Disappointment banged like a drum in Allegra's chest.

'Has she said anything that could be related to here?'

'Like what?'

'I don't know, like . . . being in a mountain hut or—'

Barry chuckled. 'Why would she have been in a mountain hut?'

'Her family were goat farmers. They owned loads of land in the valley apparently.'

'Oh! She was talking about a goat the other day,' Barry said excitedly.

Allegra felt her breath catch. 'And . . . ?'

She could hear Barry straining to give her the answers he knew she wanted to hear. 'It ate her lunch.'

Allegra smiled, the tension inside her dissolving. There would be no answers here. Her mother had been so young when she'd left, and—

'Oh, I remember she said there was a cuckoo clock she used to sit in front of and watch, waiting for the cuckoo to pop out, and it *always* made her cry, even though she knew it would be coming out any second.' He paused. 'Allegra? Are you there?'

'Yes, I—' It was hard to speak. She had just realized something. '*When her mam changed her hair from dark to blonde.*' Valentina's hair had been raven-black, Anya's strawberry blonde. The revelation brought tears to her eyes. Julia remembered Valentina. She remembered her mother!

'Oh, wait.' Barry's voice became muffled as she heard him talking to her mother in the background. 'I've got to go. Your mam's wanting her biscuits and I've had to hide them. She made me promise – she thinks she's getting too fat.'

'Yes, of course,' Allegra half laughed, sniffing as she wiped her eyes dry. 'Give her a kiss from us, won't you?'

'Always. Ta-ta.'

He hung up and Allegra leaned over the terrace, taking in the night view with a new feeling of levity. These were the moments that sustained her and she felt a new impetus to find out as much as she could about Valentina's past and why Anya had left.

A night breeze wrapped around her and she shivered as another bark of laughter erupted from the room upstairs.

She glanced up with a wry look. If she'd had any idea when she'd woken up this morning that she'd be spending it staying in the Yong chalet after all . . .

She wondered briefly if Pierre knew yet. Had Sam alerted him? And if so, would that be what it took for Pierre to make the call she'd been waiting for? Surely it could only be a matter of hours now.

She stood up and hurried back into the bedroom.

'And how the hell is this supposed to work?'

Allegra almost screamed from surprise as she saw Sam filling her doorway with chilling stillness. She tried not to show her fright. She tried not to show anything.

'You can always leave if it's too much for you,' she replied with a calmness she didn't feel, but not daring to walk another step.

'Just what are you playing at?' he demanded, advancing instead. 'Why are you even out here?' His eyes were pinned on hers, tension stiffening his jaw.

'You know why – family business,' she said, going to walk past him, but he caught her arm.

'Bullshit!' His grip was tight, his frustrations playing plainly over his face. 'You're everywhere I turn. You tried to sabotage my career, jacked in your own and yet here you are, still trying to muscle in on the deal. You need to get the hell out of here.'

'Or what?' He didn't reply, his threat empty, and she pointedly looked down at his hand on her arm. 'Are you done?'

He released her and stepped back, his eyes searching hers for clues to the game she was playing.

'Is all this just about winning?' he asked after her as she reached the door. 'Or just about beating me?'

But she wasn't about to put him out of his misery. Instead she rounded the corner and ran quickly up the steps, her heart beating pneumatically. Let him wonder. Let him wonder.

Chapter Twenty-Four

Day Seventeen: *Red Candle*

Lars was waiting for her in the same chair when she arrived the next morning, and she saw the life ignite in his eyes at the sight of her. She took a seat in the chair beside him, and he clasped her hand in his.

'You are so much the image of your grandmother seeing you fools me into thinking I am a young man again.'

Allegra smiled delightedly. 'I'm sorry I'm a bit late. Isobel hurt her leg on the night skiing yesterday, so she's had me running around like a crazy thing all morning.'

'I hope it is not serious?'

'I don't think so, no, but I think she's enjoying being waited on too much to indicate otherwise at the moment.'

Lars laughed. 'She has spirit.'

'Oh yes,' Allegra agreed.

He looked better today. His colour had improved, and the shock of yesterday's news had clearly settled, leaving only the good parts: his daughter was alive, and her family was here.

Across the room, the clock sounded the hour and a flurry of whirring cogs made her turn her head just in time to see a cuckoo pop out.

'Oh my goodness!' she laughed, jumping up to stand closer to it. The doors of the chalet opened and a man and a woman wheeled out, spinning in circles at the front and tipping forwards to kiss before gliding back into the house again, until the next hour. 'I've never seen one of those work before! Do you know, Iz and I found one in the loft at home just the other week? Iz has taken it. She thought Ferdy would love it. She's sent it off to be repaired.'

'You have a cuckoo clock?' He leaned forward interestedly in the chair. 'Can you describe it to me? Maybe I will remember it.'

Remember it? Allegra looked at him. 'Was it *yours*?' she asked in astonishment.

'Well, it could have been. That one on the wall there is a copy of the one I lost, although I've never liked it as much as the original. Giulia would sit in front of it for hours, waiting for the cuckoo to come out, and she always cried when it did. *Every* time.' He laughed, shaking his head sadly. 'In the end, Valentina insisted we stop using it. Such a shame, really.'

Allegra blinked as she sat beside him again. Had her grandmother stolen that clock too, then? 'I'm so sorry. We never knew . . .'

'No, no, of course not,' he smiled, patting her hand. 'Besides, it's only a clock. It makes me happy to think it's with my grandchildren now. That's how it should be.'

Allegra nodded.

'Do you have a photograph of my great-grandson? I should love to see him. See whether he has my good looks.' He chuckled as Allegra looked for a photo on her phone and handed it over. 'Ah yes, yes. He's like his mother. I can see that.' He looked back at her. 'You and your sister are very close.'

'Yes. Best friends really.'

'And her husband? Does he deserve her?'

'Um . . .' It was exactly the question he shouldn't have asked.

'No?'

'It's not that,' she said quickly. 'Lloyd means well enough and he's very . . . *personable*.' She knew she had made it sound like a four-letter word, but she couldn't help it. 'I just think he takes her for granted. I mean, you've seen her. She's such a catch and so fun to be around. Lloyd just . . . lies on the sofa and drinks beer when he gets in and grunts like a teenager most of the time.'

'So you think she could have done better,' Lars smiled.

'No, no,' Allegra laughed. 'Well, maybe.' She shrugged. Lars arched his eyebrows. 'Probably . . . OK, yes. Yes. She settled.'

'But you're not going to do that.'

'Absolutely not.'

'You don't believe in happy endings?'

'Let's just say I don't believe in white knights. *I* am my white knight.'

He patted her hand with a smile. 'You are a modern woman. Your grandmother would have been so proud.'

She fell still, realizing he meant Valentina, not Anya, but she well remembered the glow in her granny's eyes when her grades had begun to improve, when she'd got her first-class honours degree, her first job . . . 'Do you really think so?'

'I know it. I listen to you and I watch you, and it's like you are her, come back to me.'

'Well, we have come back to you.'

He smiled, just as the nurse came back in with a tray of coffee and pastries. Allegra glanced over at her, but Lars ignored her. He had eyes only for Allegra. 'Of course, there is still one thing we have yet to discuss.'

Allegra blinked up at him. 'What's that?'

'What are you to call me?'

'Oh.' Her mouth opened in surprise. 'We did . . . wonder what would be . . . appropriate.'

He watched her with eyes that betrayed a still-sharp intellect, seeming to understand her reluctance to move straight into terms of endearment. 'Of course, I know these things can't be rushed.'

She smiled shyly, grateful he understood.

'Although, at eighty-eight years of age, I could be for-given for asking for a *little* haste.'

His eyes twinkled and Allegra couldn't help but laugh. 'Quite!'

'You know, the word used by the local children here is "*opa*".'

'*Opa*?' she repeated, trying it out for size. It didn't seem . . . intrusive, like 'grandpa' or 'granddad'. Both those words carried a suggestion of familial intimacy to her that couldn't possibly be expected yet, but by virtue of being foreign, '*opa*' was just a collection of sounds. No pressure. 'I like that,' she smiled. 'Do you mind if I run it past Isobel first?'

'Of course. You can come back tomorrow and tell me her answer.'

'I will,' she grinned, pleased to have another invitation to visit.

Picking up her coffee and taking a sip, her eyes flitted around the room with growing curiosity. There were very few old photographs out, most of them taken in the 1970s and 1980s, it seemed, and her eyes came to rest on the cuckoo clock again. 'You know, I think the clock we found in the loft *is* very similar to yours. I remember it's got the same garden at the front, and the detailing on the balconies is almost identical.'

'It is hard for me to recall exactly.'

'You were lucky to find someone who could do a copy for you.'

Lars shrugged. 'There is a carpenter in the village who makes them. I think he still does.'

They lapsed into a small, comfortable silence.

'Can I ask you something?'

He nodded.

'Did the police contact you when they found Valentina?'

'No.'

'But why not?'

'Because I am no longer her next of kin. My remarriage invalidated that status.'

Allegra frowned to think he'd been treated as an outsider after the discovery of his own wife's body. 'But that's terrible.'

'Oh, I have known worse.' He gave a wry smile. 'It is just red tape. Besides, take away the visitors and this is a small town still. The news came back to me as quickly as the police would have done anyway.'

'Father Merete says you haven't been to church since they found her.'

His expression changed. 'No . . .' His gaze became distant, his voice faraway. 'Many of the older families in the town remember your grandmother's disappearance. It was one of the town's greatest tragedies. She was never forgotten in all those years she was lost and now there is almost an excitement about it all.' He looked back at her. 'I am not ready for that. I cannot *celebrate* that she has been found.'

Allegra fell quiet in the face of a love that had endured even through sixty years of loss, of never knowing what had happened . . . He still loved her as much now surely as he had as a young man. No wonder Granny had run . . . Who could compete with that?

'Well, she'll be able to rest in peace, at last,' she said quietly.

'Yes. Thanks must be given for that.'

They fell into another silence again, but it was light and easy, a frank familiarity beginning to grow between them. She watched him as he stared in the fire. Opa.

'Why do you think she went up to the hut that night?'

Lars's eyes swivelled round slowly to meet hers, as though weighted down by the question, and she could see from the weariness with which he shook his head how many times he had been asked that question before.

'Were you with her the night she disappeared?'

He nodded. 'We had eaten and I had gone back out to check on the herd. It had been snowing for two days, and more snow was expected for that night. It was so deep by then that we had rounded the goats into the pens for their safety. When I came back, maybe forty minutes later, she had gone.' He shrugged. 'She hadn't been feeling well and I thought she had gone to bed.'

He stopped talking and she recognized a look on his face that she knew so well in her mother's – he had retreated to another time, another place.

'I have never forgotten the moment I went upstairs and

found the bed empty. It was like someone had plunged my heart in ice.' He shook his head, over and over. 'And I knew then. I knew she was gone. There was no *reason* for her to have gone out.'

'How much later was this?'

'An hour? Slightly more.'

She had been out of his sight, then, for around two hours – and two hours of snowfall in a hundred-year storm meant her footsteps must surely have been obscured . . . 'Had anyone in the town seen her?'

'Not that evening. Not even Timo, and I believed him, though many didn't.'

'Who's Timo?'

'The boy she had been engaged to before me. A lot of people hated me for coming in and stealing the prettiest girl in town, and him most of all. It was a big upset back then.'

The revelations surprised her. 'You weren't born here?'

'No. Bern. I was a city boy. My family had a successful printing business.'

After a lifetime of stunted family conversations in which memories were equated with secrets, it made Allegra's eyes glow to hear about her great-grandparents. 'So what made you come to Zermatt?'

'You mean apart from the pretty girls?' he laughed softly. 'I came to ski with some friends before I started my apprenticeship. You can imagine my father's reaction when I told him I was staying and marrying a goat farmer's daughter.'

'Oh heavens!'

He frowned. 'People are strange, though. Her father was more against the marriage than mine. I came into it with if not a fortune, at least a modest dowry, and it was certainly better than anything Timo or any of the other locals could have given her. I told him I would give Valentina a better life than she could ever have expected, but he didn't want her marrying a "foreigner", as he called me.' He shook his head bitterly. 'Even now, all these years later, I wish he could have seen what I could have given her, that I kept my promise.'

Their eyes moved over the chalet and Allegra knew from her own Alpine holidays that this was probably worth at least 7 million Swiss francs.

'There's a saying back home – "There's nowt so queer as folk,"' she said.

Lars looked at her quizzically, clearly not understanding, just as the nurse came back in to collect the cups and plates. She was as unsmiling as she had been yesterday, and she placed Allegra's half-empty cup down so hard on the tray it slopped over the sides.

Annoyed, Allegra watched as she walked away again. 'Do you have many problems with your staff?' she asked loudly – certainly loudly enough for the nurse to hear and Allegra saw her pause by the door. She already knew from Lars's reaction yesterday that he felt less than supported by the woman.

Lars laughed, patting her hand appreciatively. 'Indeed I do, Allegra. Indeed I do.'

'So here you all are,' she said, pulling off her gloves and staring down at the three men with a shy smile. Zhou, Sam and Massi were sitting in a row at a table, all leaning back on their chairs against the wall behind them, eyes closed, their faces tilted up to the sun. In front of them were tankards of beer, almost finished, suggesting they'd been here a short while at least.

Zum See was one of the most renowned mountain restaurants, not only in Zermatt but all of the Alps, and had been easy to find. She had wandered into the tiny constellation of ancient sheep sheds and grain stores that made up the famous eatery, led as much by ear as by nose, for the noise was terrific – a perfect storm of pan-European languages as 'Pass the bread' and 'More wine?' were called at the tables in French, German, Italian, Spanish, English, Portuguese . . .

The sun had pierced the snow clouds at last and everyone clearly wanted to make the most of the rare good weather. Every table was packed, some people squeezed in round the corners with barely room for a side plate; a courtyard of sorts had been created by virtue of outdoor tables being arranged against and around the various decrepit, tumbledown outbuildings, but the ground was uneven, straw strewn across the paths. It was a contrary scene – rich customers in their designer clothes clamouring to enjoy the erstwhile peasants' delight – and she absolutely saw the appeal. In fact, she loved it. After all, she belonged to both worlds.

She took off her helmet and clipped it with all the others onto a rope that was slung between two pegs on the wall.

'Our little bird,' Massi grinned delightedly. 'I knew you would fly back to us.'

'Did you do what you needed to?' Zhou asked, immediately raising his arm to flag down a passing waitress.

'Yes, thanks,' she replied brightly. She was still buoyant from seeing Lars again and felt relaxed, even in the face of Sam's stony stare. 'I'll have a *vin chaud*, please,' she said to the waitress. She looked back at Zhou. 'Have you ordered food yet?'

He nodded. 'We weren't sure if you were coming or not.'

'No, that's fine.' She looked back at the waitress. 'Something quick – pasta?' she shrugged.

'Lemon ravioli?' the waitress asked.

'Great.'

She sat down on the bench opposite them as Zhou and Massi sat forward, their elbows on the table. Sam, naturally, had closed his eyes again, like a child pretending that if he couldn't see her, she wouldn't be there.

The guys took in her ski kit. She had gone back to the chalet to change and check on Isobel.

'How is your beautiful sister?' Massi asked, sloshing some warmed wine from a carafe into a glass for her, not waiting for hers to arrive.

'I think the novelty's beginning to wear off,' she grinned. 'Now that she's on her own and we're all skiing, anyway. I'm sure she'll be delighted to relapse later when we're all back.'

Zhou and Massi laughed.

'Will she rally for the party?' Zhou asked.

'Will she rally? Listen, she'll *rule* the party. Even from the sofa.'

'I love her,' Massi declared simply.

'I know,' Allegra smiled. She spotted the breadbasket and grabbed a piece. 'So tell me about your morning. What's the snow like?'

'In-credible,' Massi replied, pinching the air. 'Powder up to your nose.'

'He means knees,' Zhou said with a roll of his eyes.

'Wow. Where did you go?' she asked.

'Over the border into Cervinia,' Zhou said. 'It was quieter over there, and we prefer the north-facing slopes in backcountry.'

'That sounds wise. I'm sorry to have missed it.'

'Are you going to come out with us after lunch?'

'If you'll have me, thanks.'

'We thought we'd try over in Trift. The Ober Gabelhorn glacier is at the top, and there are no marked runs or lifts at all. I've never seen anyone over there, so we should have the place to ourselves.'

Wasn't that where Connor had said Valentina had been found?

'Great.' Reaching in her pocket, she found her Chanel Neige lip balm, which gave her full UV protection without making her look like a Test cricketer, and she began absently dabbing her lips, wondering if Sam intended to spend the entire lunch blanking her.

'So,' she said, putting the lip balm away again, determined to shine in his eyes like a too-bright light, 'Zhou told me you all met at Harvard Business School. What do you do now, Massi?'

'I make cupcakes.'

'*What?*' Disbelief made the word come out as a squeal. 'Sorry. It's just that . . . cup . . . You went to Harvard to make cupcakes?'

Massi laughed too. 'I know! It's insane. You should have seen my father's face when I graduated and showed him my business plane.'

'Plan. And no, you really shouldn't have,' Zhou said, shaking his head, no hint of a smile. 'His father's almost as traditional as mine.'

Massi rolled his eyes, looking suddenly – scarily – serious. '*Sì*. Mafia. They like guns, not the cakes.'

Allegra immediately stopped laughing. 'Shit, really?'

Massi's face broke into another infectious grin. 'No! But you know, as I said to him, the first thing they teach you at Harvard Business School is that eighty-four per cent of all buying decisions are based on emotion, not thought. And a hundred per cent of my cupcake sales are based on emotion. Each one is a little pot of happiness. It is why I now have seventeen branches throughout the United States, with annual turnover of thirty-four million dollars.'

Allegra's smile faded. 'I'm sorry, how much?'

'That is exactly what my father said when I showed him my accountings!' Massi grinned.

'It's still peanuts compared to my fortune, of course,' Zhou said waspishly.

'Your father's fortune,' Massi clarified. 'It's just as well for you there's a one-child policy in China. At least there's no one else for your father to give the money to instead.'

Allegra watched as they laughed, two multi-millionaires teasing each other like teenagers, throwing barbs back and forth like it was a basketball. They were all old friends, the three of them, far closer than she'd supposed. Would Zhou really encourage his father to choose her over Sam?

'So you're based in the States, then, Massi?' she asked, wrapping her hands round her warm glass.

'Boston.'

She nodded, wondering how his English could still be so lousy. 'You all seem very close. Do you get to see each other regularly?'

'This man here, he is my brother,' Massi said, gripping

Sam's arm and jolting him out of his faux sleep. 'We used to see each other most weeks, but Sam moving to London has erupted our routine. We would play every week in the racquets and tennis club. I would catch the shuttle down especially for it.' He reached over and patted Sam on the arm. 'I hope it was worth it, buddy.'

Sam, forced to contribute to the conversation, shrugged. 'Gotta go where the work is.'

'Or where the ex *isn't*, huh? You know Amy called me—'

Sam tipped his chair violently back. 'Stop right there.'

Amy? That was the name of his wife? Allegra's eyes slid between the two of them.

'But she just wanted to—' Massi protested.

'I said stop. You don't go there.'

Allegra watched as he drained his beer and immediately raised his arm, indicating a fresh round for the table. What had Amy done that was so bad he wouldn't even let her name be brought up?

She looked across at Zhou, surprised to find his eyes already on her. 'We fight like brothers too.'

'Fair enough. Who's the boss?' By anyone's definition they were alpha males, the lot of them.

Massi, shaken by Sam's warning, rallied quickly. 'Well,' he said, leaning in closer across the table, 'these two are the jokers of the pack. I am . . . I am . . .'

'The knave?' Zhou quipped, one eyebrow slightly lifted.

'No. I am the ace.'

'Huh?' Zhou frowned, confused and no doubt concerned at the prospect of Massi swerving into metaphorical territory.

'You know – I can be high *or* low.'

'And don't we know it!' Zhou quipped.

Massi shot his friend a tart look. 'I am the bridge man. I have to' – he looked up to the sky, straining for the word – 'negotiate between these two.' He thumbed towards Sam and Zhou. 'Like for hostages.'

There was a puzzled silence.

'*Really?*' she smiled, pretending to understand.

'Oh yes.' Massi lowered his chin, speaking in sombre tones. 'They are just so jealous of each other: Sam because Zhou is so rich; Zhou because Sam is so good-looking.'

'Oh jeez,' Sam groaned under his breath, not looking remotely amused.

'What? You think that is not true?' Massi asked, looking over. 'Would you be his friend if he did not have all his money? I mean, really, what else is there to like about him?'

'Massi!' Allegra shrieked, laughing.

'As you pointed out, it's his father's money,' Sam corrected drily.

'Ouch!' Zhou winced at the double punch, eyes gleaming with amusement.

'So you were listening,' Massi grinned, stretching further on the table and resting his head on his hand. 'Well, you love him but hate him too for being so rich,' he said provocatively.

'Is that so?' Sam asked laconically, drumming his fingers on the table.

'Allegra, do you think there is more to Zhou than his money?'

'Of course!'

'Thank you,' Zhou said with an appreciative smile.

'And what about Sam?' Massi asked.

She frowned, unsure what he meant. 'What about him?'

'Is there more to him than just a pretty face?'

334

Allegra stiffened. 'Well, strictly speaking, *I* never said he had a pretty face.'

Massi's mouth dropped open and he slapped Sam hard on the thigh. 'I don't believe it! Never did I think I would see the day. A woman who is impossible to your charms!

'Tell me, then, Allegra,' Massi said, drawing back to her. 'If Sam isn't a pretty face, what is he?'

'Well, I never said that either,' she pushed back. 'And besides, we're talking about you three, not me.'

'But a conversation is a two-way road. Tell me. What is Sam? In five words?'

Both Massi and Zhou were watching her intently. Sam had fixed a stony stare on the floor, but she knew from his straining stillness that he was listening. 'Well, he's Canadian, divorced,' she said, aiming for benign. Handsome, funny, good in bed, stylish, successful . . .

'That's two,' Massi prompted, and she looked back at him from far-off eyes.

Heart-broken, recovering . . . 'Ambitious, unscrupulous.'

'Four. I thought you were better at maths than that, Allegra,' Zhou teased.

Imaginative, persistent . . . 'A thief.'

She watched as Sam's eyes blazed, his mouth falling open a little in shock at the word as it resounded around the table. Massi's eyes were positively dancing with delight.

'Oh! That is . . . that is . . .' He exhaled loudly. 'Sam? That is a *beeg* accusation. What have you to say to that?'

The waitress set down his fresh drink, appraising him with eyes that suggested she would blatantly disagree with Allegra's synopsis.

'What? You expect me to dignify it with a comment?'

Massi clasped his hands together like he was chairing a panel. 'OK, then. How would you describe Allegra in five?'

He didn't even blink. 'Simple: single, beautiful, successful, lonely, bitter.' The words tripped off so quickly, no hesitation, no pause, like it was something he'd been musing on for days.

She looked away quickly, reaching for something pithy to say, but her mind had gone blank, all the blood rushing to her heart, and she forced herself to take another sip of her drink instead as a clunky silence descended like an iron cloak.

'Oh no! No, no!' Massi said, rushing to her rescue this time, like a Labrador whose loyalty was being tested. 'I cannot allow that. It is ingallant.'

Their food arrived, trailing steam ribbons in the air, and they all concentrated, even Massi, on the black pepper as it was twisted onto their plates with lavish ceremony, asking for extra *parmigiano*, some more water – anything to distract from the joke that had started off funny but fallen horribly flat.

Chapter Twenty-Five

'Just what exactly are you looking for down there?' Zhou shouted, barely audible above the engines.

'Nothing!'

'Doesn't look like nothing!'

She looked over at him, her bright eyes reflected back to her in his rainbow-tinted oil-slick goggles. He looked menacing and lean in his ninja-style all-black kit – unlike Massi, who, in baggy green and yellow, looked more like a giant jelly baby.

'You may be in line to inherit a mining company, Zhou, but see down there? One day, all that down there's going to be mine!' she laughed.

Zhou roared with laughter, but her joke wasn't as unfeasible as it sounded. Her family's old pastures were somewhere here, below them, below the snow, and had they not been sold almost sixty years earlier, she may well have stood to one day inherit her own corner of a mountain.

But it mattered not. Even without the deeds to some acres of grass, she felt connected to this place now, like a balloon tied to a rock.

She pressed her face to the window again, her breath fogging the glass. The hamlet of snow-capped huts was almost invisible from the sky. Clustered together like wind-blown cattle, it was only the flashes of blackened walls as the helicopter swooped past below them that betrayed their presence at all.

'This is a good choice, no?' Massi shouted with a buoy-ant grin. Only his white teeth were visible with his goggles on, but his curls easily escaped the helmet, wrapping round its edges like a climbing rose. Sam was checking his bindings behind them.

The slopes on this side of the resort were untouched and still boasting pristine powder. They circled a small plateau in ever-decreasing circles, the helicopter lowering slowly, and snow whirled up like a sandstorm in the desert. Sprays of snow particles blew past the windows as Zhou slid open the door, ready to jump first.

She watched him leap, arms wide, the ski poles extended like an eagle's wing tips . . . Then it was Massi's turn. He jumped almost without looking, hurling himself out with a kamikaze ebullience that was to be expected.

She was up next and she took a breath. She had helied before, but she'd never liked this bit, the pop – or the jump.

'After you!' Sam shouted after a moment, and she glanced back at him, half wondering whether he was lining up to push her out. It was the spur she needed – just in case and before he could, she leaped unaided, Sam following a few seconds after. Zhou had already taken off down the slope, with Massi in hot pursuit, both wanting to be first to make tracks in the snow, and she didn't bother this time to turn round to see exactly where Sam might be. He was breathing down her neck, she knew, and she waited for the moment he shot past her, determined to beat her and catch them up. They could hear Massi ahead, whooping with delight, and she suspected that meant he had taken the lead.

Behind them, the helicopter rose into the sky again, the drone of its blades like a jungle drumbeat. The snow was in the sun up here, and the glare coming off it was blinding even with a high-light ski mask on. Zhou and Massi's tracks snaked in front of her – like a bread trail showing her where to go – but still Sam didn't overtake. She began to slow, easing into wider, more languid turns, almost forcing him into passing her, but he remained resolutely behind.

Dammit! She wanted to stop and look around. The curiosity was killing her. Somewhere in this expanse – beneath the glacier, wedged in a crevasse – was the hut that had hidden Valentina all these years. She glanced around, trying to see anything that might indicate a hut – a sign, itinerary poles highlighting a path – but the snow lay thick and smooth, unbroken across the landscape for miles in every direction. Rocks were deeply buried, the trees sagging from the weight on their branches, and there was no evidence of human presence here apart from their own.

She went slower still.

'What are you doing?' he shouted, from behind her.

She waved with her pole, indicating for him to overtake, but to her frustration, he slowed up, matching her tracks like a ski-school kid to their instructor.

'Just go ahead. I'll catch you up!' she shouted, sweeping in ever wider, slower arcs.

'Are you nuts? The others are long gone!' he shouted back.

'So then catch them!' she shouted again, easing into a lazy turn, her eyes on the distant shadows.

He dropped down onto the fall line, picking up speed quickly, and she thought he was going to do as she'd asked. Instead, he overtook her as she made a right turn, coming to an abrupt stop in her path.

'You idiot!' she shrieked, almost skiing straight into him. She braked hard and he caught her hand to steady her. 'What did you do that for?' she demanded crossly, jamming her poles in the snow.

'We can't split up here. There are no patrols. The snow hasn't been bashed.' He shrugged. 'And the others are too far ahead now. We're going to have to stick together.'

'Jesus,' she muttered angrily, looking away. Was it too much to ask for a little solitude on a mountain? She scanned the landscape again – anything? Connor had said he'd seen the hut's roof from a walking path, but there was nothing to suggest they were near one here. They were too far from the crease of the valley; that was the problem. The helicopter had dropped them on the beautiful smooth face instead, and if she was going to have any hope of finding the crevasse, she would have to traverse the slope, away from the others.

'*What* are you looking for?'

'Nothing.'

'Nothing?' She couldn't see his eyes behind his mask – just like he couldn't see hers – but she knew he didn't buy her denial. 'You seriously want me to believe you're not trying to scope out that mountain hut where your grand-mother was found?' he asked.

Her lips parted with surprise. 'I don't know what you're talking about,' she muttered.

'No? So it's just coincidence that you're skiing horizon-tally in the very valley she was found?'

Allegra glowered at him. What exactly had Isobel told him? 'What bloody business is it of yours?'

'It isn't,' he shrugged. 'But if you'd at least have the courtesy to tell me, I could try to help.'

'You?' she scoffed. 'Help? Don't make me laugh.'

Her phone rang and she reached for it quickly, hoping it wasn't Barry.

It wasn't, but her eyes widened at the name on the caller ID. Side-slipping down the slope a little way, pointedly making a show of wanting privacy, she pressed 'connect'.

'Bob,' she said in a low voice. 'Thanks so much for your messages. I really appreciate your support. It's been a rough few days, but I was going to call y—' She straightened up. 'Oh!' She frowned. 'Oh, I see. Yes, he's right here.' She held out the phone towards Sam, still fifty metres uphill. 'It's for you.'

'Me?' Sam looked surprised as he pulled off a glove, sliding down to her and taking the phone with a quizzical expression. 'Kemp.'

He continued watching her as Bob talked, but she pulled her poles out of the ground and looped the straps round her wrists again, making a few swoops down the hill to give him the privacy she'd pointedly taken for herself, although the breeze carried his voice down to her.

'OK . . . And what did you find? . . . Right, well, I appreciate you checking that for me . . . Yes, if you could. I'll be back the day after next.'

He skied down to her and handed back the phone. 'Thanks. Apparently my phone's out of juice. He didn't know how else to contact me.'

She wanted to know why Bob was contacting him at all, but she already knew the answer: survival. Now that she had gone, he had to pin his flag to someone else's pole. 'And how did he know *I* was with you?' she asked instead.

Sam had the grace to look awkward, but at least it told her one thing: he must have told Pierre she was a guest of the Yongs after all. She was there and, he therefore had to assume, still in the running.

Yet no call.

'Whatever,' she said before he could answer. 'Let's just go.'

She felt angry with herself for being so upset at the thought of Bob working with Sam now. She remembered how unimpressed Bob had been as Sam had come in and tried to usurp her in front of her own team, calling him a 'dick-swinging tosser'. That had been less than two weeks ago, and now, how all their worlds – and loyalties – had changed.

'Allegra—'

But she skied off quickly, carving the snow in neat, short S-bends, her body articulating in strong movements as the rhythm became established. Sam stayed behind her – deliberately so, it appeared – but she didn't care. She just wanted to get to the bottom as fast as she could, away from him, back to the others.

She didn't see the edge that her right ski caught. All she saw was Zermatt advance towards her like the moon to the rocket man, as she was thrown through the air and, a millisecond later, unceremoniously dumped face first in the powder.

'Allegra! Jesus, are you OK?' Sam asked, stopping and crouching down beside her with a concerned expression.

She lay still, checking she was alive, could move, mortified. She was aware she was spreadeagled on her tummy, and as she lifted her head, she spat out a mouthful of snow. Her ski mask had been pushed clean off her face so that it hung only by the strap on the loop at the back of her helmet, and her right ski had come off. 'I'm fine,' she said with a half-frozen tongue so that her words sounded distorted.

Sam didn't move. 'You're sure? That was a hell of a wipeout. Just take a moment.'

'I'm completely fine,' she said, spitting out some more snow. Just how much of the white stuff had she swallowed? She tried to push herself up into a sitting position, but the snow was so soft her hands just pushed through it and she face-planted again – and again, and again.

'Oh my God!' she cried, somehow managing to roll onto her back instead, but with her one attached ski becoming wedged vertically in the snow. 'Urgh!' She couldn't release the bindings from the angle it was stuck at, but nor would she let Sam help, and for several minutes she tried to get herself up, insisting she could do it alone, even though it was exhausting trying to stand up again on powder – skis were essential to spread the weight and surface area of the skier, and her hands and feet just kept poling through the snow like probes.

Sam watched on, his hands resting on his poles, watching her spluttering efforts. She thought she saw him smiling a few times, but he was poker-faced every time she looked straight at him. She deplored the entire situation. She couldn't be further from the boardroom, with one leg wedged upright and the rest of her flailing on her back like an overturned beetle.

'Right, enough,' Sam said finally as she collapsed back in the snow with an exasperated cry. He pushed himself backwards to draw level with her foot. 'I'm going to turn your ski out.'

'Fine,' she panted, too tired to protest now, feeling him tugging her ski upwards, trying to loosen the snow around it. It released quite suddenly, and she felt him carefully angle the ski so that it didn't wrench any ligaments, digging its outside edge into the slope.

'Now, hold on to this,' he said, offering her his pole and pulling her up into a sitting position.

'Thank you,' she said reluctantly, looking downhill again and dusting the snow off her shoulders and back. Some of it had gone down her neck and she pulled her jumper away from her skin to give it an escape route.

'OK, now let's get your ski back on,' Sam said, casting around for it. 'Where did it go?'

'Funnily enough, I didn't think to look when I was flying through the air,' she muttered, pulling clumps of the snow from the ends of her hair. 'You saw it happen, not me.'

Sam sidestepped up the slope a little, but the snow was so deep and soft he just kept sinking up to his knees, and there was no question of him taking off his skis to look – then he'd be in the same position as her. He shaded his eyes with his hand as he searched for the errant ski. 'I can't see it.'

'You must be able to – I didn't travel that far, surely?' she said over her shoulder.

Sam tried sidestepping further up, his eyes focused on the sudden stop of her ski tracks and then fanning out from that point. 'No, really – I can't see it. It's not up here.'

'But it has to be,' she said, twisting as much as she could in her position. 'I mean, where could it have gone?'

Sam looked downhill again. 'Well, if it landed flat . . .' His eyes met hers.

Allegra looked at him in horror before erupting with laughter. Her ski had skied itself down? 'No way!' she cried. 'There is no way that could have happened!'

He shrugged. 'But it's not up here.'

She stopped laughing. They were still at the top of the mountain. They'd barely begun the run. She couldn't be without a ski, all the way at the top!

'I'd better ring the others and let them know we're OK,' Sam said, skiing back down to her. 'Give me your phone again.'

'Oh, this is just bloody brilliant,' Allegra muttered, handing it up to him with a mutinous look. It wasn't quite so funny now. This was going to be humiliating in front of Zhou and Massi. Her first run with them and she'd lost a ski! And after Isobel's disaster last night . . .

'Hi, it's me,' she heard Sam say a moment later. 'No, I know – mine's out of juice . . . Yes, it's fine, but Allegra's lost her ski . . . No, we're still looking for it . . . Just go on and we'll meet you down there . . . But keep your phone on you . . . I'm not sure you'll be able to. Look up . . . Exactly, yeah . . . It's fine. We'll deal with it . . . OK. Bye.' He handed the phone back to her and shrugged off his backpack. 'Right, well, it looks like there's only one thing for it.'

'What's that?' she asked.

'We'll have to try to change the bindings on my skis and get you down on those.'

'But what about you?'

'I'll ski on one – it's fine,' he said, rummaging in the backpack.

'No,' she said firmly. 'I am perfectly capable of skiing down on one myself.'

'I don't doubt that,' he said calmly, and sounding – to her ears – like a patient father to a tantrumming toddler. 'But it's a damned long way from here. Even just a hundred metres is going to make your leg burn, and we've got, well . . .' He stopped, but she didn't need him to say it out loud. They'd both done the Infinity race. They both knew top to bottom was a 2,200-metre drop. This mountain wasn't as high, but it wouldn't be far out from that, and the snow here was unbashed and heavier on the legs.

'Just help me up,' she said, reaching her arms. She didn't do the damsel-in-distress gig.

Sam picked up the backpack by a strap and skied an arc down to her, stopping just beside her again. 'Allegra, let me do this.'

'No. Your boots are much bigger than mine, and with the weight discrepancy between us . . . even if you've got the right tools, there's no way you can sort the skis up here. It's impossible to test the bindings on this surface – it's too soft. I'll be fine. Worst-case scenario, I'll just keep switching legs.'

He shook his head, the expression on his face showing her he clearly disagreed, but he hooked out his arm, each of them grabbing the other by the elbow, and pulled her up to standing. It was more difficult to balance on one leg than she'd anticipated – her ski boots were heavy and it was hard to keep the ski-less leg lifted.

She swallowed, looking down at the miles of virgin powder stretched out below them. 'Right, you go first. I'll follow after,' Sam said, watching her closely.

She nodded, pulling her ski mask back on properly and getting her poles sorted. She was an excellent skier, but she'd never done this before. She closed her eyes and took three deep breaths.

She set off cautiously, keeping her speed down with long sweeping traverses. Short turns would be faster, but they created more thigh burn and she couldn't carve in this snow. This would just have to be slow and pretty.

'You OK?' Sam called out after a while, and she held one pole up in acknowledgement, not stopping. But he had been right: a hundred metres suddenly felt a really long way, and even with her triathlon-level fitness, the lactic acid began to build up quickly in her quads as she couldn't ease out of the knee bend and release the muscle.

'I'm going to have to swap,' she panted after six, seven minutes, looking back up the slope and seeing how depressingly little progress they'd made. 'My thigh feels like it's on fire.'

It was easier said than done. For all the same reasons as before, it was difficult swapping skis in the unpisted, deep, soft snow and Sam had to lower her to a seated position, changing the ski for her himself, before pulling her up again.

She tried not to complain about it, but after she'd skied on each leg a few hundred metres several times, they began to burn out, her muscles exhausted and beginning to cramp, and it was harder to stay optimistic.

'Oh shit!' she cried, flopping sideways into the snow as her left leg gave out. 'We're not even a quarter of the way down and I can't . . . I just can't . . .'

Her head hung forward as she limply tried massaging the muscle. It wasn't even like she had any emergency energy on her – Isobel had eaten the last of her toffees yesterday. Sam was looking worried, his brows furrowed.

'Look, you go down on your own,' she said, watching him watching her. 'If you get me another set of skis, then you can heli back up and ski over to me. I won't go anywhere, promise,' she shrugged, joking weakly.

'Can't do that. The weather's closing in again. Look over there.' He pointed to Sunnegga, the mountain opposite, where she and Isobel had skied on the first day. It was snowing again over there, the sky a murky grey, and the light was already flattening out over here. She realized all shadows had gone on this side of the valley now and it wouldn't be long before the sky began to thicken with flakes. 'By the time I get down there and sort out some skis, they might not let the heli take off again.'

'But you don't understand. I really can't ski any more,' she said. 'My legs are shaking. I'm not even sure I could stand right now. Really, I'm not just being feeble.'

He made a sound as though the thought amused him. 'I doubt you've ever been feeble in your life,' he said, looking down at her with an expression that she couldn't read behind his mask. 'Well, there's only one thing I can think to do.'

'What is it?'

'You need to stand up.'

'Urgh, no,' she protested, shaking her head.

'Yes. Stand.' He held out his pole, pulling her to standing again. He pushed himself backwards so that he slid back on the skis, moving his legs into a wide stance. 'Now stand there,' he said, pointing to the space where he had been standing.

'What, here?' she said uncertainly, side-slipping to where

he'd indicated, her left leg bent like a flamingo's as she tried to balance with her poles.

'Right,' he said, poling forwards again so that he came to stand behind her, his skis outside hers, his voice in her ear. 'Now we're going to ski down together.'

'Oh no, we're not,' she argued, realizing his plan to bring her down the mountain like a ski-school instructor returning to the resort with a toddler between his legs.

'And didn't I just know you'd argue,' he muttered. 'Look, just let me lead. I'll steer, but you must lean when I lean. If I do the turns, you should just be able to glide and not burn the muscle out.' He paused, his voice by her ear. 'OK?'

'It won't work.' Panic scalloped her words like a pretty lace.

'Yes, it will. If you behave and do as I say. OK?'

She didn't reply.

'OK?' he repeated.

'OK.'

He went to move, then stopped again. 'You have to trust me, Allegra. This won't work if you try to lead. If you try to turn, you'll cross my skis and we'll both go flying. Got it?'

'Yes.' Her voice was small. Of all the bad ideas, this had to be the worst ever. How could he expect her to trust him, of all people? She'd prefer to be left alone on the mountain. She could dig a snow hole if she had to . . .

'And give me your poles. You can't use those. You'll trip me up.'

'Well, where am I going to put my hands?' she asked, wobbling on her one leg.

He held out their four poles across her body like a rail. 'Hold on to these.'

'I'm not sure about this,' she said, almost whispering with fear.

'I am. Just trust me.' His voice was reassuring. Kind.

And before she could talk herself out of it further, he put his weight on the outside of his right ski, setting them off.

The sudden motion and strange position took her by surprise and she lost her balance momentarily, her back pressing into his chest. He brought them to a slow stop again. They had moved six metres.

'Sorry,' she murmured, trying to peel herself away.

'It's fine. Just keep your weight forward. Stick your ass out more,' he said.

'Oh, you have got to be kidding me,' she muttered, knowing he was right. She heard him laugh softly behind her and it reminded her of a moment she'd been determined to forget in the hotel room in Zurich that first night. She refused to grin too.

They began traversing slowly across the slope again, dropping in height by mere inches.

'Now get ready to turn left on three,' he said. 'One . . . two . . . three . . .'

They turned as one, Sam's weight forcing the skis into a wide radius, Allegra's ski flat on the snow and following effortlessly. He'd been right! If she would just follow, he could lead them down.

He must have been exhausted taking on all the effort himself, but turn after turn they swooped together – after three turns, he didn't even need to count for her; she could feel the rhythm herself – Sam angling the poles down on each pivot, keeping them balanced, his body like a wall around her.

There was no sound, just the *shush* of the snow beneath their skis, the caws of rooks in the trees, their breath hard but steady. Several times her ski or confidence slipped, but Sam's own body was like a shell around her, a harbour wall keeping the boats safe.

She didn't know how long they skied like that for – thirty, forty minutes? It could even have been an hour – but exhilaration rushed through her as she saw the stepping-stone-hatted roofs of the chalets finally come into view, Zermatt seemingly rising to meet them and shortening the last section of their hard journey.

And then, as suddenly as it had happened, it was over.

She felt profoundly grateful to him – a new emotion in their fractious relationship – and so happy not to have to stand on one leg any longer; she was actually pleased to see Zhou and Massi standing waiting for them with relieved faces (in spite of the teasing that she knew would be inevitable now). And she couldn't wait to have something to eat. To get into a hot bath and ease her bruised, depleted body. To get warm again.

And yet there was something else too, something that was surprising and shocking, bewildering, illogical . . .

Because in spite of all those things, she realized she also didn't want it to end.

Chapter Twenty-Six

They decided to call it quits for the day. Allegra had to buy some new skis now, and with the weather having closed in as threatened, no one fancied skiing in blizzard conditions. They also all knew – though no one said it – how easily the situation could have turned far more treacherous. The teasing had started up almost as soon as they took in the sight of Sam skiing her down the mountain like a child, but there was also a nervy energy in the air as adrenalin and relief fused, and she sensed they were all going to let off some steam later, at the party.

Massi was keeping her company in town – Sam and Zhou had gone back to the chalet – and they rock-walked through the snowy streets in their ski boots, wolfing down waffles to recharge their sugar levels, while Massi regaled her with stories about the cut-throat reality of the cupcake business.

But Allegra – though amused – was distracted. Sam, in spite of skiing with his arms around her for several miles, hadn't met her eyes on level ground and she felt deflated by the immediate resumption of hostilities. More than deflated.

'Oh my God, that is *it*!' Massi proclaimed suddenly, making her look up. He was staring at a boutique just a few shops down and seemingly at a mannequin in the window that was wearing a dress that almost looked couture. Thousands of gold sequins had been sewn onto a fragile knitted mesh that fluted from the hips, and it had split cap sleeves that draped at the shoulder. The neckline plunged in a deep 'V', and the entire effect was of dripping liquid gold. It was a goddess dress.

She looked back at him. 'No.'

Massi looked scandalized. 'Why not?'

'I don't do gold. Nor do I particularly want to look like a phoenix.'

'It is not about you. This is Zhou's moment. His life is not so easy as you may think.'

Allegra looked at him unsympathetically. Private jets on standby? An army of staff? His every whim catered for? 'Massi, plenty of people have difficult relationships with their parents. It doesn't mean I have to dress up as a dead bird.'

Massi's mouth opened, then closed, then opened again. But instead of saying another word, he simply grabbed her by the wrist and marched her across the road.

She laughed, protesting all the way, only noticing the gift shop next to it as they passed the beautifully decorated window display.

'Hang on a minute,' she said, stopping laughing, stopping walking, her hands framing the glass to better allow her to see in. Plush fronds of fir had been arranged in swirls to create an opening like a camera's aperture, and in the middle, where Isobel's nativity scene had been, was a wooden Advent calendar – significantly larger in scale, but otherwise almost exactly the same as hers, right down to some of the gifts visible in the opened drawers: that wooden Angel Gabriel? 'He's got cheeks like Barry,' Isobel had said, and she was right. She'd recognize him anywhere. It was the same figure she'd seen in Isobel's nativity set.

Behind the glass, in the shop itself, which was painted a glossy pillar-box red, were hand-carved wooden Matterhorns, miniature rocking horses and teething toys lining the shelves. Round rattan baskets of wooden painted candy canes and angels sat by the till, and the entire wall behind the counter was given over to tens of cuckoo clocks, their pendulums all moving slightly out of time with one another.

'Uh-uh. *Andiamo*,' Massi said, scooping her away and bundling her into the boutique next door. The bells jangled prettily above their heads, announcing their arrival.

'I wanted to have a look in that shop!'

'And you can. After you've tried on the dress.'

'But I don't want to try on the dress. I already told you that.'

'A-llegra, your sister made me promise to try to get you off the shelf,' he said, folding his hands over his heart.

'Oh, I bet she did.' Allegra planted her hands on her hips.

'Come. We will try it on, you will look ravishing, and my duty will be done.'

'*We?*' Allegra realized two assistants were waiting to get their attention, their eyes sweeping up and down her waisted Moncler jacket, skinny salopettes and bespoke ski boots.

'*Guten Tag.*'

Massi replied in fluent German, while Allegra stood mutely beside him, beginning to sulk – Isobel was bang out of order on this. One of the assistants disappeared into a back room.

'Massi,' she scolded, 'I am *not* wearing that dress.'

'I am a man. I can see very well what looks good on a woman. You, on the other foot, are too concentrated on what you think looks properly.'

She thought she knew what he meant. 'It's not me.'

'Are you the best judge of you?' he asked sceptically, his thick eyebrows knitted together.

'Yes!'

The assistant came back, trailing a hanging bag over her shoulder. She smiled and inclined her head for Allegra to follow her to the changing room.

'I'm not putting it on,' she said, folding her arms and shaking her head.

'Go,' Massi said, pushing her gently in that direction. 'Just try. Where is the farm?' he shrugged.

'*Harm*, Massi! Where's the harm!'

'Exactly.'

He shooed her into the dressing room. The assistant had unzipped the bag and was draping the dress over a toile-upholstered bedroom chair.

'*Danke*,' Allegra nodded, pretty much exhausting her knowledge of German. The door closed behind her and she stared down at it suspiciously – limp and shapeless, its beauty was just a faint promise from here.

She slumped against the wall and looked at her own reflection in the mirror. Her clothes were still sprinkled with snow, the ends of her hair wet and matted together from where she'd been lying down in the drifts, her cheeks pink, her eyes uncharacteristically bright.

Her hands flew up defensively – she knew why. It was

the adrenalin: she hadn't yet come down from the drama on the mountain and her nervous system was still alive to the memory of Sam as close as a shadow, his presence like a warm blanket on a cold body.

It would pass. It was shock, of a kind.

There was a knock at the door. Massi's voice.

'Principessa Allegra,' he murmured in his velvet accent, making her name sound like a musical score, 'are you ready?'

'One more minute,' she said, hurriedly unzipping her jacket and wriggling out of her clothes. The dress – weighted by the sequins – moulded around her, the ribbed, knitted mesh beneath creating discreet transparent panels that ran down to the hem in rivulets. She looked at her reflection in the mirror. It was everything she feared.

She opened the door, shaking her head. 'Right, I tried it on. Now let's go.'

But Massi wasn't by the dressing-room door. He was across the floor at the till, the assistant handing something to him with a brilliant smile, and when he looked back at her, his eyes widened with delight. '*Fantastico!*' he cried, throwing his arms up into the air. 'Sold!'

Two minutes later, they stepped back out onto the street.

'You've just totally wasted your money. I'm not wearing it,' she said, making a beeline for the gift shop. She pushed against the door, but it didn't budge. No jingling bells, no helpful assistants rushing to make a sale. She turned back to him in a huff. 'Massi! It's bloody well closed now!'

He shrugged, nonplussed. 'So we come back tomorrow.'

She wanted to shriek with exasperation. This had to be the shop her grandfather had meant when he had been talking about his cuckoo clock. And she was almost certain the Advent calendar had come from here too, but generations earlier.

She took a step back, staring at the bijou shop that ticked to the sound of a hundred clocks and glowed red. In the middle of the snowy white silence, it seemed to her like a little beating heart.

Beads of condensation trickled down the glass door, the lights overhead morphing from blue to violet to magenta to pink like a ripple of captured aurora borealis. Thick blankets of lotus oil-infused steam buffeted off the walls and back into the tiny room again and Allegra half expected Kate Bush to suddenly emerge at any moment, with the announcement she'd come home now.

Isobel was lying on the bench opposite, her 'bad' leg in the knee brace and propped up on four folded towels.

'So, we get to keep these, right?' she asked, prodding at her non-existent 'mummy tummy' in the brand-new Heidi Klein bikini. 'I mean, once the tags are off, it's not like . . .' She wrinkled her nose with distaste.

'Yep.'

'Cool. I'd better do this again tomorrow, then. Get another one,' she winked.

'You are outrageous.'

'As if they'll even notice!' Isobel laughed. 'So, tell me about today, then. What did I miss?'

'Oh, not much. We just went off-piste; I lost a ski and almost got stranded on the mountain.'

'No!'

'Yep.'

'That could have been seriously dodgy. How did you get down?'

'Sam helped me while I skied on one leg.'

'That's it?'

Allegra shrugged. 'That's it.'

'Massi made it sound much more dramatic.'

'Listen, Massi makes reading the back of a cereal box sound dramatic,' Allegra wise-cracked.

'It's true – he's a riot,' Isobel cackled with laughter. She looked anxious suddenly. 'D'you think we'll stay in touch once . . . you know? We leave.'

'Well, thank God you are actually planning on leaving. I was harbouring serious doubts.'

'Awww, I miss my boys too much to stay, even though I could totally get used to living like this . . .' She closed her eyes as she inhaled the luxuriously lotus-scented air, as if proving the point. 'So do you think we will?'

'That's entirely up to the two of you. Why wouldn't you?'

'Well, because, you know, he's a . . . millionaire. He's a power player, a mover and shaker.'

Allegra frowned at her. 'We're still talking about Massi, right?'

'Yes! You can't deny he's successful, Legs.'

'I'm not. But that doesn't mean he's some power-tripping egomaniac who can only be surrounded by people just like him. He clearly adores you – the two of you are like very non-identical fraternal twins.' Allegra worried about her sister's persistent insecurities. How could she still think she wasn't good enough? Everyone who met her loved her.

'Yeah,' Isobel sighed, just as the door opened, letting in a blast of cold air that made Allegra shiver.

'Oh!' It took a moment for the steam to clear, but even that short word came with an accent. 'Sorry. I—'

'Hey, Sammy!' Isobel cried, bottom-shuffling along the bench. 'Come and join us.'

Sammy? *Sammy?* Allegra glared at her sister, wanting to smother her with one of those towels. What, were they best friends too now?

She looked back to the door and found Sam's gaze already on her – they hadn't seen each other since he'd released her from his safe embrace at the bottom of the run earlier and she felt strangely unsure how to behave with him if not aggressively.

'No, it's fine. You're talking. I'll go for a swim first,' he said quickly.

'But—'

'Really. I'll catch you in a bit.' And he closed the door.

Isobel turned to face Allegra, her mouth dropping wide open in slow motion.

'I know. Rude, right?' Allegra said, one eyebrow arched and pretending to look for in-growing hairs on her calf.

'What the *hell* is going on between the two of you?' she asked slowly.

Allegra froze. 'What do you mean?'

'Oh, come on, Legs! Don't tell me you're expecting me to believe there's nothing going on there. He almost had a heart attack seeing you sitting there in that bikini. And you went bright red.'

Allegra threw her arms in the air. 'We're in a bloody steam room, Iz. Of course I'm bright red! Now I know how lobsters feel!'

Isobel just shook her head. 'Uh-uh. I want details. *Now.*'

'There is nothing to tell. You already know it's because of

359

him that my entire life has fallen apart. He was the one who cornered Pierre into forcing me to quit my job.'

'Pierre got cornered?' Isobel laughed. 'Since when has Pierre Lafauvre ever been cornered, except by a posse of supermodels in a hot tub?'

'Not funny,' Allegra replied tetchily.

They were quiet for a moment, Isobel scrutinizing her sister through the steam. 'Oh no,' she murmured. 'Oh no, no, no, no, no.'

'What?'

'You're in love with Pierre.'

'*What?*' Allegra screeched. 'Don't be so idiotic! Really, Iz, even for you that is—'

'You are. I can totally see it all over your face.'

'You can't see my face in here.'

'You think he's going to see sense and divorce his teen-age wife and start a life with you, conquering the financial markets *on* your iPads, *in* his bed, *on* his yacht, *in* the middle of the Indian fucking Ocean.'

Allegra swallowed. 'I do not think that. I do not want that.'

Isobel's face fell and sympathy bled like a stain across her soft features. 'Oh, Legs. It makes perfect sense. Why did you never say anything?'

Allegra's only reply was to swivel on the bench, resting her back against the wet wall and hugging her knees in to her chest. Her voice had gone on walkabout, and the steam suddenly seemed too thin. She picked up the remote and increased the temperature by another degree.

'Can't you see it's never going to happen? You worked with the guy for six years. You were his star – it's not like he didn't notice you. If it was going to happen, it would have happened by now.'

Allegra stared harder at her knees. She remembered Bob's phone call earlier and what that meant: Pierre knew she was here. This was his chance to get her back. On side.

A sudden thought occurred to her and her head snapped up. What if that was *why* Bob had rung! Pierre had wanted to know for certain and he probably didn't think she'd return his calls right now, not after text-gate; but he'd have known she would pick up a call from her old deputy. What if . . . ? Oh God, what if he'd wanted to double-check she was here before coming to the party himself? It would be the perfect opportunity for them to talk face to face, in a neutral environment . . .

She rallied, looking back at Isobel with bright eyes. 'You're wrong, Iz. I've never had any romantic thoughts about Pierre.'

'Am I? So then tell me why you're the only one who can't see what *everyone else* can see every time Old Blue Eyes out there looks at you?'

Allegra looked at her sister incredulously. 'Honestly, there are times I think you're on drugs! I've got no idea what you're talking about.'

'Legs, the poor guy looks like he doesn't know whether to throw you over his knee and spank you or throw you over the back of the sofa and—'

'Iz! Enough! You don't know the whole story, OK? Really you don't. There is nothing between me and Kemp besides utter antipathy. I hate him. More than I've ever hated anyone in my life.'

'Really? *Anyone?*'

Allegra looked away. They both knew to whom she was referring.

Isobel blinked. 'So then what are you doing staying under the same roof as him?'

'Well, what do you think, dummy?' Allegra motioned to Isobel's strapped leg.

'Oh no.' Isobel shook her head, rebutting the point. 'You know you could have got us back to the apartment if you'd really wanted to. No one stands in *your* way.'

Allegra inhaled. 'Fine. It also turned out things aren't quite as finalized on the business side of things as I'd thought.'

'Meaning?'

'Meaning I'm still in the running for the deal.'

'*Against* Sam?'

Allegra nodded.

'Does he know?'

Allegra shrugged. 'Don't know. Don't care.'

Isobel let out a low whistle, watching her sister for a long moment. 'Yeah, well . . . you're probably right anyway,' she said finally. 'I mean, regardless of the vibes, the two of you together had disaster written all over it.'

There was a short silence. 'Disaster how?'

'Well, as much as he's really good-looking . . .'

'Yes,' Allegra prompted after a moment.

'I mean really, *really* good-looking . . .'

'Yes!' Allegra huffed impatiently. 'Got that.'

'He's not right for you. He's too easy-going.'

'Ha! You haven't seen him in meetings. He's as cold-blooded as a shark then.' Allegra remembered his chilly demeanour that morning in Pierre's office when they'd both faced the sack, his stony expression opposite at the dinner table as Zhou began to talk to her. 'What else?'

'Well, he's really funny. Have you seen his Ed Milliband impression?'

Allegra shook her head irritably. When had Isobel seen his Ed Milliband impression?

'And you hate laughing. You don't even like smiling.'

'Exactly.'

'Plus he's clearly ambitious and successful.'

'Why's that a disaster?'

'Because you are too! You'd constantly be butting heads. You do not need another winner in your life, Legs. Trust me, you'd be miserable, constantly trying to come out on top. No, what you need is a dismal failure. A loser.'

Allegra groaned, dropping her head back against the wall. She had walked right into that one. 'You are a nightmare!'

Isobel laughed out loud. 'I'm right. You'll see.'

'Bollocks.'

'Nice. Classy. Hey – where are you going?'

'To get away from you and your ridiculous conspiracy theories. I need to do a bit of work before the party.' Mr and Mrs Yong would be arriving imminently. Zhou had said yesterday they'd be at the party and she knew she had to give him her new proposal tonight, before he made his announcement tomorrow.

'I can't believe I'm going to miss the swankiest party of my life by six sodding feet,' Isobel moaned.

Allegra frowned. 'Why are you going to miss it?'

'Well, I can hardly go to a party with this thing on, can I?' Isobel pointed to the black knee brace.

'Of course you can! Just make like Cleopatra and lounge

on the sofa. You know everyone will end up coming to you.'

'No they won't. What would I have to say that's interesting to a load of billionaires?'

'Just stop that.'

'Besides, I've not got anything to wear and—'

'Check out your wardrobe, Iz. You may find there's a surprise in there for you.'

Isobel's eyes widened as she propped herself up on her elbows. 'Is there? What is it? Tell me!'

'No. Go and see for yourself,' Allegra said with a wink, much preferring to play the role of Fairy Godmother to that of Cinderella.

Chapter Twenty-Seven

She sat alone in her room, Bob's report spread around her on the bed as she stared, unseeing, at the wall, Isobel's words spinning like a top in her mind. It wasn't true what she'd said about Pierre, or about Sam. All they shared, the three of them, were ambition and a knack for making money.

She looked down at the papers again, determined not to be swayed from her planned course. What the hell did Isobel know anyway? Allegra operated in an entirely different universe, one her sister had only gleaned in films. How could Isobel possibly understand that a bumper year-end reporting was the nearest thing to a happy ending in her world?

With renewed focus, she read the charts one more time. Kemp had headed the New York office's commodities desk, and from going over, one by one, the trades that he had made on the Besakovitch fund for the past two years, she had found a clear bias to trading in stocks with an ethical manifesto, like fair-trade coffee producers in Nicaragua and organic green bean growers in Kenya. None of the traditional 'sin' stocks – cigarettes, alcohol, betting or casino companies – which usually offered higher returns, had featured in the portfolio, and yet Kemp had still managed to yield a 13 per cent profit for Besakovitch.

In addition, he had set up a secondary pot from which anonymous donations were made to a host of eminent charities: $500,000 here, $750,000 there to Médecins Sans Frontières, Kids Fighting Cancer, PeaceSyria, Water for Children Africa . . . But it wasn't an entirely selfless initiative; rather, it was a complicated tax-relief scheme that meant Leo got to make yet more money by giving some away.

She ran her eye over the main investments again. Everything seemed . . . normal. Besakovitch got the philanthropic feel-good factor of both an ethical trading policy and charitable giving, topped off with better-than-average returns. So *why* was he leaving? There had to be a reason he was sundering a ten-year partnership that had delivered on every count. And that reason had to be somewhere in this report.

Upstairs, she could hear the music start pumping as the DJ ran through his final checks on the PA system and she knew she had to start getting dressed. She didn't put it past Massi to come down here and carry her through in a fireman's lift in her underwear if she was late.

She stood in front of her wardrobe and sighed at the scant selection. With the gold dress already approved by Isobel – she had heard the scream of delight across the hallway – pretty much all she had to choose from was her skinny black ski pants, skinny black jeans and a pair of skinny black trousers. Tops-wise, she had some thermal underwear, a Napapijri Nordic jumper, a red six-ply cashmere polo neck and a black T-shirt. 'Oh, Cinzia,' she murmured, pulling out the skinny jeans and T-shirt. 'It's as well you can't see this.'

She quickly did her make-up – applying a smokier eye than usual to compensate for her minimal outfit – and changed into the all-black ensemble that had no decoration other than the tight, lean lines of her figure. Looking at her reflection in the mirror, she felt it was too plain. She tousled her hair with her fingers and applied a quick dab of berry stain to her lips, but it still wasn't quite enough and she wished she'd brought some jewellery out with her. Usually she travelled with a selection of pieces for different moods, but she'd deliberately left everything at home this time. There was something very ageing, she thought, about skiing in diamonds.

What she needed was something . . . funky, something to get a rock-chick vibe going. She wondered whether Isobel had brought any of those woven leather bracelets with her.

Leather . . . The red leather strap of the cowbell.

No, she dismissed the idea as instantly as it came. It was too unusual, it would attract too much attention, and it didn't feel appropriate to wear something so significant to a party as a mere fashion piece.

Then she remembered the rings.

She found the small cardboard box and pulled them out. The engagement ring, with its three diamonds, was too sentimental to wear to a party. It, too, carried a story that deserved more respect than to be reduced to a mere fashion accessory.

The other one, though . . . The metal was so dull and blackened it was somehow cool, and it had no intrinsic value or symbolism attached to it that she could see.

She gave a shrug and slipped it on her finger. It was better than nothing.

*

Of course, she saw him first, the last one she wanted to see. Even in a crowded room, he stood apart. On a plane, in a boardroom, in a club, at a party, her eyes found him every time. He was talking to a woman who had her back turned to the rest of the room, her brown hair swinging as she talked, one manicured hand gesticulating elegantly. She was wearing a teal dress that had a daringly low scooped back and Allegra wondered whether Sam had been treated to a tantalizing glimpse of it yet.

He was wearing a black velvet jacket, white shirt and narrow black trousers, but he hadn't shaved, the stubble glinting like metal filings under the lights and lending a rougher element to his look.

She looked in vain, instead, for Pierre's distinctive salt-and-pepper hair, barely noticing how enchanting the room looked. Heady sprays of white dendrobium orchids almost as tall as the men were grouped in huge crystal vases, and the lights had been dimmed to their lowest setting, candles a flickering accent on every surface, so that the opulent Christmas tree and Zermatt itself took centre stage in the snowy room.

The guests themselves were no less showy, in sequins and feathers, velvets and silks, the women's skin tanned and gleaming, their hair as shiny as jewels, high heels tip-tapping daintily across the wooden floors as they began to drift into the panoramic glassy corner of the room that had been set up as a dance area. Anyone in the town who happened to look up would be treated to a display of how the super-rich played: flowers, lights and ultra-short dresses.

Allegra felt a stab of doubt as she looked down at her own outfit. Should she have worn the dress herself, after all?

A crescendo of laughter rang out, a top note to the vodka-based buzz of conversation, and she saw Massi and Isobel already in full flow, entertaining a group by the vast window. Isobel really did look like a goddess in the dress, propped as she was on a tall bar stool, with her leg outstretched on the other, Massi standing by her protectively and looking like one of the town's giant St Bernards. He was wearing a black suit and pale pink shirt, no socks, his hair as wild and unruly as his clothes were tailored, perfect teeth flashing with every smile, every joke. Women couldn't take their eyes off him, she noticed, and they kept touching him like he was some sort of interactive art exhibit. She thought of cupcakes again and smiled. He was such a delicious juxtaposition: lover looks, adrenalin junkie, heart of a poet.

Allegra wanted to go over to them both; they were already fast becoming the heart of the party. For all her self-doubt, Isobel was regaling people easily – no doubt with horror stories about weaning Ferds – and the two of them made such easy company, such a good-looking couple. Were they aware of the attraction between them? They looked right together too: Isobel's bright hair and lightly freckled slender limbs against Massi's swarthy Mediterranean bulk. If only Iz hadn't settled for the first guy who'd asked for her hand.

But Allegra couldn't play yet, maybe not at all. Everyone else in the room was here to party, but she was here to work. She looked around for the Yongs – it would be good to make her pitch early before she found Pierre – but she found only Zhou, who was holding court by the Christmas tree.

'Hey!' she shouted over the music.

'Legs! Where have you been?' Zhou beamed, kissing her enthusiastically on each cheek. Legs? He'd called her Legs? Over the course of last night and today their relationship had naturally shifted from being purely professional to something more personal, but this was a quantum leap again. Then she saw the unnatural brightness in his eyes and realized he was cruising on more than just adrenalin.

She noticed he was standing with an auburn-haired woman who appeared to be trying to burrow into the crook of his arm and Allegra suspected she wouldn't be the first – or last – woman vying for an overnight stopover in the chalet with him.

She leaned in and spoke in his ear. 'Are your parents here yet?'

He pulled back, an apologetic expression on his face. 'Oh, Legs, I'm sorry. They called about half an hour ago to say they can't make it. They'll be here in the morning instead.' He squeezed her arm lightly.

'Oh,' she said, disappointed. She'd geared herself up for the meeting and it felt hard to just let the focus go.

'Hey! That's a good thing! It gives us twelve more hours to party!'

She smiled and nodded, realizing that was why he was letting loose. She knew he wouldn't be this unbridled – or off his head – in his parents' company, although it was hard to imagine them at a party like this under any circumstances, no matter how he behaved.

'Is . . . is Pierre coming, by the way?' she asked as casually as she could.

'Pierre?' Zhou said in a scoffing tone. 'Why would he be coming?'

Her heart plummeted at his scorn. 'I don't know,' she

said, as lightly as she could. 'I just thought that, you know, because you'd invited me, maybe you'd have invited him too . . .' Her voice trailed away, a weight beginning to press down on her chest.

Zhou disentangled himself from the brunette and threw his arms around her in an exuberant hug. He was definitely high. 'Legs, tonight is about fun! Not work! We are going to party and we are all going to let ourselves go.' He brought his face close to hers. 'Including you. In fact, *especially* you. OK?'

She nodded, hoping she wasn't going to cry. The tension cables that held her together felt slack suddenly. No Pierre? No Yongs? He stopped a passing waiter and grabbed her a vodka. From the taste of it, it was a double.

'Good! Now, where's Sam?'

'Sam? He's . . . he's talking to someone.'

'We should find him.'

'No! No! He . . . uh, he didn't look like he wanted to be disturbed.'

Zhou grinned. 'Trust me. He does.'

'Wait! Why . . . why don't you introduce me to these people here?' And before he could protest, she turned and burst in on the conversation of the men beside them. 'Hi. Allegra Fisher,' she said, pulling out one of her legendary smiles.

Zhou sighed, not discreetly. 'Allegra, this is Anatoly Greshnev.'

'A pleasure.' Allegra shook his hand; she knew the name: Russian gas company.

'And this is Jae Won. He's just sold his app to Google for half a billion.'

'Wow, congratulations!' she shouted. Was it her imagination or was the music getting louder and louder? 'I guess drinks are on you, then.'

'And this is Frank Kopitsch.' She knew the name again – the Alps's rock-'n'-roll architect, who designed megachalets, in fact probably this one.

She kept smiling, kept shaking hands. To have all these high-net-worth individuals in one room, much less one group . . . It was a brilliant networking opportunity to bring in a portfolio from even a couple of these guys. She looked across at Zhou, remembering his suggestion that she could start up on her own. No matter what he said, she was going to be working tonight, one way or another.

Anatoly was mid-flow about his new yacht in the Azores and she tried to listen, to look for ways in with him, but her eyes drifted and she saw plenty of other women 'working' too. She wondered about the woman still with Sam. Was she here on business?

The backless brunette was laughing at something he'd said – Ed Milliband impression maybe? – and as the woman stepped right, slightly, letting a waiter pass, Allegra, engrossed, automatically stepped right too, inadvertently standing on Frank's foot.

'Oh, sorry!' she shouted, stepping back again.

Frank, whose hair was long – 1980s heavy-metal-long – and grey, with some blond highlights at the front, clasped her elbow lightly, as though she'd lost her balance. He was wearing a black shirt and leather trousers, and was no doubt here for the networking opportunities too. She saw his gaze dragged along with a passing blonde in stacked Louboutins and a fallout dress, her arms held high as she 'squeezed' through the crowd.

'Did you build this chalet, Frank?' she asked, having to lean in to him to make herself heard.

He responded in kind. 'I did!' he said, clearly flattered to learn she already knew of him. 'Do you like it?'

'It's magnificent. I've never seen a pool with quite such a wow factor.'

'We had every tile hand-gilded,' he said proudly.

'*Really?*' she nodded, not remotely interested. 'And the glass walls and roof in here . . . just amazing.' She took a sip of her drink. Pierre wasn't coming.

'If I was to tell you about the thermal restrictions, the load-bearing calculations of the snow on the glass . . .' He rolled his eyes. 'Every time on a build I say to myself, Frank, this is the last time you are putting yourself through this. The demands are crazy; frankly, it's inhuman. And yet . . .' He held out his hands. 'I'm a sucker. My job is my mistress.'

It wasn't a great thought. She tipped her head to the side sympathetically. 'And what are you working on at the moment?'

'An eighteen sleeper in Winkelmatten. Cinema, snow room, conference room, private nightclub . . .'

'Anyone I'd know?'

'Oh yes.' He strummed a few chords of air guitar and then pretended to smoke a spliff, as if that would tell her the client's identity, as opposed to holding up a mirror to the entire music industry.

'Allegra!' The word surfed the crowd and she turned to see Massi pushing his way through the bodies towards her.

'What is *this*?' he asked, hands held out low towards her, disappointment tainting his voice.

'As well you know, I gave the dress to Iz. You've just been looking at her in it!'

Massi looked aghast at her. 'But *you* are supposed to be golden tonight,' he explained. 'The golden girl. This is what we said. Tonight is a *beeg* night.'

'Massi, I'm not auditioning for *The X Factor*,' she laughed, trying to lessen his devastation.

'But you look like . . . a member of the stuff,' he hissed, desperation in his eyes.

Frank frowned, clearly not keeping up with Massi's stranglehold of the English language.

'He means "staff",' Allegra shouted, taking another sip. God, but she had a sudden thirst on. Pierre wasn't coming, the Yongs weren't here, and she was left with an abundance of adrenalin that had nowhere to go. 'Fairytale of New York' was pumping through the speakers, Kirsty MacColl's voice clear and defiant, throwing verbal punches at her lover even as she came in for the kiss.

'But you were so sexy in the dress.' He had begun to whine. 'I wanted you to stand out of the cloud. I wanted every man's eyes on you.'

'Did it ever occur to you that maybe I don't want every man's eyes on me?' she asked, placing a hand on his arm. 'Besides, I think there are more than enough women here vying for that honour.' As if to prove her point, a rail-thin white-blonde with a tight bun and infeasible cleavage sashayed past. Frank's eyes followed again.

'But you are lost here,' Massi scolded.

'Lost is what I want,' she replied truthfully. She had wanted to hide in this crowd tonight, be visible to the only two men who mattered in her life right now. But neither of them had showed and she was left here like a lone shadow in the lights.

'Hey! Allegra?'

Another voice cut into their conversation. She turned as if in slow motion.

Max smiled back at her, a beer in one hand, his eyes on her alone as he leaned in and kissed her on the corner of her mouth, just like last time – deliberately ambiguous, much like their relationship, which had been kindled but not consummated.

He stood apart from the crowd for the same reasons as her – woefully underdressed – but he was still better-looking than was polite in a red and navy check shirt and jeans. She half wondered where he'd got the beer from – as far as she was aware, vintage champagne and vodka were tonight's tipples, in keeping with the party (and indeed chalet's) all-white Christmas theme.

'What are you doing here?' she gasped in surprise, her eyes searching the crowd for the others.

'Jacques is hanging with a girl who was invited. She said it was cool to come.' He shrugged. 'I thought you left Zermatt. You said you were only staying a few days.'

It was hard to find her voice. 'Our plans changed.'

'Because . . . ?'

She had no intention of getting into the details of her grandmother's memorial service. 'We're finishing up some family business.'

'Unfinished business, huh?' he smiled, his eyes soft upon her, and she knew he was alluding to them. 'Well, *I* am pleased. Where are you staying? Same place?'

'Uh, no . . . Here, actually.'

'*Here?*' He looked younger suddenly, as he took in the

lavish scale of the chalet. It belonged to a world that he would probably never see beyond this point. Nor would much care to.

She nodded, remembering suddenly Frank and Massi standing beside them, watching everything. 'God, I'm sorry – I'm being so rude. Frank, Massi, this is Max.'

The men nodded sternly – both suspicious of the beautiful man-child in their midst who was seemingly unaware of the glances he attracted from women and appeared to have eyes only for Allegra.

Massi took a half-step into the space. 'We have met before,' he said in a low growl.

'Yeah?' Max replied with a quizzical grin. Everything about him – his longer hair, baby beard, baggy clothes, ready smile and languid pose – marked him out as a different animal to the buttoned-up international playboys here tonight. 'So, did you ski today?' Max asked, opening up the conversation to the rest of the group, but his eyes permanently coming back to Allegra, like the swing of a compass to magnetic north.

Frank excused himself on the pretext of getting a fresh drink, most likely making a beeline for any woman who was surrounded by less men.

'Well, do you want to say, or shall I?' Massi asked her, but he had lost the happy-go-lucky smile she had already come to know and quite love.

She gave an exaggerated groan, eager to keep the tone light. She didn't quite understand Massi's undoubted aversion to Max. 'We went heli-skiing and I lost a ski at the top.'

Max immediately pulled a face that suggested he understood exactly the potential gravity of that scenario. 'But how? You are so good.'

'Just caught an edge,' she sighed, trying not to remember her hurt at Bob's phone call to Sam.

'So how did you get down?' He looked across at Massi. 'You stayed with her, yes?'

The point was subtle, but there. They were squaring up.

'I was already ahead,' Massi said, pushing out his chest. 'I knew nothing about it till the phone call from Sam. He was *with* her.'

Allegra's eyes snapped across to Massi. Had he deliberately put the stress on that word, or was it just his terrible English?

Max seemed to pick up the unusual syntax too. 'Who's Sam?'

'Sam, you remember. He is over there,' Massi said, stepping closer to Max and wrapping an arm over the younger man's shoulder, pointing out Sam across the room. 'Can you see him?'

It was easy to spot him – he was already staring over at them all.

Allegra felt her stomach twist as Massi waved, a generous friendly gesture to come over. Max's gaze strayed questioningly to Allegra and she felt her stomach lurch.

'Hey. What's up?'

Sam was standing beside them with a drink in his hand and that familiar dark look that was like a firewall – keeping everything outside out, keeping everything inside in. He didn't look at her at all and she felt the last of the afternoon's truce crumble like a stale cake. His earlier warmth on the snow had gone completely and they were back to their usual checkmate.

'Sam, I want you to meet Allegra's friend Max,' Massi said with an unnaturally light tone.

377

'Oh, yes. I remember. We met the other night,' Max said first, tipping his beer bottle in easy greeting, but the tension in their little group had tightened into a hard knot. Everyone felt it.

'I remember too.'

'You see, Sam remembers too,' Massi said, looking back down at Max, his usually laughing eyes wide and stony cold. 'He remembers *everything* that happened at the Broken Bar, don't you, Sam?'

'That's right.'

Max looked between the two older men, seemingly not intimidated by them, seemingly not as baffled by their aggression as Allegra.

'What's going on here?' she asked.

'Hey, man, it was all legal, just a bit of fun,' Max shrugged.

'Yeah. There's just the small issue of consent,' Sam snarled.

'Did she look to you like she wasn't having a good t—'

He didn't get to finish the sentence. In the next moment, Sam had rushed at him, slamming him against the wall.

'Oh my God! Massi, do something!' she cried, seeing Sam's hand drawn back in a fist, ready to fly. The people immediately around them parted, looking on curiously as Max was held up by his shirt collar, his feet on tiptoes on the ground, but there was too much noise and movement for the ruckus to be noticed by the rest of the crowd.

Massi waded in. 'Hey, hey! Leave him to me, my friend. I can throw this boy further in the snow. Leave him.'

Massi lowered Sam's arm, patting him on the shoulder as Sam dropped Max from the hold.

'Hey, what's your problem, man?' Max coughed, his eyes catching everyone's stares.

'You know exactly what my problem is,' Sam snarled, his jaw clenching again.

'You're just jealous I got there before y—'

Sam flew again, but this time Massi stopped him, blocking his path and hauling Max off his feet and through the crowd like a naughty little boy.

Allegra looked after them both in open-mouthed horror.

'What the *hell* is wrong with you?' she demanded, turning to Sam. 'Who do you think you are to treat him like that? What's he done to you to deserve being humiliated like that?'

'It's what he's done to you that's the problem.'

Allegra cocked an eyebrow. '*That's* what this is about? You're behaving like some jealous little schoolboy because he kissed me? Jesus Christ, just grow up, why don't you!'

'Allegra—'

'No! Fuck you!' she said angrily, turning away from him and darting into the crowd, past Zhou and Jae Won – still deep in conversation – past the Russian escorts showing what they had on the dance floor, past the waiters scurrying to and from the kitchen with sterling-silver trays pressed flat on their upturned palms. She ran into the lift, the doors closing as she heard her name called.

Her heart accelerated as the lift moved down and she willed it to go faster, but half a flight on pulleys took longer than on foot. Oh God, *why* hadn't she taken the stairs?

The doors opened again on the lower level just seconds later and she darted out, but it was too late: Sam was already at the bottom steps, his jacket flying behind him as he rushed at her.

'Wait!' he demanded, standing in her way.

'No!' she shouted, pushing against him to get past.

His hands closed on her elbows and held her in place. 'You don't know what's going on!'

'I know enough,' she snapped, trying to wrest her arms free, but he held her fast. 'Let me past!' she shouted. She was almost shaking with rage. She couldn't stand it with him any more. None of it. Just his presence in the same room made her lungs compress, her head spin, her palms sweat. He made the world tip off its axis so that nothing made sense: kindness felt like a trick, intimacy a cruel joke. Aggression and hostility were the only behaviours she understood in him, for they were clear to read and easy to understand, the inevitable consequences of chemistry turning toxic.

'He drugged you, Allegra.'

Her body slackened in his grip and he let her go, taking a step back.

'What?' she whispered, her eyes never leaving him, searching his face for clues.

'It's called sparkle, one of these so-called legal highs. It dissolves in your drink, makes you . . . happy, free . . .'

She watched his lips moving, but her mind was elsewhere, remembering the killing hangover the next day . . . the persistent blank about the night before.

'His friend put it in your drink in the bar. Massi saw them and alerted the managers, then told us. Apparently those guys have already been banned at half the clubs in town.'

She tensed suddenly, panic infusing her face. 'Did I . . . ? How did I get home? What did I . . . ?'

'We took you back ourselves.'

'*You* did?' She stared at him, completely unable to conjure a single memory of him or Massi or Zhou walking her and Iz back to the apartment. Oh God! She covered her face with her hands. She had thought it had been bad enough that Zhou had seen her drunk! But drugged too?

'Hey.' She felt his hand on her shoulder. 'It's OK. Nothing happened. They didn't touch you.'

She looked up at him, shaking her head from side to side. 'I didn't know.'

'I know . . . And I wasn't sure whether or not to tell you. I thought you might think I was . . . interfering or trying to scare you.' He shrugged. 'So I decided not to. I told myself the chances were you wouldn't see him again anyway, but then the next morning, before the race—'

She looked up at him.

'When he came over and kissed you, I . . .' He looked down. 'I thought he was going to try again. I chased after him all the way down that freaking mountain. Nearly took you out too, I realized, when you then started chasing me!' He shrugged.

She blinked. He hadn't done it on purpose?

'By the time I caught up with him at the bottom, Massi was already on their case, roughing them up a bit. He told them to get the hell out of town. So when they turned up tonight . . .'

She didn't know what to say. How could she have got this all so wrong? 'Can't the police do anything?'

'Technically no. They know about them and have alerted the bars and clubs owners, but the drugs are legal to buy, and there haven't been any allegations made against these guys. Not yet anyway.'

'I don't know what to say,' she murmured, looking away, before looking up at him, before looking away again.

'None of it's your fault. You were just trying to blow off some steam . . . No one could blame you for that.' He shifted position, looking awkward, and she knew they'd moved onto new ground. *Them.*

'I should go,' she said in a quiet voice, turning to move past him.

'Wait,' he said, taking a half-step towards her. 'Please. Can we just . . . talk for a bit?'

'There's nothing to say, Sam.'

'There's *everything* to say.'

She looked up at him. 'Is talking going to change what you did? Is it going to change what you said that night to Pierre? What you made him say to me?'

Sam looked taken aback. 'Allegra, I—'

She stared at him, waiting for a justification she knew he couldn't give, even while his eyes were telling her a different story.

'I had to do it.'

'You *had* to?' She almost laughed. Whatever had flickered between them for one night in Zurich hadn't been able to survive the ambition he had bared in London. 'The deal comes first, right?'

He stared at her, conflicting emotions running across his face so that she couldn't tell what he was going to say next. 'I know you understand it. We're the same, Allegra.'

'No, we're not. I never would have hung someone out to dry the way you did with me.'

'No? Then tell me this – would you have hated me if I *hadn't* turned up in London afterwards? Would there have been something between us if I'd stayed in Zurich or gone back to New York – off your patch and out of your deal?'

She looked away, refusing to go down that path. What did he expect her to say when he'd just admitted he'd deliberately thrown her under the train to save himself?

'Answer me.' He took another step towards her.

'Of course not. That was the point! There was nothing between us except a few hours to kill. It was easy because it meant nothing.'

'Nothing? You want us to keep pretending there's nothing there?'

'Who's pretending?'

He raked back his hair, keeping his hand there, an almost pitying look on his face. 'Allegra, you never *stop* pretending. You pretend that you're not lonely, that you feel nothing but contempt for me. But I know it's a lie. Every memory from Zurich tells me it's a lie.' His voice had changed and she felt her pulse begin to quicken, her body getting ready for flight. 'Why are we doing this to each other? I thought you were the smartest, sexiest, most intoxicating woman I'd ever met.'

'I'm not interested in what you think.' She took a step back, but he simply followed and she swallowed hard, hating the way his movements directed hers. She tried standing her ground, but she couldn't tolerate him standing that close and it was all she could do not to raise her arms like a barrier.

'I don't believe you.'

'Fine. Be delusional.'

She twisted away, walking round him, but he simply hooked his arm around her waist and gathered her into him, kissing her with a passion that stripped her of every conscious thought and left nothing but instinct, an instinct that impelled her to kiss him back.

He pulled away, breathless, his eyes intense and heavy upon hers as her heart beat so loudly she could feel it like a bass beat. 'I'm the deluded one? Really?'

She wanted to laugh, she wanted to cry, but she did neither, his eyes had her in a lock that made it impossible to move. She had run out of fight and excuses. And as his mouth lowered to hers again, slowly this time, she wrapped her arms around his neck and did something she'd never done in her adult life. She gave in.

Chapter Twenty-Eight

Day Eighteen: *Miniature Cowbell*

She lay in his arms, listening to his heartbeat. She knew its rhythm now; she could play it on a drum as it thumped gently beneath her cheek like the kick of an unborn baby. She thought she could lie here forever, his arm heavy and bent around her, his skin warm and tanned beneath her.

But that was a fantasy. It was already almost over. The Yongs would be arriving soon and these were their dying moments. Her eyes were still, upon the brooding hulk of the Matterhorn, which watched over them in silent constancy, the pre-dawn sky like a bruise behind it. She only had as much time as the night's span, and the sun was beginning to leach a lambent glow that even the mountains could only hide for so long. When the first shadow hit the north face, she would rise. There would be no point in lamenting it. Tears were a waste of energy, the past a dead thing. And soon this would be past like everything else.

A twist of hair fell over her face and she pushed it back, holding her arm up in the air as she noticed the ring still on her finger. She'd forgotten about it last night, her token effort at display. Was it made from tin? It really was as modest and humble as a drawing pin.

She twisted it slightly, thinking how different it was to the flashy engagement ring that had bright yellow gold and not one, not two but three diamonds, and as she did so, her eyes widened in surprise at what she saw. For there, on her skin where the ring had been, was a tiny but perfect indent of a heart.

Allegra slipped off the ring and saw, under the widest part – where one ordinarily might expect a seal or crest – a shallow heart-shaped rim. Hidden, like a secret.

Sam stirred slightly, bending his leg so that hers – slung across him – slipped into the warm space, rolling her deeper into him. Sliding the ring back on, she dropped her arm down and closed her eyes, inhaling his scent. He groaned softly in his sleep, the sound a low growl against her ear. She smiled. And her eyes stayed closed.

'Good morning.'

Her eyes flew open. Sam was sitting with wet hair on the edge of the bed, wearing just a towel and holding a mug.

'I guessed tea. Was I right?'

She nodded wordlessly, her gaze stuck on him in bafflement. What had happened? Why was he here? Why was she still *here*?

She looked out at the Matterhorn basking in full sun, the sky a speedwell blue behind it, mocking her. He put the tea on the bedside table and leaned in, kissing her on the mouth and pushing her back against the warm pillows. 'How did you sleep?'

She nodded again as she looked up at him, trying not to think how good he looked, trying not to panic. She had fallen asleep again. She had fallen asleep in his arms and now it was too late to make the discreet exit that would have told him wordlessly how things had to be.

His eyes tracked her face lazily, like he had all the time in the world to drink her in. They met hers again. 'I didn't want to wake you, but the Yongs are due soon and I didn't think you'd want to be in your pyjamas. Or worse . . . mine.'

He grinned at her, a lopsided smile with bright eyes that almost winded her. How could she want him and yet hate him at the same time?

'Thank you,' she whispered as his mouth came down on hers again and the world receded . . .

No. Her hands found his shoulders and pushed against them. He rolled back, resting his head on one hand, the smile seemingly tattooed to his face.

'I'd better get up,' she said quietly.

'Well, you can certainly try,' he grinned, leaning down and kissing her yet again, feeling her immediate response.

Oh God, oh God . . . She knew she had to re-establish a cool that would draw a line between them again, but her heart was pounding with a wildness she couldn't tame, and her emotions felt dangerously close to the surface. How could she have fallen back to sleep? Every minute spent with him was wearing her down, making it harder to leave.

'It was a good party,' she murmured as he tenderly pushed her hair away from her face. At least if they could get on to talking, that might lead to arguing . . .

'No it wasn't. It was terrible. Far too flashy. You were forty minutes late, and *he* turned up. I don't think I've ever been to a worse party.'

'Forty minutes?' She blinked up at him. 'How do you know that?'

'Why do you think I was standing where I was standing? I had an uninterrupted view of everyone coming and going. I could clearly see you trying to avoid me,' he laughed. 'Not that I had any intention of letting you get away with that.'

She wriggled away from him, jumping up from the bed, but the duvet was pinned fast beneath him, so she grabbed the nearest thing to hand off the floor. His . . . ? His shirt.

'Oh, *now* you're coy?' he asked, watching as she turned away and shrugged her arms through the sleeves, buttoning it up loosely with trembling hands. She had to get out of here, away from these words, away from those eyes, because the reasons she was here in this chalet were nothing to do with him. The chemistry between them was undeniable, yes, she'd admit that, but she hadn't come here to be in his bed. She was here because of Yong's promise, that headline in Sunday's papers, the report in the room next door . . .

She couldn't afford to forget that. She reached down to scoop her knickers and bra off the floor. Her jeans were by the door, and the sooner she got out of here, the better – his words were spinning her off in directions she couldn't take. She had only one path.

But he had other ideas, lunging across the bed and whipping her into him as she tried to scoot past. She burst out laughing as his hands skimmed down her waist with deft lightness, tickling her, pushing her into him.

'Nice effort,' he said, looking down at her in his arms and laying her back on the mattress. 'But no cigar.'

*

They agreed to stagger their entrances. Sam said he would give her a five-minute head start on breakfast before he came upstairs, but everyone's eyes still flicked over her with seemingly knowing looks when he took his place at the table. Or was that just the paranoia talking?

'Sleep well?' Massi asked, mischief in his smile as Sam reached for some grapes.

'Yes. You?' Sam replied, his face and voice neutral, even though his foot had somehow found her ankle and hooked around it under the table. Isobel was still taking breakfast in her room, although Allegra suspected that novelty was wearing thin now that there was a party post-mortem going on.

'You know me – I sleep like the dead,' Massi said, tearing open a bread roll and buttering it lavishly.

'No you don't. The dead are a lot quieter than you. You snore like a gorilla,' Zhou said. 'I could hear you all the way from my room.'

Massi tossed his head and then the bread roll at Zhou, who simply ducked and laughed.

'It was a great party, Zhou,' Allegra said, sipping her tea as she eyed her host, looking for signs of an epic come-down, but he seemed to be brimming with barely restrained ebullience, clearly still buoyed by last night's success. 'So many people. You've got a lot of friends.'

'Oh, I think we all know they're not my friends,' Zhou said with a knowing smile. 'But I agree. It was a great party.'

He carried on nodding, very pleased about something, and Allegra wondered what else had gone on after she and Sam had retired early. Zhou was playing a risky game cutting fast and loose in the chalet with the Alpine elite only hours before his parents arrived.

She shifted in her chair slightly to see whether any damage had been done to the chalet – she and Sam had been awake till three and the music had still been playing then – but everything looked as pristine as ever: no red wine on the sofas, no curtains hanging off their hooks, no rips in the sheepskin rugs, no three-legged chairs . . . No doubt because Estelle and the staff had worked as a crack team before first light, restoring everything to order before breakfast.

'I don't remember seeing *you* after the French boy ate snow,' Massi said, slopping jam on the roll.

The mention of Max made her eyes dim and she looked over at Massi with newfound appreciation. Her unsung guardian angel. 'No? Oh, I was around. Mingling, you know.' She busied herself with quartering a strawberry as Sam's foot hooked her tighter.

'Mingling,' Massi echoed, his eyes watching her closely.

'New word for you there, Mass,' Sam quipped. 'What time are your parents getting here?' he asked Zhou.

Zhou inhaled deeply at the question, his spine straightening so that he sat an inch taller. 'Their plane's due to land in Geneva in an hour. Then it's forty minutes in the helicopter to here.'

'You want us to be here as a welcoming party, or shall we scoot?'

'You should be out when they arrive. My parents will want to rest after their journey and . . .' He cleared his throat, glancing at Allegra. 'There are some things I need to discuss with them.'

'OK, then.' Sam arched an eyebrow curiously and Allegra felt her stomach lurch. This was why she should have run from the room. This was why she should have crept from his room in the black of night. How could she do her job if she let emotions get in the way?

She unhooked her leg from his and tucked it under her chair.

'Well, that should give us time to get a few runs in. Where do you fancy skiing this morning?' Sam asked, his foot clearly trying to find hers under the table.

'Gornergrat?' Massi shrugged, chewing on his pastry. 'We could stop by the snow park and do some jumps.'

'Allegra, does that sound good to you?' Sam asked, more directly. His tone was deliberately casual, but she wondered whether that alone would give them away. He had, after all, distinguished himself by being unreservedly silent in her presence to date.

'Actually, I've got some things to do in town again this morning. Why don't I meet up with you all later, again?' She said it as lightly as possible, putting her elbows on the table and sipping from her tea.

'Sure,' Sam said after a pause, resuming chewing, but she saw the question mark flash in his eyes.

'It is not another boyfriend of yours, I hope, Allegra,' Massi said, his eyes shining wickedly.

'Rest assured you don't need to beat anybody up for me today,' she replied with a smile, subtly acknowledging what he'd done for her and Iz.

'Good,' Massi said with a wink. 'Although I do not think anyone could be so bald as the French boy.'

'*Bold*, Massi! You are a nightmare,' she chuckled.

Zhou laughed too, throwing a napkin at his head.

But Sam wasn't laughing, and as she jogged down the stairs ten minutes later, he was straight after her.

'What was all that about?' he whispered, catching her by her bedroom door.

'What?'

'Pulling away from me, refusing to look at me . . .' He put his hands on her hips and drew her into him, his mouth on hers before she could protest, as though he understood that words were her best defence.

'I just don't want them to suspect us,' she said when they pulled away, unable to meet his eyes.

He put his finger under chin and made her look at him. 'And why do we have to be a secret? Why do I have to enter a room five minutes after you, anyway? These guys are two of my oldest friends. I don't think I *can* hide us from them. You must have noticed they've been trying to get us together.'

She frowned. 'No.'

'Legs, it's why Zhou invited you to stay here.' He shrugged and his ignorance of the real reason she was here hammered a crack in her heart. 'He told me after the meeting in Paris that he knew there was something between us.'

'What? How?'

'He said no one who hates each other as much as we hated each other really hates each other.'

She fell silent. She knew this was the moment to tell him why she was really here. She could be his rival *and* his lover. The two states could exist independently of each other, but the words wouldn't come. She didn't believe them, and in just a few hours from now, her career would blow them apart.

'Anyway, what *are* you doing this morning that you can't ski with us?' He stepped towards her, one hand sliding behind her neck and angling her face up to his. 'Because I don't want you out of my bed, much less my sight.'

She felt the gravitational pull between them as his eyes locked on hers and their mutual desire ignited again. Was this what Lars had felt for Valentina? Was this the all-encompassing love that would bring down the walls of her world if she were to lose him? They had fought and loved and warred across Europe – in Zurich, Paris, London and Zermatt – and she couldn't outrun him, couldn't shake him off.

The sound of footsteps on the staircase made them leap apart, but not quickly enough for Massi to miss seeing them standing together.

'You two look guilty as hell,' Massi grinned delightedly, his eyes wide.

'We're just discussing where to meet for lunch,' Sam replied, slouching against the doorframe for good measure. 'I was thinking Findlerhof?'

'No,' Massi sighed, his smile fading. 'Lunch must be back here today. We must pay lipstick to the Yongs.'

Allegra heard Sam laugh under his breath. 'Fair enough,' he muttered, pushing himself back to standing again.

'We'd better all make the most of this morning, then,' Allegra said briskly, stepping towards her room. 'See you later, boys.'

'OK, man, I see you upstairs in ten,' Massi called over his shoulder to Sam, walking back to his room.

'Sure,' Sam said back, but with his eyes on Allegra. 'Ten minutes ought to do it . . .' he murmured.

She shut the door behind them quickly as his mouth found the sweet spot between her shoulder and neck, and she closed her eyes, lost already. Her head told her she was letting herself get carried away. Her head told her not to allow this to become anything more than a straightforward case of sexual attraction, but what hope did she have? Two nights with him and her world was already spinning off its own axis. Two nights with him and she was beginning to believe she'd found someone to trust. Two nights with him and her heart was already telling her that maybe he was worth more than a deal.

Chapter Twenty-Nine

Her boots weren't tall enough for the night's newly laid drifts and puffs of snow gathered at her calves, ready to melt and drip into her jeans and socks. But she didn't notice. She was too busy waving as Massi and Sam pressed their faces to the windows of the ski train as it pulled out from the station and across the town's streets, ahead of its climb to the top of Zermatt's middle mountain.

Massi was making faces for her amusement, but although she was laughing, her eyes never once left Sam's. And long after the train had snaked into the trees, she stood looking at where they'd been, fresh memories playing over in her mind and making her heart bounce.

He'd been right. They weren't going to be able to hide it for much longer. She was distracted to the point of delirium and she hardly remembered why she was out here at all and not flying down a mountain with him, letting her body take flight and catch up with her soaring soul. She walked through the crowds with a smile on her lips that she knew, by rights, shouldn't be there, but it wouldn't come off, wouldn't die down.

Her feet knew where to take her now and she moved with the careless eyes of a local, unseeing of the majesty of the mountain arena, the pretty glitter of the Christmas lights. She walked past the wooden gift shop again and her feet stopped. The drawer of the Advent calendar numbered '18' had been opened since yesterday to reveal an ornate wire star that had been threaded with white and red glass beads, but her eyes fell again to the fat-cheeked wooden angel in the fifth drawer.

Allegra pushed open the door and wandered in. It was warm inside the little shop, a red carpet bouncing a rosy glow up the walls, which were covered with shelves of wooden figures, musical boxes, doll's houses and animals; puppets dangled by their strings from the ceiling; the traditional cuckoo clocks hung on the wall behind the long red wooden counter – as shiny as any sleigh – their faces all set to different times.

A young girl, maybe eighteen or nineteen, smiled up at her as she walked along the far wall, by the Christmas gifts and decorations. Her hair was long and tied in a loose plait, and she was wearing a traditional red waistcoat and full skirt – no doubt to please the tourist trade. '*Guten Tag*.'

'*Guten Tag*,' Allegra nodded, smiling back, as she cast her eye lightly over the shelves. A pile of Angel Barrys were heaped in a shallow basket and she picked one up.

'English?' the girl enquired.

Allegra nodded.

'Would you like help with anything, or are you happy to browse?'

'I'll take this, please.' She brought it over to the girl, who smiled and immediately began wrapping it in tissue paper.

'That is sixteen Swiss francs, please.'

Allegra handed over a twenty, her eyes falling to the cuckoo clocks behind her. They were, after all, one of the reasons she'd come in. 'Could you tell me a little more about those?'

The girl half turned as she counted out Allegra's change. 'These are very special pieces. All hand-made by my father and grandfather. The roof, you can see,' she said, pointing out the one nearest to her, 'it is made from one piece of wood, so there are no hinges or nails, and the little stones in the garden are off these mountains. There are over six hundred and fifty separate pieces in each clock.'

'Wow.'

'Yes,' the girl beamed, delighted by Allegra's reaction.

'Is your grandfather still making them?'

She gave a shrug. 'Slowly, now. His eyesight is not so good.'

'Oh.'

The girl handed Allegra back her change and the Angel Barry, now gloved in a small paper bag.

Allegra hesitated, not wanting to leave so quickly. She had so many questions she wanted to ask, but wasn't quite sure how . . .

'So this is a family business, then?'

'Yes. My family have been carpenters for five generations. We are very proud.'

Allegra nodded. 'My family were goat farmers.' She said it almost shyly. It felt strange saying the words out loud for the first time, taking ownership of a history she'd never known.

'Oh.' The girl nodded politely. After a moment, she added: 'Here?'

'Mm-hmm.' It was Allegra's turn to shrug. 'Not any more, though. Sadly. We can't claim to be five generations of anything.' Well, five generations of women – *a long line of mothers*, the family joke – but now didn't seem the time.

A little silence blossomed and the girl gave a tiny, embarrassed shrug.

'Actually, I was admiring the Advent calendar in the window,' Allegra said, picking up the slack again.

'Oh yes. In truth, it is too small for a window display, but we sold our last nativity scene and had nothing else to put in. I have tried to make it fit with the leaves.' The girl gave an anxious frown. From this angle, the window did look far too big for the calendar.

'It looks wonderful,' Allegra said encouragingly. 'It really caught my eye . . . Is it a local . . . speciality? I've never seen an Advent calendar like that before.'

'Yes,' the girl said, bowing her head politely. 'And they are becoming more popular. People enjoy coming in and choosing which gifts they want to put inside the drawers. It makes it very personal. No two are ever the same.'

'No, I bet. It's a great idea.'

'Many people like the Angel Gabriels.' The girl nodded towards Allegra's purchase, in her hand.

'Oh yes, right . . . Yes, I bet they do. He's cute. The cheeks . . .'

The girl smiled politely and Allegra hesitated at the natural pause. She knew she should leave now. Instead, she placed her hand on the counter. 'To be honest, the Advent calendar, I've already got one and I think it may be one of yours.'

'Ours?'

'Yes. It's really old, but it's even got an angel like this one. We found it in the loft at our house.'

'In England?'

'Yes, but our mother's from here and . . .' She stopped, not wanting to bore the poor girl with her convoluted family history. 'Well, given the clock and the calendar, it seems more and more likely they came from here.'

The girl looked even more surprised. 'You have one of the clocks too?'

'Yes, but not here. The clock's back in England being repaired, but I've got the calendar with me.' She shrugged, a little embarrassed. 'Ours is a lot smaller than the one in your window, obviously – I couldn't travel with one that size – but I've been enjoying opening the drawers each day. And *I* don't usually do Christmas.' She realized she hadn't opened today's. Sam had been far too distracting for that.

'Could you bring it in? I know my father would love to see it.'

'Really? You think he'd be interested?'

The girl nodded eagerly. 'I know he would.'

'OK, well . . . is there any particular time?'

'He is with suppliers today, but he will be in the workshop all day tomorrow. I will tell him to expect you.'

'Great,' Allegra shrugged happily. 'Well, then it's a date.'

'A date,' the girl repeated, smiling back too.

Allegra walked out onto the street, feeling like another piece of history was slotting into place. If the clock were from here, perhaps the girl's grandparents had known Valentina. Allegra could never bring back Valentina for her mother, but maybe, just maybe, she could bring back stories about her.

The door of the coffee shop next door opened and a waft of crêpes drifted onto the street as a gaggle of cute snowboarding girls loped out with neon-yellow trousers hanging off their hips, baggy beige jackets falling to their thighs and thick knitted 1970s-style headbands keeping their ears warm.

Allegra cut in, deciding to buy a *tortin* for Isobel. She had been right about her sister's high spirits beginning to plummet – not only was she fed up with missing another day on the slopes, but drinking on painkillers had significantly worsened today's hangover and she was now five days without Ferdy and Lloyd, meaning that even Massi was having to work hard to make her smile. The only blessing was, she'd been so swaddled in her own misery this morning that she hadn't noticed Allegra's suspiciously rare radiance.

The queue was almost to the door and she took her phone out of her pocket while she waited, mayday-texting Lloyd to send photos of Ferdy over to his wife. There were no new messages for her. The flurry of sympathy calls had tailed off sharply as she kept her head down – out of sight, almost forgotten – and she didn't know how to keep explaining away Pierre's continued silence any more. He knew she was here; he had to know she was still in the running . . .

The expansion in her chest began to narrow again as she realized just how much last night had complicated things, and she made herself remember what Sam had done at the dinner – the antagonistic whispers he'd admitted to, just seconds before he kissed her.

She closed her eyes and inhaled slowly, making herself remember that *she* was the good guy in all of this. It was one thing to give in to desire, quite another to give up revenge, and defeating Sam was her only way back to Pierre. He wouldn't hesitate to do the same to her.

'Miss Fisher?'

She opened her eyes to find Father Merete standing beside her, two coffees-to-go in his hands. 'I'm sorry, I hope I didn't interrupt your prayers.'

'Oh, I . . . I wasn't—' she spluttered, before seeing the twinkle in his eyes. 'Oh.'

He smiled. 'Are you feeling ready for tomorrow?'

She nodded. 'You were right. The undertakers have been excellent. As soon as we'd dealt with the paperwork, they took over and managed everything for us. I rather feel I haven't done enough.'

'The fact that you're here and doing this at all is enough.'

She shrugged, still not comfortable with taking any credit for her actions. This was duty – or at least, it had started out like that. 'Oh, by the way, I met my grandfather. After we spoke, my sister and I went round to see him.'

'And?' Father Merete looked pleased.

'He's just wonderful. I saw him yesterday too, and I'm hoping to get over there again this afternoon. It's been incredible talking to him about the past. I've already learned so much about my family from him and we've barely even begun.'

'I am happy to hear that. I hope it has restored his spirits to have you in his life too. Did he say whether he will attend the service tomorrow?'

'Yes, he's coming.'

'That's good. I was very concerned about him. I went to the house several times to visit, but Bettina would not let me in.' His brow furrowed. 'She kept saying he was rest-ing and could not be disturbed.'

'Yes, she was very off with us too. She's a bit of a dragon, isn't she?' The queue moved forward and she shuffled along to keep up.

He chuckled. 'Well, I have to remind myself it can't be easy for her being confronted with the reappearance of Lars's spectacular first wife. I would imagine no woman wants to feel second best.'

Allegra remembered what Lars had said about her grandmother's flight for that very reason. 'I guess not, but then who's she to get so personally involved? She's just his nurse. What does it matter how she—' She saw his expres-sion. 'What?'

'Bettina is Lars's wife, not his nurse – well, not offi-cially.'

Allegra felt the hairs on her skin prickle. 'Oh.'

'Does that matter?'

'No, no. I just . . . didn't realize.' She remembered how she'd dissed Bettina, thinking she was upstart staff, and Lars had laughed.

She was almost at the front of the queue now. She could see the sugar-sifted *tortin* sitting under the glass.

Father Merete held up the cups in his hands. 'Well, I should get these back to my assistant priest before they're cold or he'll switch over to the Anglicans. Apparently they do better coffee than me.'

Allegra smiled, appreciating the attempt at levity, but she felt unsettled somehow, not only to realize that Lars had never introduced Bettina as his wife, but that she was so much younger than him – at least thirty years, surely? But then again, why shouldn't he have remarried? Was he supposed to live his life alone, especially after Granny had deserted him in such terrible circumstances?

Anya . . .

Father Merete turned to leave.

'Father,' she said, turning back, 'can I ask you something?'

'Of course.'

'For all the years Valentina was missing, they couldn't have issued a death certificate for her, could they? Not without a body.'

'That's right. Although there's what's known as a presumption of death after seven years. A death certificate can be issued then, even without a body.'

'So then how could my grandfather have remarried my aunt only a year later? Technically he would still have been married to Valentina.'

The priest looked at the floor for a moment and she could see he was considering his words carefully. When he looked back up, his eyes moved left and right to check no one was listening in. 'You have to understand things were different back then. Life here, in the 1950s, it was not like you see now, with thousands of visitors. These villages were tiny: everyone knew everyone. When your grandmother disappeared that fateful weekend, there was no way she could have survived – everyone would have known it, including the priest.' He paused. 'We run our lives to bureaucracy now, but back then a death certificate was just a piece of paper, and part of the role of the parish priest is also to help the living to live. Do you understand what I'm saying?'

She nodded, understanding absolutely. Lars and Anya's wedding had been illegal.

'*Ja?*' the woman behind the counter asked, leaning forward to get Allegra's attention.

She turned in surprise, startled by the intrusion.

'I'll see you tomorrow,' he smiled, heading off with the coffees, which had stopped steaming.

Allegra watched him go with an uneasy heart. What he had said made sense, but she still didn't understand.

Chapter Thirty

'Oh, hey! Look at you!' Allegra said in surprise as she stepped out of the lift. She had been hoping to disappear into her room unseen – she wanted some time to regroup after the morning's events – but Isobel was walking in wobbly squares on crutches around the lower-ground-floor hall.

'Good, right? I've been going round in squares for the past hour.'

'Did the doctor say you should be doing this yet?'

'Who do you think gave me the crutches, silly? He said he's very pleased with my progress.' Isobel pulled a proud face.

'He wouldn't have been so pleased if he'd seen you propping up the bar last night.'

'Actually, the bar was propping me up.'

Allegra had to laugh: her sister had an answer for everything.

She walked across to her room and Isobel hobbled in after.

'By the way, I'll get the dress dry-cleaned for you,' Isobel said, falling with relief on the bed and making herself comfortable. Allegra was grateful it was late enough for the beds to have been made and for Isobel not to realize hers hadn't been slept in.

Allegra, who was hanging her jacket up in the wardrobe, turned back to her. 'Iz, don't be daft. It's for you. I want you to have it.'

'But I can't keep a dress like that! It must have cost a fortune!'

Allegra gave a wry smile. 'Massi bought it, and besides, it is much more you than it is me.'

'But are you absolutely sure?' Isobel asked, leaning forward for added earnestness.

Allegra sighed. 'I am.'

'Cool,' Isobel grinned, falling back into the cushions again. 'Well, you know if you ever want to borrow it . . .'

'Yes. Thanks.' Allegra sat down in front of her dressing table and put on some moisturizer; Sam's constant hijacks this morning had thrown her completely off schedule.

'Ooh, what was in today's drawer?' Isobel asked, picking up the Advent calendar beside the bed.

'Oh, I . . .' Allegra twisted quickly on the stool. 'I haven't opened it yet.'

Isobel looked up at her, hearing the strained note in her sister's voice.

'Well, you'd better open it, then,' Isobel said, holding it out towards her.

'No, really,' Allegra protested. 'It's fine. You do it.'

'Legs.'

'Honestly, you do it. It's only a drawer. Just a fun little habit.'

'Legs, get over here or I really will open it myself.'

'OK, well' – Allegra hurried over – 'if you're that insistent . . .'

She sat down on the bed beside her and slid open the twentieth drawer. Both women peered in at the object inside: a miniature cowbell with red leather strap, identical but for scale to the one that Valentina had been wearing when she died.

'How can it be so diddy?' Isobel gasped, picking it up and holding it to the light. A tiny tinkle rang out. 'Ha! It works!' she trilled delightedly.

'Can I see?' Allegra asked.

Isobel handed it over and peered at it more closely. 'Is that a "G"?'

'Where?'

Allegra held the loop directly in front of the window so that the light could pour through. A silhouette of a 'G' fell onto the bed beside Isobel's legs.

'It is,' Isobel said, puzzled. 'Weird. I wonder what that stands for?'

Allegra laid it flat in her palm. It was so small the entire thing barely stretched across. Unlike Valentina's, this was too small and had to be for decorative purposes only.

'I love it,' said Isobel. 'I'm slightly regretting letting you have this now. All I got was a ticky old clock that won't tock.'

'Yeah, but think of the choking hazards, Iz. Ferds would have been living in the shadow of threat the whole time this was in the house.'

'Yeah,' Isobel frowned, before catching sight of Allegra's face. 'Oh, ha bloody ha!'

Allegra chuckled. 'Anyway, they'll be able to repair the clock for you and you'll have the last laugh.'

'Actually, they already have. They're delivering it tomorrow, Lloyd said.'

'Cool. By the way, did I tell you I thought I found the place they came from?'

'They?'

'The calendar and the clock.'

'No!'

'Yes, I think it's from the same place you bought the world's most expensive nativity set. They put a calendar like this one, only bigger, in the window the next day and they've got loads of clocks on one of the walls too. Did you notice them?'

Isobel wrinkled her nose. 'Not really. I was probably a bit overexcited at the time about getting the nativity stuff.'

'How unlike you! Well, anyway, I'm taking this in to them tomorrow. Lars has got a similar clock to yours and he told me he'd had it made here to replicate one he lost – which must be the one you've got, don't you think? . . . What?'

'You called him Lars. I thought you said we had to call him "Opa" from now on.'

'I didn't say we *had* to.'

Isobel looked at her sister with eyes that knew her too well. 'Come on. Spill.'

'There's nothing to—'

'Legs!'

'Fine,' Allegra sighed. 'Apparently the Rottweiler nurse is actually his wife.'

'*What?*' Isobel bellowed. 'Who told you that?'

'The priest.'

'Oh.' She paused. 'Well, I guess *he'd* know.'

'Yes.'

They were both quiet for a moment.

'That's really quite grim,' Isobel muttered. 'We're supposed to be finding our' – she waved her hands in the air, clutching for words – 'cuddly, sweet granddad, not some dirty old perv.'

'It doesn't make him a dirty old perv to have married a younger woman, Iz.'

'She's scarcely twenty years older than us,' Isobel pointed out with an unimpressed expression.

'Well, maybe he . . .' Allegra searched for the words. 'He needed a nurse *and* a wife and he decided to . . . economize?'

Isobel's nose wrinkled even more. 'That just makes him sly.'

Allegra gave up. 'Oh, I don't know. What I do know is that we have to get ready and be upstairs in forty-five minutes. Zhou's parents are having drinks in the sitting room.'

'Oh *shit!*' Isobel hissed. 'You don't mean I've got to go up there too.'

'Well, you can hardly hide out in their own house. They have to at least meet you!' Allegra laughed in exasperation.

'But they're the . . . I mean, they're the . . . actual . . . scary ones.'

'If you mean they're rich, yes. But that doesn't make them scary. I've met Zhou's father and he's very nice. You'll like him.'

Isobel looked back at her with a panicked expression. 'You're sure?'

'I promise. Now go and get changed and let me have a shower.'

'OK.' Isobel hopped off, more wobbly on her crutches than before, back to her own room.

Allegra shut the bedroom door behind her and turned,

falling back against it hard as she found Sam standing by the bathroom door, one arm raised above his head on the frame, in just his boxer shorts.

'Sam! What the hell are you doing there?' she whispered furiously, her hands over her heart as she pulled herself upright again on wobbly legs. 'How long have you been in here?'

'I'm sorry!' he laughed, amused by her reaction. 'I heard you coming up in the lift and came in here to surprise you, but then Isobel came in too! What was I supposed to do? I couldn't think of a single damned reason I could give her as to why I should be standing in your shower.'

'So you *hid*?' An amused grin cracked across her face. 'That's pretty demeaning.'

'Tell me about it,' he smiled, with an expression that spelled out their affair as clearly as a 'Sam hearts Allegra' tattoo.

'But how did you even get in without Iz seeing you? She said she'd been walking in the hall for an hour.'

He tossed his head in the direction of the sliding doors and her eyes scanned the balconies behind him. 'You climbed over the verandas?'

'You're making it sound more impressive than it actually was,' he grinned. 'But if you'd like to believe I'm heroic, by all means . . .' He walked towards her with a look that made her heart as skippy as an antelope. 'Not that there's any point in us going to these lengths to hide. She'll probably guess the moment she sees us – and that's if Massi doesn't tell her first. We're not fooling anybody apparently; he said on the train this morning it was like watching children hide sweets under their pillows.'

'Oh.'

She went still, knowing what he was really saying – he wanted them to go public; he wanted this to be more than just two nights and one morning of crazy, stupid recklessness that could undo both their careers.

'I've pitched for the deal,' she blurted out. 'On my own.'

A silence bloomed and she rushed to fill it. 'You know, with the new proposal I drafted?'

He didn't reply.

'Remember? When I forgot to reschedule the meeting?'

'All I really remember is you standing in front of me with a bare back and your dress ready to fall down.' A light glimmered in his eyes at the memory.

The joke threw her. Him not shouting threw her.

'You . . . you don't seem upset.'

He shrugged. 'Why would I be upset?'

'Because I'll win the deal, Sam. My package is amazing. I've never done such a good job. There'll be no way they can turn me down.'

A smile played on his lips. 'Legs, no one in their right mind could turn you down.'

She stared at him. He'd called her Legs? He thought this was funny? 'I don't understand why you're not freaking out.'

He smiled, his eyes so soft. 'Listen, don't you think I knew the second Zhou coerced you into staying here that he'd got you in on some pitch ticket? I didn't flatter myself to think you had come to pick things up where we'd left them in Zurich.'

She blinked in bafflement. 'So then you're not . . . ? It's not a problem?'

He laughed, walking over and wrapping his arms around her. 'Legs, I'm not going to throw my toys out of the pram if I find myself on the wrong side of the conference table to you. Your ambition and brilliance and tenacity are some of the things I . . . I admire most about you.'

She blinked at the near miss. They both knew what he'd almost said, and as his mouth covered hers again, she knew this thing between them was fast getting out of control.

It was Mrs Yong's laughter that she heard first, the crystalline sound of femininity blowing through the house like a spring breeze as Massi and Sam stood beside her in front of the lit fire, glasses in hands, polite smiles on their faces.

Sam was wearing a navy suit, no tie, freshly shaven and freshly showered. If they only knew, she thought with a flutter in her stomach as she approached; what they'd been doing twenty minutes ago in that shower had been as far away from clean cut as it was possible to get.

Mr Yong and Zhou were nowhere to be seen and Massi looked back at her with grateful eyes, like a bored child at an adults' party, Sam with adoring ones that paid no heed to her pleas to keep their relationship a secret from the Yongs – at least until the details of the deal had been announced.

But this was no time for distractions. The moment of reckoning was upon them all and she squared her shoulders as she walked, making rapid visual deductions with each step. Mrs Yong was taller than she had expected – five feet eight and very slim, with jet hair styled short. Pearl globes were fastened at her ears and throat, and she wore a navy wool Valentino skirt suit with a satin bow at the neck. Her face was beautiful, so finely boned she was almost birdlike, and as Allegra came to a stop in front of her, she showed that her smile had been passed to her son.

'Miss Fisher, I have heard so very much about you.' Her handshake was firm and perfectly pitched, her English better than most Brits'.

'The pleasure is mine, Mrs Yong. I am deeply honoured to have been invited into your home, especially at such a special time of year. You must be relieved to be here at last.' Out of the corner of her eye, she noticed Sam's stare change as he slowly realized she was wearing his pale pink shirt with her black trousers. He was already up here when she'd darted into his room and pinched it in panic, once she'd been faced again with the limitations of her wardrobe out here.

'I am. It does become very wearing living in hotels all the time, and this is our favourite home. Estelle does a marvellous job of making everything so inviting. Don't you agree the town is just so pretty at this time of year?'

'It's magical,' Allegra smiled, fiddling with the rolled-back cuffs. 'It's my first visit here, so I've been non-stop enchanted.'

'Sam and Massi have been telling me how much skiing they've been doing. Apparently the snow's wonderful this season.'

'Oh yes, we're so lucky with this early fall. It's certainly among the best I've known.'

'They're talking about potentially doing the Haute Route later in the season. Do you know it?'

'Chamonix to Zermatt? I've never done it myself,' Allegra said. 'Do you ski?'

Mrs Yong laughed again, that light tinkling sound skittering over the polished surfaces like a sprite. 'Well, if you asked my son, he'd say no, I don't. I am not what you would call a speed freak. I like to keep my skiing . . .' She thought, considering the word carefully. 'Tidy.'

'Tidy. I like that,' Allegra smiled back. 'I should keep it in mind myself. I grew up with a speed freak for a sister, so in trying to keep up, I've learned to ski by clattering down everything without any style.'

'Yes, your sister. Isobel, isn't it? How is she?'

'Much better, thank you. In fact, she should be up any minute. She was getting changed when I passed her room just now. She's finding it rather slow going, getting used to the crutches.'

'Of course she is. Oh dear, the poor thing. What rotten luck taking that fall.'

'Oh, talk of the devil.'

Estelle came into the room, sweeping chairs and rugs out of the way like a minesweeper as Isobel followed several seconds behind her, panting and with flushed cheeks, her long encased leg held out in front of her as she planted and swung her way into the room – wearing last night's gold mesh dress.

A stunned silence greeted her arrival and Allegra felt her smile freeze.

Oh good God. Who did she think she was lunching with? The Kardashians?

Isobel stopped moving as she took in everybody's sombre clothes – work shirts and trousers, low-key couture – and a look of such abject horror and panic ran across her face that Massi, Allegra *and* Mrs Yong all advanced towards her in a rush. But it was Mrs Yong who got there first.

'You must be Isobel,' Mrs Yong smiled, putting her arms lightly around Isobel's shoulders and guiding her towards the sofa. 'I'm Lucy Yong. Do take a seat here.'

'Oh, really I-I'm fine,' Isobel stammered, trying to smile, but her mouth tipping grotesquely down, perilously close to tears.

'But you must be so tired having to get about on those things,' Lucy Yong insisted. 'And to be perfectly honest, *I'd* be glad of the excuse to sit. My feet are killing me.' She smiled, perching on the sofa beside her and directing Estelle to place the cushion on the ottoman for Isobel's leg. 'Are you chilly? It is quite cool in here.'

Isobel looked at her blankly, before realizing a rope was being thrown out to her. She nodded.

'Estelle, would you get my cream cardigan from the bedroom, please? It's the Loro Piana.'

'Yes, Mrs Yong.' Estelle left the room at almost a sprint.

Allegra, who had walked back to the fireplace and was now standing beside Sam, wanted to throw her arm around their hostess's shoulders and weep with gratitude. Such small mercies . . .

But they were all out of time. The sound of voices came into the hall, growing nearer, and Allegra realized Mr Yong and Zhou had been in the study. She realized they must have been discussing her proposal.

In an instant, her mouth dried up and she swallowed, her eyes flitting anxiously to Sam, who had the nerve not to be looking concerned at all. She felt something graze her wrist and looked down to find his finger stroking her gently. When she looked back up at him, he just winked.

'Oh . . .' Mrs Yong glanced back at Isobel, who looked like she was trying to dig her way down and hibernate in the cushions. 'Really, he's very distracted at the moment. Don't worry a bit,' she said as Mr Yong came into the room.

'Ah, husband,' Mrs Yong smiled, getting up from the

sofa and reaching towards him with a gracious arm. 'It is cool in here. Come and join us by the fire.'

He strode across the room with a march that was scarcely less than an imperial goosestep, staring at Allegra as he approached, and she knew from the fractional tilt of his head that he had seen the pitch. Nothing in his body language told her, though, which way he was going to go.

'Miss Fisher, it is an honour to see you again,' he said formally, walking up to her and bowing.

'The honour is mine, Mr Yong.' Her voice was assured, her movements minimal as she echoed the bow, and they both fell into the roles they had assumed at their first meeting in Zurich, even though they were now in his home. 'I am humbled to be invited to your home at this special time. Your son has been a generous and thoughtful host.'

'My son makes me a proud father,' Yong replied, the formalities observed.

Allegra bowed her head in reply, not daring to look across at Isobel. She could only imagine the look on her sister's face right now.

Yong looked over to Sam, his back erect, holding his champagne glass by the stem, one hand in his trouser pocket. 'Sam.'

'Mr Yong. Happy Christmas.' They shook hands.

'You and my son have not been terrorizing the locals, I hope.'

A half-smile twitched the corner of the mouth that had last kissed hers only twenty minutes earlier. 'Categorically not, sir. We're far too old for that kind of mischief these days.'

Yong smiled, his face softening exponentially. 'Good. There are only so many times I can bribe the mayor.'

Allegra glanced down at her own drink as the ease between the two men stood in stark contrast to her rigid formality. What if Zhou had been wrong? Yong circled back into space on the floor and she sensed the moment had come for the decision. After weeks of waiting, it was here as suddenly as a slap.

He was about to begin talking when Estelle suddenly came back into the room with the cherished cardigan in her hands and hastened over to Isobel, sliding her arms in with a speed and efficiency that would have brought pride to a military sniper.

Mr Yong looked astonished to notice the broken young golden woman sitting obscured by cushions on his sofa.

But Mrs Yong had that covered too. 'Husband, you recall that Miss Fisher's sister, Isobel, is staying with us too? She is a good friend of Zhou's, and Dr Baden insisted she should not be moved until her leg improved.'

Mr Yong looked at his wife, perplexed but obedient. 'Of course. Of course,' he said, hesitantly bowing his head at Isobel as she hesitantly bowed back, clutching the cardigan closed over her chest, and using a large cushion to obscure her legs. 'You are . . . healing, I hope?'

'I am, thank you.'

'Good. Good.'

'And your doctor's just lovely. He's been really nice to me – all your staff have.'

'Well, that's good to hear.'

There was a tiny silence. 'Thank you very much for letting us stay.'

'It is my great pleasure.'

'Your home is lovely.'

'Thank you.'

'The wallpaper in my room is—'

Oh God. Allegra could see her sister beginning to relax with the billionaire she'd been so frightened of meeting, and she gave a sudden cough, pretending to choke a little on her drink. Isobel had no idea of the enormity of this moment.

'You OK?' Sam asked, his hand immediately on her back and patting her lightly.

She nodded, recovering quickly, just as he twanged her bra strap.

Mr Yong, grasping the opportunity to withdraw from Isobel's gracious company, walked to the centre of the room again.

Isobel glanced across at Allegra – knowing exactly what she'd done – and as Allegra looked back, Isobel crossed her eyes – an age-old trick that never failed to make Allegra laugh and had always got her into trouble when their father had asked them to be on their best behaviour. But for once it didn't work. Yong was about to announce who had won and she was too nervous for childish pranks.

Mr Yong dropped his head down as he considered his words and Allegra felt her heart begin to accelerate.

'I would like to begin by saying that I am so pleased that you are all here today. I have waited a long time, it feels, to make this announcement.' His eyes flickered over Allegra and Sam, revealing nothing, and she wondered whether Sam felt as she did at this moment – the adrenalin spiking her brain, her hands tingling as she held the crystal glass, butterflies taking wing in her stomach.

'I know that it probably strikes you as . . . superstitious to consult the stars for something as trivial or arbitrary as a date, but in my country, we place much store by the traditions and wisdom of our forebears, and if I am a man of my time, I am also a man of my country. This is simply how we do it.'

He paused and Allegra felt her mouth go dry.

'But I am glad too that Zhou has asked to have his friends present at this momentous occasion. It is the modern way and I try to embrace that too – believe it or not.'

Allegra processed that he was trying to make a joke and she laughed politely. Zhou was coming slowly into the room behind his father, and beside him, a petite Chinese girl with straight black hair and a fringe that tapped her eyes. She had wide cheekbones and a pretty pointed chin, her mouth pressed tight like a bud, and Allegra guessed her to be eighteen or nineteen.

A sister? She had heard that some particularly wealthy Chinese were able to buy their way round the one-child policy by paying a substantial fine. Why *wouldn't* the Yongs do that if they'd wanted another child? Money was no object.

She looked at Zhou as he came to stand beside his father. The memory of him at the party last night, of him lobbing the bread roll at breakfast this morning seemed farcical, absurd now. He was standing with almost military bearing, his palms flat against the sides of his thighs, his gaze fixed on a point on the wall behind his mother's head, his expression utterly neutral, his eyes flat.

She looked back up at Yong, forcing herself to focus. Everything she had been through in the past few weeks had been dovetailed into this moment. This was what it had all been for – the thrill of the win, the kill.

She hung her attention on his words, waiting for her name, willing it to enter this room and fill it, pushing out once and for all any other emotion.

'. . . is a decision that has been taken with utmost care and integrity, not only to preserve the historical high regard of the Yong dynasty name but also that going forwards. We have taken many months to consider every aspect of this partnership, and in the final step, my advisers have, today, confirmed our highest hopes. And so I am very happy to formally announce that . . .' Yong's eyes swung over their small group like a swing's shadow on the grass.

She waited, an offhand joke Massi had made yesterday drifting back through her subconscious. '*It's just as well for you there's a one-child policy in China . . .*'

'. . . our only son and heir, Zhou Yong, is now formally engaged to Min-Wae Hijan.'

The girl didn't stir as a stunned silence erupted. Allegra saw Sam's head whip round sharply to Zhou's, but no one else moved. Not Zhou himself, not Massi, not her.

Zhou was engaged? *That* was the big announcement? She looked across at Sam. Had he known? But Sam was staring across at Zhou with an expression she couldn't read.

She didn't understand. Zhou had expressly told her to be here for this. He had said his father would be announcing his decision then. Had she really put herself through all the turmoil of the past thirty-six hours for an *engagement party?*

She looked back at Zhou, but his eyes remained fixed and distant on the spot beyond his mother's head, and she realized how unhappy he looked. The change was marked. How easily he had laughed with his friends, how vital he'd seemed out of his parents' shadows. Was this as much a surprise to Zhou himself as it was to her? Neither Zhou nor any of the others had ever said a word about him becoming engaged.

She looked back at the so-called happy couple. From the physical distance between Zhou and Min-Wae, and their mutually isolated body language, it seemed more than likely that the marriage was arranged. She looked across at Massi as though he held the answers, but he too was limp with surprise, his expansive bonhomie completely vanquished in the face of the Yongs' austere formality. And as she stared, her brain began to buzz with static interference. Anomalies and slips of etiquette began to crowd her mind . . .

Mr Yong hadn't greeted him, she realized. He had welcomed her and Sam – even Isobel, when he'd found her – with a fastidious social diligence, but he had ignored Massi completely as though he wasn't even there. Zhou and Massi were old friends from Harvard, just like Sam, and Massi was no scrounger – he'd built his own empire – so why would Zhou's father do that?

But as his eyes rose to meet hers, she understood exactly. *You snore like a gorilla.*

A friend's tease, a lover's privilege.

Chapter Thirty-One

The chalet was so quiet it was as though Death had visited. Lunch had been a disaster: the food was barely touched, and the conversation flickered as weakly as a flame on green wood. Eyes slid like they were on ice – skittish and flighty. Entire conversations were carried on looks, and the celebratory scene at the table was no more real than a mirage: Massi wouldn't look at Zhou; Zhou wouldn't look at his father; his father wouldn't look at Min-Wae.

Neither one of the happy couple had said a word, not one, and it had been down to Sam, Allegra and the Yongs to fill the silences that kept opening up like sinkholes, threatening to swallow them all. But they knew. She knew from the way Mrs Yong insisted on discussing the upcoming couture collections in Paris after Christmas – talking about her and Min-Wae visiting Mr Valentino's and Mr Lagerfeld's ateliers in January without once looking at the girl she was locking in to a sterile marriage. She knew from the way Mr Yong collared Sam on the iron-ore surplus in Australia that he knew. They knew, but they were resolute in their actions. Fortunes and names needed to be preserved. This marriage would happen.

Massi had broken the stalemate first as coffees were brought out, saying something about a headache, and Allegra had watched in frigid sorrow as he left, heavy-footed and silent. But it had been the cue they had all been waiting for, and the rest of the party had dispersed minutes later, scattering to their rooms like lead shot, agreeing to meet up at 6 p.m. for drinks before venturing out for dinner – Mr Yong had arranged for a Cat to get them all up the mountain to a private yurt, where the Michelin-starred chef Michaele Lambretto was cooking for them.

Allegra was lying on the bed, her head full of other people's sorrows, when Sam put his head round her door. He had only been able to shoot an apologetic look over to her as he had made a beeline from the table to Massi's room and she had heard the low hum of their voices as she'd passed the door.

She propped herself up on her elbow, her heart leaping just to set eyes on him again.

'Hey.' He smiled, though his face was tense. 'I'm just going to go out with Massi. He needs to . . . uh, vent.'

'Sure, OK,' she murmured earnestly, her eyes wide, wanting to help but not sure how. This was between families and old friends, and she had no place in either camp. 'What's happening with Zhou?'

'He's at a private appointment at some jeweller's with his parents and Min-Wae.'

'Oh God. Poor Zhou. Surely he's not going to go through with it? He has to say something.'

Sam's eyebrows hitched up sceptically. 'You think?'

'Well, of course! His parents can't just condemn him to a life of misery like that. They must know!'

'Of course they do, but it's not that simple. Zhou's the very visible son and heir to one of China's biggest companies – with a father who's so old school he had to consult on the engagement date.'

'But as their only son, they must want his happiness above all else?'

'It's different over there, Legs,' Sam sighed. 'Homosexuality was considered a mental illness in China until just a few years ago.' He saw her expression. 'I *know*. So the poor guy's effectively got to choose between Massi or his family.'

Her face fell. 'Is there anything I can do?'

His eyes flicked over her tenderly and he came into the room, unable to keep his distance at the door another moment. 'Just be here when I get back,' he said, kissing her until she flopped back into the pillows again, his hand skimming her lightly and making her eyes close. 'God, you'll be the end of me,' he murmured, wrenching his hand away with visible effort.

She watched his back as he crossed the floor again, feeling almost ashamed that she should be so happy when other lives – just metres from her – were collapsing in on themselves.

The door closed with a click and she listened to the timbre of their serious voices in the hallway, Massi's signature exuberance replaced by a flat, tight anger, then the retreating sound of their feet on the steps and an empty hush filling the void they left behind.

A minute later, she had poked her head round Isobel's door. 'Hey, you.'

Isobel, who was lying on her tummy on the bed, looked up at her with wet cheeks. 'Oh, Legs, it's just so awful,' she cried, burying her face in the pillows again.

'Oh, Iz, no! You look lovely. It was just a surprise, that's all. I thought you carried it off very wel—'

'Not the *dress*! Massi!' she wailed. 'How can they do this to him?'

'Oh.' Allegra sank onto the bed beside her. 'Yes, I know.'

'Why can't they see he's the best thing that could ever happen to their son? I mean, they've been together eight years. It's not like they don't know what's really going on.'

Eight years? Allegra looked at her sister in astonishment. 'You knew?'

'Well, not about the engagement obviously.'

'No, but . . . you knew they were gay? You knew they were together?'

Isobel blinked at her in disbelief. 'Of course! How could you not?'

Allegra looked away, shaking her head. Kirsty was not only married but divorced? Zhou and Massi were together? Other people's personal lives were forever a mystery to her. She had no ear for gossip, no appetite for heart-to-hearts.

'Oh my God! I can't believe you didn't know!' Isobel gasped, half laughing, half weeping. 'How could you not know?'

'I'm not a people person like you,' Allegra muttered, pulling at some lint on her trousers.

'Jeez, you don't say.'

Allegra threw herself back on the bed beside her annoying little sister, her arms over her head.

Isobel looked sideways at her, giving a big sniff as she wiped her eyes dry. 'So loverboy's gone out, then.'

'Yeah – what? No! I mean, who?'

Isobel cackled with laughter. 'You are priceless! I swear to God watching you trying to lie is the best part.'

Allegra groaned, throwing her arm over her face. 'Just leave me alone. It's been a long day.'

'I bet it has,' Isobel said in a dirty voice.

'Ugh!'

'Come on, give me the goss. You know I won't stop till I know every nasty little detail.'

'No.'

'Legs!'

Allegra lay there for a moment before looking slyly at Isobel from the crook of her arm. She knew exactly what would shut her sister up. 'Hey, fancy a new bikini?'

'Oooh!'

The air was warm on their faces as Allegra opened one of the double doors and they stepped into the spa suite a few minutes later. Lights from the gold-tiled pool rippled on the ceiling, refracted thousands of times over by the twirling crystals of the chandelier, and Allegra had to prompt Isobel to move out of the way – and breathe.

'Holy cow!' Isobel gasped, eyes wider than they had *ever* been, as she hobbled towards one of the cantilevered loungers, upholstered with Tiffany-blue cushions.

'Now you're sure you're going to be OK in the water?' Allegra asked, slipping off her towelling robe and stepping in.

'Yep. Dr Baden said hydrotherapy was the best thing for it. Just get me that lilo, will you?'

Allegra brought the floating chaise longue over to her – not sure this counted as hydrotherapy – and supported Isobel as she held on to a rail and struggled down the submerged steps. It was easier when they were waist deep; the water was as warm as baby's milk and Isobel hoisted herself relatively easily onto the lilo, giving a whoop of joy as she found a waterproof TV remote in the cup holder. 'Jeez, just when you think things can't get any better . . .'

Allegra tipped her head back and began to float, her eyes tracking the chandelier overhead as she drifted ever closer to it, then beneath, then past to the far end, where Isobel had managed to get the giant plasma flashing colours but no sound. Her toes touched the wall at the end and she pushed herself off gently, going back the way she'd come, hands sculling lightly by her hips, as her mind ran over the strange events of the day – heady exhilarations interwoven with revelations that had left her feeling un-settled and anxious.

She did ten lengths like that, almost motionless, floating weightlessly beneath the skin of the water, before Isobel finally got the sound system working, sitting up with a splash as Daft Punk came on so loud the water rippled from the vibrations.

'Could you turn it down?' Allegra shouted, above the noise.

'What?' Isobel cupped her ear, waggling her shoulders to the beat.

'Turn it down!' She motioned frantically.

'Oh.'

A moment later, the decibel level dropped to merely thunderous, and as Allegra watched Miley Cyrus twerking – or was it tworking? – she realized she'd gone cold turkey on her Reuters habit. She'd become so wrapped up in the events here it seemed hard to believe the world was still going on outside these mountains.

'Could you possibly put a news channel on for me quickly? Just for a few minutes.'

Isobel wrinkled her nose as she flicked over. 'Honestly,

Legs, you are such a grown-up sometimes. This is the most rock-'n'-roll pool I've ever seen and you want to watch BBC News.'

But Allegra had already tuned out. Her attention was on the correspondent, who was standing in a hard hat and filing a report from Syria as shells exploded in the near distance behind, plumes of thick dust clogging the sky. Her eyes quickly scanned the red ticker tape with the pertinent bullet points running across the bottom, getting up to speed. She looked back at the live images and, particularly, a white truck parked in the corner. She recognized the logo.

'Just turn it up a little,' she murmured.

'Tch, turn it up, turn it down, make your mind up,' Isobel muttered mindlessly under her breath.

'. . . six months ago reported fears that charitable aid convoys to Syria may be abused for non-charitable purposes and as cover for smuggling extremists into the country. The Charities Commission is now investigating whether in fact a suspected American suicide bomber in Syria had travelled there as part of a humanitarian convoy assembled by PeaceSyria in August 2014 . . .'

PeaceSyria. PeaceSyria. Allegra held her breath.

'Legs, what on earth is wrong?'

Allegra looked at her. 'When did that reporter say the bomber travelled?'

'August, was it?'

'That was four months ago . . .' Allegra murmured. 'And the notice period to withdraw investments is twelve weeks. Besakovitch is pulling out *today*.' She looked at her sister. 'He must have known. He must have found it out somehow and *that's* why he's going.'

'Who is? *What?*'

'Sam drew down quarterly dividends of $750,000 and paid them through to PeaceSyria as part of the tax break on Besakovitch's fund.'

'Who's Besa-what's-it?'

'The founding investor at PLF. After ten years of bloody good returns, he's suddenly running and no one knows why. But this is why. It *has* to be. The timing fits.'

'Why can't it just be a coincidence? Surely people take money out all the time?'

Allegra shook her head, certain she was right. Links and connections that remained invisible to most people shone like gold thread on a spindle to her, and with those timings so aligned, she saw the impossible tension immediately: money from an ethical trading pot invested in a warmonger's charity? Of course he was running!

'Not of this size. Not after ten years. Leo and Pierre made each other.'

Pierre . . .

'Legs?' Isobel was watching her closely, like a child seeing their father cry.

Allegra's eyes widened as her brain began running faster and faster through the potential end-case scenarios of this. 'Oh God, I've got to tell Pierre! This could . . . this could destroy him . . .' she whispered, slapping her hand to her forehead. 'Any suggestion of links with terrorists and it'll be investigated by the CIA and then it's only a matter of time before they trace the donations back to PLF.'

'Well, I'm sure you can explain to them that you didn't know,' Isobel said weakly, struggling to grasp the seriousness.

'You don't understand – the markets run on confidence.

If PLF becomes linked in any way to terrorism, everyone will pull their money. No one will touch him.'

She looked at Isobel urgently, remembering something, sensing a lifeline. 'When is Zhou getting back? His father *has* to sign with PLF today. He'll be locked in for three months. It'll be a public vote of confidence in Pierre. It'll buy him some time.'

Isobel looked frightened. 'Legs, there is no deal.'

'I know *not yet*. But later—'

'No, Legs,' Isobel interrupted, looking serious for once. 'There is no deal. Massi told me last night. He was drunk.'

'What?'

'He said Zhou's dad's here for a merger. That's why they're in Switzerland.'

Allegra stared at her sister with an anger that bordered on madness. 'Don't be ridiculous!' she snapped. 'They're investing, not merging.' God, did her sister even know the difference? 'I've had meetings with them in Zurich, in Paris. Zhou was desperate to get me out here.'

'It's Glen-something. Gleneagles? No—'

'Glencore?' The word came as a whisper. Her sister had never heard that name before, she knew that. There was no way Isobel randomly knew the name of the biggest commodity and mining company in the world, which had a listing on the Hong Kong stock exchange and was headquartered here in Baar.

'Massi says Zhou got you out here because he feels bad about what he did to Sam.'

Allegra didn't ask what he'd done to Sam. She didn't trust her voice.

'Sam tried to pull out of his wedding to Amy. He didn't want to go ahead with it, but Zhou was his best man and thought it was just cold feet. He made him go through with it. Apparently the marriage lasted four months and now she's slagging him off left, right and centre and taking him to the cleaners.' She shrugged apologetically. 'So when Zhou saw how Sam was around you, he tried to do something about it.'

'But . . . that doesn't make sense. Zhou wouldn't get his father to table long and bloody *boring* meetings with me across Europe just to do a spot of matchmaking for his friend . . . I mean, come on!' she shouted as Isobel just stared back at her with a frightened look of apology on her face. The proverbial messenger . . .

Allegra stared back, her head spinning. No. There was a deal here. It didn't make sense. 'Massi's wrong and I'll tell you why.' She began jabbing her finger in the air as her brain sped up to warp speed, cooling under pressure. 'The timings don't work for that to be true. I was en route to meeting Yong when I met Sam. He was on the plane, but I had *already* made contact with Yong by then. The deal came first. Sam came after.'

Isobel shrugged hopelessly. 'Look, I don't know, Legs. I'm just telling you what Massi told me Zhou told him.'

They blinked at each other beneath the chandelier, which swung almost within touching distance of their heads. Allegra felt so much information was being machine-gunned at her she was in danger of falling. She didn't know what the Zhous were playing at, and she didn't know how this tied in with Sam. And she wouldn't know until they all came back and she could confront them. In the meantime, she had to keep focused. Limit the damage where she could . . .

'I've got to tell Pierre,' Allegra said, wading through the

water in giant strides and hauling herself out. Without even grabbing a towel, she ran along the side of the pool.

'Hey! What about me?' Isobel cried, paddling furiously and trying to get back to the edge of the pool again. But Allegra couldn't stop. Not right now. She ran up the stairs as silently as an owl on the hunt, only beads of water on the ground marking her flight.

She grabbed her phone from the table and called Pierre without hesitation. All the pride, all the longing, all the hope that he would do the right thing and make the first move – she forgot it in an instant. She had to warn him what was coming.

He picked up on one ring. 'Fisher.'

She swallowed at the sound of his voice, so assured, so familiar, so certain she'd be back. 'Have you seen the news?'

'Many times.' She could hear the smile in his voice, imagine the glimmer in his eyes. He loved playing games.

'I mean about PeaceSyria. Do you know what's happened?'

There was a pause. 'Tell me.'

'They're being investigated as a cover for getting terrorists into Syria. Besakovitch paid out over two million dollars to them in charitable donations over the past year.'

Her words were met with silence.

'Pierre, do you understand what I'm saying? He effectively funded them and the CIA will trace the money back to you. The firm will be implicated, and innocent or not, this mud will stick. Doubt will be enough. Everyone will pull.'

'Not with Yong on board, Allegra.' A note of calm pervaded the words and she wondered whether he had a brandy in his hand, London spread beneath him like a rug. 'He's bigger than Leo. He's the honey to the other bees.'

'No . . .' Her voice cracked. How could she break this to him? 'It's all been a game, Pierre. They're not investing. They're merging with Glencore.'

Silence rang out again, but this time it was taut, vibrating down the space between them like a garrotting wire.

'Pierre?'

'Then what the fuck have the past few weeks been about?'

She shook her head, pinching her forehead with her hand as she sank back onto the bed in her wet bikini. 'I don't know. A bluff maybe? They were trying to throw everyone off the scent until they announced the real deal? I haven't seen Sam yet. I haven't got the full facts. I'm just telling you what I know.'

She heard the sound of his breathing getting heavier, his footsteps on the floor as he began to pace.

'The fucking bastard. After everything I did for him . . . *everything* I did and he goes and fucks me over anyway.' His words were low and jumbled, an indistinct stream of fury, and Allegra frowned. Was he talking about Yong? 'I bent over fucking backwards to meet his demands. He said he'd keep it quiet! That was the deal. We had a deal!'

'Who had a deal?' she asked in a weak voice.

'Who do you think? Sam fucking Kemp! The man who kicked off this whole sorry mess in the first place! He made the investments and yet somehow I'm cleaning up his pissing mess!' Pierre was shouting, venom colouring his words red, his voice straining to match his fury.

'Pierre, I don't understand. What's going on? You have to tell me.'

There was another beat of silence, a heavy, weary sigh. Pierre's voice, when it came back, was flat. 'Sam came to me telling me about the fuck-up with Leo's money back in October. Rumours on the news desks at some of the papers got back to some of our contacts in finance . . . I told Kemp to go public. If we blew the whistle on it, we could disassociate ourselves, it would prove our innocence, but he said what you just said – that even the suggestion of any involvement would ruin us. The fund would be finished. He said he had a better idea.'

Allegra covered her mouth with her hand, waiting for him to continue as her mind began freewheeling and gathering speed with his every word.

'He said he couldn't keep Leo from pulling out, but he'd managed to get him to promise his silence – that fat bastard's even more interested in his reputation than we are about profit. Then Sam told me he knew the Yongs were looking to invest outside China and that he'd make it happen. He convinced me to keep quiet about the charity while he got the deal.' His voice changed. 'I had to go along with it, Allegra. I had no choice. I couldn't tell you what was going on. If you were involved, you could have been implicated.' He paused. 'But I couldn't afford to lose Sam either. If I put you before him . . .'

He didn't need to finish for Allegra to understand. It was all so clear now. If Sam didn't get what he wanted, he could have left and leaked the information at any time. It wasn't a question of innocence, it was a question of association – and PLF was the goliath that would take this fall.

She was almost scared to speak. Each question she asked opened another secret, the lies winding round the truth like ribbons on a maypole: wrapping, obscuring and hiding something that was really very plain and simple. 'He was blackmailing you.'

He had held all the cards; he had controlled this game from the start: Pierre was *his* puppet. But what about her? She had stood in his way from the first meeting, fighting him at every step, refusing to concede a single point. Had he underestimated her ambition, her determination to win, to never give up? Had he thought she'd just roll over and die?

Or had he played her too? Had he worked out that her weakness wasn't in her head, it was in her heart?

She thought back to the beginning, the very beginning – his seat on the plane just ahead of hers, the lingering smile, the late-night knock on her door . . . He'd not only known she was flying out to see the Yongs, he must have been the one to dangle them in front of her in the first place. He'd known her CV, read up on her trades. Why hadn't she seen it was just all too neat, the way he'd pitched up in her life, his friendship with the son a coincidence too far?

Even this afternoon . . . She remembered Sam's unusual calm as Yong had prowled and paraded looking for big words for his big announcement. Sam had known none of it concerned him. And when she'd told him she was here to pitch, he'd just smiled, almost laughed, almost told her he loved her.

That was the worst part of it. That was what made him most dangerous. Not just what he'd done, but what he'd almost made her believe.

Chapter Thirty-Two

Day Nineteen: *Blank Scroll*

The night seemed without end, but when daybreak did come, the sun split open the inky sky like a cracked egg, pouring sunlight over the valley, and Allegra felt a tangible relief to have survived it. Blinking into the dark had made her feel like the only person alive, and as the streets began to fill with noise – deliverymen shouting, metal screens rolling back in the jewellers' windows, jingle bells tinkling on the horses' reins on their runs to the station – she watched from the balcony with ashen eyes.

Her body was cold. Even with her snow boots on, a towelling robe wasn't enough against the mid-December temperatures and she was forced back into the hotel room to order a breakfast she knew she wouldn't eat.

Isobel was still asleep in the huge bed that Allegra hadn't even climbed into, her leg elevated on a cushion. The suite had been all that was available at such short notice – the town was fully booked now for Christmas – and there were still rooms Allegra hadn't been in yet. Isobel, by contrast, had hopped from one to the other, her excitement on mute as she kept looking across at Allegra with concerned eyes. She had understood enough from the conversation in the pool and Allegra's silent tears as she'd hurriedly packed not to question their abrupt and rude departure. She had understood enough to agree with Allegra that they couldn't go back to the little apartment for the last night; it would be the first place Sam, Massi and Zhou would look when their escape was discovered, and Allegra had made Isobel swear on Ferdy's life that she wouldn't call Massi and tell him where they were.

Arranging the scatter cushions against the headboard, Allegra climbed onto the bed and tucked her cold feet into the sheets and blankets, trying to feel some warmth, trying to feel anything at all.

The movement was enough to make Isobel stir with a small, sudden snore, lifting her head with a groan a few moments later. She blinked groggily into the light, seeing her sister beside her staring vacantly at the wall. That woke her up.

'Hey,' she said brightly, propping herself up on the pillows. 'How'd you sleep?'

There was a ten-second delay before Allegra seemed to hear.

'Sorry, what?' Allegra blinked, turning to her.

Isobel took in her sallow complexion and the dark moons cradled beneath her eyes. 'It doesn't matter.' Hauling herself further up the bed and rearranging her pillows like Allegra's, she sat upright too.

Allegra didn't seem to notice and they sat in silence for a few minutes.

'Hungry?'

Allegra blinked at her blankly again. 'What?'

'Are you hungry? You look pale and you didn't eat last night. Shall I order some breakfast?'

'Oh, uh . . . I've already done it,' she murmured.

'Oh. Right. Cool.'

Isobel laced her fingers together, wondering what to say. Her sister's distance frightened her. She'd seen it only once before, many years ago, and that had been the prelude to before . . . well, the Allegra she was now. Allegra mark II. Allegra redux.

'Have you opened the drawer yet?' This time she anticipated her sister's questioning look and was pointing to the Advent calendar on Allegra's bedside table.

'Oh . . . No.' Allegra lifted it and handed it to Isobel.

That hadn't been the response Isobel had been hoping for. 'Don't you want to open it?' she asked, holding it back out to her. But Allegra just shook her head and resumed staring at the wall.

With a sigh, Isobel slid open the drawer. Inside was a small square of paper that had been folded down and secured with a red satin ribbon. The knot was tight and difficult to unpick, but she eventually managed it, unfolding the paper slowly.

'Eh?' she scowled.

Her tone caught Allegra's attention this time. 'What's wrong?'

'There's nothing on it. Look, it's blank. What's the point of that?'

She held the piece of paper out for Allegra to take, passing it through a sunbeam that was falling across the bed. Isobel took it back again. 'Wait a sec . . .' She sat fully upright, holding the paper directly into the light. A small bubble of laughter escaped her. 'I don't believe it! Look!'

Allegra didn't even bother to arch an eyebrow in curiosity. The paper was blank.

'It's got an invisible message on it.'

Allegra tutted.

'Seriously! Hold it up to the light.'

'There is no such thing as an invis—' But as Isobel held the paper directly in front of her eyes, Allegra saw what she meant. A line of handwriting could be seen on the page as faint as a watermark. 'But . . . how? Who had invisible ink when this was put together? It's over sixty years old if Mum had it as a baby.'

'Legs, the "how" is the easy part: don't you remember we'd write invisible messages on our midnight feasts and read them with our torches?'

Allegra blinked. She didn't remember much about their childhood. She didn't allow herself to.

'Lemon juice! I can't believe you can't remember that,' Isobel said disappointedly. 'The question we should be asking ourselves is, *why* did someone write a message in invisible ink?' An idea came to her. 'I bet Mum wrote it. Maybe it was a special message to Santa for something,' she said brightly.

'They don't have Santa over here.'

Isobel sighed at her sister's depressing insistence on factual correctness. 'Let's see . . .' she murmured, grabbing the hotel notepad and pen beside the bed and slowly writing down what she could make out. '*In einem Meer von Menschen, meine Augen sehen immer für Sie,*' she said eventually, her nose wrinkled with confusion. 'That mean anything to you?'

'You know I never did German. You're the one who took it to A level.'

'No, I didn't.'

'Well, you took it to GCSE.'

Isobel gave her sister a peculiar look. 'I flunked the mocks and had to take general studies instead.'

Allegra frowned. 'I don't remember that.'

'No. Because you were too busy with your nose stuck in books to notice.'

They fell quiet, both realizing that their lives had already begun to diverge by then – Allegra finding solace in perfectionism and achievement; Isobel in parties and inappropriate boyfriends.

'Do Google Translate on the iPad,' Allegra said instead. The last thing she needed was to go back there. It was going to be hard enough getting through today.

Isobel obeyed without argument. 'Huh,' she said a moment later. '"In a sea of people, my eyes will always look for you." Crikey, that's romantic.'

'Well, it's not a message for Santa,' Allegra murmured, certain it had to be for Valentina. She thought of Lars – Opa, she tried the word out again for size – and the portrait of his beloved, lost wife. No one could enter or leave without seeing her. She still dominated his house, his entire life.

Because that was the big problem with love. She understood now why her mother had dissolved so completely in her father's wake. She understood why the sight of her – as Valentina's double – still brought tears to an old man's eyes. Real love was unrecoverable, terminal; it followed you through your life and to the grave. There was never any going back.

She didn't realize the tears had started to roll. It was only when Isobel wrapped her arms around her shoulders and began rubbing her back that she was aware anything was wrong at all.

*

'Right, I won't be long. Are you sure there's nothing you need me to get for you while I'm out?'

'Nope, I'm good,' Isobel said, comfortably positioned on the balcony with cushions and blankets, a hot breakfast arranged in front of her.

'Well, just be dressed when I get back. We need to be in church in an hour.'

'Sure. No problemo,' Isobel grinned, holding up her Buck's Fizz with a wink.

Allegra walked briskly down the corridor to the lifts, where a young couple, younger than her, held the doors for her and she stared at the ceiling as they whispered and giggled in the corner.

She stepped out into the lobby, which was rendered in a warm palette of greens, pinks and light woods, and where fur-trimmed women in grey capes fluttered through like moths. 'Can you arrange a late checkout for me, please?' she said in a quiet, flat voice to the receptionist. 'I'll need the suite until after lunch.'

'Of course, Miss Fisher,' the receptionist replied, tapping quickly on a keyboard and printing out confirmation of her request. She tipped her chin low, looking back at Allegra discreetly. 'Also, you had some visitors last night, Miss Fisher.'

Allegra made herself stay still.

'As requested, we told them no one of your name was staying in the hotel.'

'Thank you.'

'Is there anything further I can do for you today?'

'No. Thank you for your help.'

'A pleasure, Miss Fisher.'

Allegra slid on a pair of shades and stepped out into the

blinding whiteness, her heart beating like a trapped bird in her chest. The cold was ascetic and raw, and she felt as though her skin had been flayed and her nerves exposed, but at least now the world was restored to its rightful order. White was white; black was black. There were no rainbows or pink tints in this filter, and she was seeing clearly again as she walked back down the Bahnhofstrasse, her arms swinging, eyes dead ahead. People moved out of her way, the way they usually did in corridors, but she didn't thank them. There were no smiles within her, no warmth, just the cold, hard satisfaction of victory at last. She had won. Out of all the lies, one good thing had emerged. There may be no deal to bring home, but she didn't need that, not with Pierre waiting for her back at the office tonight now that she was the only one he could trust. They would fight Sam together. They would weather the storm that was coming their way – together. She had got what she'd wanted all along.

Hadn't she?

Somewhere in the distance, she heard the drone of a helicopter lifting up from the heliport and she wondered if it was Zhou's or just another billionaire out for the morning. The bell above the door jangled as she stepped into the gift shop and the dark-haired girl looked up with a bright smile. The sound of the ticking clocks filled the room as she shut the door behind her, locking out the chatter from the street.

'Oh! I did not expect you so soon,' the girl said in surprise, glancing at the carrier bag in Allegra's hand. According to the sign on the door, they had been open barely ten minutes.

'I'm leaving tonight and I can't get here later,' Allegra said briskly, vaguely aware that her manner was in sharp contrast to her shy excitement yesterday, but she wasn't the same person she'd been even twenty-four hours ago and there was nothing she could do to help that. 'Is your father here?'

The girl hesitated. 'He's in the workshop. I can get him for you.'

'Or I can come through, whichever is quickest. I'm pressed for time.' Allegra shrugged impatiently.

'Oh . . . OK,' the girl said. She lifted a small hatch and Allegra passed swiftly through the counter to the back. She followed the girl into a tiny corridor with a staircase running off the back, a stepladder propped up against one wall, and a WC sign on a door.

The girl paused so that Allegra almost trod on her heels and had to jump back. 'Opa!' she called up the stairs.

They ducked through another open doorway – the ceilings were very low – before descending some steps into a small room out the back. A long but narrow window ran along the rear wall, with benches covered with blocks of linden wood, curled shavings carpeted the floor, tools hung on the walls by hooks, and a man with his back to them stood planing something in a clamp. Behind him, old black-and-white framed photographs clustered one section of the wall. She could see the distinct silhouette of the Matterhorn in the background of some of them, even from across the room.

'Papa.' The man turned as the girl spoke to him in Swiss German, his eyes steady on Allegra. He was wearing a full-length leather apron and seemed to be a few years older than her – in his mid-fifties – with very thick, dark hair that had begun to grey at the temples. His eyes too were dark, and Allegra saw his daughter had inherited his underbite.

He wiped sawdust off his hands as he walked towards her. 'Nikolai,' he said, shaking her hand. 'My daughter tells me you think you may have an early Advent calendar of ours?'

'I think there's a good chance, yes,' she nodded. 'May I?' She indicated to the bench and he nodded, wiping more shavings onto the floor. The girl disappeared and came back a second later with a brush and began sweeping the floor.

Allegra put the bag on the bench and drew out the small green cabinet. She watched Nikolai closely as he lifted it, scrutinizing not the decorative paint effects but the joints in the corners, on the drawers. He held it away on outstretched arms and peered at the backplate.

He looked up at her. 'Everything about it suggests it is one of ours – the dovetail joints, the scalloping across the front here, the size of the drawer knobs – and yet I do not recall our ever having made one so small. All the ones we make are at least twice the size.'

'Yes, I did notice that myself when I saw the one in your window, but some of the gifts inside my calendar you still seem to be making, and I have a cuckoo clock that I also think came from here.' She saw his eyes glance over at the deflated bag. 'It's being repaired by a specialist in England.'

'That is a shame.' He blanched at her words. 'What makes you think the clock came from here too? It is true we are the only carpenters in Zermatt who still make them, but thirty, forty years or more ago . . . if it is the same vintage as this.' He ran a hand over the calendar. 'There were several families who made them.'

'My grandfather here has a replica of the one that is now

ours. He thought it was lost and said he had a copy made locally.'

'What is his name?'

'Lars Fischer.'

The man's expression changed. 'Then I can tell you for certain the clock did not come from here – and so it is unlikely this was made by us either.' He put the Advent calendar back down on the open bag on the bench.

'But . . .' Allegra looked at him in bewilderment, confused by the sudden about-turn. She drew open the fifth drawer and held out the new Angel Barry. 'I have exactly this angel back home.'

Nikolai frowned, staring at the figure with a confusion that she sensed matched hers. 'Then it is a coincidence. Just an angel.'

'Well, I don't believe in coincidences,' she said after a pause, putting the angel away in the drawer and carefully replacing the Advent calendar back in the bag. She didn't know what was going on; she didn't understand why Lars's name had provoked such hostility, but a slur against her grandfather was now a slur against her. Not that it mattered anyway whether or not the Advent calendar or the clock came from here. It was just a detail, an irrelevance, a bit of colour to a story she may or may not get to tell her mother one day.

'Papi,' Nikolai said, looking at someone behind her with an anxious expression.

Allegra turned to find an elderly, white-haired man staring back at her, his hand shaking on a walking cane. But he wasn't looking at her. His eyes were on the Advent calendar on the bench.

Slowly, he advanced until he was level with Allegra, his

free arm outstretched as he touched the small cabinet with something approaching reverence.

Allegra looked questioningly over at Nikolai.

Nikolai was watching his father closely too, as though worried he might fall. His eyes briefly met Allegra's. 'This is my father, Timo.'

'Timo?' She had heard that name before.

Her voice broke the elderly man's spell and he looked at her for the first time. And as she saw the shock come into his face – just like it had in Lars's – she remembered.

'You knew my grandmother,' she said quietly, more to herself than anyone.

But he could only nod – telling her, at least, he understood English – and she knew he was seeing not her but Valentina, the woman he had been engaged to before Lars had come to town.

She rested her hand on the top of the Advent calendar too. 'Did you make this?'

His eyes fell to her hand. 'I did.'

She swallowed. There was something in the way he said those two words that caught her attention – the gravity in them, like he was in the dock, making an admission . . .

She followed his gaze to her hand and, on it, the tin ring, still on her finger – the one Valentina had died wearing, the one that conspicuously didn't and couldn't match up to the showy three-diamond studded engagement band. Without thinking, she twisted the ring and exposed the perfect heart indented in her skin. Discovered in the twilight, she had forgotten it again in the glare of the day. Until now.

Somewhere in her mind, the spindle began spinning again, spooling out loops of golden thread that, if she followed them, would take her down paths she hadn't considered before now, although the clues had been there all along – such as the love note Isobel had discovered only an hour or so ago, also hidden in plain sight.

A secret love.

She watched as he opened the twelfth drawer and pulled out the tiny flat metal hoop – also tin, also engraved with hearts. And as she realized what it was, she suddenly understood why the secret could never have been kept. Because as Timo held out the baby bangle and met her gaze, she saw that the eyes looking back at her were her own.

Chapter Thirty-Three

A murmur rose from the congregation at the sight of Allegra, Valentina's ghost, as she walked to join Lars in the front pew. He was sitting alone – no sign of Bettina – a wheelchair folded and propped against one of the white pillars, his blue eyes watery as he watched her advance like a bride.

'I thought something had happened,' he said with relief as she followed after Isobel, who hopped into the pew, and she knew that he was referring as much to her absence yesterday afternoon as to here. He could have no idea it was a minor miracle she and Isobel weren't more than ten minutes late. What Timo had told her, upstairs in the little flat above the workshop, she could have stayed there for days, just listening to his stories.

'Isobel can't move very quickly, that's all,' Allegra replied, her eyes averted as she pretended to fuss with Isobel's crutches.

Lars shot her a quizzical look – they had taken to greeting each other with squeezed hands and a kiss on each cheek – but the organist had started playing now that the sisters had arrived, and everyone stood, launching into the first hymn.

Being in Swiss German, neither Allegra nor Isobel could

read it – the tune was unfamiliar too – and Allegra subtly looked around the congregation instead. She had been taken aback by the sheer numbers as she'd come through the door; she had expected it would be simply her, Isobel and Lars here today, but every seat had been taken, to the point that the chaplains had had to take some chairs from the nearby cafes to accommodate extras.

She could see the little group huddled together at the back: Timo, Nikolai, Leysa and Noemie. They would not join her and Isobel at the front in the family pews.

Allegra glanced over at Lars. He wasn't singing either, staring instead at the lavish portrait he'd had removed from his own hall and placed on an easel.

Allegra looked back at it too, taking in her grandmother's narrow face, high forehead and planed jaw, the strong eyebrows that were currently enjoying a fashion moment (and had seen Allegra herself stopped several times at parties as women asked after her regime), the dark hair swept back from her beautifully boned face with the band of flowers, and her lips which, though not fleshy, were sensuously dark as if just kissed. This was the woman who had refused to remain just a name, just a correction on a family tree whose only buds were women. She would not be forgotten or overlooked. More than sixty years dead and she still drew a crowd.

As everybody sat down again and Father Merete began speaking, she remembered how Lars had cast the finger of suspicion on Timo when she had asked him what had happened the night of Valentina's disappearance. He had been testing her, she saw that now, seeing whether the name registered and how much she knew about her grandmother's past. Well . . . She glanced over again, catching sight of his wet eyes and trembling lips, but she didn't mistake it for lost love this time. She was on to him now and she knew fear when she saw it.

The chalet swarmed with life. Laughter filled the rooms; conversation soaked into the walls as people jostled and circulated and shared memories of a woman who had been dead three times as long as she had lived. The flowers and the art, the rugs and the antiques faded into mere backdrop against the stories of her beauty, the tales of her temper, and Lars sat in his chair in the drawing room with a fierce pride that she had been his. Beside him, newly positioned, was a sepia-tinted photograph taken on their wedding day, showing them both standing stiffly in the style of the day, Valentina in clotted-cream lace and Lars in a narrow black suit, tie and hat.

Isobel was sitting on the sofa to his left. She had wanted to stand, preferring to stay with Allegra greeting guests in the hallway, but her knee was throbbing too much, and after forty minutes, she had had to admit defeat, sitting on the sofa with a rigid smile as Lars paraded her in front of his friends like a show pony. It hadn't gone unnoticed by her, the tone of disapproval that greeted Anya's name as their likeness was compared and agreed, and Allegra hadn't had a chance yet to tell her sister about the morning's developments. By the time she'd got back, Isobel was already waiting for her in the lobby of the hotel, and they were too late for her to delay the memorial service even a minute further. What she had to tell her couldn't be compressed into one sentence or even one day.

Allegra kept on passing the visitors through to Lars, but only after they'd obliged her small request. She scanned the visitors' book that the Mont Cervin concierge had speedily bought and delivered to Lars's chalet before the service had ended, with the result that it was already three-quarters full. All the townsfolk who'd wanted to pay their respects in church and back here had happily obliged her request of sharing anecdotes and memories of Valentina for Julia, her little girl, who'd left here when she was barely more than four years old. The pages were filled with black script, and one or two people had even slipped grainy black-and-white photographs of Valentina in the pages, she saw, which would need to be secured later. Allegra smiled a little as she saw, too, the local spelling of her mother's name – Giulia – and remembered the 'G' dotted out on the leather strap of the baby cowbell. The significance of it had passed her by when she'd first seen it, but now it was obvious what the 'G' stood for. The cowbell was a father's gift to his secret baby daughter.

A finger tapped her shoulder and she looked up to find the lean, bristly face of Connor Mayhew staring down at her.

'Mr Mayhew,' she said in surprise 'Goodness, thank you so much for coming.'

He nodded awkwardly. 'It seemed right to pay my respects.'

Allegra stared up at the man who'd found her grandmother, the man who'd set this entire sequence of events into motion. She thought it seemed right he was here too.

'Can I get you a drink?'

'No, thank you. I . . .' He glanced around the lavish chalet, as though looking for someone. 'I should go now.'

'Oh. That's a shame. Well, I'll tell my grandfather you were here.'

'No—' he said, too quickly. He gave a tight smile. 'Please don't.'

She paused. 'Why not?'

'He would not appreciate my presence here.'

'Why not? He'd be so grateful that you've taken the ti—'

Connor gave a wry look that suggested he thought she was being deliberately ironic.

'You must be aware that the history between your grandfather and the SLF is difficult.'

'No. Why does my grandfather even *have* a history with the SLF?' she asked, her eyes probing his face for answers.

'Miss Fisher, I don't think now is the—'

'On the contrary, now is exactly the time, Mr Mayhew.' She took him by the elbow and, glancing into the sitting room and seeing Lars in full flow from his fireside chair, she lowered her voice. 'He's not my grandfather.' She stopped him from saying anything with a brief shake of her head. 'I only found out today.'

'So then all this—' He indicated to her dutiful-granddaughter routine, meeting and greeting guests.

'Is for appearance's sake only.' She took a deep breath. 'Everyone in the town who knew her has come and I've been trying to speak to as many of them as possible. From what I've learned today, I think that he may well have played a role in my grandmother's disappearance, so if there's anything relevant you know that could help me shed light on what happened . . . anything at all . . .'

Connor stared back with those clear blue eyes that hid nothing and kept no lies.

'The SLF believes – but cannot prove – that your grandfather was complicit in an agreement between local

452

landowners to sell the local pastures to developers before the zoning maps could be drawn up.'

She shook her head. 'What's a zoning map?'

'It is a map that identifies low-, medium- and high-risk avalanche areas. Low-risk areas are zoned yellow, medium are blue, and high risk are red. Much of Zermatt would have been classified as a red zone, meaning no development would be permitted there. But your family's farm and several others were sold off to developers before the classifications could be enforced.'

'Because they would have been in the red zones – and therefore worthless?' she asked.

'Fischer says he was just being a businessman. The government and SLF had been talking about bringing in the maps for years, but there were many delays and legal wranglings. It was only when the winter of 1951 hit that they were rushed through, but by then it was too late: development had begun and fortunes had been made.'

'So you're saying even though Zermatt is developed in a red zone, Lars knowingly went ahead and put hundreds of thousands of people's lives at risk, just to build his fortune?'

He nodded. 'Fischer calculated the risk – he knew if the SLF could not prevent, we would have to cure. And so we have. We have invested hundreds of millions of francs in creating anti-avalanche defences: building reservoirs, planting forests, as well as hard structures. Advances in understanding and predicting avalanches have taken giant steps forward since the 1950s and Zermatt is now safe. But it is the ordinary taxpayer who has had to foot the bill for his greed.'

Lars had traded other people's safety for his own profit? Allegra looked away, ashamed to have ever thought she was like him, ashamed to have ever shown the old man a moment's kindness. 'How many people know about this?'

'Barely any. Some of the old locals here have their suspicions, of course, but we could never confirm them. It would not have been politic for this to come out. If it had become public knowledge that some of the country's most famous ski resorts had been knowingly developed in red zones, the scandal would have been devastating. Fifty per cent of all Swiss live in avalanche terrain, and too many livelihoods are at stake to undermine the tourism industry here.' He looked at her closely, watching as her eyes darted side to side, digesting the revelation. 'I trust I can depend on your discretion with this information.'

She nodded. 'Of course.'

'Good. I don't know if that is any help . . .'

She shrugged. 'It gives me a more accurate sense of his character, if nothing else.'

He took a step back and held out his hand, a signal that their private conference was at an end. 'Well, it's been a pleasure meeting you, Miss Fisher,' he said in a louder voice. 'If ever I can be of assistance . . .'

She gave a weak smile as he walked into the lift, his eyes – she saw – moving between her and the portrait back hanging on the wall behind her, as the doors closed.

She turned to look at the painting herself. Valentina stared back: strong, independent, passionate, young. Only twenty-one and a mother. What had made a woman like that run into the mountains during a hundred-year storm? What had made her own sister flee just two years later with her child? Until she knew the answers to those questions, secrets would hang in the air like smoke over water.

The party was nearly over. Guests were taking their cue from one another and leaving in polite groups, bundling into the lifts with their coats still not on, their cheek muscles tired from the laughter of the afternoon as they regretfully departed the grand chalet for their own more modest homes.

But there was still one person who hadn't come to say hello. Allegra gave the cue they'd agreed on and walked back through the hall. It was empty, with just a few wine glasses on the windowsills to indicate the merriment that had blown through the house. She could hear only the sound of voices in the sitting room and she stopped at the sight that greeted her. Isobel was laughing with Lars, her leg propped up, explaining something with bright eyes and excited hand movements.

Allegra felt her stomach tighten. She had left them alone too long. She should have told Isobel this morning; she should have said something before Lars had had a chance to get his hooks into her, because now . . . now the betrayal would be so much worse.

She watched Lars clap his hands in delight at Isobel's punchline and she wondered whether he'd suspected her doubts in the church. Maybe he had seen something in her face – a face he already knew so well, of course – and known he had to switch teams.

'Legs!' Isobel beamed, noticing her standing by the door. 'Come and take a seat. You must be shattered! Have you got face-ache?'

Allegra smiled as she walked across, sitting protectively

next to her sister and handing her the cream leather-bound visitors' book that was now all but full of memories. 'For Mum's good days.'

Isobel looked down at in her surprise, but her nose soon began to wrinkle as she flicked through the pages. 'Uh, sis – it's all in German. And I hate to say this, but I don't reckon Barry's German is going to be all that, do you?' she chuckled.

'It's OK. Timo's going to translate it for us.'

'Who's Timo?' Isobel asked, without looking up. She had found one of the photographs and was squinting at it.

'Our grandfather.'

Isobel's head snapped up and all Allegra could do was let her see the truth in her eyes. If she could have told Isobel another way, she would have done, but this needed to be done overtly and swiftly. Lars couldn't be given anywhere to hide.

The sound of the walking cane on the floor told her Timo was coming through, Nikolai by his elbow, and she watched as Lars's face set hard and fast.

'Legs? What's going on?' Isobel asked in a nervous voice as the two men came in, Nikolai helping his father into the armchair opposite Lars and going to stand behind him. The two old men stared at each other coldly, their bodies too old for fighting, but there was war in their eyes.

After a moment, Timo turned, his gaze falling to Isobel, and a look of unbidden affection softened his face at the sight of her.

Isobel looked at her sister. 'Legs, tell me what's going on. *Now.* I mean it.'

'Lars was Valentina's husband, but he wasn't Mum's dad.'

'Are you saying Valentina had an *affair*?' Isobel's face took on an incredulous expression and Allegra knew her sister was thinking, Did people do stuff like that back then?

Isobel turned back to Lars sympathetically. 'Did you know?'

'No.' Lars's response was lightning-quick, but his eyes were on Timo, his lips curled in a sneer. 'I knew he was in love with her, just like everyone else. There was nothing more to it. He wanted what he couldn't have.'

'So did you, old man,' Timo replied calmly.

'*I* married her.'

'I'm not talking about Valentina.'

Another silence fell as they waited – waited for Timo to elaborate his accusation, for Lars to defend, but they were like boxers in the ring, circling each other, gloves up, each waiting for the other to throw the first punch.

'It has been a great party here today. You must be in no doubt now about his great love for his first wife.' Timo was looking at Isobel again.

She shook her head uncertainly.

'No. How could you? His love for her is famed. You can imagine how hard it must have been for Anya to follow in her footsteps. And as for poor Bettina, well, is it any wonder she carries a face like a storm?' he shrugged.

'What are you doing here in my house?' Lars said in an ominously low voice. 'I want you out of here.'

Timo's expression changed, looking almost pleased, as he addressed Lars directly now. 'I know you do, just like you wanted Valentina out of the house that night. You knew what you were doing when you told her I was waiting for her at the hut. You knew you were sending her out to her death.'

'That is a lie!'

'No. It is the truth. You know it and I know it, but what does it really matter when we both know I cannot prove it?' he shrugged. 'Proof has always been our problem, Fischer, has it not? For when Valentina died, I had no proof that Giulia was mine. In the eyes of the law, you were her father. But we could all see in her eyes that *I* was; every time you looked at her, you saw the truth. You knew it, but you could not prove it either. A checkmate.'

Lars didn't respond, but his hands were clawed into the armrests, his complexion turning steadily redder.

'Just tell me what you told her,' Timo said, leaning forwards in his chair. 'Even if I had proof, there's a statute of limitations, is there not, on how long a manslaughter charge can be pressed?'

'You are a *fool*,' Lars hissed.

'I am a fool who has had sixty years to think about this, and my guess is that you told her she'd be waiting for me there. What is . . . ?' He said something in German to Nikolai, who thought for a moment.

'A double bluff?'

'Yes. Double bluff.' Timo looked back at Lars. 'It's the only possible reason she would have gone up there.'

'Why would I have done that? I loved her.'

'But she didn't love you. She despised you. You tricked her into marrying you with promises of seeing the world beyond these mountains, of living like a lady, but she quickly found out you had overstated your wealth. And when you started your campaign to get her to sell, she realized exactly why you had married her.' A shadow passed over Timo's face. 'But I think perhaps she couldn't hide the sickness from you. Three days trapped in the house with you during the storms and even you guessed her condition? And that was when you realized you were out of time. One child that looked like me . . .' He shrugged. 'Maybe you could pass it off. But two? Everyone would know. You knew she was going to leave you – and take the farm with her.'

'You lie!' Lars roared, so loudly that Isobel jumped, his eyes bulging like a gargoyle's as spittle collected on his chin.

'Oh, don't worry. I knew how stubborn she could be. Believe me, I spent *years* trying to get her to walk away from the farm, to just come away with me so we could start a new life with Giulia somewhere else. But that deathbed promise . . .' He shook his head sadly. 'She could never forgive herself for defying her father in marrying you and she felt she owed it to him to stay, no matter what beatings or threats you punished her with. She wouldn't leave for me, the man she loved, and she would never sell for you, the man she hated – not even as Giulia grew more like me by the day, spelling out our secret.' Timo's voice trembled at the mention of his daughter, but the look in his eyes never wavered. 'Valentina had made a promise and she was prepared to die to keep it. And die she did.'

Allegra felt like she could hardly breathe as the words filled the room like bellows. She knew what Timo was doing here: pushing, humiliating, carousing Lars into confessing. It was the only card he had to play, because the accusations he was throwing out there . . . Without proof, it was just theory.

'I never raised a hand to her,' Lars snarled, quieter again.

'It was how our affair started up again, Lars,' Timo said with almost a chuckle and a shrug, riling him up again.

'She was hiding up in the huts, pretending to shepherd the herd but waiting for her bruises to go down . . . And of course everyone bought that. They all knew you were no farmer. "Lars wouldn't know a goat from a cow," they used to say, and they were right. Six months after her father's death, you had almost run the farm into the ground, over-stocking the pastures and starting that roundworm epidemic. We would have laughed if it hadn't been so tragic.'

He was quiet for a long moment. 'And it was tragic. It almost killed me watching her trying to keep that farm going as you made one bad decision after another. Were they deliberate? I've always wondered. Were you deliber-ately trying to fail so that she would have no option but to sell?' He nodded. 'Maybe. Maybe you did. I think you probably tried everything – but with the zoning maps coming and a new baby on the way, you could not wait any longer. She would not sell and you could not make her. You sensed your opportunity for fortune was going to slip by like a salmon in the river.'

'I don't have to listen to this. If you're so sure I'm such a monster, why don't you go to the police with your big ideas? I'm sure they'd be interested to hear the ramblings of a bitter, poor old man who lost the woman he loved to one of the richest and most powerful men in the area.'

Timo's eyes shone. 'If only I had those deeds, I would, old man.'

Lars's face changed.

'*They* were what you needed, weren't they? That's what Anya told me.'

'Anya? What does she have to do with this?'

'Everything, of course. It's why you married her. Everybody knew she was sweet on you, and you made a convincing show of falling apart after Valentina's death. The marriage stood up to scrutiny even if it was indecently fast, but there was no time to lose, was there? Because she had inherited the farm, not you.'

Allegra frowned, interrupting. 'Wait, surely inheritance law means the farm passes to the husband as next of kin?'

'Ordinarily, yes. But with no sons in your family for several generations, a clause on the deeds of the farm states that it must pass down through the bloodline to prevent the farm from passing out of the family through marriage.'

'"You come from a long line of mothers,"' Isobel murmured under her breath, her hand on Allegra's arm.

Timo was back to watching Lars closely. 'You married Anya thinking you could easily persuade *her* to sell. She was gentler than Valentina; she would do anything you asked.' His voice changed like a capricious wind. 'But she was more like her sister than you had supposed. You underestimated her!' Timo jabbed his finger delightedly towards Lars. 'And when you got rough with her too, she started to think that maybe her sister's death had been more than an unlucky accident.'

Allegra cut in again. 'Were there *any* circumstances in which Lars could have inherited?'

Timo turned to her with a grim expression. 'Only if the bloodline stopped.'

'Stopped. You mean' – her eyes scoped his – 'if Anya and Julia died?'

He nodded. 'Only once the clause was null would the farm would pass to him as Anya's legal next of kin.'

Allegra and Isobel both looked at Lars with horror. It was obvious now why Anya had run; and without proof that Julia was his, legally Timo couldn't do anything to protect her either.

'Sorry, there's something I don't get,' Isobel said, half raising her hand like a student in class. 'Granny didn't die until 2001, and Mum is still very much alive.'

'Yes.' Timo nodded.

'So then if legally the farm has passed down to Mum, how did *he* sell the farm?'

'With Anya gone, she was as good as dead. There was no one to argue the farm wasn't legally his, and those who may have known about the clause . . . Well, Lars was clever enough to be generous where it counted. He could afford to be. When he sold the land, he made six, seven, eight fortunes.'

Allegra stared at him, her brain racing. 'So where are the deeds now?' she asked urgently.

Timo's eyes slid back to Lars, narrowing into slits. 'I wish I knew. I've never seen them.'

'Didn't Anya tell you?'

'She didn't know either. Valentina had hidden them. She couldn't let *him* find them – if they'd fallen into his possession, that would have made her . . . What is the word? Disposable?'

Everyone fell silent. Allegra couldn't bear to look at Lars any more. What was the point in all this? Histories and feuds and wars that had lasted three generations were blowing around like leaves in her mind, and just when she thought everything was beginning to settle, another wind disturbed them all again. But there wouldn't be any victories here tonight. Nothing had changed. There was still no proof. She had heard enough, and they had a plane to catch. Feeling nauseated by the lies that had defined every generation of her family, she got up, helping Isobel to her feet. Nikolai moved forwards too – a silent bodyguard – as Timo got out of his chair.

'Shouldn't we . . . ?' Isobel protested feebly, but Allegra shook her head.

'Let's just go,' she murmured, keeping her eyes down. The only justice they would have here was knowing, at last, the unproved truth. It would have to be enough.

'The truth will out, old man,' Timo said, his voice weaker from the strain of the battle, Lars watching in silence as their small group shuffled and hopped their way to the door. This was his only punishment – to watch the family that wasn't his walk out on him for the last time. Did he even care?

It was like Timo had said at the beginning: proof was their problem. Without the deeds they couldn't prove motive, or that he had sold the farm illegally.

The mountains were still keeping secrets.

To all intents and purposes, Lars had got away with it.

Chapter Thirty-Four

It was after ten in the evening before they approached the arrivals hall at Heathrow, Isobel enjoying the envious stares of the other passengers as they were whisked past on the special-assistance buggy, Allegra holding her crutches.

She was dead on her feet – she hadn't slept in nearly thirty-six hours, and the day's events had made it impossible for her even to nap on the plane – but she couldn't stop yet. Pierre was waiting for her in the office. He had said he'd wait for her, as long as it took, an ambiguity in his words that she'd never heard before.

Her stomach clenched with nerves again and she wished she had time to go home for a shower and change of clothes. She had woefully under-packed and all her clothes had been worn several times over. Then again, if she'd known half of what was coming her way, she never would have gone at all – racing down the mountains, dancing on barrels and getting drunk with dangerous strangers had been the easy part. She had found angels and demons on this trip, sifted the truth from the lies, and she was back on home soil with a new past and a brighter future. She would be there in the hour.

'You OK?' Isobel asked, putting a hand on her knee.

'Of course,' she smiled, banishing Sam Kemp from her thoughts.

'You were amazing today.'

'No.'

'Yes. Mum would have been so proud.'

Allegra hesitated. 'I'm just sorry we can't do more.'

'We can only do what we can do, Legs. Besides, look what you've got for her.' She patted the memory book sticking out of her bag. 'Stories to share for the good days, like you said. That's worth more than revenge.'

They rounded the corner into the arrivals hall, with the buggy's orange lights flashing and a warning beep alerting stragglers to move out of their path. There were still hundreds of people milling about – some lovers being reunited, many of them bored drivers with names written on whiteboards.

'Oh my God!' Isobel squealed suddenly, clapping her hands across her mouth as she caught sight of Lloyd in his curious trapper hat waving Ferds in his baby-blue snowsuit and a 'Welcome home, Mummy!' banner, which had been made of five A4 sheets sellotaped together and decorated with felt-tip rainbows and hearts. He saw them coming through like VIPs and in the next instant disappeared, running round the back of the crowd and emerging in front of them moments later, forcing the buggy driver to perform an emergency stop.

'Oh, Iz,' he said with a tender croak in his voice as he saw her knee brace, reaching down to kiss her just as Ferdy grabbed her hair. Impressively, Isobel managed not to shout, simply winding her index finger into his little fist and feeling the strength of his squeeze as she bent down and kissed his snub nose.

'Does it hurt?'

'No. Champagne helps.'

He laughed, looking up and noticing Allegra. 'Hey, Legs, how've you been?' And he reached over to give her a kiss on the cheek as Isobel held Ferdy in her arms.

'Nice artwork,' Allegra said drily, her eyes on the banner. 'Must've taken you some time.'

He chuckled. 'Yeah, well . . . Ferdy helped.'

'I can't believe you've kept him up this late,' Isobel mock scolded, clearly delighted.

'Sleep was not an option. He was desperate to see you. We both were.'

Isobel looked up at the tone in his voice and Allegra looked away discreetly as he kissed her again. Maybe it was true – absence really does make the heart grow fonder.

'Seeing as you've got someone picking you up, I'll give you the wheelchair to use in the car park,' the driver said gruffly to Allegra. 'Just bring it back to the passenger enquiries desk over there.'

'Will do. Thanks,' she smiled, gathering Isobel's crutches and hopping down.

'I swear he's grown another foot,' Isobel said a moment later as she settled in the wheelchair, gazing down at her baby son.

'Really? There were definitely only two earlier.'

'No, I mean—' Isobel managed before catching sight of Lloyd's expression and dissolving into giggles.

Allegra pulled the bags as Lloyd pushed Isobel and Ferds in the wheelchair and they found the car in the multi-storey car park. It was snowing hard, for London, and a bitter wind pitted the soft-blanketed ground, garlands of tinsel wrapped round the trolleys a visitor's first sign that

Christmas was almost here. Fifteen minutes later, they were on the M4 and heading back into London in Lloyd's trusty black Golf, Ferdy fast asleep in the car seat beside Allegra in the back as Lloyd set the blowers to 'max' to warm them all up. Isobel looked like she was in a wind tunnel, her hair blowing back dramatically from her face as she filled Lloyd in with the new family history and he squeezed her good knee, looking at her like she was a goddess.

Just wait till he sees the gold dress, Allegra thought to herself, picking up a battered copy of today's *Times* and thumbing through it. If she got a cab over to the office from Isobel's house, she could squeeze a shower in, too, while she waited. Isobel must have something smart she could borrow. A suit she wore for funerals perhaps?

The thought of funerals made her eyes fall to the tin ring on her hand. She still hadn't taken it off and she felt in no hurry to do so.

'. . . wasn't an Advent calendar at all, see, but like a memory box,' Isobel was saying. 'There's a bracelet made with holly berries that he picked the day Mum was born.'

'Holly berries? Aren't they poisonous?' Lloyd frowned.

'I *know*, right?' Isobel said animatedly. 'You could *never* put them near a child.'

'Social services would be straight in,' Lloyd agreed.

In the back seat, Allegra sighed and carried on reading.

'And then there's like this little wire heart threaded with edelweiss. He and Valentina picked it together in the summer before Mum was born; Valentina dried it out above Mum's cot . . . And, and . . .' Isobel twisted in her seat. 'What else is there, Legs?'

'The lucky leaf,' Allegra murmured, not looking up.

'Oh yes! He caught lucky leaves too! He put one in a

little leather booklet because he said sometimes you need luck on your side.' Isobel joshed him with her arm. 'See? You always thought I was just making it up, but that's where it comes from!'

Lloyd rubbed her thigh. 'I shall never doubt you again.'

'Wait till you see him, Lloyd. He looks just like . . .' She wrinkled her nose, clicking her fingers. 'Oh! What's Pinocchio's dad called?'

'Geppetto.'

'Right. He looks just like him. Little white moustache and twinkly eyes. And he was the one who made the cuckoo clock too. That was why Granny took it: another thing for Mum to have from her dad. Isn't that sweet? Plus he still lives in the same house he was born in. All his life in one place – can you imagine?' After leaving Lars, they had just had time for tea together in the apartment Timo shared with Nikolai, Noemie and Leysa before leaving for the airport.

'Not really.'

'I mean, it's tiny. Just a room above the shop really, but so homely, you know? And he made all the furniture. Ha! Linley eat your heart out!'

Allegra wondered whether her sister was going to take a breath before they reached the river.

'So did he never marry, then?' Lloyd asked, swinging them off the Hammersmith flyover and down towards Fulham.

'No, he did, but not till twelve years later. He said he used to go up the mountains all the time trying to find Valentina, but eventually, you know . . . He had to move on with his life.' She shrugged. 'It's really sad. His wife died four years ago and now he lives in the apartment with his son Nikolai, Nik's wife, Leysa, and their daughter, Noemie. She's seventeen . . . She is seventeen, isn't she?' Isobel twisted in her seat again. 'Legs? Legs, what is it?'

Allegra blinked back at her, the newspaper flat against her lap where she'd dropped it. 'Glencore's gone up thirty-nine per cent today.'

'Glencore?' Isobel paused, concentrating hard. 'Oh, that's the company I told you about, isn't it?'

'And I told Pierre.'

Lloyd glanced back at her in the rear-view mirror, getting the gist immediately, as Isobel's mouth dropped open – even she understood what that meant.

Chapter Thirty-Five

Day Twenty: *Empty. Light Trace*
of a Circle on the Drawer Base

'Legs, bacon sarnie?' Isobel called across the kitchen.

'Huh? Uh, no. No, thanks.' Allegra shook her head, her nose almost to the TV screen as she watched the footage again, the twentieth time in an hour, of Pierre being led to a patrol car in handcuffs, flashbulbs popping.

A sandwich was thrust in front of her nose. 'Eat. You are no use to anyone dead on my kitchen floor.'

'Uh . . .' She accepted it obediently. Took a bite obediently. Chewed obediently.

As soon as Isobel walked back to the worktop, she put it down.

'Legs!' Isobel said in a warning voice, her back still turned as she shook the ketchup bottle.

'Sorry.' She picked up the sandwich and took another bite, but it was like chewing sawdust.

The producers cut back to the presenters in the studio, all sitting in bright colours with bright smiles as they discussed again the very serious charges and failures in risk control that had allowed the trades to happen. But it didn't matter how many times they said them, or rearranged the

470

words – 'arrested ... billions ... liquidity squeeze ... whistle-blower' – they always led to just one meaning: insider trading.

Allegra had been flicking through the various twenty-four-hour news channels since the story had broken, devouring the details with macabre intensity.

'I can't believe he thought he'd get away with it,' Isobel said, glancing over at her as she cut her sandwich in half.

'Desperation,' Allegra murmured, her own sandwich forgotten again in her hands.

'Greedy bastard, more like. He was arrogant enough to think he'd covered all the angles, but anyone with half a brain could see the timings were too tight.' She picked up her sandwich and took a bite, leaning against the worktop as she scrolled through her texts.

'Mmmm . . .' Allegra replied, her eyes on a still image of her own office building. 'Wait . . . What?'

'Huh?'

'You said the timings were too tight.'

'Yeah, a second between the trades? I mean, come on! Even I know you can't input something that quickly.' Isobel rolled her eyes, her hand over her mouth as she talked and ate at the same time.

Allegra stared at her. 'What timings are you talking about?'

Isobel swallowed, her eyes glancing at the screen. 'They said about the timings on there, didn't they?'

'No. They haven't released any operational information whatsoever. The press don't have access to that kind of information yet.' Allegra's eyes narrowed as she stood up. 'Where did you hear about the timings?'

'Nowhere.' But she had put her phone behind her back.

'Iz—' Allegra said in a warning voice, advancing towards her and holding out her hand. 'Give it.'

'There's nothing—'

'Now!'

Isobel shook her head, but Allegra reached round and snatched the phone from her hands anyway. Massi had signed off with a line of kisses and a smiley face.

Her jaw dropped. 'I told you not to call him!' Allegra shrieked, realizing in a flash the 'mole'.

'No, you told me not to tell him where we were staying in Zermatt and I didn't. But we're home now.' She gave a feeble shrug. 'And technically I didn't call.'

'Texting is the same thing and you know it,' Allegra muttered furiously as she flicked through their lengthy correspondence. Half of it was her sister commiserating as he and Zhou tried to work out an escape plan from the arranged marriage. But the other half . . .

She looked up at Isobel with a furious glare.

'Legs, I had to give him some kind of explanation about why we left! Sam freaked when they got back and we weren't there, and obviously *you* weren't picking up his calls. Massi just wanted to know we were all right and to find out what was going on. I told him what happened in the pool with Syria and how that meant I had to tell you about the merger and then you went off to warn Pierre. I never told him where we were staying.'

Allegra's head tipped sharply. 'Sam knew I'd told Pierre about the merger?'

'I guess. So?'

Allegra looked back at the screen. Whistle-blower.

'Look, Legs, I know you're mad with him, but you've

got to speak to Sam. Massi says you only know half the story. Sam was on to Pierre weeks ago apparently.'

'How?' she asked in a brittle tone. What had Sam seen that she'd missed?

'You were right. It is something to do with the charity guy in Syria.'

'Leo Besakovitch?'

'Yeah, him. He got wind of the rumours and wanted to know how exposed he'd been to more bad investments. Sam went back over the trades and saw a load going from his fund into the . . . home thingy . . . ?'

'You mean the house account? The firm's money?'

'That's it. But they all happened at weird hours, Sam hadn't authorized them, and the trades had your initials on.'

'*Mine?*' Allegra felt weak. No . . .

'That's why he came over. Zhou's dad was having talks with Gleneagles anyway, and he agreed to have a couple of meetings with you, pretending to want to invest. Apparently it worked for him because it took any attention away from his real meetings and it meant Sam could get in on the deal and start finding out what was going on.'

'That's why Yong said he didn't want to work with a woman,' Allegra said sharply, things beginning to fall into place.

Isobel shrugged. 'I don't know. This is just what Massi told me. He said Sam realized almost immediately it wasn't you. One of the trades happened overnight in Zurich, apparently, when he'd been with you himself.' Her eyebrow raised up suggestively, as though half expecting an explanation from Allegra, although she wasn't so foolish as to ask. Not now, anyway.

'At any rate, it meant if it wasn't you, it had to be someone with access to your login. So he got one of your analysts to help.'

Allegra inhaled sharply. Bob?

'And they traced the . . . you know, the computer routes . . .'

'IP addresses?'

'Yes, those! Back to – guess where? Pierre's offices. Massi says that's why Sam goaded Pierre at that dinner. He said you wouldn't give up trying to get the deal, so he had to get you to quit somehow, because then, if the trades happened and you'd left the company . . .' She arched an eyebrow.

Allegra wasn't sure which was more incredible: that Pierre had gone to such lengths to destroy her or that Sam had gone to such lengths to save her.

She looked away, feeling the ground tip and rock like a ship in the ocean as clarity dawned, the game revealed at last. Pierre had been setting her up. And the only way for Sam to save her career had been to destroy it. She remembered Sam's anger when he'd seen her in Zermatt, Zhou going off-plan as he tried to assuage his guilt about Amy and drew Allegra back into the game again.

All the other tiny discrepancies that had seemed odd but insignificant rushed back in a swarm too: the Lindover slip-up in the meeting that told her he'd been prying, her phone opened onto Pierre's message when she woke on Monday morning after he'd walked her home, not her bare back but her files accessible to him after she'd entered her passcode in front of him when she'd brought up her diary, Bob's phone call on the slopes . . .

'Just call him, Legs.' Isobel's hand was on her arm, concern in her eyes. 'Let him explain; I'm probably getting half of this wrong.'

Allegra looked back at her through dull eyes, remembering the first time she'd set eyes on Sam. If she'd had any clue then how interconnected they would become – lovers, enemies, colleagues, allies . . . If she could go back to change anything about that night, what would she change? All of it? One thing? Nothing?

In a sea of people, my eyes will always look for you. The bold poetry of the words, the simple longing that leaped from them had been like a chime from her own heart because she couldn't forget how her eyes always searched for him – right from the first instant on the plane. He could be everything, but hadn't Zermatt shown her that love was terminal, unrecoverable . . . ?

She shook her head. Some risks weren't worth taking.

'For God's sake, Legs, he's not Dad!'

Allegra looked up at her sister in surprise. 'What? Why would you say *that*?'

'A blind man could see how crazy Sam is about you. He wouldn't have done all this if he was going to leave you.'

'Iz, you don't understand—'

'Yes, I do. I understand perfectly. I know exactly what went on back then, and I know there's nothing you could have done to change it. You were amazing that night in the church. Christmas Eve and the whole school stopped just to listen to you sing. I remember Mum's face as she watched you. I don't think she breathed once during the whole verse.'

'Iz—' Her voice was a croak. She remembered it too – their mother sitting with a rolled-up copy of the *TV Times* on her lap, to read because she'd arrived an hour early to bag the front pew – her eyes shining with pride and utterly oblivious to the devastation the quiet man in the grey over-coat and brown scarf would wreak on them all the next morning.

'You were absolutely perfect.'

'No.'

'Yes. But it didn't matter what you did or how perfect you were, he was never going to stay, Legs, and what he did to you was cruel and unfair.' Isobel was standing beside her now. 'He made you believe you could change things that were already unstoppable; but he never had any intention of staying with us. He was just buying time; he always wanted them more.'

Allegra looked away, remembering how hard she'd tried, all those teenage nights she had stayed in to revise while Isobel found wild escape in partying, hitting the scholarship stream within a term of trying, taking the lead in the play, breaking the long-distance record at school, singing the solo in the choir . . .

And when he'd gone anyway – the very next day, to enjoy Christmas morning with his other family – she hadn't stopped. Others would have buckled, given up, but she'd taken two jobs around lectures to pay her way through uni-versity when everyone else was on pub crawls. And after graduation, she had sat in high-end strip clubs – the only woman in there wearing more than a thong – as she wooed clients into signing on the dotted line because it brought her the success and security that was a two-fingered salute to the father who'd left.

Her mother may have crumbled as the bills came in with no way of paying for them, Isobel may have run from the truth that he had other children he loved more, but she had filled the gap he'd left behind. She had turned her sorrow into ambition and used it to save them, making sure that no one had the power to imperil them again. Their fates would not rest on the caprices of whether someone loved them enough or not.

Isobel hesitated. 'I saw them one time, you know.'

Allegra frowned. '*You* did? When?'

'In a restaurant in Kew about three years later. They were just talking, nothing much. The boy was on a Nintendo. I remember thinking he looked about your age.'

'Yes, I thought so too.' Allegra sank back into the memory of the moment that had changed everything. 'It's funny, there's so little I can really remember before it happened, but I can recall that one day so clearly. It was in the park, four days after my thirteenth birthday. I couldn't understand why Dad was playing with these other kids when he barely even spoke to us.' He'd been gone within seven months.

'I wished you'd told me what he'd done, challenging you to give him a reason to stay.' Isobel's hand was on her shoulder. 'It would have changed everything I felt about him. I never would have wanted him to come back if I'd known how he'd tricked you. I never would have wanted to keep his name.'

Allegra looked up at her. 'How *did* you know?' She had always kept his 'pact' with her a secret, too ashamed to admit that she'd failed, even to her mother, who'd insisted the failure had been hers.

'It was something Lloyd said, actually. He was talking about how driven you are and I told him how you didn't used to be, but that you'd changed literally overnight into this mega-swot, just when Dad started staying away more, pretending to be on the rig, even though we all knew it was forty days on, forty days off, like we couldn't count or something.'

She sighed. 'Lloyd figured you must have thought you could stop him leaving by becoming the perfect daughter.' She shrugged. 'And as soon as he said it, I knew that was it! I remembered what you said to him at the front door when he was going and it all made sense at last.'

Allegra's eyes flickered away, wet with unshed tears. She remembered that like it had happened yesterday, too – crying at the front door as he put on his coat, the Christmas presents untouched and unwanted beneath the tree. *'But we had a deal. You promised.'*

'Lloyd thinks you've never trusted anyone since, and especially not him, the token adult male in the family. He thinks you don't think he's good enough for me and Ferds. He said sometimes it's almost like you're auditioning him.' Isobel's voice wavered. 'You don't do that, do you?'

Allegra hesitated, seeing her scorn through his eyes. 'If I did, I didn't mean to,' she replied after a moment. 'I just don't want anyone to hurt you again. You're my little sister. It's my job to protect you.'

Isobel smiled, sitting on the arm of the chair beside her. 'Legs, it's his now. *He's* my safety net. He always catches me, even when I go too far.' She gave Allegra a meaningful stare and Allegra thought of her sister's brush with Brice. 'And he knows that sometimes I don't feel as lovable as he thinks I am.' She bit her lip. 'Hey, we're all works in progress, right?'

Allegra smiled. 'I guess so.'

'Just trust me on this, will you? Pretty much the only

thing I know more about in the world than you is men, and Sam's one of the good guys, Legs. Give him a chance.'

Allegra looked back at the screen – a new set of experts were giving their opinion on the scandal, weighing in and adding momentum to the juggernaut that would sooner or later bring her name into the mix.

She had been saved from this, Sam had saved her, but he had also lied to her every step of the way and Isobel still didn't see that it wasn't a white knight Allegra needed – it was someone she could trust.

Chapter Thirty-Six

Day Twenty-Four: *A Likeness*

'Because it would happen on Christmas Eve,' Allegra muttered to herself as she darted around Ikea with a trolley that was the size of a flatbed lorry, trying to load up a flat-pack kitchen table with stacking chairs, floor lamps and several nests of tables that could be separated, one in each room. If she'd thought Selfridges was bad the other week . . .

Hmm, she stopped in front of some giant fluffy sheepskin rugs. Were these good, or would Isobel worry about dust mites or something? She grabbed three anyway.

Lloyd was in the Poplar flat, unscrewing the arms off her sofa and trying to get it down the stairs, while Isobel was at theirs packing up her cutlery and crockery and unloading the fridge of the enormous Waitrose order that had been delivered about forty minutes before the pipe burst and the ceiling fell down in their sitting room. Half the joists could be seen, and no one had fooled themselves for one minute that Isobel was going to contemplate her son spending his first Christmas dodging plaster ceiling missiles.

She checked her watch. Eleven twenty-six. The beds –

the world's two most expensive beds, which had required a £200 express-delivery surcharge – were arriving anytime after one. Everyone else could sleep on the floor, and Ferds had his cot, but both Timo and her mother needed proper beds. The thought of the reunion again this afternoon almost made the floor drop away from her and she squeezed her eyes shut and counted to five.

What else? Towels? How many? Five sets? She took eight, just in case. Oh, and bedding. She'd need that too . . .

She grabbed things from the shelves as she passed, pushing the trolley with a groan and feeling like she was a muscleman heaving a lorry.

The queues at the tills stretched halfway to Surrey, but the Golf was less elastic and she had to unpack almost all the furniture, stamping on cardboard boxes in the car park, before she could cram it in, driving all the way to Islington with her head held at a right angle.

Lloyd was just parking his white van – begged from an ex-City friend who'd decided the area's local wealthy residents would pay more for a 'posh plumber' they could trust – when she turned into the street, driving along at a slow crawl as she checked the house numbers for the one that was actually hers.

The street it was on was family dominated, with the buildings inhabited as houses, not flats, and in every window she could see tall, handsome Christmas trees and majestic wreaths nailed to the front doors.

'Christ, Legs,' Lloyd muttered as she hopped out of the car to join him.

The sale may have been completed five weeks ago, but this was the first time she was actually seeing for herself how £3.7 million translated into bricks and mortar, and it was far bigger than she'd envisioned. Five storeys in total, it was stuccoed on the ground and basement floors, honey-brown bricks on the upper levels. The white door was embellished with a glazed crescent, and the metal-work balconies outside the long, narrow Georgian windows bowed as though blown. When she put the key in the door, the lock was stiff and reluctant to turn, as though sulking with her for its long neglect.

'Here, it's probably frozen,' Lloyd said, barging her gently out of the way. 'Let me try.'

She watched as he blew on it, rubbing the copper plate with his hands before blowing on it again.

It worked a treat and they both stepped in with wide eyes, curiosity finally catching up with her critical invest-ment faculties as she looked down the long hallway that ballooned out into a kitchen at the back. Oak floors – too treacly in colour for her liking – ran through every room like excited children. The walls, depressed in their grubby, taupe-painted skins, were stained with greasy handprints and flecked with small circles of exposed plaster that looked like scars from where mirrors and pictures and photographs had once hung. The marble fireplaces in the reception rooms were still mottled with wax crusts, a box of Swan matches left on one windowsill. The chandeliers – which she'd thought too grand and fussy anyway – had gone, the exposed wires left dangling in express defiance of building regulations. So often it was the richest people who acted cheaply.

The kitchen was less expensive than it had looked in the photographs – ply backs to the drawers obfuscated by expensive handles, the granite worktop merely entry-level grade. The garden was pretty and generous for London, though, its long, narrow proportions emphasized as overgrown shrubs in beds on either side practically met in an arch overhead, the grass dotted with prickly dandelions and scorch marks from the neighbourhood cats.

She wandered through the ghostly house, Lloyd at a polite distance, her hi-tech, blacked-out running kit – she had left it at Isobel's the other week and hadn't been home yet to get another change – at odds with the domestic palette of creams and blues and taupes, her neon mesh Nike Flyknits flattening the deep-piled carpets. The staircase was beautiful – tight and winding, but with a mahogany handrail that fluted in the palm, inviting a careless leg thrown over and a Peter Pan-style ride to the bottom.

She stopped in the doorways of the bedrooms – the master bedroom was too large for one, the nursery for children she didn't have, guest suites for friendships long since lapsed. Only a week ago, this house could have felt like a sharp slap in the face, but now she felt its walls close around her like arms. Today, at least, it was perfect.

She patted Lloyd on the shoulder. 'Come on, then,' she smiled. 'We'd better get this place shipshape before Little Miss Health and Safety gets here and closes us down.'

Three hours later, it was getting dark. The first street lamps were beginning to switch on, and the houses opposite glowed a warm, honeyed colour, the windows like television screens as the lives inside were illuminated to show children racing through rooms, their parents wrapping presents and straightening pictures, drinking wine, some of them dancing.

What did her windows show? Allegra wondered, as she fixed the wreath to the door, the finishing touch to their afternoon's labours. She jogged down the steps and looked back in.

It certainly didn't have the lifestyle finesse or colour-matched sophistication of her neighbours yet. The orange and yellow plastic chairs sat uncomfortably with the veneered pine table, and the floor lamps looked like they belonged in a loft in Wapping, not a Regency house in Islington. And yet . . . flames were leaping from the fire Lloyd had managed to get going (after a heroic last-minute dash to the petrol station for smokeless coal), Noemie was sitting on one of the sheepskin rugs, rolling a ball for Ferdy, and Barry was single-handedly hoisting the giant eleven-foot Christmas tree into position in the corner by the window. But it was Timo she couldn't take her eyes off, sitting on her battered too-small sofa with her mother's hand in his, neither one of them speaking, an expression on both their faces that transcended words.

Isobel was sitting by their feet, a blond and chestnut box, which Timo had made especially, balanced on her lap as she pored over the photographs he had shown Allegra in Zermatt. They were the reason she'd been late for the memorial service; it had turned out Anya had kept her promise as well as her secret. She had written faithfully, and inside were hundreds of letters tied together in a ribbon, all with British stamps and postmarked Hampshire, each one padded with black and white – and later, colour – photographs, and folded drawings of stick men and flowers and rainbows and horses.

Allegra liked best the photo of her mother standing in front of a mossy wall, aged eight, with bobbed hair and freckles and a hand-knitted cardigan buttoned up to the neck; she had easily recognized her grandmother's looping script, carefree and confident, on postcards from Babbacombe in Devon with red cliffs and sandy beaches; Julia and Anya standing outside a caravan somewhere windy — their hair whipping around both their faces so that wide smiles were all that could be seen; a faded photograph of snow-domed Ben Nevis in Scotland jokily captioned 'Big. But not big enough.' No, it wasn't the Matterhorn.

And then there were the later Kodak photographs — the pigment more intense and clear — of two little girls, one with a gap between her teeth, sitting on some stone steps, ice creams with Flakes sticking out of them, and grubby knees peeking out from apple-patched skirts . . .

'Legs!'

The voice that had been honed to carry over a windswept Welsh field floated easily to her ear and she hurried back in to find Barry standing at the bottom of the stairs, a glass of wine in his hand.

'Behind you,' she smiled, closing the door with a soft *thunk*.

'Oh, there you are. It's time.' He handed her the glass, shooing her quickly into the room.

Leysa came through from the kitchen. Calm and quietly efficient, she had worked out how to use the oven quite easily – Allegra had been sure it 'didn't work' – and the goose inside it was turning golden.

Nikolai, Noemie and Timo were standing in front of the tree, which was almost bare by British standards – no tinsel, no fairy lights, no angels, no stars. Instead, some narrow red candles were attached, by virtue of counterbalanced clips, to the ends of the branches, from the very top of the tree to the very bottom, bare flames flickering in the fronds.

Isobel looked like she was going to hyperventilate, Ferdy held close in her arms as she began to rock. 'I'll be honest – I'm nervous. Fairy lights would be safer.'

Leysa laughed. She made fifty-two look beautiful, with chocolate-brown eyes that were doe-soft and dewy olive skin, and she held out her hands to take Ferdy for a cuddle.

'Maybe you could have pretend candles but with, you know, LED lights? That way if Ferdy was to touch them, they wouldn't burn him, *and* the risk of us all being burnt to death in our beds would be vastly diminished.'

Lloyd hugged her around the shoulders and planted a kiss on her forehead and Allegra saw her sister's body relax. 'Iz, we've cut away the branches that were too close. It'll be OK. They've done this for many years.'

'Everyone is ready?' Noemie asked, standing by the light switch. Barry was positioned next to Julia – just in case – but her eyes were already on the tree.

Nik nodded, pressing 'play' on an iPod, and the first vaulted notes of 'Ave Maria' filled the air, just as darkness drenched the room and the simple, undressed tree glittered in its own elegant illuminations. Allegra saw Julia's hands fly to her mouth as she looked around the room in almost childlike wonder – was this tradition something she distantly remembered from early childhood?

Allegra looked around the new house with similar awe herself. Isobel's collection of scented candles flickered on every surface, the Advent calendar had been given pride of place on the mantelpiece above the fire, and the nativity set was in the bay window, arranged in the traditional Swiss tradition of an Advent window.

Isobel leaned over to her. 'For someone who doesn't "do" Christmas, you sure have a funny way of showing it.'

'Ha, yes, right,' Allegra smiled, nodding, pretending to laugh. But she felt like the boy with his thumb in the dyke, holding back something much bigger than him, and she could only hold the pose for so long. Here she was, at last, in a house that had become a home, with strangers who had become a family and yet, as ever, they were one person short.

Only it wasn't the one she'd been missing for the last eighteen years. It was the one she hadn't seen for the past four days.

'What was in the last drawer, by the way?' Isobel's voice drew her out of her reverie.

'Huh?'

'In the calendar.' Isobel jerked her head towards the Advent calendar sitting in the window.

Allegra's eyes widened. 'How would I know? I was in Ikea at dawn and I've not seen it all day. You were the one who wanted to be in charge of the decorations.'

'Oh, please.' Isobel rolled her eyes dramatically. 'Like that's an excuse. It's Christmas Eve. This is the big one. It's what the whole calendar's been counting down to!'

'Why didn't you open it, then?'

'Duh. Because it's yours!'

'It's ours.'

'No.' Isobel patted her shoulder. 'It's very definitely yours. I've got the clock. Go on.' She grabbed the glass from Allegra's hand and pushed her bossily towards the fire place. Allegra took the Advent calendar over to the window seat and opened the final drawer. Number 24.

She blinked at what she saw there, her hands beginning

to tremble at the sight of her own likeness staring up at her – not an image of Valentina this time, but the cameo from the PLF Christmas party. Her mouth parted in astonishment as she carefully lifted it out.

What on earth was it doing here? She thought back to that night. . . . She had given it to a waiter to throw away. She was certain of it. So how could it be here? Who had put it here?

The silhouette sagged lightly against her fingers as her eyes traced the note-perfect form. Unthinkingly, she turned it over. 'Open the door' was written across the back.

What?

She looked up, out of the window, past the steady rise of the snow on the sills. Had the lights been on, she would have seen only her reflection, but the gentle light of the candles kept the room in relative darkness and she could easily see the figure standing at the bottom of the steps, watching her.

Her heart pirouetted defiantly at the sight of Sam, his hair flecked with snow, a red scarf wrapped several times round his neck and his hands under his armpits as he kept his feet moving in the cold.

She turned away, looking back into the room at her family, but no one was paying any attention to her, it seemed. Nikolai and Lloyd were crawling around at the base of the tree, looking for the presents with red bows on that denoted the special Swiss Christmas Eve preview, a tradition they intended to continue, Timo, Julia and Barry were all together on the sofa, and Allegra had to assume Isobel had taken Ferds with her back into the kitchen with Leysa.

Silently, unnoticed, she got up and walked to the front door, pressing her hand to the wood for a moment, before opening it.

Sam stared back at her from the top step. 'Hey.'

She immediately looked down, away from those eyes that made everything so difficult, those eyes that had been looking into hers when he'd said his last words to her: *'Just be here when I get back.'* An impossible request.

'Allegra, if I could have told you earlier, I would have done.' They were straight into it.

'So why didn't you, then?'

He hesitated. 'I wasn't sure where your loyalties lay. I thought after you quit, when you saw what he was capable of and how disposable you were to him, maybe I could tell you. I wanted to. I wanted everything to be open between us. But then you pitched up in Zermatt still trying to get the deal, and I thought you might be trying to win it for Pierre still. I couldn't be sure you'd trust me over him.'

She swallowed, embarrassed and ashamed that he'd so accurately assessed her tangled emotions about the man who'd been more of a father figure to her than her own.

'You know that Pierre had planned it all so that if suspicions were raised, they'd be led to you?'

Allegra nodded. Isobel had got her facts right. 'How did *you* know it wasn't me?'

He almost laughed. 'You mean, you looking like you wanted to punch me when I gave the Garrard tip wasn't convincing enough that you're straight?'

'So you did have doubts about me.'

He shrugged. 'I needed *absolute* proof. I gave you Garrard, and Pierre, Demontignac. He acted; you didn't.'

His expression changed, his eyes on her mouth. 'But for what it's worth, I realized before we got in Crivelli's car it couldn't be you.'

'*How?*'

'I was reading up on you in New York, trying to get the lowdown on who you were, long before we actually met. It was your name on the trades and I was so sure when I got on that plane that I knew how things were going to pan out. I thought I had you. But then when I first saw you and you saw me . . .' His voice faded at the memory and she thought her knees might buckle at the look in his eyes. 'No one who was involved in criminal activity would have blushed to their fingertips like that. They just wouldn't.'

'I'm not a blusher,' she protested weakly, aware that that wasn't the point.

He took a step closer. 'I'm afraid you are. It's one of the things I love about you.'

'You . . . ?'

He nodded, toe to toe with her now, one arm beginning to snake loosely around her hips, the other trailing down her nose onto her lips. 'Mainly, though, it's the gap.'

'You like my gap?' Her hand flew to her mouth.

'I love the gap. The gap kills me.' He gave a slow smile. 'As long as you have a gap, you'll have me.'

'Well, I guess I could work with that,' she murmured, as his grip around her tightened and she remembered how it felt to be in his arms: the feel of him as he'd brought her safely down the mountain, the heat of his hands on her arms as he stopped her from running at Zhou's party, his hands everywhere else as they finally succumbed to what was inevitable between them when the fighting stopped.

And as he kissed her, her fingers fiddled with the little tin ring and slid it sideways, the secret heart visible, at last, for all to see.

When they walked into the house together, no one seemed surprised; in fact, Lloyd appeared to have a beer ready-poured for him, and Isobel was rushing around – as quickly as is possible in a knee brace – with a tray of canapés and speaking in a very fast, very high, overexcited voice.

'Ready for the next bit?' she trilled with exquisite ambiguity, standing in front of them both, offering Sam a vol-au-vent but her eyes firmly on her sister.

'Finally? Yes,' Allegra smiled, throwing her arms around Isobel's neck, knowing full well her sister had been complicit in planning and scheming this. No doubt Massi and Zhou were standing on the street corner ready to launch into carols.

'Good,' Isobel laughed, having to dab at her eyes, before throwing her arms around Sam's neck too. 'Good. Because we have to get these presents opened before Ferds goes down or he'll become overtired and I'll never get him to settle.'

'Nightmare,' Allegra laughed, slapping her sister on the arm.

Leading Sam by the hand, she went over to the sofa, where Timo, Julia and Barry were still sitting. Barry's eyes met hers briefly and she knew from the way he nodded that now was a good time.

'Opa, Barry, Mum, I want you to meet Sam.'

Julia's eyes brightened at the sight of him and she leaned forward, covering his hand with hers. 'Are you the one who's going to look after my girl?' she asked intently.

Allegra looked across at him, crouched down in front of her mother. He already had, more than Julia could ever know.

'Yes. I'm the one,' he smiled.

Julia's eyes slid over to Allegra's in delight. 'American,' she mouthed, as though this fact might have passed Allegra by.

'Canadian,' Allegra grinned, flashing her gap and making Sam take a half-step back to her again, his arm round her waist.

'Here, for you.'

They turned. Isobel was holding out two envelopes with red bows attached. Allegra took them with a wry smile. 'A present for Sam?' she asked her sister. Isobel winked. 'It was obviously considered a foregone conclusion that I was going to let you in,' Allegra said archly, handing Sam the one with his name on. His only reply was to kiss her again, a smile playing on his lips.

Behind them, they saw Lloyd handing the wrapped memory book to Julia and the framed photograph of Granny, Julia, Isobel and herself to Timo.

'Don't get too excited. It's probably an iTunes voucher,' Allegra joked, her smile fading as she pulled out a folded, thick cream sheet of paper from her envelope. 'What . . . ?' She gasped, her hand slapping over her mouth and making everyone turn. 'Who . . . who had this?' Her eyes swung over Timo, Nik, Leysa, Noemie, but they were all staring back at her blankly, and she looked at Isobel with a dumbstruck expression.

'What is it?' Isobel frowned, hobbling over and peering at it over her shoulder. She frowned as she took in the elaborate sloping black script. 'I can't understand it. It's all in Ger—' Her hand slapped over her mouth too. 'Oh my God!' she screeched. 'The deeds!'

Nik ran over. 'The deeds? You mean . . . for the farm?' He read them quickly, looking across at Timo and nodding.

Tears sprang to the old man's eyes and his hand found Julia's, squeezing it tightly as his head began to nod.

'Who found this?' Nik asked, repeating Allegra's question.

'I did,' Lloyd said, beaming and clearly pleased he'd been able to keep his surprise a secret. 'Well, strictly speaking, it was the clock repairers who found it. They said they found it in the back compartment of the cuckoo clock.'

'Valentina hid them in there!' Allegra said.

'They've been here with us all along!' Isobel half laughed, half shrieked. 'And poor Granny never even knew, I bet. If the clock made Mum cry, she wouldn't have put it up. She probably just boxed it away and forgot all about it.' Allegra blinked down at the papers in disbelief. It was the proof they had needed. It wouldn't get the farm back – that was long gone now. The world had changed and Zermatt with it, but Lars would lose everything and Timo could finally know some peace. Valentina's death had changed her family's identity, trajectory and destiny, but she had been loved then and she was loved now. Families endure, and theirs hadn't ended with that sheared slab of snow.

'I guess this puts quite a bit of pressure on my present now, then, huh?' Sam said in her ear.

He opened the envelope, pulling out a large copper-brown horse chestnut leaf. He twirled it by the stalk between his fingers. 'Oh. Ummm . . .' He grinned.

'It's a day of luck,' Allegra laughed, falling into him and resting her cheek against his shoulder. She thought she could just stay there forever. 'Iz is big on that. It's not her fault; it's a genetic thing. She gets it from our grandfather.' She looked down at the leaf. 'It's a real shame I only got those deeds,' she sighed. 'We could have been lucky together.'

He chuckled, his fingers tilting her face up to his, so that she was looking into his eyes. 'Oh, baby,' he grinned. 'We already are.'

Acknowledgements

I decided to set this book in Zermatt following a happy family ski trip there last year. The mighty Matterhorn really is something to behold and rightly attracts visitors from around the world. As I began to research the area in greater detail, I discovered the tragedy of the January 1951 storms and became fascinated by how much the town had changed within two generations, developing from a rustic farming community to one of the ritziest resorts in the chic international ski scene. Much of what you've just read is true and accurate – the world-class slope-side restaurants such as Zum See, Findlerhof and Chez Vrony (to name a few) are worth the ski pass alone, and the Broken Bar is the regulars' favourite nightspot. But I have, of course, made full use of my artistic licence, and although the SLF and avalanche zoning maps are real, Zermatt is not and never has been – to my knowledge – classified as a red zone. I'm paid to make things up and so I do. With abandon.

I owe a huge debt of thanks to my great friends the Becks – Johny, Carina, Coco, Codi and Dita – who practically live there through the winter months and have given me the insider's guide to that beautiful town. I adore the lot of you.

To my editor, Caroline Hogg, your steer on this book has

been invaluable. Thank you so much for your patience and calm as I struggled, suitably enough, with a ski injury that knocked me off schedule – although I hope you'll agree it at least brought a commanding authenticity to Isobel's corresponding scenes!

To my agent, Amanda Preston, thank you for reading between the lines of my 'trying to be brave' tweets and taking charge on this book. You're always several steps ahead of me in this crazy, mad, fun business and I know how very lucky I am to have you in my corner.

Finally, to my family, you're not the reason I write; you're the reason I breathe. I couldn't love you more.

PLAYERS
by
Karen Swan

Friendships are strong. Lust is stronger . . .

*Harry Hunter was everywhere you looked – bearing down
from bus billboards, beaming out from the society pages,
falling out of nightclubs in the gossip columns, and flirting
up a storm on the telly chat-show circuit.*

Harry Hunter is the new golden boy of the literary scene.
With his books selling by the millions, the paparazzi on
his tail, and a supermodel on each arm, he seems to have
the world at his feet. Women all over the globe adore
him, but few suspect that his angelic looks hide a darker
side, a side that conceals a lifetime of lies and deceit.

Tor, Cress and Kate have been best friends for as long as
they can remember. Through all the challenges of
marriage, raising children and maintaining their high-
flying careers, they have stuck together as a powerful and
loyal force to be reckoned with   living proof that
twenty-first-century women can have it all, and do. It is
only when the captivating Harry comes into their lives
that things begin to get complicated, as Tor, Cress and
Kate are drawn into Harry's dangerous games.

Prima DONNA

by
Karen Swan

Breaking the rules was what she liked best.
That was her sport.

Renegade, rebel, bad girl. Getting away with it.

Pia Soto is the sexy and glamorous prima ballerina,
the Brazilian bombshell who's shaking up the
ballet world with her outrageous behaviour.
She's wild and precocious, and she's a survivor.
She's determined that no man will ever control her
destiny. But ruthless financier Will Silk has Pia in
his sights, and has other ideas . . .

Sophie O'Farrell is Pia's hapless, gawky assistant,
the girl-next-door to Pia's Prima Donna, always either
falling in love with the wrong man or just falling over.
Sophie sets her own dreams aside to pick up the debris
in Pia's wake, but she's no angel. When a devastating
accident threatens to cut short Pia's illustrious career,
Sophie has to step out of the shadows and face up to
the demons in her own life.

Christmas at TIFFANY'S

by
Karen Swan

**Three cities, three seasons,
one chance to find the life that fits**

Cassie settled down too young, marrying her first serious
boyfriend. Now, ten years later, she is betrayed and
broken. With her marriage in tatters and no career or
home of her own, she needs to work out where she
belongs in the world and who she really is.

So begins a year-long trial as Cassie leaves her sheltered
life in rural Scotland to stay with each of her best friends
in the most glamorous cities in the world: New York,
Paris and London. Exchanging grouse moor and mousy
hair for low-carb diets and high-end highlights, Cassie
tries on each city for size as she attempts to track down
the life she was supposed to have been leading, and with
it, the man who was supposed to love her all along.

The Perfect
PRESENT
by
Karen Swan

Memories are a gift . . .

Haunted by a past she can't escape, Laura Cunningham
desires nothing more than to keep her world small
and precise - her quiet relationship and growing
jewellery business are all she needs to get by. Until the
day when Rob Blake walks into her studio and
commissions a necklace that will tell his enigmatic
wife Cat's life in charms.

As Laura interviews Cat's family, friends and former
lovers, she steps out of her world and into theirs – a
charmed world where weekends are spent in Verbier and
the air is lavender-scented, where friends are wild,
extravagant and jealous, and a big love has to compete
with grand passions.

Hearts are opened, secrets revealed and as the necklace
begins to fill up with trinkets, Cat's intoxicating life
envelops Laura's own. By the time she has to identify the
final charm, Laura's metamorphosis is almost complete.
But the last story left to tell has the power to change all
of their lives forever, and Laura is forced to choose
between who she really is and who it is she wants to be.

Christmas at CLARIDGE'S

by

Karen Swan

The best presents can't be wrapped . . .

This was where her dreams drifted to if she didn't blot her nights out with drink; this was where her thoughts settled if she didn't fill her days with chat. She remembered this tiny, remote foreign village on a molecular level and the sight of it soaked into her like water into sand, because this was where her old life had ended and her new one had begun.

Portobello – home to the world-famous street market, Notting Hill Carnival and Clem Alderton. She's the queen of the scene, the girl everyone wants to be or be with. But beneath the morning-after make, Clem is keeping a secret, and when she goes too f one reckless night she endangers everything – her ho e, her job and even her adored brother's ve.

Portofino – a place of wild beauty and old-school glamour. Clem has been here once before and vowed never to return. But when a handsome stranger asks Clem to restore a neglected villa, it seems like the answer to her problems – if she can just face up to her past.

Claridge's – at Christmas. Clem is back in London working on a special commission for London's grandest hotel. But is this really where her heart lies?

The SUMMER WITHOUT YOU

by
Karen Swan

Everything will change . . .

Rowena Tipton isn't looking for a new life, just a new
adventure; something to while away the months as
her long-term boyfriend presses pause on their
relationship before they become engaged. But when a
chance encounter at a New York wedding leads to an
audition for a coveted house share in the Hamptons –
Manhattan's elite beach scene – suddenly a new life
is exactly what she's got.

Stretching before her is a summer with three eclectic
housemates, long days on white sand ocean beaches and
parties on gilded tennis courts. But high rewards bring
high stakes and Rowena soon finds herself caught in the
crossfire of a vicious intimidation campaign. Alone for
the first time in her adult life, she has no-one to turn to
but a stranger who is everything she doesn't want – but
possibly everything she needs.

It's time to relax with your next good book

THEWINDOWSEAT.CO.UK

If you've enjoyed this book, but don't know what to read next, then we can help. The Window Seat is a site that's all about making it easier to discover your next good book. We feature recommendations, behind-the-scenes tales from the world of publishing, creative writing tips, competitions, and, if we're honest, quite a lot of lists based on our favourite reads.

You'll find stories and features by authors including Lucinda Riley, Karen Swan, Diane Chamberlain, Jane Green, Lucy Diamond and many more. We showcase brand-new talent as well as classic favourites, so you'll never be stuck for what to read again.

We'd love to know what you think of the site, our books, and what you'd like us to feature, so do let us know.

 @panmacmillan.com

facebook.com/panmacmillan

WWW.THEWINDOWSEAT.CO.UK